THE
FATEFUL
TEXT

GEORGIE GEE

BALBOA.PRESS

A DIVISION OF HAY HOUSE

Balboa Press books may be ordered through booksellers or by contacting:

Balboa Press
A Division of Hay House
1663 Liberty Drive
Bloomington, IN 47403
www.balboapress.co.uk
UK TFN: 0800 0148647 (Toll Free inside the UK)
UK Local: (02) 0369 56325 (+44 20 3695 6325 from outside the UK)

Print information available on the last page.

ISBN: 978-1-9822-8536-4 (sc)
ISBN: 978-1-9822-8537-1 (e)

Balboa Press rev. date: 11/15/2022

About the Author

Throughout my life I have struggled with many health issues that resulted in my regularly being in and out of hospital, from a small child into adulthood, until I was diagnosed with Ehlers Danlos Syndrome type 3 at the age of 38. This is a condition that affects the connective tissues, in a nutshell, they are far too soft and as the connective tissue holds one 'together' both through the skeleton and the internal organs, it explained why I had so many problems. However, having received this diagnosis, that was where it ended, the NHS offered no further help or advice, and I was left to get on with it.

From then on, I made it my purpose to do the very best for myself. I have spent my life proactively doing everything I can to make myself as well and as healthy as I possibly can be. I've studied health and wellbeing from many different angles for 20 years now and learned from some amazing people along the way who have afforded me life changing and empowering information.

For many years my world revolved around exercise and diet and I was doing very well. In my quest for any knowledge to do with health and well-being, around seven years ago, I came to learn of the principles of the holistic lifestyle. I became very interested in the concept of treating my 'being' as a whole, mind, body and spirit. This incredible approach, combined with the knowledge I already had of exercise and nutrition, took my health to a whole new level and it has completely changed my life. I learned on my journey that it's impossible to have a healthy body without a healthy mind because the body is a physical manifestation of our thoughts and feelings. We need to address it all to be healthy, happy and whole.

I now lead a normal life and one wouldn't know I had a problem now unless I told them. I'm very proud of the level of wellness I have managed to achieve for myself with this knowledge and am truly passionate about creating awareness of the difference this approach can make to one's health and wellbeing.

In my opinion, since we have been faced with this pandemic, it has NEVER been more important for individuals to take responsibility for their own health and wellbeing.

I had always wanted to write a novel and so, I decided that I would write a beautiful love story, with all the basic principles of the holistic lifestyle laced throughout as an enjoyable introduction to this healthful and life changing practice. I hope you enjoy it.

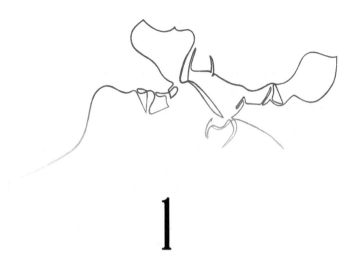

1

Lexi walked round the house checking that the doors and windows were locked, picked up her suitcase from the hall and stepped outside. As she locked the door, the neighbour's cat spotted her and came trotting across the garden for a fuss. Lexi bent down to stroke it.

"Sorry Pepys I haven't got anything for you today," she said as she stroked his thick, black fur. He responded by rubbing the side of his face affectionately into her. She stood up and loaded her case into the car, ensuring the cat wasn't under the car before she got in, set up her sat nav and went on her way.

Lexi was a 50-year-old mother of two grown up children; she was a Holistic Lifestyle and Exercise Coach married to her husband, Nathan for twenty years. Four days earlier her life was jogging along nicely. She was happy at work, happy at home and her life was what one would call 'sweet'. However, three days ago this was all to change.

Nathan was away on business; his work regularly took him away from home. Lexi was at the end of a long day at work at a gym fairly close to where she lived. She had just finished teaching her last class of the day; she switched off the lights and locked up the gym studio, then headed to the reception desk where she handed over the studio keys. The lad on reception looked up as she approached the desk.

"Good one tonight?" he enquired.

"Yes, excellent thank you," Lexi replied. She loved her job; she loved exercise and everything to do with health and wellbeing and was extremely passionate about what she did, totally driven by it.

"I'm going to hit the sauna before I go home," she said, finishing with "see you in a bit," and walked off in the direction of the changing rooms.

She opened her locker and checked her phone. She noticed a 'missed call' from Nathan and called him back. "Hey, how was your day?" she asked.

"Oh, good thanks, and you?" came his reply.

"Yes, fine thanks. I'm a bit knackered to be honest, I've covered someone else's classes today so I'm going to relax in the sauna for a little while and unwind before I go home. How did last night go?" Nathan was currently working on the final stages of a big project that he'd been working on for the last 18 months.

"Oh, you know, nice meal. We got most of the business done over the table and then spent the rest of the night in the bar!" he replied jovially.

This wasn't an unusual statement from Nathan.

"Lol, typical," she laughed. "How many of you?"

"Five of us."

"Suitable hangover this morning then?" she enquired.

"Not too bad," came the reply.

"Ok, well, I'm going to get off now, see you when you get back tomorrow, bye, love you."

With their brief exchange complete, Lexi popped her phone back in the locker and pulled out her towel and swimwear. She removed her sweaty kit and had a nice, hot shower to relax her tired muscles. Towards the end she turned the water down cold, cooling her body right down, taking her breath away and making her gasp a little; then she turned the water back hot again to finish. When she was done, she popped on her bikini and headed for the sauna.

"Oh, bliss," she exclaimed as she lay her tired body down on her towel on the wooden bench, the heat on her skin instantly relaxing her. There was just one other lady in there who had just participated in her class. They had a little chat and after twenty minutes or so, a very 'spent' but suitably chilled-out Lexi, gathered her belongings from her locker and put on her pj's to drive home. It was now 9pm and she didn't see any sense in getting dressed just to go home and get undressed again!

Heading back towards the reception desk Lexi saw two of the male gym staff pick up a girl and throw her in the pool fully clothed. It was her birthday, and this was the ritual at the gym when there was any kind of celebration. They were all a little high spirited and counted to three as they swung her over the pool, cheering as they let go on 'three' and she flew out of their hands and hit the water.

"You rotten lot!" she exclaimed, dripping wet as she climbed out and they all laughed. By now there was quite a group of staff at the reception desk, socialising and congratulating the birthday girl. At that point Lexi's phone bleeped to alert her to a text. She fished in her bag for her phone, opened up the message and froze...

Paul was one of the other personal trainers who worked there; he could see from Lexi's expression something was quite obviously wrong.

"Are you ok Lex?" he asked. Lexi and Paul were very good friends, having worked together for over four years at the gym. They were very like-minded and got on very well both in and outside of work. She looked at him and passed him her phone, presenting him with the message she had just received from her husband.

'Hey sexy minx, you left your knickers on the floor! P.S. You were amazing last night xx'

"Oi oi!" Paul winked and lightly elbowed her in the side.

Lexi's serious expression remained as she turned to her unknowing friend and said, "Nathan has been away since Monday Paul.

The jokey expression on Paul's face instantly dropped as her words sunk in.

"Oh shit, Lex!" Paul exclaimed "No way! I'm so sorry, Jesus! What are you going to do?" he asked, horrified at the situation that he found unfolding in front of him.

Lexi looked at the message again and said, "I'm going to reply to him, that's what I'm going to do!"

She replied to her husband saying, "I don't think that was meant for me, was it?"

Within about fifteen seconds Lexi's phone started to ring. She didn't really need to look to see who it was.

She answered the call saying, "There really isn't an awful lot you can say right now is there?"

"Lexi please!" came her husband's anxious voice from the other end.

She gave him no chance to say any more, "Please?... Please what Nathan? Please ignore that last message? Or is it more a case of, please let me off this once?" Her voice cold and stern.

"No!" Completely flustered Nathan began to fumble for his words. "I mean…"

Again, she didn't allow him to continue, "What do you mean Nathan? Exactly what DO you mean?" She pressed the red button finishing the call and tossed the phone into her bag, a mixture of anger and upset raging up inside of her. She took a moment to breathe and tried to get control of the stress response that was now surging through every cell in her body. She managed to compose herself to a degree, aware of the celebrations still happening all around her and then exclaimed to Paul, "Oh my God, I didn't see that one coming!" Her cheeks were already flushed from the sauna, but now her jaw started to quiver as she spoke. Paul put his arm around her and led her away from the celebrating crowd.

"Jeeze Lex, I honestly don't know what to say!" he was absolutely 'crushed' to see his friend being dealt such a nasty blow.

"God Paul, I would never have expected this in a million years!" she said in disbelief as their conversation became more private.

"What are you going to do?" he said concerned.

"Right now, I have absolutely no idea… Oh… my… God!" she said slowly as the horrible reality of what had just happened kicked in.

"When is he due back home?"

"Tomorrow evening,"

"Are you gonna be ok? I mean, I don't mind coming back with you if you want me to, if you don't want to be on your own?" He offered supportively.

"Aw, bless you sweetie, no, honestly, I think I need to just get home and think this one out by myself, but thank you anyway," she assured him.

"Ok, I'm here if you need me hun."

"Thank you, sweetie, I know you are and that's really kind of you," she said kissing him on the cheek.

"Hey, I know you'd do the same for me," he gave her a reassuring hug as he kissed her cheek.

"Right, I'm going to go," she said heaving her heavy bag onto her shoulder.

"Drive carefully," he said. He could see how shaken Lexi was by this despite her effort to be calm and added, "Text me to let me know you get back ok please."

"Yeah, will do," she said turning towards the foyer to leave.

As she pushed through the heavy glass door her strong exterior began to slip away, the tears started to roll down her face and she had a shaky feeling in the pit of her stomach. She walked through the car park, opened the car door, slung her gym bag on the back seat and launched herself heavily into the driver's seat. She took a big sigh reaching into her handbag for her phone again. She opened up Nathan's message and sat staring at it, almost as if she hoped it'd go away but of course it didn't, it just continued to glare back at her in all its horror. Her shoulders began to shake, her breathing started to heave and finally she gave in to her battered emotions and started to cry. She sobbed for a full five minutes, either bawling into her steering wheel or staring back into her phone whilst hugging herself with her free arm, trying to process this awful burden of knowledge. Eventually and after quite some time she managed to compose herself enough to drive the car. She started up the engine and drove home.

2

Lexi pulled up to her house and parked in darkness. She'd forgotten to put the outside light on before leaving for work. As she walked up the path, Pepys, ever eager for a fuss, came trotting straight out from under the hedge to greet her making a little 'brrrp' sound. Bending down to pick him up her tears started to flow again; she momentarily consoled herself, hugging him into her like a furry teddy bear. The cat oblivious to her emotional state, just purred loudly as she buried her head in his comforting fur and cried. After a few minutes she popped him back on the ground, 'cuffed' his fur off her face with the back of her sleeve, picked up her bags and unlocked the front door. She walked in, switched on some lights and just stood looking around in a daze for a few minutes.

"What on earth am I going to do?" she said out loud to herself. She went into the kitchen, picked up a sage stick and lit it, letting it burn for a few moments and then blew it out allowing the smoke to flow from it. She then proceeded to walk through the house wafting the smoke into every corner, high and low with a feather, almost on autopilot as her tangled thoughts played over and over in her head. This was a ritual she performed every day to cleanse the energy of her home. On her holistic path she had also become very spiritual and this was one of many things that had become part of her daily practice.

Once she had 'smudged' the house, she returned to the kitchen, poured herself a glass of water and went upstairs; she brushed her teeth and went into the bedroom. She'd only finished decorating it about a month ago; it was all shiny and new in beautiful aqua and purple tones with a lovely new bed, all new furniture and an eye-catching rug on the floor to finish it off. She'd been so thrilled with it and now she was sitting there not even noticing it as she sat alone with her thoughts, wondering to herself, "How on earth am I going to handle this?

Once more she broke down and cried but just at that moment her phone 'bleeped', it was a text from Paul to see if she'd got home ok. "Bless him," she said to herself out loud and replied to his message. She lay on the bed with the light on staring at the ceiling. A short while later her phone bleeped again and again it was Paul; clearly worried about her.

"I hope you're ok, I haven't been able to stop thinking about you. Lord only knows what must be going through your head right now, please do call me if you need me."

He was a sweet man, only 24 years old, a personal trainer following the same path as her, they both went on courses together and were fiercely passionate about their jobs, their own lifestyle choices and the health of the planet, they gelled very well both as work colleagues and as friends.

"I'm ok, I think. Well... Quite honestly Paul I don't know what to think, I'm just so shocked. Obviously, he can't deny this, he's sent me a message intended for her, but

I have no idea what 'this' is! I've no idea if this was a one-night stand or if it's an affair that's been going on forever? I simply have no idea; all I do know is that it's happened!"

Their messages started back and forth.

"What do you think you'll do?" he asked.

"I really don't know, it'd be different if the message had said, "I'm so sorry, you're a lovely girl but I'm married and that really shouldn't have happened! But no, he was sounding quite pleased with himself. As far as I could see from that message, there was certainly no sign of 'regret' in there anywhere. I can't help feeling that whatever he says, his only true regret at this present moment in time is pressing the wrong contact number on his phone!" She was now convincing herself.

"Could you forgive him if it was just one night?" came the obvious question.

"Oh Paul, don't! I really don't know. Right now, I feel like the rug has well and truly been pulled out from under my feet, I don't even want to think about it"!

As she was tapping in her reply to Paul her phone received another text message, this time it was Nathan. "Can we talk?"

"Arseholes!" she exclaimed out loud to her phone.

With absolutely no intention of replying to him she finished her message to Paul. "I'm off to bed now, thank you for caring. X" she finished.

To which he replied, "Take care lovely lady, I'm here if you need me, you know that, just call me. Lexi, you are worth so much more than this. X" His kind words provoking her tears to flow once again.

She took her phone downstairs and put it on charge. She read both of Nathan's messages again and shook her head.

"What on earth am I going to do?" she said again to herself.

She went back upstairs and lay on her bed; all sorts of things were going through her mind.

'How long has it been going on?" Was it someone he got talking to in the bar?'

As she kept thinking about how it might have come about and all the possible scenarios, she worked herself up until she made herself angry.

"Bastard!" she shouted out from the silence, but then her rational side argued back at her, 'actually, as horrible as it all is, if he hadn't sent that message to me, I would be none the wiser'. Then another thought occurred to her, 'if this is an affair and it's been going on for a while, he's also been sleeping with me!' So, for the rest of the night Lexi tortured herself, with every kind of awful scenario imaginable whirring around in her head.

She spent the whole night tossing and turning, finally managing to get to sleep around 4.30 am, the alarm rudely awaking her at 7am. She wearily sat up in bed and drank her glass of water. She felt awful; she had a heavy, tired head and an obviously low mood. She pulled the blind up and sat in bed looking around her, slowly coming back to terms with her reality. It hadn't been a bad dream. This had happened and in about twelve hours he'd be walking through the front door to face the music. She wasn't tearful now, just numb and very tired; she went downstairs and made a coffee, took it back upstairs and got herself showered. After putting her make up on, she then went back down and made her breakfast, all of this on a very slow, methodical autopilot. Only managing to stomach half of her green smoothie, she grabbed a banana and her kit bag and went out of the door to work.

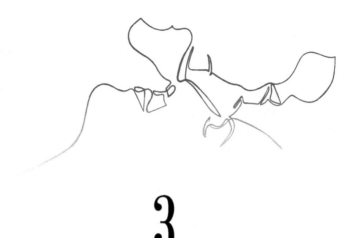

3

One thing to be said for being in the fitness industry, you don't get time to think or dwell! She took two classes in the morning and another two in the afternoon as well as two personal training sessions. It's impossible to overthink when you've got to bounce about like the energiser bunny and motivate people, so the day passed by quickly. After her last class she went in the gym to stretch out.

Angie, one of the other gym staff came over for a chat.

"Hey Mrs, how are you?" she asked cheerfully plonking herself down next to Lexi.

"Ha, don't ask!" Lexi replied, her tone giving away the heaviness inside of her.

"Seriously, that bad, eh?" Angie frowned at her response.

"It doesn't get a great deal worse I'm afraid Ange!" and she told Angie the events of the night before as they sat on the mats together.

"So, what are you going to do then?"

Lexi sighed, "I really have no idea."

"When's he back?"

"Tonight," Lexi replied, shrugging her shoulders and giving Angie a look as if to say 'Any suggestions?'

Angie sat back on her heels. "Wow Lexi, I can't say I envy you right now! So, you know nothing about her or whether it's been going on a while?"

"Nope," Lexi shook her head, "nothing at all, just that it's happened." She turned to her, "What would you do?"

Angie thought for a moment, "Well you have to hear him out. Let him explain himself, you can't make a decision when you don't really know what's gone on, he might have been pissed and not even known what he'd done till the next day!" she said trying to think outside the box and give her friend the best of bad scenarios.

"That maybe so, but in the text message I received he didn't exactly have his tail between his legs!" Lexi said in a very matter-of-fact way and told Angie what the message had said.

"Oh lordy!" she cringed with empathy.

"Exactly, I have so much going through my head right now Angie... Why now? For goodness's sake! We've got through the kiddy stage where they seem to drive a massive wedge between you both and then all the teenage trials and tribulations that followed on after that. This should be a time when we get to relax and enjoy our time together again. I honestly didn't see this coming and now I'm wondering, if we can't resolve this, we'll probably have to sell the house and go our separate ways. Quite honestly Ange, the thought of a mortgage at 50 and struggling to make ends meet is frightening me but not as much as staying with him and not being able to trust him, or always thinking that, maybe I'm not enough for him!"

Her eyes filled with tears as her emotions began to surface again.

Saying nothing, Angie sympathetically placed her hand on Lexi's arm as she continued, "Angie, I'm 50 and in the space of one day, I've gone from being happy-go-lucky and enjoying what I would describe as a happy and 'safe life' to sitting on the top of the crap-heap not knowing where I'm going to be in a week's time!" As she expressed herself, her brow furrowed with worry.

Angie put her arm round Lexi and gave her a hug, "Try not to overthink this hun, I know it's easier said than done but hear what he has to say first before you make any decisions, you don't know the full story yet. I know it's not going to be pleasant, but you might be able to work things out between you, you just don't know until you have all the facts," she said, desperately trying to sound positive. They finished their exchange; Lexi went to the changing rooms, grabbed her kit bag, and left the gym. Questions, going round and round in her head like a tornado; she threw her bag into the boot and drove home.

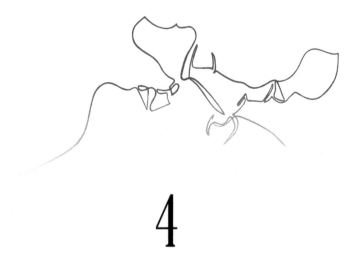

4

Nathan wasn't home yet. Lexi went into the kitchen and started to prepare some food, then shot upstairs to have a shower. She stood under the hot, powerful jets of water, stinging her skin and just let her mind go blank. The heat was relaxing her, making her feel tired after her energetic day's work on top of her restless night the night before. In a lethargic manner skipping her usual hot/cold routine she bent forwards allowing the hot jets to hit her back and stayed there until the water started to lose temperature. She switched the water off and leaned out to grab her towel, catching sight of herself in the mirror, her face looked terribly stressed. She stared at her reflection for a moment, not liking the sad and troubled image that stared back at her. She stepped out of the bath and went to the mirror. Lexi strongly believed in the law of attraction and that what we give out, we draw back to us. She also believed that the words we speak and the thoughts we think shape our reality.

Our words are spells (that's why it's called spelling) and the more strongly we connect to them and the more feeling we put into them, the more strongly the universe takes them as an affirmation. Lexi regularly did affirmations, both for releasing and bringing in. As she stood in front of the mirror, she heard the front door open then click shut, bringing her abruptly back into the present moment. She faced herself, took a breath and looked deep into her own eyes and connecting with every word said, "I release the need within me to be a victim and I now take back my power". She repeated this over and over, then blew 'life-force' into her words by blowing hard into the air, she grabbed her dressing gown, put it on and went downstairs.

Her legs felt weak as she went down the stairs. She walked into the lounge and there he stood, awkwardly awaiting her initial reaction. How was she going to be? Will she start yelling and screaming? To be honest, he knew it would be no more than he deserved.

Nathan was an attractive man. Medium height, warm brown hair, quite fit for his age and he looked after himself going to the gym 3 times a week. It went with the territory being married to an exercise professional. Although he wasn't quite as fanatical as her about the principals of health and wellbeing, he was a good-looking man and had never been short of female admirers.

She stood in silence and looked at him. She could feel the strain in her throat as she tried to choke back her tears. He could see her wrestling with her emotions and stepped forwards reaching out to her with his arms.

"No!" she said sternly, instinctively stepping backwards and putting her hand up like a stop sign.

"Don't touch me! I don't want you anywhere near me!" she recoiled.

'Here we go,' he thought, bracing himself. "Ok I won't touch you; I'll stay here. But we need to talk, I've been trying to work out what I was going to say to you all the way home in the car. I just feel so terrible," he said, almost as if he needed sympathy.

"Oh, diddum's! How awful for you!" she responded sarcastically.

A little voice inside his head said, "Yep, take that one on the chin, sunshine you asked for that!" He then offered, "I just want you to know that nothing like this has ever happened before."

"Oh really?"

"Yes, really!" he protested as she continued.

"So, it's the first time you've ever done anything like this and you've been caught out straight away? Do you really expect me to believe that Nathan?"

"It's true, I promise you, that's the truth!" he said trying his best to reason with her.

"Yeah, well, your promise isn't exactly held in high regard right now Nathan!" and before he could say anything else, she added, "Why Nathan? Why now"? Throwing her hands up in the air. Nathan's head dropped, "I don't know," he shrugged.

"You don't know?" She glared at him, "what kind of an answer is that? Am I not enough for you? Do I bore you?"

Nathan shook his head, "No, no, no, nothing like that, it just wasn't like that!"

"Oh really? What was it like then?" she persisted.

He ran his hands through his hair and sat on the arm of the settee trying to figure out what he could say that would limit the damage. Of course, the damage was already done and no matter how carefully he chose his words he wasn't going to make the situation any better.

"We've both been working on the project and spending a lot of time together, the deadline is in little over a month, it's been manic! You know it has babe?" He looked at Lexi searching for some kind of understanding but this pathetic look only fuelled her fire.

"So, you thought you'd have a shag and relieve a bit of the tension, did you?" she mocked.

"No, Lexi! No!" he protested, "I never set out for this to happen, please believe me, I feel fucking terrible," he said raising his voice now in sheer frustration.

"Good! I'm glad you feel fucking terrible!" she said raising her voice to meet his.

"Yeah, ok, I asked for that. But please hear me out. It was never my intention for this to happen. We'd all been working really hard on the merger, there is just so much still to do before the deadline. We had dinner, working all the way through, then we sat in the bar after dinner still working but we'd had a few drinks. I don't know, it just kind of happened."

Lexi just stared at him silently.

"It just happened Lexi," he repeated looking up at her earnestly. "I'm so sorry, really I am."

The tears started to roll down Lexi's face.

"It just happened," she said croakily, lightly shaking her head and before he could come back with anything else she added, "How old is she?"

"Thirty-five".

"Was she good?" she asked as Nathan visibly 'cringed' shaking his head and saying

"Lexi, please don't do this."

"Please don't do what? Please don't want to find out about the lady that you've been unfaithful to me with? Why not? I want to know!" She protested really raising her voice again now, "Is she more attractive than me? Is she better in bed than me? Tell me, don't be shy, shyness didn't stop you shagging her in the first place!" Her tongue razor sharp now.

"Please Lexi, this isn't getting us anywhere," he said desperately trying to diffuse the situation, but Lexi wasn't having any of it.

"Tell me about her, I want to know. I want to know what it is about her that was worth pissing all over 20 years of marriage, she must be very special!" She could see Nathan was visibly shaken by this statement. He shook his head as he said, "I didn't piss all over 20 years of marriage!"

"Didn't you?" She questioned, looking him straight in the eye "What did you do then? Did you think of it as just a bit of fun and I'd be ok with it?" He squirmed but she didn't give him a chance to answer. "No. You didn't! What you didn't think was – that you would be stupid enough to send your lovers message to your wife by mistake!"

He observed her energy change; her upset had now turned to anger. She walked into the kitchen and started to carry on with the dinner, not that she'd be able to eat anything. She started to throw things noisily into the pan for a stir-fry; Nathan followed her into the kitchen.

"You still haven't told me what it is that's so special about her," she carried on not letting the point go and also not looking up from what she was doing.

Sighing he wearily replied, "We're on the same team, we work well together…"

"Have you always fancied her?" she interrupted.

"No! Honestly!" he protested, "It's like I said, we've been working so hard to get everything in place for the merger, it's all been so intense, we had a few drinks and it, it just happened. If I could turn the clock back I would, honestly." He reached out for her arm but she surreptitiously manoeuvred herself just out of his reach. She placed the pan on the hob and started cooking.

Inside her head she was so angry and what had sparked that anger was his reaction when she had said he'd pissed over the marriage, because he so clearly didn't think of it like that. In her head she felt he had trivialised it, as if she was the one making a 'big thing' of it, it was this that had angered her and with it came an innate strength she never knew she had.

She cooked in silence as he stood leaning against the doorframe watching her, not knowing what to say next. He realised that this wasn't going to be like one of his 'deals' at work, this wasn't going to be at all easy. He struggled to think of something constructive to say that wouldn't land him any deeper in it. He knew he was in the biggest trouble of his life, that was obvious, but he hadn't bargained for the 'pissed all over the marriage' bit! Surely, she wouldn't leave him over this… surely? It simply hadn't dawned on him that the situation really could be that serious. As she carried on cooking, he started to feel a streak of panic going through him. He thought back to the night in question, had he known this would be the result he would never have done it. But 'done it' he had, and now he was facing the aftermath. It was actually easier when she was upset, now she was angry he was going to have to tread very carefully indeed.

She dished up the dinner and took hers to the dining table. She wasn't at all hungry but having done so much physical work during the day she had to put away some much-needed, good quality nutrition and calories and she ate what she could.

He came in with his food, put it on the table and broke the silence by saying, "I can't handle this babe, what can I do? There must be something I can do! I just need to know we're alright."

Lexi didn't even look up from her plate, "We're far from alright Nathan!" She snapped back.

Of course he knew this, he was just desperately trying to undo the damage. "I know, I know, it's just... Oh God! Honestly, I'd do anything to turn the clock back, I truly would."

She put her cutlery down, looked straight at him and said quietly but precisely, "But that's just it, isn't it Nathan, you can't, can you? You can't turn the clock back and take it all away. It's happened, you did it and at that point in time it was exactly what you wanted to do. And, what's more, I'd lay money on it that if you hadn't sent me that message by mistake and you had got away with it, it would've happened with her again and again and again."

Nathan dropped his knife and fork on his plate and slumped back in his chair, looking into his lap and shaking his head. Not because he disagreed with her but because he simply couldn't argue with her. She'd hit the nail right on the head.

She picked up her plate and went into the kitchen, popped it in the dishwasher, got herself a glass of water and went upstairs.

"Arsehole!" She muttered under her breath as she reached for her toothbrush. "If he thinks it's all just going to be ok because he's said sorry, he's very wrong!" She finished in the bathroom and went and laid on the bed with a book, she'd shut the bedroom door just to confirm that he wasn't welcome in there. She lay on her belly propped up on her elbows and read for a bit but found herself re-reading the same paragraph and then page over and over. She was just going through the motions; not really taking any of it in, her head was elsewhere. Where her brain once was, now sat this huge, tangled mess of questions, accusations, anger and blame. Her neck and shoulders felt sore and stiff with tension. She shut the book, rolled onto her back and lay looking at the ceiling. In a bid to quieten her mind she focused on her breathing, first making her breaths deep and slow into her belly and then she started closing one nostril with her finger on alternate breaths to create a calming effect.

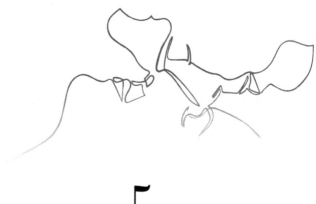

5

The next thing she knew it was 4.30 in the morning and she needed the toilet. She got up and went to the bathroom, from the landing she could hear Nathan snoring in the spare room, she returned to her room and went back to sleep. She woke to hear Nathan in the shower. Looking at the clock, it was 6.40am. Lexi only had one class on a Friday, late morning and then had the rest of the day off, which she enjoyed as it gave her a nice easy end to her week and a longer weekend.

The shower switched off in the bathroom and she could hear him moving about. Next, the bedroom door opened. Lexi was lying on her side with her back towards the door and pretended to be asleep while he got his clothes out of the wardrobe, she felt him go still. He stood there with his clothes in his hands and looked at her asleep. He was absolutely full of regret. He went over to her, bent and kissed her cheek, then turned and left the room to get dressed and go to work. Lexi didn't move, still pretending to be asleep. The only tell-tail sign of her being awake (that had gone unnoticed) was the tear that fell from the corner of her eye, onto the side of her nose, ran over the bridge of her nose and then dripped onto the pillow.

She waited for the front door to click shut behind him then got out of bed and went to make some coffee. Some very, very strong coffee! She had no need to be up this early but there was no way she'd have been able to fall back to sleep. She took her time and ambled from one thing to another before it was time to leave for work.

She had a heavy heart, she felt so terribly hurt and upset about the whole situation, but his words kept ringing through her head, "I didn't piss all over 20 years of marriage!" With this thought at large in her head she muttered to herself, "Yes you have Nathan, that's exactly what you've done."

She got to the gym where Paul was at reception, "Hey hun, how are you?" He bent forward and kissed her cheek over the reception desk. "How's it all going? I haven't been able to stop thinking about you," he said. He could tell by her posture that she was very unhappy.

"I'm not really sure to be honest," She sighed, sounding drained. "I totally believe he regrets it, but I'm not convinced of 'why' he regrets it. I don't think it's because he's hurt me, I think he regrets it because of the mess he's found himself in, and that's not helping me any!" It was time for her class, time to put her stuff in the locker, have a quick warm up and then put on her happy Mrs Motivator face!

At that point her phone pinged alerting her to a text message, it was Nathan.

"We need to get away and talk this through, I've booked us in to a hotel in Norfolk for the weekend. It'll do us good to get away and talk this over properly, we have to sort this out."

She stared at the phone for a moment and then said out loud, "What can we say in Norfolk that we can't say at home? Twit… He thinks if he takes me somewhere fancy, I'm going to forgive him just like that?... Well, sunshine, you may be going to Norfolk, but you'll be going there on your own because there's absolutely no way I'm dancing to your tune!" she said defiantly. She returned her phone to her locker and went to take her class.

It's amazing where you seem to get that extra strength when you're angry. She did her class, bounced about in her usual style, no one participating in the class would've been any the wiser that her world had fallen apart. She finished the class, showered and left the gym sharpish.

Once home, she got on her computer and looked at spa hotels and weekend retreats. She found a nice one in the Peak District; it was a large stately home turned into a hotel and spa. The estate had three converted barns in the grounds that were part of the complex, with use of the spa but self-catering. "That'll do nicely," she thought. She got the phone number off the Internet and called the hotel direct, yes there was a self-catering dwelling vacant and she booked it.

She got her cool box out and started to put together food to take with her, she preferred it this way. Lexi was very fussy about what she ate, pretty much everything was organic and absolutely everything, without exception was cooked from scratch. She liked to know where her food came from and how it was grown or raised. She tried not to change her lifestyle much, (if at all) when she was away from home.

Into the cool box went the meat she'd bought for the weekend, some freshly made bone broth, eggs and what veg there was, she'd have to stop and get some more shopping on the way. In a holdall, she put her Nutri Bullet (can't live without that!) Coffee beans (organic of course!) Coconut oil, spices, most of her supplements, tea bags, phone charger and anything else she thought she might need that didn't fit into her suitcase. When she went away, which was quite often as she went on courses at least three times a year, she was careful not to upset her rhythm in any unnecessary way. She always took food, drink and supplements and tried to stick to her daily routine where food, exercise and rest was concerned.

She was so used to packing for trips she had it off to a fine art. From experience she'd learned that there's nothing worse than being away from home, stuck in a hotel room on your own with nothing to do in an unfamiliar area and not having something you realise you need. For this reason, she had a regular 'check list' and a good system. She loaded the cool box into the boot with the holdall and finally went inside to bring her suitcase down and lock up the house. By the time Nathan got home she'd be well on her way and unavailable to be manipulated by him!

6

She set off on her way stopping for petrol and some groceries and, "Ooh, wine! Don't mind if I do!" she said out loud as she picked it up. Organic of course! She was determined to nurture herself. Her journey took her well over three hours and fortunately, with the state of mind she was in, the journey was both pleasant and uneventful.

As she turned into the estate it was just stunning. Trees lined the road either side, the main building was just magnificent, made from stone with original leaded windows. She parked up, got out and took in the amazing building in all its splendour, "Wow!" she exclaimed in awe as she took it all in. She spotted a notice saying, 'reception this way' and followed the arrow. She had to go through a massive arched doorway with a wonderful, heavy, carved wooden door. She absolutely loved this kind of place. There was an entrance hall with a standing suit of armour at the side and through an intricately carved, wooden hatch stood a very attractive lady, slim and elegant with brown hair tied back in a very tidy fishtail plait. She had beautiful high cheekbones and her name badge read Selina.

"Can I help you?"

"Yes please," Lexi replied, I made a booking earlier this afternoon in the name of Mrs Cooper.

"Oh yes, here we are," replied the receptionist. "If you go to the far end of the car park there's a track to the left, down there are three buildings, you're in the one at the far end."

"Thank you," Lexi said as Selina handed her the key. She got back in the car, drove through the car park and up the tiny track.

It was lovely; the buildings were really old, crooked and full of character. She parked up outside her little barn building, got out and took the holdall and cool box from the boot and made her way up the little path. Unlocking the old wooden door, she went in. It was cosy looking, with a settee facing a little wood burner and a small pile of logs against a gorgeous, exposed stone wall. There was also a television and round the back of the sofa, there was just room to walk through between it and the breakfast bar. On the other side of the breakfast bar was the kitchen area. She walked beyond the kitchen area to find a bathroom with a massive bath with 'jets' in the side of it and an over-head shower. Beyond that, a sweet little bedroom, very country, with rose patterned quilt and curtains and a pretty window, again in lead with a wide ledge you could sit on. She went to the window and looked out, it was absolutely charming, "Good choice," she verbally congratulated herself.

She went back to the kitchen, put all her food away and set her familiar stuff up in the kitchen as she would like it, she then unpacked her case. It was now just after six and wouldn't get dark for another couple of hours, so she decided she would go for a run to loosen up after sitting in the car for three hours, have some dinner and then finish off with a nice magnesium bath (like I said, she took everything!) She got her kit on and off she went.

First, she went into reception to ask Selina about a possible half hour route she might take. The receptionist was straight on it, picking up a local footpath map and showing her a couple of options. Off she went with her iPod on and lost herself for a while. The footpaths were well sign posted and, once in her rhythm, she enjoyed the beautiful countryside around her. Her directions had taken her down a hilly field and along a small river, just perfect. She ran through a dense wooded area and, as she came out the other side there was the biggest, blackest cloud in front of her!

"Mmm, I don't like the look of that!" she said to herself. She'd been out about twenty minutes and by her calculation she was now just over a mile away. She decided to 'step-it-up' as the cloud seemed to get bigger, darker and lower, then, "uh oh!" Yes, the rumble of thunder! "Shit!" she exclaimed, feeling her adrenaline starting to pump, she loved a good thunderstorm from the safety of her home but wasn't quite so keen to be out in one! She could see the grounds of the stately home off in the distance. 'Thank goodness for that!' she thought. The rain had started to come down hard now and the wind had started to join in making it sting her skin. She ran on, keeping her pace faster than her usual 'comfy' pace but not so fast that she'd burn herself out. The thunder boomed again, "Oh no!" she whimpered pressing on; it almost seemed to be following her. By now she was feeling quite anxious to be out in it with very little cover as the storm started to generate more and more power.

At the same time, coming along the winding country roads, Conrad carefully navigated past the first casualties of the storm; the wind had torn down some branches that had fallen into the road. He was on the last leg of his journey and very tired as he'd been travelling for fifteen hours. Conrad was one of the co-directors of an international company that dealt in security software. His business took him all over the world; he lived in the States and regularly had business in England as well as many other countries. He lived in Los Angeles; he was single, though only just. He'd been in a relationship that had lasted just over two years, his girlfriend had lived with him and enjoyed all that his ample salary had provided for her but unfortunately in Conrad's world, work came first. He was completely driven by his passion for his job and he was very good at it. Only when work was over, the project neatly tied up or the deal safely closed, did he have time for his private life.

This had proved to be the one thorn in his side for all his adult life; he was a shrewd and intelligent businessman. His sense of 'self-worth' was measured purely by what he'd accomplished in his career, that and only that was what defined him, what drove him and unfortunately, what found him single over and over again. He wasn't a bad lover or partner, he didn't mistreat women emotionally or physically, he simply didn't put them first when he was on a roll. Whenever there was a big project, he was incredibly focused; his work took over his every waking moment. He was always chasing that deal and as a result he was now 41 with a string of failed relationships behind him, the most recent finishing just two weeks ago. His girlfriend had enjoyed the lifestyle he had provided for her but, as a result of being left to play alone all too often, she had finally 'played away' to fill the empty space he should have been there to share with her.

He was very handsome with dark hair. He was of medium height, had a nice, trim body, he was attractive and had a very likeable personality that could literally charm the birds out of the trees. He enjoyed female company, he had a very nice side to him, his charm went a long way with women, he used it well and never had any shortage of women admiring him.

As he neared his destination the storm seemed to generate more and more energy. The trees were frantically blowing about, the rain got heavier and heavier, it was getting harder and harder to see to drive. Nearing the entrance gates of his hotel, he just about made out the figure of a woman running and obviously battling against the driving rain, "I wouldn't want to be you right now, love!" he muttered to himself. He was about to pull along-side and offer her some shelter when there was an almighty clap of thunder, and with that she literally shot off like a bullet from a gun and he lost sight of her in the poor visibility through the windshield.

Lexi had just turned into the gates of the drive up to the manor house; she was absolutely soaked through to the skin by now and was really having to battle against the wind and rain. This was not what she'd bargained for when she set out, the storm was right above her now and she was quite frightened. At that moment there was an almighty clap of thunder right above her head, its deafeningly 'crack' so powerful the ground shook beneath her feet. It scared the life out of her and prompted her into an outright sprint for home and safety. She made her way up the little track, shaking and out of breath, her heart pounding in her chest. Then, as she got to the little wooden door, she said to herself, "Key! What did I do with the key?" Just then it dawned on her it had been in her hand when she'd gone to the reception. "Oh bollocks!" she exclaimed to herself and turned and headed back across the car park towards the reception.

As quickly as it had started, the rain had now calmed to a spit. Lexi walked back across the car park and as she walked round the corner toward the reception area, Conrad had got out of his car and was getting his suitcase out of the boot. He spotted her fluorescent top and realised that she'd been the lady he'd seen just a few moments earlier.

"Not the best day for it!" he addressed her as she walked past the car.

"I have to admit it wasn't my best sense of timing!" she replied, as she continued towards the entrance. She was so wet the water was literally dripping off her!

"That was quite hairy wasn't it," he said jovially.

"You could say that! It came on so suddenly. It was absolutely fine when I left!" Lexi replied.

"I saw you up by the gates," he continued, "I was going to offer you a lift, but you just shot off! I don't think I've ever seen anyone move so fast!" he laughed.

"Tell me about it, it's amazing how fast you can go with the right motivation, I don't think I've ever been so frightened! But thank you anyway." She smiled at him 'That was nice,' she thought to herself. Selina was still there on duty; she took one look at Lexi and said, "Oh, my goodness! Are you ok? I've been thinking about you! It all changed so quickly, didn't it? I did wonder if you'd got caught in it or not."

"Yes, I think we can safely say I did!' Lexi said laughing, "Did I leave my key here?" she asked.

"Yes, you did, here it is." Selina reached back and took Lexi's key off a hook and handed it to her.

"Thanks," she said taking it from her.

Conrad took her all in as she stood there. She was soaked from head to toe, her hair was in a soggy ponytail on her head, her wet, fluorescent yellow top stuck to her body, she was very slim and athletic, his eyes happily scanned her as she stood there.

Despite her age, Lexi was functionally quite strong and very fit. She was driven more by what her body was capable of doing rather than aesthetics, her athletic frame was a happy by-product of the lifestyle she lived. She took her key and went to leave.

"How long are you here for?" Conrad asked.

"I'm just here for the weekend." She replied. "I've only just got here, I went for a run because I was stiff from driving!" she explained, "What about you?"

"Yes, I'm here for the weekend too, I have business not far from here next week," he replied.

"It seems like a beautiful place," she continued, "so far I think I've made a good choice… apart from the run of course! Have a nice weekend," she said smiling at both Selina and Conrad.

"And the very same to you, I hope we bump into each other again." Conrad said with a look that stayed on her just a little longer than it should. She smiled a little bashfully and patted her soggy, wet hair back consciously as she thought to herself, 'I don't think I could look a lot worse!' On the contrary, as she walked away Conrad thought to himself, 'The weekend just got interesting!'

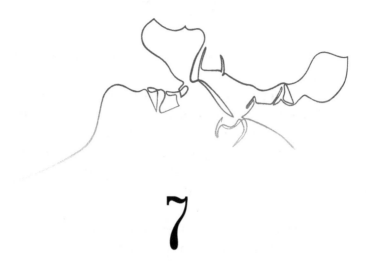

7

Lexi left the reception building with a smile on her face, Conrad's attention had given her a bit of a lift and right now that was exactly what she needed. She returned to her dwelling, stepped inside and took off her soaking wet running kit as she stood on the doormat, wrestling with the wet, clingy material, then took it in the bathroom and hung it on the towel rail. At that point she decided to run her bath before she ate, as she was now feeling cold and was shivering from being wet through. The hot, steamy water started to fill the bath as she added some of her magnesium flakes and then a beautiful 'heady' fragrance rose in the air as she added some of her relaxing essential oils. She went into the kitchen and got some water. Her handbag was sitting on the breakfast bar. She went over and got her phone out, there were 17 missed calls from Nathan and five messages. "Oh, here we go!" she muttered as she opened her messages to hear…

" Where are you hun? Call me when you get this."

"Lexi, please don't do this to me, we need to talk, you know we do!"

"Please come home hun, I can make it up to you I promise."

She listened to three messages from Nathan all sent within the space of an hour followed by another and another, "Lexi, let me know you're ok please, I know I deserve this and I totally understand you, but please come home now so we can work this out." and lastly, "Lexi please, when you get this call me, you've made your point, just come home now please."

She listened to the messages without any reaction or emotion; looking at her phone she said to it,

"You don't honestly think I'm going to make it that easy for you, do you?" She returned the phone to her bag, picked up her water and headed back toward the bathroom.

She got in the bath and turned the water jets on so the bath was bubbling away nicely. She slid down so her shoulders were under the water and let out a big sigh as she relaxed, being gently 'pummelled' by the water. She was miles from home, Nathan couldn't possibly find her or try to manipulate, or force her into his way of thinking. This was her space to sort it out in her head, in her own way and she didn't feel the slightest bit bad about it. She considered it her prerogative to have time to think things out and not be pushed or bullied by Nathan. He was a problem solver by nature, he would just try to make things right and bombard her with whatever plan of action he thought would get him back where he wanted to be. No! She was going to do things her way.

A good half hour later, she emerged from the bath a whole lot more relaxed and started to think about food. Lexi was fanatical about her diet. Her belief was that one of the best investments you can possibly make in your quest for good health is to put the best quality food in your mouth.

She loved cooking and enjoyed the ritual of preparing her food. She liked to know where her food came from and that it hadn't come into contact with chemicals, antibiotics or growth hormones. Also being a very spiritual person, when she sat to eat her meal, she always thanked her food for giving its life to nourish her and support her life. She'd bought some chicken to use in a stir-fry for this evening; she'd also bought some diced beef to make a curry, some salmon, salad and lots and lots of vegetables. Lexi was gluten intolerant, so she didn't have any grains in her diet but made up for it with a nice assortment of colourful vegetables with every meal.

She chopped her vegetables and sautéed them in a pan with some of the chicken, a big dollop of coconut oil, some lovely, fragrant lemon thyme, chopped chives, Celtic salt and black pepper.

"Mmm, lovely," she said, as the aromas filled the air and within five minutes she was happily and ravenously tucking in. After her dinner she sat and read for a while. It was getting dark now so she got up, checked the door was locked and drew the curtains. She was shattered; she'd had no, or very little sleep the previous two nights, so at this point she decided it was time to go to bed. As she was leaving the kitchen, she spotted her bag. Just out of interest she got her phone out, there were three more missed calls from Nathan and one message.

"Lexi, please come home, please? We can still go away for the weekend; I really, really want you to come back. I'll do anything you want, absolutely anything, please let me make this right again, at least give me a chance, please!"

She sighed as she read the message, "still go away for the weekend," she retorted with contempt to the phone,

"I don't think so somehow, try asking your tart to go with you!" she muttered.

She walked into the pretty little bedroom, went over and drew the curtains and put the bedside lamp on, all the time reflecting on why she was there. She took her clothes off and got into bed. Lying there she thought to herself, "Is this how it's going to be? Cynical comments and back biting because I've lost all respect for him?" She agonised with herself. "I truly don't see how we can ever get our relationship back on track, I really don't. He says it's the first time it's ever happened, but he's been travelling with work for years, it could've happened hundreds of times for all I know. I only have his word that he hasn't done it before, and what about future trips? I could never trust him again; I'd be constantly wondering if he were up to something while he was away. Do I still love him?" She thought long and hard, "I'm really not sure, to be totally honest, I know it's the 'hurt' talking but I'm truly not sure." She lay flat on her back with her palms turned up and concentrated on her breathing and the gentle ticking of the clock. She consciously emptied her mind of all that was spinning round in it and gradually drifted off to sleep.

Meanwhile, back at home, Nathan tipped the last drop of a glass of whisky down his throat, popped the glass on the table and picked up his phone. Still nothing from Lexi, he was now feeling a bit drunk and very, very sorry for himself. He was well aware that the situation he found himself in was purely of his own doing, he accepted that, but he hadn't bargained for her being so difficult and sabotaging his efforts to try and make amends. She was simply making it impossible for him to reach out to her; she was making it impossible for him to even begin to show how much he regretted his actions. There was so much he would be prepared to do to make things better if she'd just give him the opportunity. Feeling terribly frustrated that she wouldn't even give him a chance, he went into the kitchen, saw the last of the whisky in the bottle, poured it into the glass and knocked it straight back, then staggered off to bed.

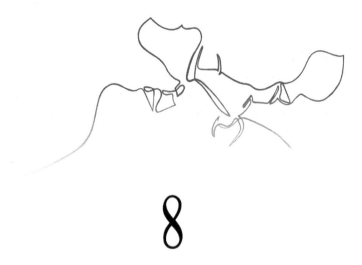

8

Lexi awoke to the sunshine streaming through her curtains; she sat up and drank her glass of water, her eyes following the straight beams of light that penetrated through tiny gaps in the curtains. She got out of bed, went to the window and drew them open, "What a lovely day!" she said to herself with certain delight as she looked out at the pleasing view. Humming as she went into her little kitchen, she put the kettle on and made up a concoction of herbs and spices in a cup then added hot water to it, stirred it and knocked it straight back for her morning liver cleanse tonic. She then made herself a nice fresh pot of organic coffee, poured herself a mug, added a knob of butter and then parked herself on the wide window ledge, savouring both the strong aromatic coffee and the pleasing view. Once she'd finished her coffee she went and got her kit on, tied her hair up and went out to the car and got some equipment out of the boot. There was a substantial area of grass at the end of the track by the car park that was perfect for what she had in mind.

She took out of the car boot some weights, a kettlebell, a couple of medicine balls, a skipping rope and a 'battle rope' and then put together a little circuit for herself. She loved being outdoors and exercised outside all year round. Once she was set up, she happily got on with her workout and totally lost herself in it.

At one point a young man had parked his car in the parking area and seeing Lexi working out across from the car park, he got out and went over to her.

"Good morning!" he said.

"Oh! Good morning!" Lexi replied a little surprised, as she hadn't seen him coming over.

"You look like you're on a mission!" he said.

"Ha, no, not really, just doing my thing. It's a lovely morning for it, isn't it?" she replied.

"It certainly is," he agreed. "I'm Charlie, I run the gym in the hotel." He put his hand out to shake hers. "It's not huge but I'm confident it's got everything you'll need in it; you'll have to pop over," he said.

"Oh, thank you," she said shaking his hand, "I haven't been and taken a look yet, but I will definitely be paying a visit over the course of the weekend," she confirmed.

"I take it you're in the fitness industry?" he asked.

"Yes", she replied.

"Thought so, you can just tell, can't you?" he winked; she carried on with her work out as they talked.

He was pleasant, mid to late twenties and had a very friendly way with him. They chatted about their trade and their education, where they had both worked and then went on to talk about the area, what was about, the villages and tea shops etc. She was nearing the end of her workout. She lay down on the grass to do some core work and then made use of Charlie as she did some reverse curls. She held onto his ankles to stabilise herself as she bought her legs and bottom off the floor and he pushed her legs back down again as they came up toward him.

"Thanks for that," she said, appreciating his input.

"No worries, you might as well make use of me as I'm here!" He jested and then added. "No doubt I'll see you at some point over the weekend then?"

To which she replied, "Oh yes absolutely, I'll definitely be paying you a visit."

And with that he went on his way to work and left Lexi to round off her workout.

Conrad woke up with a heavy head from his jet lag. He was in the main part of the hotel in a very grand room. It had beautiful wooden furniture and heavy, good quality soft furnishings also in the old country style of the rest of the hotel. He bumbled out of bed almost falling over his own feet; putting the little kettle on he went to the toilet while it boiled. He opened one of the complimentary sachets of coffee from a selection in a small wicker basket by the kettle and poured the water in. There was a yoga class over at the gym studio in twenty minutes, he did yoga regularly, he felt it benefitted him and helped him to relax a bit. Still in his boxer shorts he pulled back the curtains and let the dazzling sunlight flood into his room as he stood looking out of the window taking in the eye-catching grounds and drinking his coffee.

It was most certainly a charming setting, beautiful trees, endless grass, a lovely lake with all kinds of different ducks, a rose garden and an herb garden, it was a perfect retreat from the chaos of business life and long-distance-flights. As he stood by the window, sipping his coffee and gradually coming 'to', his eyes scanned the aesthetically pleasing grounds. His eyes rested upon the pretty, old outbuildings right across the car park and then fell upon the movement of a little lady out on the grass by the car park, instantly recognising her as the lady he'd seen the day before.

He opened his French windows and stepped out onto the balcony to get a clearer look. Completely oblivious of her observer, Lexi skipped, jumped, threw heavy balls about in every direction and did a whole range of other exercises in her little circuit.

He was mesmerised and stood watching her as he sipped his coffee forgetful of the time. All at once he looked at the clock, "Oh, bugger!" he exclaimed as he realised he'd now missed the start of his yoga session. He refilled his coffee and then went back to the window, his eyes widening as a young man walked over to her and started to make conversation.

"Nut's!" He exclaimed but kept watching all the same, the young man stood and talked to her for about ten minutes before going on his way. He then watched her as she started throwing cartwheels and doing handstands on the grass, 'not something you see every day!' he thought to himself, smiling.

After she'd rounded off her workout with a bit of 'play' Lexi started clearing up her equipment from the grass and heading back to the car park area.

Noticing this, Conrad quickly threw on a vest and some loose sweatpants, he made his way through the hotel corridors and reception and out towards the cars. When he got there, there was no sign of her. He went to his hire car and opened it, fumbled with something on the back seat for a second and as he stood back up, there she was, coming back across the car park with some balls and weights in her arms. She was walking towards the little track where her car was parked.

"Good morning!" he called after her.

"Oh! Hello again!" she said with surprise, "How are you?"

"I'm good thanks, and yourself?" he said, eager to get a conversation going with her. Of course, that was never difficult with Lexi!

"Yes, great thank you, did you have a good rest after your journey?" she replied.

"Yeah, great thanks, I've just been watching you work out, you completely wore me out while I drank my coffee!" he jested. Feeling a bit brave she said, "Oh, you should've come and joined in, it's always nice to have some company." Thinking on his feet he replied, "I thought you had got company?" Fishing now, to see whether this other male was competition.

"No, he works here, he just came over for a chat and to be nosey I think!" she said dismissively. Feeling a small sense of relief, he said, "Do you want a hand with any of that?" gesturing towards her arms full of equipment.

"No, I'm good thanks," she replied, "mind you, I would appreciate it if you could just open the boot for me, if you'd be so good," she said nodding towards her car.

They walked towards her car, he opened the boot, and she launched herself at it, relieving herself of the weights and balls. As her back turned towards him, he noticed she was covered in grass and mud.

"Jesus you're filthy!" he exclaimed.

Lexi glanced back over her shoulder and replied, "Yes, the grass was a bit dewy, lovely out there though, I prefer to be outside in the fresh air, it suits me."

"It looked like hard work to me!" he added.

"Ah, but very satisfying!" she smiled back at him.

He was intrigued, "Do you work out like that every day then?" he asked.

"No, not like that every day, I work out most days," she replied, adding "but I do something different every day and obviously I have rest days."

He was quite impressed by this, "So, what are your plans for the rest of the day?" To which she replied, "No major plans, I'm just pleasing myself, I thought I'd go and grab a sauna after this."

Thinking on his feet he said," Oh, that's exactly what I was about to do!"

"Oh, I'll probably see you over there then," she said with a smile.

"Great, I'll see you in there, what's your name?"

"Lexi!" she replied.

"Nice, I'm Conrad!"

They smiled at each other.

"I'll probably see you in a bit then," she said and with that Conrad went back over to his car, took something out of the boot (so it didn't look like he'd only come out to talk to her) and then went back to the main hotel building. Lexi smiled to herself, went inside and made up a green smoothie for her breakfast, which she knocked back with her herbal supplements and then she got everything together for her trip to the spa.

9

Lexi walked over to the main building. It was very grand and beautifully kept, with lovely old features, a massive staircase leading up to the hotel rooms and an enormous chandelier in the reception area. A different receptionist was on duty today, Lexi asked the way to the spa and if she needed a coin for the lockers. She found out what she needed to know and made her way to the ladies changing rooms. She popped on her bikini and got her towel and toiletries together; in the shower she washed the grass and mud out of her hair and then rubbed conditioner in and put it in a knot on top of her head to leave in while she had the sauna.

As she entered the sauna, Conrad was already in there lying up on the top shelf relaxing with his eyes closed. She opened the door and with that he stirred.

"Aw, sorry," she said apologetically.

"What for?" he replied.

"You looked peaceful it seemed a shame to disturb you!"

She walked over to him and placed her towel on the middle shelf and lay down on the towel.

"No, not at all," he said watching her get settled below him, his eyes taking in her body. "What do you do for a living?" he asked.

"I'm a Holistic Health Practitioner, Exercise and Lifestyle coach,"

"Yeah, that figures, I thought it must be something like that,"

"What about you, what do you do?" she asked.

"I work for a company that designs and installs security software systems for companies,"

"Oh, interesting. So, I take it you're not from here then?"

"No, I live in the states, I was born here but moved over when I was ten. I travel a lot with my business and I come to England a lot, probably once every month to six weeks. I enjoy it, it keeps me occupied." He smiled, "You here alone then?"

"Yes unfortunately" she replied with a regretful tone in her voice.

"Oh? Unfortunately? Why so?" he fished.

She sighed, "It's all a bit of a mess really, I've kind of run away."

He listened intently as she explained her situation to him then exclaimed, "Jesus, what an idiot! I bet he's climbing the walls right now! You mean he has absolutely no idea where you are? Good for you. You make him sweat! I don't blame you!" he said with conviction.

Lexi appreciated this show of support, "What about you? Are you married?" she asked.

"Ha, no! I'm in a kind of similar situation to you though, I split with my partner a couple of weeks back, I caught her out messing with another guy." Then added, "Well, a friend of mine actually."

"Ex friend of yours now, I should imagine!" she added ironically.

"Exactly! Yeah, I'm still smarting from that one a bit!" He went on to explain, "I've had a lot going on and there's been a lot of travelling lately, so I can understand her being pissed at me for not spending enough time with her, I do get that and claim full responsibility for it." He said earnestly,

"It's not really what she's done so much as how she did it, I just feel well and truly 'stung' by it, to be honest, I just didn't think she'd be the sort to go behind my back, let alone with my friend."

Lexi could see he was still a bit upset by this.

"I don't think anyone sets out to cause that kind of hurt Conrad, I think it all depends on their need and how strong that 'pull' is, the hurt is a by-product of their weakness," Lexi said trying to soften the blow.

He turned on his side, looked at her and said, "Do you really believe that?"

"I have to!" she replied, "If I don't what have the last twenty years been about?"

He looked at her, as she appeared to reflect on herself and her own situation.

"Yeah, sorry, of course you do, I can see where you're coming from." He sat up and said, "I bet you he would do anything to turn the clock back right now though, he must be gutted! So, do you know what you're going to do then?" he asked.

"Right now, I have no idea, I came away to think about it, to give myself some space to work out in my mind what it is I want and how I might want to resolve it but quite honestly, I keep drawing a blank. All I keep thinking is, if he hadn't sent me that text, I'd be none the wiser and he'd probably still be at it, I just can't seem to get that scenario out of my head," she admitted.

"Mmm, it's a difficult one," he agreed, "what about your family?" he asked.

"My children are grown up, my son lives with his girlfriend and my daughter is at University, neither of them knows that any of this has happened yet." At that point Lexi started to get a bit over heated. "I need to cool off for a moment," she said and left the sauna for a cold shower.

No messing about, she was straight in there under the ice-cold, powerful shower, letting the cold water run down her body cooling her core temperature.

Conrad watched her through the glass, "Blimey she's either brave or mad!" he thought to himself.

Lexi returned to the sauna and took up her previous position. "Do you have any plans while you're here?" she asked.

"I have some preparation to finish off for a big conference next week. I'm in the middle of something quite important, so I'll get some work done on that this afternoon. What about you?" he asked.

"Oh, I thought I'd go out for a nice walk this afternoon, it's such a pretty area, I'd like to get a feel for the place. I drove through a very picturesque village on my way here; it's about two miles away if you turn left out of here, so I think I'll head there today. There's another, slightly larger village going in the other direction, I thought I might explore that way tomorrow." She made up her mind as she spoke then added, "I also have a massage booked in at 6pm, so that'll finish my day nicely."

Feeling the heat now getting a bit too much for her, she said, "I think I'm cooked; I'm going to have to cool down." She picked up her towel and water.

Not wanting the conversation to end there, Conrad also got up and they went out into the shower area. He watched her under the cold shower, again finding it hard to take his eyes off her and just so he didn't appear to be a coward, once Lexi had stepped away, he got under the cold shower.

"Fuck that's cold!" he exclaimed and jumped out again very quickly!

Lexi found this quite amusing and giggled; there was something about her he really liked.

"That was nice, I feel good after that," she said.

"Yeah, me too."

"Well, it's been nice talking to you," she added as she picked up her stuff to go.

"Yes, and yourself," he replied, adding, "It'd be nice to catch up with you later if you're around, are you eating in the restaurant this evening?"

"No," she responded, "I'm over in the self-catering bit, I bought all my food with me." A little disappointed by this he asked, "Don't you eat out then?"

"Yes, I do," came her reply.

Keen to not let her walk away without fixing a date with her he asked, "Would you like to have dinner with me tonight, no strings, just nice company?"

She looked at him and thought to herself, why not indeed?

Smiling she replied, "Yes, I'd like that very much."

Trying not to look too triumphant he asked, "Great, what time do you think? How long is your massage?"

"45 minutes," she replied, "so I could be ready for about 8pm, if that's ok?"

"Sounds good to me," he replied, happy he'd managed to fix a date with her.

As she turned to go, she added, "Shall I meet you in the bar?"

"Yeah, that'd be great, see you in the bar at eight then." He smiled to himself as he picked up his towel and headed off to the changing rooms.

Lexi showered and washed her conditioner off back at her apartment. She got dressed and let her hair dry while she had some lunch and then tidied herself up. With her hair dried and a bit of make-up on, she picked up her iPod and handbag ready to set off. She pulled her phone out; there was nothing new on it. "Finally, he gets the message!" she said putting the phone away as she stepped outside and locked the door. She called in at reception on her way out to pick up a local map, then stepped out into the sunshine, selected the music she wanted to listen to, popped her earphones in and started on her way. She really couldn't have picked a better day to be there. The sun was out, she had the whole afternoon to herself, which was a very rare occurrence for her and happy, she went on her way.

Conrad showered and had lunch in the spa. He returned to his room, got his computer out and started his preparation for the week. After an hour or so, he sat back from the screen, his eyes were sore, still tired from both the travelling and the time difference. He thought about Lexi for a moment and smiled to himself. He got up and opened the French windows to let in some fresh air to see if that would help him to refocus on his work. He managed another fifteen minutes and then sat back again rubbing his eyes. He started to realise that this was a lost cause; he couldn't concentrate on what was in front of him. He looked outside, it was a lovely afternoon, and thought to himself that a walk would've been nice, but she'd be gone by now. "Damn!" he exclaimed out loud. He then packed away his computer, put some trainers on, picked up his wallet and left for the car.

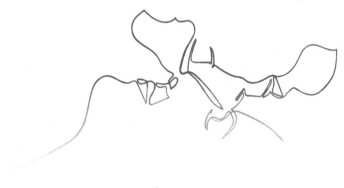

10

As Lexi was walking along the country road, she felt her phone vibrating in her handbag. "Here we go!" she thought to herself as she took out her phone. It was her son Eddie. "Uh oh!" she exclaimed as she looked at her phone displaying his name. She pressed the green arrow, "Hiya, you ok?" she asked.

"Mum, where are you?" came his anxious voice from the other end.

"Why?" she asked.

"Dad says he can't get hold of you," came the frantic reply, "he said that you've had an argument and he doesn't know where you are!"

"Oh, has he now!" she said, thinking to herself, 'So, because he can't get his own way, he has to involve the kids,' Lexi was absolutely seething!

"I've come away for a bit of space Eddie, I am entitled to that after what your father has done. I take it he's filled you in on it?" she enquired.

"He said you've had a massive argument!" Eddie said with concern.

Seeing red now, Lexi retorted, "That'd be about right! So, he's involved you when he's not even prepared to say what he's done, what a yellow belly!"

"What has he done mum?" Eddie asked.

"Your dad's been with another woman Eddie, that's what he's done!" Lexi replied, not to intentionally upset him but really there was no other way of saying it.

All went quiet on the other end of the line at this statement.

After a few moments Eddie asked, "Do you know that for sure mum?"

"Yes, sweetheart, I know that for sure, and I'm really cross your dad has involved you. I've come away to think things through and he keeps calling me and not giving me any space, so I've ignored his calls." she tried to explain. "I'm really sorry you've had to find out like this Eddie but it's something I've got to figure out for myself in my own way." She insisted.

"You are going to go back though, aren't you?" Eddie asked, his voice now getting quite high.

"Eddie, I don't know what I'm going to do right now, I haven't had enough head space to sort out my thoughts yet," she replied honestly.

Eddie, who was now getting very worried, jumped in with, "But you can't split up, you can't!"

Lexi could hear that her son was getting in a real 'flap'.

"Sweetie," Lexi tried to reason, "I also can't go home to a man who has not only betrayed me but now seems to think that any approach is fair game as long as he gets his way. I will NOT be bullied about this, not by him or by you! I know exactly why he's called you and what his game is and he's the one who's at fault here!" Her voice quivering with emotion.

"But mum, you can't leave him, we're a family, you have to forgive him, you have to" Eddie pleaded. Lexi, now feeling under tremendous pressure from her son retorted with, "I don't have to do anything Eddie, please just give me some space, I really can't believe he's dragged you into all this, the selfish bastard!" She was crying now as her desperate son tried to convince her that if she went home everything would be all right and they could live happily ever after. On and on he went, his voice getting ever 'shriller' by the moment. In the end Lexi just said, "I'm sorry Eddie, I'm going to have to go!" As she took the phone from her ear, she could still hear her son ranting down the other end as she pressed the red button.

Placing her phone back in her bag Lexi was now absolutely sobbing at the injustice of it all; how dare he involve the children; she felt like she was getting it from all angles.

Conrad got into the car and decided to go for a little drive into one of the villages, just to see if he could see Lexi about. He turned left out of the estate, remembering that she'd said she was going that way and drove in the direction of the next village. After a mile or so he spotted her up ahead.

"Ah, bingo!" he said to himself out loud, cheerfully. But as he neared her, he could tell by her body language that something was wrong and as he came alongside her, he could see that she was not only crying but that she was clearly, terribly upset. He pulled up on the verge and quickly got out.

"Lexi! Whatever's wrong?" he said as he darted towards her.

Lexi just sobbed uncontrollably.

"Hey, hey, come here," he said softly and put his arms around her in a concerned way. She held onto him as her upset poured out of her, they stood for a few minutes until she managed to gather herself enough to get her words out and explain what was wrong.

"I'm so sorry," she sobbed.

"Hey, don't apologise," he said, "What an earth has happened?"

She stood back from him, searching in her bag for a tissue.

"I've just had a frantic call from my son, Eddie."

She blew her nose, took a breath and contained herself enough to talk.

"Because I wasn't answering his calls, Nathan, my husband, in his wisdom, has decided to call our son and get him alongside."

With this statement she started crying again, sobbing out her words,

"It's just so unfair, I would never have involved the kids until I knew exactly what was what!"

He stood facing her with his hands on her shoulders, as she explained with red eyes and a runny nose the conversation she'd just had.

"I couldn't bear for him to blame me for not forgiving. He can't expect me to just accept the situation and go home, it's so unfair!" she protested.

"Hey," Conrad tried to reason with her, "He's shocked and upset. This is his initial knee-jerk-reaction, give him time, I'm sure he'll see it in a different light when it's sunk in properly and he's had time to think about it."

"And anyway," she continued, "what kind of message is Nathan giving him by involving him like this, it's just so wrong!"

Conrad put his arm round her shoulder and gently led her towards his car.

"Come and sit down for a moment." He led her to the car and they sat on the bonnet.

"You have to do what is best for you, I'll lay money on it after he's had time to think about it and see it from both sides, he won't blame you, he'll come around." Conrad tried his best to convince her.

"I hope so, I couldn't bear it if he blamed me, it's so unjust!" Lexi sniffed.

"Trust me," Conrad added, "He's in a panic right now, that's all. This must be a massive shock for him. I'll bet you hear from him again before the day's out and he'll be different, mark my words, just give him time for it to sink in."

"Do you think so?" Lexi looked at Conrad with pink eyes, he felt absolutely wretched for her.

"I'm absolutely sure of it." His words seemed to calm her a little.

Noticing this he added, "I think a walk is the best thing for you right now. Actually, I quite fancy a walk too, that's unless you would prefer to be alone?" he quizzed not wanting to be pushy.

"No, not at all, that'd be nice, you've been very kind. Thank you. Where were you off to anyway?" Lexi asked.

"Oh, I was just going to look for a paper shop," he said fibbing slightly.

Conrad parked the car off the road in a field entrance so that it wouldn't be in the way, locked it up and they started to walk in the direction of the village and talk. The conversation went from Lexi's situation to Conrad's situation and then on to their lives and work and slowly Lexi's mind began to settle.

After about forty minutes they found themselves entering the village. Such a pretty village with beautiful stone houses just like on a chocolate box.

"Oh look, there's the paper shop," she said, and they went in.

Without wanting to admit that he didn't really need the paper shop, he walked round and picked up a few things. He got to the till with some biscuits, crisps and a bottle of coke. Lexi took a sideways glance at his purchases and thought to herself 'clearly not into healthy eating then!' Lexi just picked up a bottle of still mineral water and they paid and left.

They walked along through the village and came across a little coffee shop.

"Fancy a cuppa?" he said.

"Ooh, yes, that'd be nice," she replied. They went inside and ordered a pot of tea. Feeling peckish, Conrad also chose to order a massive piece of carrot cake.

"Do you fancy anything?" he asked.

Lexi took a look in the glass cabinet and spotted a gluten free chocolate brownie and asked for that.

They sat at the table and she poured the tea from the teapot. At that point her phone bleeped to indicate there was a text message, she picked up her phone and saw that it was from Eddie. With a concerned look on her face, she opened the message, mumbling, "Mmm, here we go!" And opened it to read.

"I'm sorry mum, I know you must be very upset, I'm sorry for earlier, I love you E xXx"

As she read the message there was look of relief on her face. Observing this, Conrad asked,

"Everything ok?" As he did, Lexi turned her phone round and showed him the message. Conrad felt quite relieved for her.

"Told you, didn't I"? He said.

"You did," she said smiling like a massive weight had been lifted from her.

"Feel better now?" he asked, though he didn't really need to, her face said it all.

"Absolutely, yes," she said whole-heartedly, "I'm so relieved."

"Good, that's one problem out of the way, I think you have quite enough on your plate right now," he finished.

At which point Lexi said, "It looks like you also have quite enough on your plate too!"

She gestured to his oversized piece of cake. He started to tuck into his carrot cake and she, her brownie. "Mmmm, this is lovely," she said. Conrad forked off a rather large chunk of cake and tried to fit it in his mouth not very efficiently! "Have you got enough on there?" she laughed as he finally got control of his mouthful and reached for a napkin.

"Wow! That's amazing, try some," he offered.

"No thanks, I'm gluten intolerant," she replied.

"One little bit won't hurt, surely?" he questioned, to which she replied,

"Sweetie, if I have any of that I'll be guffing like a bison for the rest of the afternoon, trust me, you'll be glad I didn't!" They both laughed, he liked her way of just saying it how it is with no apology, he found it endearing. He smiled at her, reaching for the pot, asking, "Would you like another cup?" Sliding her chair back she replied, "Ooh, yes please but first I need to get rid of the one I had lunch time!"

He laughed as she got up and headed towards the sign that said 'toilets' and couldn't help but watch her as she left the room. She was wearing cut-down denim shorts with a blue and white check short-sleeved shirt and these, rather odd-looking trainers with separate toes in them. He liked her walk and watched her bum as she disappeared from the room.

Lexi returned to the table and sat back down.

"That's better!" she said with a beaming smile.

"What's with the weird trainers then?" He was intrigued.

Lexi looked down at them, "Have you not seen these before?"

"No, I haven't, they're rather weird!" He observed.

"They make you use your feet properly," she said and as he stared at them, she lifted her foot in the air to give him a better look. "I think they're great," she said, "I wear them all the time."

He smiled at her sitting there with her foot up in the air and said, "I'm really pleased I met you this weekend Lexi, I'm really enjoying your company."

She felt a certain glow at his words, she smiled softly back at him and replied, "And I'm really pleased I've met you too."

Her eyes searched his face, she was taking him all in, he was very handsome, but she was well, aware that she was quite a bit older than him.

As she gave her soft, sincere reply he felt a flutter of excitement deep inside. Despite her situation, he would happily go for her if she was in the right place emotionally, married or not, that was simply how he felt. He fancied her but equally he admired her passion and drive.

"I can see you live sleep and eat your trade, you're clearly very passionate about it, that's so good to see in someone and it's not something you see very often. Most people just do whatever brings the most money in". He observed continuing, "Given the right circumstances what would you like to do, or where would you like to end up in your career... would you like your own gym?" he asked.

"Oh, wow! Now you got me, I've always loved the idea of it but I think I came into the industry a little too late for anything like that to be honest," she replied

"What do you mean by that?" he questioned.

"Well, I didn't start in the industry till I was 38 and spent seven years just interested in the exercise and nutrition bit. It's only been the last five years I've been studying the whole holistic side of it and it's really a whole other world. I've got so much out of it, my knowledge of how to achieve health and wellbeing has grown tenfold and I love the difference I can make to people's lives. I've always dreamed of running something of my own, but I think I'm a bit too old now to take on anything as big as a gym, I wouldn't really want the stress of it to be honest, certainly not on my own anyway."

As she was rambling, he did the math and said," But that would make you 50?"

"Yes, that's right."

"Fuck off! You're never fifty!"

"Sshhh!" she leaned in with her finger over her mouth looking sheepishly around to see if anyone had heard.

"Yes, I am fifty," she confirmed, "Deal breaker, eh?" She laughed giving a half wink.

"No, not at all, blimey, you've surprised me though, I thought you were about my age," he said in disbelief.

"Well, thank you, that's what healthy living does for you!"

"Well, if that's what it does, maybe I should be employing you!" he said very impressed.

"It wouldn't be out of the question, but I think the time difference might be a problem!" she said. He was straight back with, "Where there's a will there's a way!" backed up with, "And there's always good old Skype or Zoom!... No, seriously, I would be more than interested. I mean, I try to keep myself quite fit, I do yoga, I have the occasional smoothie but to be honest, it's hard when you're travelling all the time."

"Hey, don't worry, I'm not judging you!" she chipped in.

"I didn't think for one moment you were," he replied, "but I think you probably would do if you saw my wine cabinet," he paused, then continued, "and you most definitely would if you saw my fridge," then his lips curled at the edges and he started to laugh as he finished with, "and abso-fucking-lutely, if you went through my bin!" Lexi giggled at his honesty.

"Have you got a business card?" he asked.

"Yes," she said picking up her bag. She took a slim, silver box out of her handbag and produced her business card, he took it from her and read it.

"You do parasite testing?" he looked up at her quizzically.

"Yes, it comes up quite a lot," she replied.

"Seriously?" he said almost in disbelief.

"Yes," she continued, "It's estimated one-in-three people are playing host to a parasite and I'm talking here, in this country, you don't have to be from some far-flung country to get parasites."

"You're shitting me!" Conrad was astonished.

"Nope," she shook her head. "It's a common problem."

"Blimey, well, I've learned something today," he said shaking his head, adding, "you're really into all this aren't you?"

"Yes, I'm extremely passionate about it," she said with conviction.

"It shows," he smiled and then he produced a card from his pocket. "Here, this is my card, not that you're ever likely to need security software but you never know!"

She took the card, read it and popped it in a zip pocket of her handbag. They finished their tea, "You all done?" He asked.

"Mmm, that was lovely," she said as they got up from the table. Lexi decided she'd pay another visit to the toilet as she'd had two cups of tea and it was going to be at least a couple of miles back. Conrad insisted this was his treat and while she was in there, he settled up and they went on their way.

They walked a little way along the road and then decided it would be nicer if they walked back on the footpath rather than the main road. Lexi got the map out of her bag and they worked out a route that would take them off road and bring them out close to where they had parked the car.

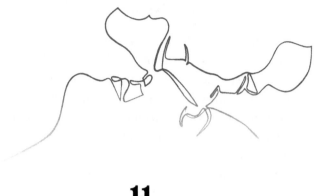

11

It was a lovely walk up a huge hill; Lexi was going 'great guns' in front of him. As they got about three quarters of the way up Conrad was flagging a little, but Lexi kept her stride and reached the top ahead of him.

"Oh wow! This is just amazing!" She exclaimed as she got out her phone and switched it to camera. As Conrad approached, she was climbing up onto the bottom rail of the fence to get a better view. The old, crooked fence was unstable and bowed towards her as it took her weight. "Oooer!" she exclaimed bending forwards to try and counterbalance the movement. Conrad grabbed her by the hips to steady her, "I've gotcha," he said, "Take your pictures." As she steadied, she was so aware of his hands on her, it felt nice so she took her time!

Conrad held her at the top of her legs near her hips and stood to the side of her admiring the view, so conscious of his hands in contact with her body.

"Wow, just look at that, absolutely awesome," he said.

"Isn't it, I'm pleased we've come this way," she replied.

"Yeah, good call," he said as their eyes took in the landscape rolling down the other side of the hill. There was a field with two horses in, a little fence running down the length of it, with stables and beyond that a pond that had two weeping willow trees hanging into it at the bottom.

"It's like a paradise!" she said taking her pictures. "Just breath-taking."

"Totally," he agreed, as she climbed back down from the fence aided quite unnecessarily by his hands, by now he was reluctant to take them off her.

As they walked together down the footpath, he kept feeling he wanted to take hold of her hand but stopped himself in case she was offended in any way.

She was in heaven, she felt so nice compared to how she'd felt earlier. She'd been so upset but now she was completely relaxed and much happier, enjoying both her surroundings and her company. She felt grateful to Conrad, he'd really lifted her spirits, she felt like she wanted to hold his hand but thought she'd better not, he might take it the wrong way.

As they walked down the footpath the two horses noticed that they had company and gracefully strolled towards the fence,

"Oh, hello there!" said Lexi and instantly held her hands out to them.

Conrad watched her as she started to pet them, stroking their faces and patting their necks. She stood back and took her phone out.

"I have to get a picture of these beauties!" she said. As she stood back to get the shots, the horses were reaching their heads right over the fence, craving more of her attention.

"Here, give me your phone, I'll take one of you with them," he said, and she handed it over and stood in between the two horses as he took a couple of pictures. "Perfect!" he exclaimed.

"Let me take one of you with them," she said.

He obliged, handing the phone back to her and she took a couple of shots. "Let's have a selfie with them?" he suggested, they both huddled in to get the shot.

"Oh, that's a fabulous one!" she chirped, really enjoying herself. They took a few more and then she said, "Thank you my lovelies," as she petted them a little more before they carried on their way. As they walked on, the camera became quite a source of entertainment, it was a good camera; you could do all sorts with it.

They neared a little pond with a gnarled old log by it. She sat down on it and tipped her head up towards the sunshine and Conrad sat next to her. Sitting with her eyes closed, she took a deep breath and gave a relaxing sigh as she exhaled. "Ok?" He asked.

"Mmm, it's lovely, isn't it?" She replied, "I feel really at peace here." She undid her trainers, slipped them off and placed her feet on the grass giving out another contented sigh as she did so, the sun was beating down and the birds sung happily in the trees and bushes. Conrad watched her peaceful expression and smiled, she opened her eyes and asked, "Do you ground yourself?" "No, I can't say that I do." He replied.

"It's very good for you," She continued, "It's mother nature's natural anti-oxidant, like a free multi-vitamin, the earth releases negative ions and when we are barefoot on the earth, we can absorb these negative ions."

"The only time my bare feet touch the earth is when I'm on holiday," He replied, "It would never occur to me to do it otherwise. I live in a penthouse apartment, I go from the lift to the car, from there, to the underground parking lot and then in the lift to my office!"

"All the more reason for you to try and make time to do it then." She replied, "Especially with the amount of time you spend in the air and travelling on the road. Don't you ever have lunch in the park?"

"Man, no! To be honest I'm usually grabbing my lunch on the go, lunch is something I do between appointments most of the time!" Lexi gave a little frown at this, "What does it do for you then?" He asked.

"Well, it has lots of benefits really... It helps you to heal better, it can also help you sleep better, it reduces cortisol, the body's main stress hormone, which means you will recover from stress more quickly, it can help to reduce chronic pain, it will increase your energy." As she rambled on, he cut in, "Seriously?"

"Oh yes, it helps to relieve muscle tension and headaches, it helps to reduce inflammation in the body and when you're grounded you are completely protected from the harmful effects of electromagnetic frequencies.

"Wow! I'd better get my trainers off then!" He said, enthusiastically tearing away at his laces, kicking off his trainers and socks and placing his bare feet on the grass, feeling the soft grass under the soles of his feet. He also closed his eyes turning his face to the sun and took a deep, relaxing breath and as he exhaled, he expressed. "Mmm, this is nice." Lexi took a little side-ways glance at him; he looked relaxed and 'in the moment'.

"It's important to make time for yourself, quality time." She broke the silence; "You have a very high-pressured job, it's important to bring your body and mind back into balance. We all need to take time out from our chaotic schedule and quiet the mind, otherwise you're on a constant roll of fight or flight and that's hard on the adrenal glands, they never get a rest and that's not how they are designed to work. Over time, if you're not taking time to bring about this balance, it has a negative impact on your immune system, your digestion, your hormonal system and just about everything else. What do you do to relax?" She asked.

"Usually, it involves a bottle of wine!" He laughed as he replied.

"Do you ever meditate?" She asked. "No, not really, I do chill out and listen to music though." She looked at him, "Well that is a good way of having some down time, but it also depends on what you're listening to as to what you would get from it. Have you ever listened to a guided meditation?" She asked.

"No, never, it's not something I've gotten into, I take it you do it all the time then?" "Well, not all the time but I do try and make time daily to quiet my mind and be present. It all depends on how much time I have really, sometimes it's a full-on meditation, other days it's ten minutes of mindfulness or even a 'mindful' walk. It definitely helps me manage my stress better and makes me more productive, even if it is only ten minutes, unplugging and giving the mind a break makes a huge difference." She continued, "This kind of place is perfect for practicing mindfulness, just to focus on and take in everything that's happening around you, feeling the warmth of the sun, feeling the breeze, listening to the birds and insects, watching the clouds drift by, being conscious of the scent coming from the trees. I find it's easier sometimes to be 'mindful' and focus on the here and now, rather than trying to completely empty my mind." They sat for a few minutes, mindfully taking in their surroundings.

After a while Lexi said, "Does it feel good?" "Yeah, it does." He replied in a relaxed voice, his eyes calmly scanning his surroundings. "Do you fancy having a go at a guided meditation?" She asked. "Right now, I'd be open to anything. "He replied, totally at peace with himself. "Okay, get yourself comfortable." She said and with that he had a little wriggle and settled himself in for the experience.

Lexi turned to face him, placed one hand at the top of her chest and the other on her belly, just below where her ribs finished. "Place your hands like this to begin with," she instructed, "And when you breath in, I'd like you to consciously breath right down as if you want to fill up your belly with air, make sure your bottom hand rises first and the hand at the top of your chest doesn't move until the last fifteen per cent of your breath. So, draw your diaphragm down to breathe into your belly, then allow your ribs to expand outwards and lastly allow your upper chest to rise and we'll take a few deep breaths like this." They both sat and took four or five deep slow breathes.

"Now, on this next breath, as you exhale slowly, I'd like you to imagine little holes appearing in the souls of your feet and out of those holes I'd like you to imagine roots tumbling out and starting to penetrate into the earth." Conrad did so. "Now I'd like you to imagine these roots breaking through the layers of the earth, twisting, winding and anchoring you securely into the earth, growing deeper and deeper, down and down until they come to the centre of the earth, where they will find a big ball of warm golden energy, this is the healing energy of Pachamama. Now wrap your roots around this golden ball of energy, feel it's warmth on your roots and start to draw this energy up your roots as if sucking up through a straw. Draw this wonderful healing energy right up to the souls of your feet and once it's there, invite it into your body. "As Conrad sat there with his eyes closed, he could clearly visualise this energy. "Now I'd like you to visualize this golden energy filling up your legs, right up to your pelvis, into your abdomen, let it fill your body, up to your chest and allow it to fill your heart space. Keep drawing this energy up until your body is full of this golden, healing energy." They both sat, breathing deeply for a few moments, then she continued. "Now that you are filled with this energy, I'd like you to take your attention way up, as if you're looking out of the top of your head from the inside directly up to the heavens and then I'd like you to visualise a bright white light, which isn't hard, because the sun is beating down on us. I'd like you to focus on this light, this is divine healing light and I'd like you to draw it down like a beam towards you until it reaches the centre of the top of your head and once it's there, I'd like you to invite it in…" She paused to give Conrad time to visualise this. "Now I'd like you to imagine your head is filling with this divine, white healing light, past your eyes, down to your mouth, then your neck, continuing down to your chest where it's going to infuse with the golden, healing energy of the earth. Keep your breathing deep and efficient, with every breath in, I'd like you to imagine drawing in more and more of this energy until you are filled with this nourishing infusion of both energies. Feel your body glow, feel your cells reacting to this positive charge as you are now fully connected to the energies of heaven and earth combined. Your roots are now being cleansed and nourished by Pachamama, with every breath in you are saturating yourself with these energies and with every breath out you are releasing all the toxins that don't serve you." They sat for a few long moments in this mind-set as if they were being charged like a couple of batteries.

Though this was completely alien to Conrad, he felt quite open and accepting of it.

After many moments, Lexi softly broke the silence saying, "Now that you have completely charged your body I would like you to start to unravel your roots from the ball of golden energy and start to draw your roots back up through the layers of the earth, unwinding and retracting them until they are back up at the soles of your feet, where they will neatly tuck in and the little holes will close. Then I'd like you to consciously disconnect from the white light and watch it travel back up from where it came. Feel how good your body feels, place your hands over your heart... smile and give thanks to the heavens and earth for this healing."

They both sat in silence for a while longer, the usually snappy, on-a- constant-roll Conrad, was quite content to sit with this feeling. He was surprised at just how different he did feel. After a while he took a deep breath and exclaimed, "Wow! That felt amazing, I feel like it actually did all happen." She smiled and answered softly, "It did." And gave him a knowing wink.

"Thank you." He said still feeling incredibly calm, yet pleasantly energised. "You're most welcome." Came her reply, "Imagine the difference it could make if you made time to do that, or something similar to that daily." She offered. "Yes, I can actually, that was a totally new experience for me." He said with conviction, "Good." Lexi said as Conrad reached into his plastic bag and got out the coke, unscrewed the top and took a swig.

"Want some?" He offered the bottle to her.

"No thank you sweetie, I don't drink anything like that really," she replied politely, adding, "neither would you if you knew what it does once it's inside you!"

She undid her water and took a good drink of it. He looked down at his innocent looking bottle of 'pop' and then smiled as he thought to himself, 'Somehow, I feel I have a lot to learn from you!'

There was a stile opposite them that they would have to go over as they proceeded with their walk. Lexi now energised and back in the moment, had the idea to balance the camera on the thick wooden post using a large rock to prop the camera up and set it to the timer.

"Are you ready?" She called as she pressed the button then promptly shot off to sit beside him on the log. They struck a pose just as the camera fell over!

"Ah, bugger!" she said.

"Try again" he said.

She went and set it back up again, pressed the button and ran for it, this time it worked.

"Ah excellent!" It was another nice picture totally capturing both the beauty of the place and the relaxed atmosphere between the two of them.

After a few minutes they set off again, over the stile and through a wooded area. The camera came out again, they took pictures of each other poking their heads out from behind trees, doing silly poses on a sawn-off tree stump and to complete the album, one last selfie sitting on another log. He held the camera away and leant in towards her with his arm round her, she beamed into the camera and just as he pressed the button, he turned his head towards her and kissed her cheek. The picture captured the moment beautifully, her eyes smiling and wide with surprise as he planted his lips on her. They both laughed, he hoped that she hadn't minded but it was obvious by her face that she hadn't. She was thoroughly enjoying his attention and as they made their way along the footpath, she consciously touched her cheek where he had landed his kiss and smiled to herself.

She started to get her bearings as they neared the edge of the wood, she was quite sure this was the wood she had run through yesterday. Yes, she was right, as they came to the edge of the wood there was the main road, now they just needed to find the car. Ten minutes later they arrived back at the car, it was now 4.45pm. They jumped in and Conrad drove them back to the hotel.

"I really enjoyed that, thank you," she said beaming.

"Me too, I'm pleased I came out now," he agreed.

As she got out of the car he asked," Are you still on for tonight or have you had enough of me now?" Thinking out loud, she said, "I don't think it is possible to get enough of you!" then quickly added,

"Well yes, I am, but a thought has occurred to me… I didn't pack a frock. I have a smart pair of skinny jeans and a top, but I didn't pack anything 'dressy'. I hadn't bargained on being invited out, it's so posh in there I'm not sure jeans will go down at all well."

She had a point; it was very posh.

"We could cancel the restaurant and eat in the bar?" he suggested but Lexi quickly offered,

"Or I could cook for us, I've bought loads of food with me, and it'll need to be used."

Conrad pondered and then replied, "It just seems a shame if you're going for a nice massage to have to start cooking when you get back, also I can't go eating all your food!" he said, not wanting her to go to any trouble.

"No, not at all, I enjoy cooking, anyway if you like curry, I'll put it on as soon as I get in, prepare the veg and leave it cooking while I go for the massage. It'll be no trouble, I always take lots of food with me wherever I go and besides, I think you're nice enough to share my food with." She smiled with another half wink.

"If you're sure?" he replied, "I'd love to, at least I know it'll be healthy!"

"Oh, totally healthy! All organic and cooked from scratch, mind you, I don't do rice, I have vegetables instead but if you can't face your curry without rice, you could always nip back to the village and get some?"

Happy with her invite he replied, "No that's fine, I'm cool with that, we'll have it your way." Then added, "Text me when you're ready, that way you don't have to race about."

"Ok, see you later then," she smiled.

"Yeah, I'll look forward to it."

With that she happily trotted back to her dwelling.

She got in and started straight away on the curry; meat, bone broth, onion, garlic, coconut cream and a lovely mixture of spices, in it all went. She gave it a good stir and turned it down to a simmer, took a quick look at the clock, still half an hour before her massage. She got out her phone, one text message from Nathan.

"Please, I just don't know what to do, I'll do whatever it takes."

Speaking to her phone she said, "Yes, I know you'll do whatever it takes, you've made that quite evident, even if it means using our children to get your way!"

She wasn't impressed with how he'd approached the situation at all, the way he'd tried to manipulate her and then used their son. She asked herself was this coming from the heart or was it Nathan the 'problem solver' just trying to put things back the way they were? Could they ever really go back to being the way they were? Right now, the way she was feeling toward him, she'd lost a massive chunk of respect for him and really couldn't imagine it.

She went over to the spa ten minutes before her appointment. It was so plush in there and lovely fragrances filled the air. She sat in the waiting area on a red velvet chaise longue. There were other ladies in the lounge area sitting in white bathrobes, comparing their nails and feet where they'd obviously had manicures and pedicures. When Lexi's name was called, she followed a lady through to one of the treatment rooms, she was booked for a back and shoulder massage. She got onto the treatment couch, which was quite toasty and warm.

The massage was pure bliss, she felt herself drifting away and as she drifted so did all her stresses. A couple of times she nodded off and then 'jumped' as she momentarily, flicked back into consciousness. She was so relaxed; this was just what she needed after her harrowing experience. When the massage was over, the masseur told her to take her time getting up and went and got her a glass of water. Lexi sat up on the couch and drank her water feeling a little 'woozy'. She caught sight of herself in the mirror. Despite the fact her hair was all scragged back and she'd been lying face down with her face through a little hole, her face looked nice and relaxed, so different to that of three nights ago, when she'd got out of the shower. After about five minutes she got herself together and left the spa. She was now thinking ahead to Conrad coming over, suddenly she was no longer spaced out as she felt a pang of excitement in her tummy at having him as her guest.

She got back to her dwelling; it was a little cooler now. She checked her curry, it was yummy, the veg were in a pan waiting to be sautéed and really nothing more to do until they were ready to eat. She spotted the two bottles of wine on the worktop and opened one to allow it to breathe.

She went into the bathroom, washed her face, brushed her teeth and put on a little make up. She tidied her locks up and then dived in the bedroom to get dressed, putting on a pair of black skinny jeans that had a coating on them making them look like leather, with those, a nice little black and red fitted top, and she topped it off with her favourite mixture of organic, chakra balancing essential oils that she used as perfume. She took a look at herself; it would have to do, as it was now time to text her dinner guest.

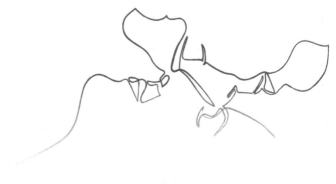

12

As she heard the knock on the door, she felt her tummy turn over; she hadn't realised just how much she'd been looking forward to this, she opened the door and there he stood, the perfect vision, freshly showered, black jeans and trainers with a nice deep purple shirt, "Come in!" She said welcoming him.

"Wow, check you out, sexy lady!" he said giving her the once over.

He bent forward and kissed her cheek, she inhaled him as his face was next to hers, he smelled amazing.

"Wow, you smell nice!" she said.

"I was about to say the same!" he replied.

"Are you sure that's not the curry?" she cut in teasingly.

"Ha, no, although the curry smells good too. I've bought some wine with me." He held up the bottle. "I forgot to ask if you drink alcohol?" he said with a tad of concern but was instantly put at ease as she replied,

"Yes, don't panic, I do. I did bring a couple of bottles with me as well, organic of course!" She said in a playful tone.

"I didn't even know you can get organic wine; I take it I have a lot to learn!" he jested.

"It would appear so!" she said playfully as she took the wine from him. "Thank you, I've already opened one to let it breathe, so we'll start with that."

He followed her into the kitchen area; she took the lid off the curry, stirred it and gave him the spoon with some of the sauce on.

"You'd better try that just in case."

"It'll be fine, I eat anything," he said taking the spoon from her and sipping the sauce off. "God, that's lovely!" he said smacking his lips, more than pleasantly surprised by the lovely infusion of flavours.

Lexi smiled a little triumphant smile at his enthusiastic approval.

"So, this is your own sauce then?" he enquired, "Not out of a jar?"

"Nope, all from scratch," she proudly confirmed as she went to the fridge and took out a small side salad. Conrad eagerly peered into the fridge as Lexi opened it, he was surprised to see how fully stocked it was.

"You bought all this food here for yourself?" he said, hardly able to believe his eyes.

"Yes!" she replied casually.

"I can understand people enjoy cooking, but I can't get my head round going to all that trouble just for yourself. Don't get me wrong, I'm not saying you're not worth it!" he laughed. "It clearly pays off to eat healthily, I just couldn't imagine going to all that trouble just for me," he said with honesty.

"It's just a case of thinking ahead and being organised. If you don't think ahead, you find that the food that is quickest and easiest to grab is usually not the best quality food," she explained.

"Tell me about it," he admitted, "since I split up with my girlfriend it's been a takeout on the way home from work or a McDonalds!" He knew that would provoke a response as the words left his lips!

"Eeewwww!" Lexi pulled a face, "I'd rather go hungry than eat that rubbish! Right, enough of the lecture!" she said taking two glasses out of the cupboard, "would you like to try some of this wine?" She showed the bottle to him.

"Yes please, I certainly would," he said eagerly and with that she poured two glasses out.

"Hungry?"

"Yes, very," he said, and she took the pan of vegetables over to the hob and put it on.

They sipped their wine and chatted in the kitchen while she tossed the vegetables in the pan. She set the meal up on the breakfast bar; there were two stools to sit on that pulled out from underneath it.

"This looks and smells absolutely amazing!" Conrad was impressed.

"Good, tuck in," she said, and they started to eat.

She watched as he ate, the expression on his face was a picture.

"This is so good! I mean really, I'm not just saying that, it's just lovely, so many flavours, I wouldn't have a clue how to cook this."

Lexi beamed happily at his compliment and added, "It's not hard, just a case of throwing it all in really."

"Mmmm." He tucked into his meal, clearly, thoroughly enjoying it. Lexi could tell by his expression that he wasn't just being polite; he was clearly enjoying every mouthful. They ate, talked and drank happily together and when they'd finished their dinner they were still deep in conversation. Lexi now started to get a bit fidgety on the high stool, "Shall we go and sit more comfy?" she suggested, gesturing toward the sofa.

"Yeah, that'd be good." He got up and picked up both plates and took them over to the sink.

"Oh, leave them, I'll do them later," she instructed him.

"No way!" he said, "You've provided me with… I have to say the most amazing meal, the very least I can do is wash up!"

"Aw, that's nice." She thought that very sweet of him, she went to the sink with him, there wasn't really that much to do, once the plates were rinsed, they picked up their glasses of wine and went and sat down.

They sat on the little settee with suitably full bellies, relaxed and a both a little 'looser' from the wine. Their conversation went from Lexi's situation to the practicalities of what she would have to do should she decide, she couldn't carry on with Nathan. She expressed her concerns over money, the gym didn't pay very well and she had only recently decided to drop some of her evening classes. Firstly, because there were now younger and enthusiastic staff at the gym that would gladly take on the evening sessions and secondly because she'd worked most weekday evenings ever since she'd started in the trade and simply wanted a break from it. Lexi had decided to wind things down a bit after her 50th birthday and for the first time since she'd been teaching classes, she now only had one late finish a week and had been enjoying her new, easier hours, she'd also found it easier to fit her studying in with this new timetable.

Since Lexi had dropped her late hours, she'd noticed that she had more energy. Her job was very physical; she had come to realise that three or four classes a day was really quite enough for her now and if she increased them again, like when she covered other people's classes as well as her own, she was aware of it having a negative impact on her. If she had to get a place of her own, it would mean without any shadow of doubt that she'd have to take on more hours again.

"Oh, it's so hard, I just don't know, I really don't, and then there's the dating again bit," she agonised.

"What do you mean?" he asked.

"Well, I know so many women of my age that have found themselves single again. They all go on these dating websites, it scares the life out of me, the thought of doing that."

"Why?" he asked.

"Well, obviously they choose someone they like the look of, find out what they have in common and all that but then they go and meet them and the first thing I always say to them is, "does anyone know where you're going? I mean, you really don't know whom you're meeting, I think it's quite worrying!" she said with concern.

"But that's how everyone does it now Lexi, anyway, surely you must meet people at the gym?" he queried.

"Yes, I do but it's not really ethical dating a client is it!"

He looked at her and added, "You must have men 'come on' to you at the gym though, surely?"

"Well occasionally," she admitted.

Straight away he added, "I bet more than occasionally! If you worked at my gym, I'd have had a go by now!"

He gave her a cheeky smile; she laughed bashfully.

"It does kind of worry me though, you know 'that' side of it." A slight awkwardness rang in her voice.

"Why?" he said, a small frown rippling his forehead.

"Well, don't get me wrong, I'm happy with my body. I am what I am, my body is a result of what I have done for my genes through my lifestyle, and I am quite proud of what I am capable of doing physically at my age, but, well, I haven't had my boobs done or anything."

"Does that matter?" he quizzed.

"It doesn't to me personally," she replied, "and to be honest I've never really thought about it until now. At my age, I wouldn't expect my boobs to still be up under my chin. I've had two pregnancies and I breast-fed both of my babies. Those beautiful babies are now two strapping young adults and personally I think it's a small price to pay. I've always been fine with it where Nathan and I were concerned but then he's seen me go through all those changes and he was instrumental in them. I'm just not sure how confident I'd feel with someone else now," she pondered.

Conrad noting the slight 'dip' in her confidence said, "You seem to be forgetting you sat in the sauna with me for half an hour this morning and it all looked pretty good from where I was sitting."

She smiled appreciating his kind words. Conrad shifted himself slightly toward her and continued,

"And I really don't think you have anything to worry about Lexi."

He was absolutely besotted by her and in that moment, he felt the need to get closer to her; he took her hand and she didn't resist him. Lexi felt herself 'catch' her breath as he gently stroked her palm with his fingertips. She felt a tingling sensation going right through her, traveling from her hand, up her arm and then down through the very centre of her body to her vagina. She shifted slightly at her awareness of this and felt very conscious of how hot she was starting to feel between her legs.

Conrad, enjoying his closeness to her said, "Lexi, I have no idea what was going through your husband's head that night." He said with such sincerity. "The more time I spend with you the more I think, what the hell was he thinking? To be honest, if I had you waiting at home for me right now, I'd even consider winding up work early and trust me, that's not something you'd hear from me very often!"

Lexi laughed feeling extremely flattered by this. "Oh! Steady on there," she countered, "I didn't think anything got you away from your work?" Using his empty glass as an excuse to stand up and move to the kitchen, she felt she desperately needed to pull her tight jeans away from her now, rather hot crotch!

As she got up he jumped saying, "Sorry, was I going too far?" a little concerned.

"No, not at all," she was quick to confirm, "quite the reverse to be honest, I was just feeling a little hot."

"I'm not surprised," he said with burning desire, "you look hot!"

She gave a sweet, feminine giggle at this and dropped her eyes slightly saying, "That's a very kind thing to say, thank you."

"I wasn't being kind," came his instant reply, as he looked at her intensely.

His eyes were like fingers touching her body, the chemistry was almost visible between them, she couldn't remember the last time she'd felt so aroused just by being near someone. He got up from the sofa and stepped toward her, he took her hand gently again, his touch was amazing and she felt like her whole body was now 'flushed'. He pulled her gently by the hand toward him and enveloped her with his other arm as he pulled her in and kissed her. She felt his soft, moist lips on hers accompanied with the small, enjoyable prickle of his neat little 'goatee' beard. He teased her lips open with his and pulled her firmly into him as he put his tongue in her mouth. His kiss was amazing; she hadn't felt quite so desired for a long time. She was lost in him, completely lost in this beautiful moment and as he kissed her deeply, she felt like she was simply going to melt.

"Are you ok?" he whispered.

"Yes, I am," her breath heavy as she sighed back saying, "I can't believe I'm doing this."

"Do you want to do this?" he asked softly.

"Yes," she replied without having to think about it.

He drew her in again kissing her deeper and deeper and more and more passionately making her murmur a little. He picked her up off the ground; his arms enveloped her and held her close to him. As he did this, she instinctively wrapped her legs around him and they continued kissing, entwined in each other. He then loosened his grip slightly, allowing her to gradually slide down him, enabling her to feel his erection against her body through her jeans until eventually her feet came back into contact with the floor. She looked at him now in a state of sheer desire, his hair was all 'ruffled' and his shirt half hanging out, the top two buttons undone. She zoned in on the bit of his chest that she could see, leaned in and kissed it. He instinctively cupped her face with his hands, lifting her head up and kissed her mouth passionately before taking the focus of his kisses more delicately now to her chin and then her neck. Lexi's head tilted back accommodatingly as he did so, and as he did this, Conrad reached down and started undoing her jeans, her stomach now felt like it was full of butterflies.

His lips came back up to meet hers, one hand now cradling the back of her head as he slipped his other hand inside her knickers and pushed his finger up inside her, making her gasp as he did so.

"You ok?" he whispered breathily.

She couldn't answer him; all that came out was a gentle groan.

"Jesus, you're soaked!" he said as he could now feel her evident excitement.

Her breath heaving, she whispered, "You excite me so much."

"That's good, because you've been exciting me since the moment I laid eyes on you!" He said, his eyes taking in the picture of absolute pleasure on her face. He continued for a while longer, his eyes searching hers, she looked longingly at him.

"Take me to bed Conrad," she whispered and of course, he didn't need to be asked twice. He took his hand out of her knickers and picked her up again, she wrapped her legs back round him and still kissing her, he carried her out of the kitchen.

"This way?" he asked.

"Yes," she said breathily as he carried her through to the bedroom and then let her feet down to the floor again.

He took the bottom of her pretty top in his hands and pulled it up over her head and off. He kissed her mouth, then her cheek, then her neck and down to her shoulder. Slowly he moved his kisses down until he kissed the top of her chest. As he did so he took her bra strap down with one hand and looked at her face to make sure she was comfortable with it. Oddly enough, having said she would probably feel self-conscious, she felt fine. She was completely lost in the moment; she didn't even think about it as he took her bra off, she was more concerned with getting his shirt off. She unbuttoned it and dropped his shirt to the floor, then kissed his chest as she reached down and started to undo his trousers and push them and his underpants down toward the floor.

Taking her by the face and kissing her, Conrad moved forward, stepping out of his clothes and simultaneously guiding Lexi backwards towards, and finally onto the bed.

They kissed passionately for many moments, then he gently kissed her chin and down onto her neck. He continued to direct his string of gentle kisses down until he reached her chest, running his tongue over her breast until it came upon her nipple. He kissed and sucked it gently as it obediently popped up for him. He cupped her other breast and teased her nipple with his fingers, she groaned as her nipples hardened and became more and more sensitive. At this point he looked up at her face, she was in ecstasy. He kissed below her breasts and down toward her belly button; he played with her belly ring with his tongue as she squirmed at the tickling sensation. He then started to kiss below her belly button and gently took hold of her knickers, as he went to pull them down, he noticed the slightest 'flicker' of something in her.

"You ok?" he whispered softly.

Gasping, she replied, "Yes I'm ok, just a bit shy."

"Don't be shy with me babe," he said sincerely.

"I've had two babies," she whispered, still breathless.

"I don't care if you've had ten babies! I want to give you nice feelings," came his instant reaction. This prompted him to come back up to her face again. He kissed her lips reassuringly, keeping his eyes on her face as he pulled her knickers down and then parted her legs with his hand. He penetrated her with his finger again, she groaned and began to move her hips instinctively. Oh my, he was good with his fingers!

Her belly started to jump and twitch with the delightful sensations he was affording her, she certainly didn't seem shy now! His trail of kisses carried on downward until they reached her clitoris, her senses now radiating tingling messages out all over her body as he kissed her gently, then started to lick her.

"Oh!" She moaned, as he started to tease her with his tongue, quick little darts followed by softer heavier strokes, her excitement was evident, her breathing becoming faster. He penetrated her again now with two fingers as he carried on stimulating her with his tongue, she was experiencing the most pleasurable sensations, it felt glorious, her whole body surrendering to the euphoria.

"Oh, God," she cried out in the heat of the moment. "Oh! Oh! Oh!" she cried as she had the most powerful orgasm; but he didn't stop there; he carried on and on, changing his technique, taking her to different heights. Then, all at once she cried out, "Oh, stop! Please stop!"

He stopped and came up to her face, "Ok?" he said.

"Oh, God!" she gasped, "I need a drink of water."

Her mouth had dried up where she'd been breathing so heavily for such a long time. There was a glass of water on the bedside table where she'd been getting ready earlier, she sat up and sipped the water finding it hard to even close her throat to begin with.

"Oh, wow, that was so, so amazing," she said between sips, still breathless.

"Why did you stop me then?" he quizzed.

"My throat was so dry I could barely swallow."

He touched her face "Ok, now?"

She kissed him. "Yes, I'm more than ok," she sighed, her breathing now beginning to recover.

She put the glass down and kissed him. He was the perfect image sitting there, his body so pleasing to the eye, he was just stunning and that most amazingly horny look on his face. Lexi wanted to give him every bit of the pleasure he'd just given her. He lay down beside her and propped himself up on one elbow then putting his other hand on her thigh.

"You ready to go again then?" he leaned forward and kissed her thigh, then shifted as he kissed it again a bit higher up. Lexi bent forward, bought his head up to her face and kissed him on the lips.

"I'm a bit too sensitive right now," she said pushing him onto his back on the bed. She crawled over to him and kissed him; she was in absolute heaven right now. "The universe does love me after all!" she said looking at him, taking him all in.

She kissed his forehead, eyebrows, nose, mouth, chin, Adam's apple, then started to run her tongue down over his chest, visiting both nipples; he groaned and closed his eyes, his hand in her hair. She licked more firmly now down his solar plexus in short, firm, downward strokes to his belly button. No fluff, thank goodness, that would've killed the moment! She kissed his belly button then firmed her tongue more, increasing the pressure as she moved down towards his pubic bone, as she did so, his penis rose up in anticipation. He exhaled heavily and groaned slightly as she took his penis in one hand quite firmly and then put her mouth over the top of it.

She shifted herself round and got between his legs. He let out a sound of utter pleasure as she massaged the shaft of his penis firmly and then licked the tip with her tongue. She looked up at him. His face was a handsome, erotic picture. She kissed down the shaft of his penis and over his balls sucking one into her mouth, tickling it with her tongue and then the other. Still massaging him she kissed her way back up to the tip and took him back in her mouth.

"Oh, my God, that's so nice!" He cried out.

She smiled to herself, she had both hands on him now massaging firmly up and down as she sucked and licked him. He cried out as he announced his arrival, she took her mouth off and finished him off with her hands as his sperm shot up over his belly towards his chest.

At this point whispering in a sweet voice, "Sorry, I don't swallow!"

He let out a massive exclamation of relief, "Oh, babe," he said breathless.

She smiled at his heaving body; she was still kneeling between his legs, her arms stretched up now holding him above the hips. She massaged his body gently.

"Come here," he said reaching for her hands.

She crawled up and lay beside him snug in the 'crook' of his arm, her head on his shoulder, and his arm around her. He slowly stroked her skin with his fingers as they lay and cuddled for many blissful minutes, both of them feeling immensely satisfied and relaxed.

Lexi needed another glass of water; she went to the kitchen and poured two glasses, tucking the kitchen roll under her arm she returned to the bedroom. She put the water down and tore some off, then sat a straddle Conrad and started to wipe him down; he watched her as she did so. He utterly desired her; he loved how he felt with her, their chemistry felt so strong, as if every mere touch sent sparks flying between them.

Sitting on him, she gently continued to wipe him down; he bought his arms down from behind his head and took hold of her hips, encouraging her to rock gently back and forth on him. They enjoyed this for quite some time. As Lexi became more aroused, she began moving her hips more, which provoked him to firm his grip on her, urging her to rub harder against him making her groan, he then pulled her up towards him.

"Come up here," he said as he wrapped his arms around her hips pulling her up to his face. Lexi held onto the headboard for support, looking down at him as he started to stimulate her again. With his hands on her buttocks, he pulled her firmly toward him and penetrated her with his tongue; this had her crying out in sheer delight, her back arching as she threw her head back in ecstasy.

She became aware her knees were starting to hurt in this position.

"Sorry, I'm going to have to move," she said, getting off and lying beside him.

He stroked her face and kissed her, to which she said, "Conrad... I want you; I want you now!"

His penis had by now resumed to full working order. He kissed her again tenderly and got between her legs, she looked at his rock-hard penis as he took it in his hand and said, "Do you want this?"

"Oh, yes," she whispered breathily.

He got on top of her and kissing her, he guided himself in, Lexi letting out an ecstatic cry as he entered her.

He started slowly at first; they were just feeling each other. It felt so good just feeling him inside her and his skin on hers, their bodies coming together in slow, passionate waves and then he got faster. He held himself up at arm's length with his eyes fixed on hers and thrust into her more firmly now as she cried out in sheer delight. He then knelt up and pulled her legs up straight, so they were running up his chest with her feet up by his shoulders. Holding on to her thighs he thrust into her, harder and faster, her boobs happily and unashamedly bouncing around all over the place with every thrust.

"Ohhhhhhhh," she cried out as he now joined in the chorus making equally rapturous noises. After a little while she said, "Do it to me doggy style!"

With a gravelly voice he said, "You like that, yeah?"

"Yeah," she gasped back.

He flipped her over and held her hip with one hand as he guided himself in again with the other. She let out another elated wail as he entered her. Oh, that felt so good. He was holding her hips and driving firmly into her as she was pushing herself back onto him, as she did, she could feel his balls slapping into her, the penetration was just amazing, provoking rhymical grunts and whines to the speed and intensity of their thrusts.

"Oh, yeah," he moaned as he got closer to coming.

She could feel he was getting close and started to stimulate herself from the front to bring things on a bit, which excited him all the more. He thrust hard into her, holding her tight and then cried out as he reached his orgasm. They became still, gasping and panting from the exertion. Placing his hands around her waist he encouraged her upright, her back still toward him. She instinctively raised her arms and draped her hands round the back of his neck as he scooped his arms around her front, enveloping her as he kissed her neck. She turned her head to the side, and he kissed her tenderly.

They remained this way for a few moments then Conrad shifted himself to lie on the bed pulling Lexi with him, where they lay holding each other, all sexed out and blissfully chilled. As they lay wrapped up in each other's arms, they dropped off to sleep.

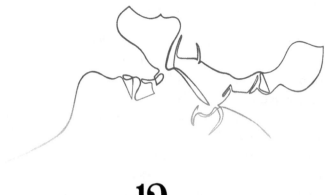

13

Morning came, and Lexi gradually became aware of Conrad's body still entwined with hers, they'd hardly moved during the night and were stuck to each other where their skin had been in contact all night. She opened her eyes and as she did Conrad, became aware of her movement and was also stirring.

"Morning!" he said dozily.

"Morning!" she replied and snuggled into him, he kissed her head as she lay with her head on his shoulder and gently stroked his chest with her fingers.

"You ok?" he asked.

"Mmm, very much so," she said contentedly nuzzling into him, she put her arm and leg further over him and he pulled her in with his other arm.

"No regrets?" he asked.

"Absolutely not!" she replied, "How could I ever regret such a pleasurable experience?"

He kissed her head again, then they both lay there for a while just enjoying the feel of lying with each other. Her mouth was dry and all the water had gone.

"Would you like a cuppa?" She offered.

"Aw, yes please," he replied and with that she got out of bed and walked toward the kitchen. As she got to the bedroom door he said "Hey!"

She stopped and looked back round at him, he looked at her standing naked in the doorway, his eyes scanned her body as she stood there, then he simply gave her a playful wink, she laughed, shook her head and went on her way. She put the kettle on, ground up some coffee beans and went to the toilet while the kettle was boiling.

She caught sight of herself in the bathroom mirror and smiled.

"Wow, who would ever have thought this would happen!" she said to herself, "I'm so happy. This is so odd, I'm supposed to be here crying my eyes out, worrying about my future, and yet it all couldn't be further from my mind! The universe has decided to soften the blow for me and I for one, am happy to accept this beautiful gift."

She made a pot of coffee and popped two mugs on a tray with some coconut oil and a spoon. As she came back into the bedroom, he lay and watched her walk towards him with the tray.

"A tray, my, we are posh!" he said teasingly.

"Posh but there might be a problem, I don't have any sugar or milk because I don't do either, are you ok with it black?" she asked, continuing with, "I either have mine with coconut oil, butter, or both, bullet proof."

Conrad hadn't got a clue what she was talking about!

"Well, I've never had it either way and what's bullet proof?" he enquired.

"With butter and coconut oil, whizzed up with a blender," came the reply.

"Butter? Sounds weird!" he said pulling a face.

"It's nice, creamy," Lexi assured him.

"I think just black will do for now please!" he said settling for the most recognisable option.

She poured the coffee into two mugs, he looked on with a funny expression on his face as she put a spoon of coconut oil in hers, then sat himself up as she passed him his and got back in bed.

Conrad got halfway through his coffee and then decided he needed the toilet; he popped his mug down on the bedside table.

"Need to pee," he said as he got up. As he got to the bedroom door, Lexi said, "Nice arse!" He gave her a wiggle and disappeared out of the room. She smiled to herself and snuggled down with her coffee and her thoughts of last night. Wow, it really had been such an experience, so very nice, and she had absolutely no regrets, she had no feeling of guilt, it had done her the world of good. Her self-esteem had fallen through the floor having had the double whammy that, not only had her husband been unfaithful, as if that wasn't bad enough, but also, the woman was 15 years her junior. It's a nasty knock for anyone, but for a fifty-year-old to experience this scenario, it's almost like saying "You're no good any-more," as if you've simply been cast aside for a newer model. Conrad had come straight to her rescue there. He had been so attentive from the outset; he had made her feel good about herself straight away which had gone a long way to re-instating her self-worth and esteem after such a cruel blow.

She heard the toilet flush and the taps going and then Conrad appeared back in the room. She'd put her coffee back on the table and lay watching him; her eyes went the full length of him as he walked towards her.

"I am one lucky lady," she thought to herself.

He stopped a few feet from the bed and looked at her.

"What?" she said.

"Take off the covers," he said.

She threw the covers back and lay there naked; both their eyes now fixed on each other.

"Open your legs," he said, barely louder than a whisper.

She felt that 'hot' feeling go through her again and she obliged. He looked down at her, taking her in, then moved onto the bed. He kissed her as he put his hand on her knee and then ran his fingers up the inside of her leg, giving her all kinds of pleasurable sensations. Still kissing her, he penetrated her with his finger and then sat back on his heels, as he continued, watching her facial expression. Lexi, was spellbound by his touch.

Her breathing started to change and she began to move her hips to accompany his touch, he turned his finger forwards gently tapping on her G-spot.

"Mmmm," she gently groaned and threw her head back.

"Look at me, Lexi..." he commanded, "I want to see the pleasure on your face."

She looked at him as he fixed his eyes on hers, watching her expression. Oh goodness, this was really doing it for her! Every time the sensation got too great, she wanted to toss her head and every time she broke eye contact, he bought her back until she was writhing, gasping, crying out and eventually bought to orgasm with her eyes fixed on his. Wow, that was a new one on her, so incredibly erotic. Who would ever have thought, four days ago, that she'd be having such a wonderful time now?

As she 'came' Conrad watched her face, he considered it to be a thing of beauty to be so deeply engaged with her in a moment of such pleasure. As she cried into his eyes, he looked deep into her soul, he loved that she'd allowed herself to become that 'vulnerable' for him. He lay down next to her and caressed her in his arms.

After a while she sat up and finished what was now a cold cup of coffee.

"Eewwww! That must be cold now?" he exclaimed.

"Yes, it is, I'll make some fresh in a minute."

She looked at him lying there; she literally couldn't get enough of him. Her eyes acknowledged the coconut oil on the bedside table and she picked it up, she opened it and scooped some out into her hand. Slowly she rubbed her hands together melting the oil and without breaking eye contact she took hold of his penis and firmly massaged the length of it. Conrad placed his hands behind his head, cupping his head to bring his face up enough to watch her. She watched him relax as she draped herself over his legs, so that her arm was in a more effective position, as she increased her pressure, he slightly tilted his head back and closed his eyes.

"Oh no Mr! You don't get off so lightly, I want you to look at me!" Lexi now commanded.

He engaged with her and then shared his gaze between her eyes and what she was doing to him, the oil felt good and she had an amazing touch. She placed both hands on him and started sliding them up and down him with a slightly wringing motion, which most certainly got his attention!

"Oh fuck, that's nice!" he exclaimed.

She smiled at him, took him in one hand, pushed his legs apart with the other and massaged his balls as well as his penis, their eyes totally engaged with one another.

As she went to change her technique again, he sat up. They were eye to eye, he took her hand off him and encouraged her onto her back, tucked his hand into the small of her back and pulled her down to the edge of the bed where he got between her legs. Without breaking eye contact he entered her; it was just so incredibly intense. Lexi's entire body was tingling. They gyrated away for a short while; he was getting very close.

"God, I'm close, I want you to come with me."

"I'm not quite there yet."

"Have you got a vibrator with you?" he asked.

"Yes."

Reaching into the bedside drawer, she took out a little pink vibrator and they resumed. He penetrated her slower but firmer as she placed the vibrator on herself. Instantly it was having the desired effect, as the vibrator magnified her sensations into something quite spectacular that complimented the stimulation, she was getting from him. Whilst their bodies were heaving and crashing together, their souls were doing a different kind of dance. Their eyes didn't leave each other for a second, they gasped as they came together and in that heightened moment their souls totally entwined one another. What a moment! Never had she experienced such a connection before. She felt like she'd shared something very special with him, which quite overwhelmed her, her eyes filled with tears with the emotion of it all.

His eyes searched deep into her as they both reached their physical 'high', it was so very intense to experience one another at such a level, no barriers, nothing to hide behind, it was a pure, raw and complete act of giving to each other. As he saw her tear up, he kissed her tenderly on the lips and caressed her, "Oh, babe, this is something else." he whispered.

They lay holding each other in silence, contemplating what had just happened, both of them feeling they had experienced something very deep and special. Their encounter had now turned from a bit of casual sex to a more spiritual and emotional experience for them.

After quite some time, Lexi propped herself up on her elbows, "Shall I make some more coffee?" His arm was still draped over her body as he lay there; as she shifted to leave the bed, he gripped her not allowing her to go. She embraced his arm and hugged it into her.

"No, I'm not going to let you go, I want us to stay in this moment for ever," he said holding onto her. "Mmm, I know what you mean, I had no idea when you came over last night that I would be feeling like this today," she said truthfully.

"And how do you feel?" he asked.

She looked down at him, put her hand out and stroked his face.

"Right now, I feel amazing. If someone had told me as I was leaving home on Friday morning that this would happen, I would never have believed them. For a start, I wouldn't have believed that I'd have been in the right frame of mind to even contemplate anything like this, let alone go to bed with someone I'd only just met. The whole point of me coming here was to get away from Nathan trying to bombard me with his tactics or bully me into forgiving him. I came to give myself time and space to sort out how I feel and how I want to tackle this in my head, I haven't exactly been doing much of that have I?" She took a breath and continued, "I believe everyone comes into your life for a reason Conrad, either as a blessing or a lesson. Right now, I see you as the biggest blessing that could've happened, I'm so pleased that you were here this weekend, I'm so pleased we've had this together," she said with total sincerity.

"Me too." He kissed her a little peck, then again, and again.

"Right, coffee!" She got up, grabbed Conrad's shirt and put it on and went to the kitchen; within a moment Conrad had followed her out there in his boxers.

"What was that coffee you mentioned with butter?" he asked.

"Bullet proof," She confirmed, "want to try some?"

"Go on then, I'll give it a go," he replied as she ground the coffee beans and boiled the kettle.

She made the coffee then put a couple of ounces of butter and a heaped spoonful of coconut oil in her blender, poured in the coffee and whizzed it all up till it just looked like a normal cup of white, frothy coffee, transferred it into two mugs and passed him his.

"Enjoy!" she said holding out her mug for them to 'chink' mugs in a cheers fashion.

"Thank you." He had a little look of suspicion on his face as he sniffed it and then tasted it.

To his surprise, it tasted good, "Mmmmm, actually, that's really nice! I'd definitely do that for myself." Lexi smiled a little triumphant smile to herself as they went and sat on the sofa. It was now 10am, Conrad suddenly noticing the time tutted, "I still haven't finished my preparation for tomorrow yet, I'm really going to have to get it done at some point today but to be honest, I'd rather be with you." She smiled.

"Really? I haven't driven you crazy then!" she said jokingly.

"Yeah, you have, but only in a good way, trust me." He winked playfully, adding, "What did you want to do today?"

"Oh, I'm easy, I didn't really have any firm plans," she said dismissively.

"You wanted to walk to the other village, didn't you?" he remembered.

"Yes, but I could do that while you're working, or I could go to the gym over at the hotel," remembering she still hadn't paid Charlie it a visit.

"What about if I get my work done and you go to the gym. When I'm done, I'll come and find you and then maybe we could walk out that way early evening. There's bound to be a pub there, we could have a meal and then walk back, it won't be dark till around 8pm," he suggested.

To which she replied, "That sounds perfect to me."

They drank their coffee and then Lexi said, "I'm hungry, I'm going to do some breakfast, would you like some?"

"What are you going to have?" he asked.

"I'm going to have a green smoothie, but I can do you some eggs if you'd prefer?"

She got up and started preparing her smoothie. He watched as she heated her bone broth, added some kale, avocado, asparagus, blueberries and a couple of different spoonsful of powder and whizzed it all up. Then she whisked up Conrad's eggs and scrambled them; she served them with slices of avocado and tomato.

"Wow, that looks nice, thank you!" he said adding cheekily, "Which is more than I can say for yours!"

"Ha, I had a feeling you might say that" Lexi said in jest, "have a taste."

She held it out to him, offering. He looked at the thick green gloop.

"Seriously?" His cutely wrinkled forehead was telling her he clearly wasn't keen on the idea!

"Go on, try it!" she said, and he carefully took a sip, swallowed and then smacked his lips.

"Actually, it tastes better than it looks," he said with surprise.

"You see, you just need an open mind, there's probably a higher nutrient content in that one cup than most western kids get in a week!" Lexi confirmed. They had their breakfast as Conrad asked her more about her food choices and how she made her bone broth.

"I always use organic bones and save all my vegetable chopping's to go into it. People have historically boiled bones and carcasses to get the collagen, but the real magic is to add organic apple cider vinegar, this leaches all the minerals out of the bones and into the water. If you're using a slow cooker, you need to leave it for three days to do its thing."

"Three days, seriously? God, there's a lot to this holistic living then, that'd be near impossible with the amount I travel!" He concluded. "Ah, but you can use a pressure cooker providing the pot isn't made of aluminium or coated with any non-stick material," Lexi added, "there are some out there that are stainless steel, which won't leach any harmful metals or chemicals into your food, and it only takes two and a half hours in a pressure cooker, so it's much quicker, or you can also buy ready-made off the internet but it needs to be grass fed and outdoor reared."

"Mmm, I'll have to think about that one," Conrad pondered," I think I'll get my head round eating better first, especially with my travel.

"You can still make far healthier choices wherever you are, you just have to think ahead," she explained, "when you return from a trip, always shop on your way home so you have good quality food to hand straight away. Make a list, whilst you're travelling of all the meals you intend to eat for three days, breakfast, lunch, dinner and snacks and stock your fridge, this way you don't fall into 'take-away' mode out of convenience. So, you will be buying lots of lovely vegetables and protein and lots of berries, nuts and seeds for smoothies and healthy snacks but back off on the grains, most people eat far too much in the way of carbohydrates when, in reality we don't need them, they make it hard for you to control your blood sugar, which creates inflammation in the body and brain and affects mental clarity. Buy grass fed organic butter, organic ghee or cold pressed virgin coconut oil and use it to cook with and put it in your coffee, or a nice knob of butter on your vegetables. Honestly, if you stuck to it for a month, you would feel very different; trust me. So, basically, all the time you're at home between trips, you shop every three-to-four days with a plan of what you would like to eat. Just bear in mind when you're buying food to choose food with the least human intervention, the longer the shelf life of your food, the more likely it is to shorten your life! So, buy everything as near to its natural state as possible. I can also help you with recipes and meal ideas, that's all part of it. I guarantee you, once you get used to it, and it becomes a habit, you won't want to go back to how you were eating before. You won't want to reach for muesli, pasta or pizzas because you won't like the taste of them anymore and you will certainly notice when you do eat them how horrible you feel afterwards. Your mental clarity is completely different without all that sugar and preservatives. Once your body's had clean food in it, it'll tell you that it's happy. It'll make you feel energetic and vital and once your body is in that place of perfect balance and you recognise your body 'feeling good', you'll equally start to notice when it's not happy.

Your body constantly gives you feedback of whether it's happy or not, it's just most people don't know how to read and recognise it. I truly believe that the vast, majority of people have no idea of how well their body is capable of feeling," she said passionately. Conrad, now completely sold on her enthusiasm said, "I really am going to do that when I'm at home, you've really inspired me to take this on, it's just going to be difficult when I'm away." He confirmed.

"It's not impossible, even if you're travelling, it's just a case of planning ahead. Source food places on the Internet close to where you're staying so you know where you can buy good quality food. I don't have MSG, wheat, soy or gluten. I always go for a place that advertises food freshly cooked on the premises if I'm eating out. If they truly do prepare everything on the premises, then it shouldn't be that hard to give me what I ask for. Like this evening, if we find a little pub, I tell them what I avoid, I order a meat or fish dish and ask if I can have extra vegetables instead of rice or pasta with a knob of butter on them. It's not difficult and you honestly feel so much better, you have so much more energy."

They chatted on for a while longer.

"We'll have to sort something out online for when I get back!" He said, and then his tone changed slightly as he asked, "You will still do it, won't you? I mean whatever you decide when you get back?" A little concern was 'telling' in his voice.

"I'd like to do that," her eyes dropped in thought, "I just don't know what's going to happen or how I'm going to feel," she said with honesty.

"Feel about me?" he asked.

"No, I know how I feel about you." She tenderly placed her hand on his leg. "Just how I'll feel about everything really. If I do give him another chance, I think it might upset me to talk to you because I know things are bound to be strained between us initially, I can't see it be anything else, a lot of damage has been done and it'll take a lot of work on both sides to recover our relationship now. I feel if I'm still in contact with you I will just keep thinking back to the wonderful time I've had here with you. I think it'll make me not try as hard as I should when, I suppose, I really should give it my all after 20 years."

She fell silent for a couple of moments obviously deep in thought, then added, "Oh, Conrad, this is going to be so hard for me, I love my family, we always have such a nice time when were all together." Her face was troubled, she was torn, she'd been so hurt by what Nathan had done and his attitude towards all of it but she loved her family and didn't want to lose it. Conrad could tell she had a lot of thinking to do.

Conrad looked at her; he could visibly see her wrestling with her thoughts.

He reached over and touched her cheek, "You have to do what you have to do honey and I won't pressure you either way. Your decision is your decision." He leant forward and planted a huge kiss on her forehead, got up and went back into the bedroom. Within a couple of moments, he came back out with his jeans on, he figured now would be a good time to disappear and get some work done and give Lexi space to sort her head out.

Lexi was now standing in the kitchen.

"Hey, I'm gonna go back and grab a shower and get that work done," he said.

He held her by both shoulders and kissed her then put one hand behind her head and kissed her some more.

"I'm gonna need my shirt back, please," he said as he gently rolled it back and down her arms leaving her naked.

He kissed her again as he popped the shirt on and did two buttons up.

Looking at her standing there naked as the day she was born he said, "Oh, my God, I can't believe I'm walking away from you like this!"

She smiled a sensual smile; he made her feel so utterly desired.

"You go and get done what you need to, and I'll see you later," she said on a more practical note. One last kiss and he headed for the door, then he turned back and said, "Trust me, you are very hard to walk away from!"

She laughed, "Have you got much to do?"

"I reckon an hour and a half should do it," he estimated, "I'll come over when I'm done."

"Ok," Lexi said watching him as he went out through doorway.

As he did, he paused for a second, looked back at her and smiled. Closing the door behind him it occurred to him that, after today, there was a chance he might never see her again and he felt his heart sink a little at this thought because he realised deep down that he didn't want that to happen.

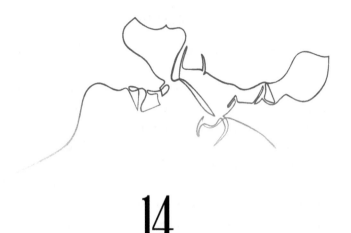

14

Lexi walked back into the bedroom, throwing herself on the bed, she pulled the corner of the quilt over her and just lay staring at the ceiling, her dilemma at large in her head. She did love her family life but if she couldn't forgive Nathan and give him another chance, all of that would change. As it was, despite her son living with his girlfriend and her daughter being at uni, they were very close, getting together often at weekends and always had a family holiday together, could she bear to lose all that? Equally, could she go back to Nathan knowing what he'd done, with the total uncertainty that this is the only time it's ever happened? And is it the only time? Or is it the only time he's been caught? Questions, questions, questions, all spinning around in her head like a Catherine wheel. How would she feel about having a physical relationship with Nathan again? To be fair, she considered she'd now done just as bad. She wondered how Nathan would feel when she went home and told him of her weekend romance. She felt she would have to tell him, she wouldn't be able to keep that one to herself and besides, if he couldn't forgive her, it would be one hell of a double standard.

If she hadn't met Conrad, she'd have had a miserable weekend tearing herself apart and gone back to Nathan, and probably both of her kids, putting pressure on her to put it all behind her and move on. As it was, she had met Conrad and she considered he was like her 'angel'. He'd made her feel attractive when she'd felt like a fifty-year-old cast off. He'd gone out of his way to comfort her when she was upset and shown her such kindness and empathy. But above all, he'd given her the most exciting, sensuous encounter coupled with the deepest spiritual connection she'd ever experienced. As she thought back over all that had happened between the two of them last night and this morning it made her positively glow and that then begged the question, could she move on and forget Conrad for the sake of her family?

"Aaahhhhhhhh," she cried out in frustration. Oh, what should she do? What indeed? This was going to be hard. Although she shouldn't bring Conrad into the equation, bearing in mind she didn't really know him, she felt that they'd be so good together. They were so happy in each-others company, they just seemed to 'fit' each other perfectly in every way, shape and form; it would be so hard to break contact with him. On the other hand, if she kept in contact would she then wish to be back in his arms again? Lexi felt that was a huge probability.

She got off the bed, went in the bathroom and stood in the bath showering herself down. She brushed her teeth, applied some mascara, finally she brushed her hair up in a 'pineapple' on top of her head, threw on some kit and headed off to the main building to the gym.

Over at the gym she was pleasantly surprised at its set out. All too often when she went to a gym (especially a hotel gym) it was all machines and a 'token' set of weights in the corner, this gym was great. A proper squat rack, cross cable machine, individual weights, dumbbells, physio balls and plenty of space to set out a good workout, as well as the obligatory row of six different CV machines. Lexi sussed out her plan of action and as she did so, Charlie spotted her and ambled over.

"Hello! You made it over here then!" he said chirpily.

"Ah, hello Charlie, yes, I thought I'd get some weights done today. I'm very impressed," she said, unconsciously nodding her head in approval as her eyes scanned the gym floor, "your gym is very nicely set out."

"Thank you," Charlie smiled proudly, "it's all just been re-done, and I had the say of what I wanted in here," he said, clearly very pleased with it.

"Brilliant, do you get very busy?" she enquired.

It was very quiet but by now it was just after 12 noon.

"Yes, the gym opens at 6.30am and we have members in from the local area, not just hotel guests, so first thing until 8.30 there's a regular handful of members and obviously again after 5pm. The rest of the time it's mainly hotel guests."

She listened as she set up the squat rack.

"Need any help?" Charlie offered.

"That would be great if you wouldn't mind spotting for me."

Lexi got on with her workout with Charlie affording her his attention. They talked about the industry, education, training, what they've done, what they would still like to do etc. She did a nice workout of squats, deadlifts and lunges as well as some upper body exercises, as per usual she got so into it she lost all track of time. As she got on the floor for her last set of glute-bridges, Conrad peered through the glass door. Charlie was still there nattering and helping her get the best out of her workout. "Come on, push, hard, directly up, give me two more," he instructed.

She pushed her last one out then lay for a few moments, motionless on the mat from exertion, the barbell still across her hips and her skin glistening with beads of sweat.

Conrad watched her unnoticed for a couple of moments; he loved how totally committed she was really giving it her all. He walked over to Lexi and Charlie.

"Hey, how are you getting on?" he said as he approached them.

"Hiya," she looked up and chirped happily, "I've just finished my last set."

She introduced Conrad to Charlie and they stood chatting for a while about the gym, the spa, how the place was run; Conrad could see Lexi was really impressed.

"Have you been in the pool yet? The pool is also really nice, it's a saltwater pool and hot tub too so you don't have to worry about strong chemicals."

This went down very well with Lexi.

"Ooh, I hadn't realised that I tend not to use the 'wet side' because it's usually all so full of chemicals, I usually just tend to use the sauna."

Lexi looked at Conrad, "Fancy a swim?"

"Yeah, I'm up for that."

Lexi thanked Charlie and they both left the gym to get their swimming stuff.

Lexi walked back to the main hotel, Conrad had walked back from his room and was waiting for her; they went into the pool changing rooms, got changed and met up the other side. The pool was lovely, it had water 'jets' you could stand under that were all different shapes and felt different as you stood underneath them, pummelling your back in a nice massage. Around the edge of the pool was a ledge to sit on that also released bubbles of air so wherever you sat you had a bubble massage up your back.

"Oh, this is fabulous!" She said as she relaxed back on the ledge enjoying the 'trickle' of bubbles running up her back. Conrad joined her and rested back on the ledge, his side and leg touching hers as he took her hand under the water and held it. They enjoyed sitting there for a while and then they decided to go in the bubble tub, which was at the side of the pool. It was much warmer, like a bath and the bubbles were fiercer. They both relaxed back and let the bubbles rock them about, it was just perfect after her workout, and she felt completely relaxed. They spent about fifteen minutes in there and then they walked over to the other side of the pool were the sauna and steam room area was, there was also an area with wooden spa beds to lie on. When they got there, they lay their towels down and sat on two of the beds.

Time was getting on, but it was so nice in the spa, they were really enjoying the facilities and relaxed atmosphere and because it was so nice outside, there weren't many other people in there. Next, they went into the sauna and got settled.

"What time do you have to be up in the morning?" Lexi asked.

"6.30," Conrad replied, "I have to be on the road for 7.30."

They both laid in silence contemplating the sudden, realisation that had hit them both. Their beautiful 'encounter' was now drawing to an end. The two of them had found themselves so far removed from the outside world and had got themselves so completely wrapped up in their experience of each other it was like being in a different world. In a few hours, it would be time for them both to return to the 'real world', Conrad back to his hectic life and Lexi back to the mess from which she had come.

"We don't have very long now do we," Lexi said looking up at Conrad on the top shelf.

He turned on his side to talk to her.

"It's going quickly, really, really quickly," he replied in a sad voice.

"If you've got to be up early, you're not going to want to be up late tonight so why don't we just chill out here and take our time, just enjoy it and then go back to mine. I'll cook dinner, I have two salmon fillets in the fridge and I still have loads of vegetables left?" He didn't argue, he thought it was the perfect way to spend the last part of their time together. "Yeah, that'd be nice," he said, both of them went quiet as they contemplated everything that had happened since that first meeting in the car park to the present moment, and on to 'what, if anything' after they leave this glorious retreat.

Lexi needed to cool down and left the sauna for a cold shower, she stepped under the jets and let the freezing water take her breath away. It was a welcome distraction from what was going through her head, which could only be described as a 'sinking' feeling at the thought of saying goodbye to Conrad. She didn't want to think about it, she didn't want it to happen, she wanted to turn the clock back twenty-four hours and live it all over again. She'd been so happy, she just didn't want it to end, the very thought made her feel sad.

Conrad watched Lexi walk out to the showers and get under the cold one; his eyes didn't leave her. They took in every inch of her from head-to-toe, he cast his mind back over the last two days and it occurred to him that in a very short space of time he'd grown very fond of her. He didn't want the weekend to end, he also couldn't imagine them simply going their separate ways in the morning, he just couldn't bear the thought of not seeing her again.

Lexi came out from the shower and went back to the long wooden spa seat; she sat down and had a drink of water. Conrad came out of the sauna, went under the shower and then moved over to the other seat. They looked at each other and she smiled a 'sad' smile, knowing exactly what each other was thinking.

"Let's just enjoy this afternoon, eh?" He said in a soft voice as he reached over and touched her arm. "Yeah," she replied with a more convincing smile than the last one.

"We haven't been in the steam room yet; do you like the steam room?" She asked.

"Yeah, sounds like a plan," he said trying to sound a bit more upbeat.

They went over to the steam room; Lexi opened the door and the steam poured out. She stepped in with Conrad just behind her, he pulled the door to as she cast her eyes around the steam filled room, getting her eyes accustomed to the atmosphere whilst also checking that she wasn't about to sit on someone's lap by mistake! A quick recce by Conrad had drawn the conclusion that the room was empty. Conrad stepped up behind Lexi and slipped his arms around her waist, hugging her as he kissed the side of her neck, she instantly responded by raising her arm and touching the side of his face. He moved his hand up and gently touched her face turning it toward him, he kissed her lips, she turned to face him, they embraced each other, passionately kissing and holding each other.

"God, I don't want this to end," he whispered.

She just held him tight thinking exactly the same thing.

"Oh God, this is so unfair," she said.

"Sssssh," he said, and they stood just holding each other, making the most of their embrace that seemed to fit each other so perfectly.

"Oh, Conrad, the more I try to think this through the more confused I'm getting. I can't bear the thought of losing my family, right now that's bothering me more than Nathan" she said as their embrace continued.

"Yeah, I know hun," he said as she carried on.

"But I can't bear the thought of us coming to an end either, I know I barely know you, but this has been so special. Oh God, I feel so confused inside my head." Stress was starting to tell in her voice.

"Hey, don't get yourself upset, please don't, you don't have to make any decisions right here and now. Like I said, you have to do what it is you have to do; I'll respect your decision either way. I don't want us to end either, I truly don't, but equally I don't want to stand in the way if there's any chance you could be happy again in your family. It would be wrong of me; I don't want you to make any decisions that you might end up regretting, Ok?" he said looking right into her eyes.

"Ok," she nodded.

As she responded to him, he kissed her on the lips and then took her by the hand.

"I think we need to go and cool off."

They left the steam room, showered off and then went in the pool again.

"I'll race you!" He said trying to change the mood.

"You might just regret that!" she responded taking the challenge.

They both launched themselves forward and raced a length of the pool. It was a close one, but Lexi just about got there first.

"Bollocks! I don't believe you, what are you super woman?" he said.

"No, just very competitive, if you challenge me, I will always rise to it!" she confirmed.

"Ha, what about under water?" he countered, figuring he may have a better chance.

"Let's give it a go, shall we?"

They counted to three and then submerged and went for it; again, they were pretty even. They started playing games, swimming through each other's legs and generally messing about and then they swam over to the ledge at the side of the pool and relaxed in the bubbles again.

It was now 4.30 and having had a late breakfast but no lunch, they were both getting hungry.

"Shall we go back and have some food? My belly thinks my throat's gone on strike!" Lexi announced.

"Sounds good to me," came his reply and with that they picked up their towels and walked towards the changing rooms.

"I'm going to have to wash my hair," she said.

"No worries, I'll go back to my room and pack away anything I don't need so it doesn't take me any time in the morning; text me when you want me to come over."

He gave her a kiss and they went their separate ways.

Lexi got her toiletries and went in the shower. She felt quite subdued and tried to think things out in her head as she stood under the powerful darts of water. The weekend was quickly running out of time; she had a decision to make, and it was a big one. She washed and conditioned her hair as everything spun around endlessly in her head. She thought of her children, her family time, she couldn't bear to see that come to an end. Her thoughts turned to Nathan but just thinking about him made her angry. "What an arse!"

she said out loud, "If only." But then she corrected herself in her thoughts, if only what? If only he hadn't hit the wrong button on his phone, absolutely not! She was pleased she had found out but why, oh, why, did he have to do it and ruin everything in the first place? Everything was fine, they were happy, or were they? Was he? Surely if he'd been that happy he wouldn't have done it? But if he hadn't, she wouldn't be here now and wouldn't have met Conrad. None of this would've happened and she wouldn't be faced with making such a difficult decision.

She got out of the shower no closer to a decision than when she'd gone in. She got dressed and headed back for the barn, where she prepared the vegetables and then went to put on a little bit of make-up, just to tidy herself up. She checked her phone, there were no calls or messages, good, she thought to herself, that's one less thing to worry about. She then sent Conrad a text to come over.

Back at his room Conrad packed away everything apart from the toiletries and clothes he'd need in the morning. He opened his computer, checked that he'd covered everything he was going to need for the morning and then packed it all away ready. He went over to the little basket of complimentary drinks and made himself a cup of tea, sat back in the plush chair that was in his room and reflected on the whole situation. He'd been upset that his recent girlfriend had done the dirty on him but more out of the principle of how she'd done it rather than the fact that he'd lost her. The truth was, yes, he did let his work take over, but he felt that, had he been crazy about her, maybe he would've been stricter with himself over work and not neglected her? He'd been with her for two years but couldn't honestly say, hand on heart that he'd ever really been in love with her, in fact it was her that pushed to move in with him and he went along with it.

He could see how it had gone wrong; he wasn't so far up himself that he couldn't see his own faults. He knew that he'd let her down many times when they'd had plans with friends and he'd ended up working late. One evening he'd arrived at the restaurant when they were halfway through their meal and another time he didn't make it at all. In fact, the reason they split was because he had asked his friend to step in for him for a charity event that she had booked to go to and yet again, he was caught up in an important project. He'd thought to himself, "I can't do that to her again, I'll see if Wayne can go, so she isn't on her own". He cared enough not to want her to have to go on her own, but the thought hadn't occurred to him to simply not work and go himself. When he'd called her to explain, she really, quite understandably had the ache over it. He'd expected her to give him a hard time the following day but she didn't; she said nothing at all. That was because something had happened between herself and Wayne that night, which was where it had started.

As he sat there thinking about it, he thought to himself, "Would I be like that with Lexi?" In his heart he felt his answer was "No." He honestly didn't think he would be. He didn't know what was so different about her. From the first moment he saw her, he'd been attracted to her, she'd intrigued him from the word go. He liked the way she was a real 'doer', he loved how she had so much drive and passion for life, how she totally believed in everything she stood for; he found that really enchanting. He loved her personality, he loved how he found it so easy to talk to her and of course, ultimately, he'd loved how they had been together in bed, it had just been so right, so, so damn right. He sighed; he didn't want this to end but he could see just how upset she'd been. As much as he would want to continue seeing her, he lived thousands of miles away and couldn't expect her to wait around video calling him for weeks on end until he came back on business. That would be worse than his last relationship!

He stood up and went to the window and looked out on the splendid grounds. His eyes scanned the area towards the converted barns; he remembered how he'd watched her out on the grass yesterday morning. It seemed like ages ago, so much had happened since then, what a difference a day makes. He'd had other women when he'd been away before when he hadn't been in a relationship. He'd met women, had a night or two with them and gone on his way thinking nothing of it, but this just felt different, and it had from the very start. Just then his phone bleeped, it was Lexi.

"Ready when you are, xXx."

He put his cup down, did a quick scan of the room to make sure everything was ready to go and set off for Lexi's.

He tapped on the door.

"Come in!" she called, and he walked in. Lexi was in the kitchen, everything was on the hob, cooking. "It'll only be about two minutes," she said.

"Great, I'm starving now!" he said.

"Me too, it's always the way when you've been swimming, I think."

Conrad looked at what she was cooking and said in disbelief, "I can't believe you bought all this food just for you!"

"I'd rather have too much and take it back home than not have enough, I hate being hungry, I'm not very nice when I'm hungry!" she admitted.

"I find that very hard to believe!" he said with a little frown.

"No, honestly", she explained, "When I'm hungry I get a bit panicky and snappy!"

"D'you know what?... That's one thing I really like about you," he said with conviction, "you're so honest, what you see is what you get, you just say it the way it is. I wish more people were like you, life would so less complicated!"

Lexi shrugged her shoulders saying, "I speak my truth from the heart, that way you always know where you are with me. I can't see the point in being any other way," she said in a matter-of-fact way. She'd almost finished cooking on the hob; she took a little pot over to the veg and sprinkled something in.

"What's that?" he asked.

"Grated lemon rind," came the reply.

"Okay," he said in a quizzical manner.

"It goes well with the salmon and lemon peel is a good way to raise your glutathione levels," she confirmed, then registering the blank look on his face added, "Glutathione is the body's major antioxidant, so good for everything really, especially good for the liver. More-often-than-not, it's the bits that people throw away that can do you the most good!"

Conrad just looked at her in wonderment.

"I really hope I still have the opportunity to learn from you Lexi." He said.

Lexi looked up at him as she started to dish up the food.

"Well, if I can't, I will most certainly put you in touch with someone who can. The team of people I have learned from teach all over the world, one of the many students has set up a Facebook page just for people who have trained with them. On there we all share experiences as well as put questions out there. If we've come up against a problem, we all help each other. All I'd have to do is ask if there's anyone in your area and they'd get back to me, we all have similar knowledge so there wouldn't be a problem finding someone for you."

"Oh, okay," he said, when what he was really thinking was 'But I don't want to learn from 'anyone', I want to learn from you!'

Lexi finished dishing up the dinner and placed the plates on the breakfast bar then got the knives and forks out. "There's still a bottle of wine here, would you like some or would you rather not if you need to be up early?" she offered.

"Yes, that'd be great thanks, it's still quite early."

She opened the wine and poured two glasses.

"Here's to what's turned out to be a wonderful weekend, and also to the beautiful experience I've had here with you."

She raised her glass.

"Likewise, lovely lady," he replied.

They chinked glasses and looked each other in the eye as they took a sip, Conrad looked down at his dinner.

"This looks awesome, thank you, I think I've lived better the last two days than I've done for months!" Lexi beamed, "You're most welcome, I've enjoyed cooking for you, it's lovely to see someone really tuck into their food and enjoy it."

"It's easy when the foods this good," he said picking up his knife and fork and they both tucked into their food ravenously.

"Mmm, that's bloody amazing," he said, "really, really nice."

She smiled, "Good."

Finishing his meal, he put his knife and fork down and picked up his wine. He looked at her searchingly, thinking maybe it's time to steer the conversation round to the situation at hand. He took a sip of his wine.

"So how do you feel about 'us' and our beautiful experience then?"

"I'm not sure 'exactly' how I feel. I feel very privileged, like something very special has happened. I've been in a relationship half my life with the same man. Don't get me wrong, we have always had a good sexual relationship, but I suppose the dynamics change when the kids come along. You just make time for it, for the 'act' of it, or physical relief of it, but maybe along the way somehow the spiritual side of feeling each other gets lost in rushed, stolen moments, but if I'm truly honest, I don't ever remember experiencing the kind of connection I've had with you."

He stroked her arm, "Yeah, I know what you mean, it was special for me too."

She carried on, "This is so out of character for me. I only had a few boyfriends before I met Nathan, two of them longer relationships, five and two years and three others that lasted around six months or so. I've never had a one-night stand in my life. In my day you just didn't do that, if you slept around you were a slag! I've only ever had sex when I've been in a relationship with someone, these days it's all different, apparently anything goes! But for myself, I just would never have thought it possible to experience something like this with someone I've only just met. I would never have thought it possible to have had the experience I have had and have the feelings I'm experiencing after just forty-eight hours, but I have and I'm so grateful I have… but again, if I'm really honest with you, I'm feeling quite confused."

"Mmm," Conrad gathered his thoughts for a moment, "It's true people have evolved to see sex as almost a recreational thing these days and I have to admit I've had quite a few women, both in relationships and also as casual partners," he admitted frankly. "I've never been married or had children, so my relationships have only revolved around me and the other person... and my work!" He felt he should add. "I don't feel that if a woman sleeps with me, she's a slag. I also don't feel it should be considered any different for a woman than a man providing you're both willing, I can't see that there's any harm in it. When I first saw you in the car park all soaked from the rain, I instantly fancied you," he admitted. "I don't know, you just 'appealed' to me and, don't get me wrong now, but straight away I hoped something might happen. Then as we'd talked and I realised your situation I felt if anything, it was less likely to happen, it didn't stop me thinking about you though... you kept popping into my mind and when I drove to the village yesterday it was in the hope that I'd bump into you again. I purposely went that way because I knew you were going to be there somewhere," he explained.

Although Lexi already, somehow, knew this in her heart, his confirming words warmed her.

"I'm so pleased you did," she said softly, "I feel my afternoon would've been very different had you not turned up. Conrad was quick to respond, "It upset me to see you like that Lexi, I would've done anything to help if I could... and at that point, quite honestly sex couldn't have been further from my mind, but I still felt I wanted to be around you."

He reached over and held her hand as she confirmed, "Yes, I've really enjoyed being around you too."

He went on, "Last night was amazing and this morning was more amazing still, if I'm completely honest with you I hadn't bargained for feeling like this at all. It's nice; it's more than nice! It's been bloody amazing, and I'd like to think that it wouldn't just end here. I know we live thousands of miles apart and your side of it is complicated, but I'd like to think we would see each other again after this, to me it just feels too good to walk away from."

He hesitated slightly then sighed, "But equally I realise that you've been married a long time, you have a family and it would be wrong for me to stand in the way of you trying to work things out with Nathan." He looked at her as she gazed straight ahead unconsciously nodding at his words. Lexi knew in her heart that she was going to have to go back home and try to work things out. She sat in silence still nodding slightly caught in that thought, her eyes then elevated up to Conrad's and as soon as they connected, she started to cry.

"Hey, come on baby."

He leant forward and put his arms around her, he knew exactly what was going through her mind and then, reading her emotions, he knew.

"It's ok hun," he said.

Feeling his heart sink, he cuddled her into him.

"You have to do what is right for you, I totally get that."

She now sobbed and he began to cry with her, holding her tight, not wanting to let her go, feeling her chest heaving.

As he held her in his arms he said, "All I ask is that you keep in contact for a while… I don't mean carry on behind his back; I wouldn't want you to do that. I mean, give it your best and see how you truly feel and then let me know that after a week, two weeks, or whatever, that you've definitely made the right decision and that you're happy."

He sat back slightly; his hands on her shoulders looking into her eyes.

"I want you to be happy Lexi, truly I do, but I also want you to know that for me, this wasn't just sex and I won't just leave here and move on, I think we both know it was so much more than that."

He hugged her into him again, "Let's go and sit down."

They got up from the breakfast bar and went over to the sofa, the two of them now knowing and accepting which way this was going to go. Lexi had made her decision; she would have to do 'the right thing' by her family as opposed to what her heart quite obviously and truly desired.

Dropping on to the sofa, he pulled her toward him and they lay together just holding each other, her head on his chest, he, stroking her back, no words were spoken for quite some time, they were simply just 'being'. She sunk into him and absorbed herself in the feeling of simply cherishing the contact between them that was soon to come to an end. Like re-charging a battery, she was absorbing his beautiful energy and he, hers, taking each other in in the stillness.

After some time, Lexi moved slightly.

"You ok?" he said.

"Not really, no!" she replied, "Why does life have to be so complicated?"

Conrad sighed. "You know you have to do this... I know you have to do this. You have to go back and see if you can make it work, there's too much at stake for you. Right now, the thought of not seeing you again is killing me, honestly, I feel like I'd do anything to keep this going but I'd be selfish to try and stand in the way of you doing what you need to do."

Time was now moving on; they still just lay together on the sofa. Conrad decided it was time to make the break, they both knew it was coming but they were both avoiding it; the longer it went on the harder it was going to be.

"I think I'd better go back to my room, I don't want to, but I think we are just going to tear each other apart the longer we put this off."

Lexi felt a certain despair rip through her at his words, she didn't move, she just continued hugging into his chest, breathing him in. A few more minutes went by.

"Come on hun, we have to do this," he said giving her a gentle nudge.

Tears started to trickle from her eyes as he made a start to get up. They both got up from the sofa, Conrad faced her, both of them now tearing up.

"I don't want to say goodbye," she cried.

"Oh, babe me neither, but it's got to happen, and I think we're just prolonging the agony. I think it would be wrong of me to spend the night here now. You have made a decision; you now have to give it your all, if I stay you'll already be going back on your decision. I have to step away now, as much as I hate it, it's the right thing to do. You need to be able to focus on what's ahead of you." They stood holding each other.

"Promise me you'll message me to say you're alright please, I need to know you're ok and happy. I want you to give this your best shot. Equally, if you find you're not happy and you change your mind all you have to do is call me and I'll arrange to come back over."

Lexi nodded, tears rolling down her face. Conrad made his way to the door, as he did so he felt almost 'ill' at the thought of walking through the door and leaving her, but he knew he had to do it. Lexi followed him to the door, he turned back, and they embraced again.

"This is so unfair," she sobbed, "Why does life have to be so unkind?"

He held her now trying to hold back how upset he was.

"Hey, we've had a beautiful experience, we've found a wonderful connection, we have to be grateful for this, many people go their whole lives without ever experiencing something like this, I consider myself so lucky to have met you. He hugged her and then said, "I'm going to go now because this is just going to get harder and harder the longer I leave it." Despite the fact she felt like her heart was being 'ripped' out, she knew he was right.

He kissed her gently on the lips, then again, then a deeper, longer, parting kiss, inside a little voice said softly to him, "Enough now." He turned and went through the door, closed it and then summoned up all his inner strength to keep walking. As a general rule Conrad wasn't an overly emotional man but as he walked away, he not only cried but also struggled to catch his breath with the weight of his sadness.

"What the fuck have I just done?" he said to himself. He made his way back to his room, opened the door, went in and threw himself down on the bed.

15

Lexi stood looking at the closed door, with tears still rolling down her face, for what seemed like eternity. She hoped that the door would open again, and Conrad would walk back through it; of course, that didn't happen. She felt like her heart had been torn from her body; did she really want this? No, of course she didn't want this, but this was how it was going to have to be if she was to commit herself completely to her decision.

She felt a sad emptiness inside as she finally walked away from the door; she spotted the wine on the breakfast bar. "What the fuck," she thought. She poured herself a huge glass and started to knock it back in the hope that it would help her to sleep, though, in reality, it would take more than a glass of wine to achieve any kind of tranquillity in her head. The night slowly rolled by, both Lexi and Conrad tossed and turned in their separate beds, the thought that each other were only a stone's throw away was almost too much to bear. Lexi watched 2am, 3am, 4am pass by and eventually dropped off to sleep. She'd set her alarm for 9am as she didn't have to vacate the apartment till 11am and she had the day off.

At some point Lexi stirred, Conrad looming large in her mind. She looked at the clock; it was 7.15am. She dived out of bed and into the bathroom; she brushed her teeth and quickly put on the first clothes that came to hand. She picked up her key and ran out of the door towards the car park. As she reached the car park, Conrad was coming out of the hotel entrance, he spotted her and instantly he felt his heart leap; he quickly made his way over to her.

"I'm so sorry," she said, "I don't want to make this any more difficult for you, but I couldn't just let you go without seeing you."

He dropped his case and embraced her.

"Oh, babe, that's ok."

He cuddled into her, holding her, inhaling her, taking in as much of her as possible. He looked her in the eye then reached forward and kissed her; he hadn't prepared himself for this, it was just so hard for him.

"Promise me you'll let me know you're ok and happy?" he said.

"I will, I promise," she said, her eyes taking him in for one last time.

He put his case in the boot and closed it, then turned to her one more time.

"Take care lovely lady."

He held her one more time, kissed her on the lips and then broke away. She stood back as he opened the car door, he didn't want to go but could feel himself starting to 'well up' again and knew that he needed to get in the car or else he would be begging her to change her mind.

He started the car and rolled down the window.

"I hope you work it out, I truly do, I want you to be happy, just remember though, if you're not happy, I want to be the first to know."

She nodded as he put the car into gear, she stood back and he drove away. She watched him disappear out of the long drive and with a heart that felt like a ton weight, she turned to go back to her apartment. Alone once more, she felt empty. She knew she was doing the right thing as far as the family was concerned but at the same time, she felt a gut feeling that she'd just turned her back on her soul mate.

Back in the apartment she made a strong coffee, took it in the bedroom and started to pack, anything to busy her sad and confused mind. She heard her phone bleep in the kitchen and went to open the message.

"The hardest thing I have ever done is to walk away from you xxx."

Her tears began to flow as she typed her reply.

"And the hardest thing I've ever done is to watch you go and not stop you xxx."

Lexi went into the bathroom, looked at herself in the mirror and said, "You're doing the right thing, this will get easier. He was sent to bring you joy, not pain, think yourself lucky that you've had this, you're doing the right thing." But in her heart she wasn't convinced. She showered, tidied herself up, packed, had some breakfast, packed up all her kitchen stuff and then loaded the car. Going back inside, she took one last look around, checking in each room that she hadn't left anything behind and as she did, she hugged herself as she remembered the wonderful things that had happened there and felt truly grateful. She then went out of the door and locked it, stopping to look over at the main building and then back at the pretty barn that had been her little paradise.

"Who would ever have thought it?" she said to herself.

She went to the car, drove across the car park, dropped the keys in at reception and thanked them very much. Getting in the car, she set up her sat nav, took one last look around then, with a sigh, put the car in gear and took off. She drove down the tree lined avenue to the gates and as she indicated to turn out, she took one last look at the beautiful manor house in her rear-view mirror and felt her heart ache a little as she turned out of the drive and on her way.

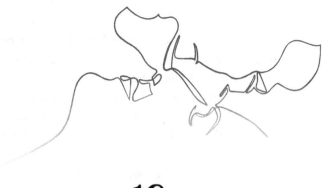

16

It was a bright, sunny day and she took her time driving back home. She felt quite relaxed as she didn't expect to hit home till about lunchtime and Nathan wouldn't be home till around 8pm. That would give her plenty of time to get in, settled, unpacked and get straight in her mind how she was going to tackle Nathan's response to her return. She knew he wouldn't be happy, he wouldn't be happy with the simple fact that she'd taken the initiative to take herself off in the first place, but he'd be even less impressed when she told him of her activities that weekend, for which she had absolutely no conscience and felt no guilt. She was the victim in all of this; he would simply have to deal with it if they were to move forwards.

She had a good journey back and stopped at the supermarket to restock food on the way. All the best-laid plans went out of the window as Lexi pulled up at home to see Nathan's car on the drive.

"Oh shit!" she exclaimed, as she now felt that she would be walking into an ambush from him. She got out of the car and took her luggage and shopping bags out of the boot, put them all on the step and then opened the door. Her heart started to beat faster as she walked in carrying two of the bags with her. She took them through to the kitchen; there was no sign of Nathan. She went back out and got the rest in. She placed the case at the bottom of the stairs and took the kitchen stuff through to the kitchen and left it there to go to the toilet.

She could feel herself becoming more anxious by the moment at the anticipation of facing Nathan; she went to the toilet and washed her hands. As she did so, she looked at herself in the mirror, aware of her heart beating faster and faster against the walls of her chest, she took a deep 'belly' breath in, held it at the top for a couple of seconds, then exhaled slowly, instantly calming herself, then she did it again. She looked deep into her eyes as she looked in the mirror, then, connecting with every word she said, "I stand in my power with confidence, I speak my truth from the heart and act from the heart with love. I trust the universe to guide and support me. She repeated her words over and over, then blew life-force into her words.

She returned to the kitchen to unpack, as she did, Nathan appeared in the kitchen doorway. She felt her stomach turn over at the look on his face. She took a deep breath and reminded herself that whatever happened from now, he was the 'catalyst' in all of this, none it would've happened had he not been unfaithful, this gave her the inner strength that she needed.

"Hi," he said, looking pathetic.

"Hi."

"Where have you been?"

"Away," came her obvious reply, which grated on Nathan somewhat, however, he kept his voice calm.

"Yes, I realise that I've been worried about you."

Defensively she replied, "Worried about me or worried about you?"

"Lexi!" He went to speak but she broke his patter.

"No, Nathan, don't make this about you, don't you dare insult me by playing the victim here. You didn't honestly think I was going to dance to your tune, did you? Did you really think we'd go away for the weekend, and it would all be hunky dory?"

He looked at her through 'pinkish' eyes and started to speak, "I thought…"

She spouted over the top of him; "You thought you could throw money at it, Nathan! You thought you could take me to a flash hotel, grovel a bit and it would all be back to normal! Well, I'm very sorry to piss all over your fire but there was no way on this earth I was going to let you manipulate me like that. Absolutely no way!"

Nathan heard her out and then replied, "Okay, so you made your stand and I can understand why you did that but can we now at least try to sort this out?" She looked at him, she looked into his face, the face she had woken up to for the last twenty years and as she did so, tried to evaluate exactly how it was she was feeling about him.

As she looked at him, she could see he must've spent the whole weekend drunk. He was an absolute mess; his eyes were pink with massive, dark circles under them. He was unshaven and looked like he hadn't touched his hair since Friday morning before he'd gone to work; he was a total mess. She didn't feel the slightest bit sorry for him, she felt no warmth towards him at all, she thought he was pathetic. He'd clearly spent the entire weekend feeling sorry for himself because it hadn't worked out how he'd planned, rather than sorry for what he'd done to her.

Looking at him, she felt yet another chunk of respect for him slipping away.

"Nathan, I don't even want to look at you right now," she said as her gaze dropped to the floor. She went to walk past him and as she did so, he grabbed her arm, just a little too hard. She pulled it out of his grip.

"If you think for one moment that kind of approach will get you anywhere, you can forget it," she snapped at him.

"I'm sorry. Lexi, please, let's just talk, you're making this so hard," he begged.

"Well, I'm terribly sorry to inconvenience you!" She said sarcastically.

"I never meant to cause all this hurt, I would never have put our marriage at risk," he tried to reason.

"But you did Nathan! That's exactly what you did. Did you think I'd just take it on the chin and move on from it?"

He was searching for the right words, but it seemed that every time he opened his mouth, he was making it worse. The truth of the matter was, she just didn't want to hear it, it was then that she came out with it. "I met someone while I was away this weekend." Her heart pounding again as her words were delivered.

Nathan visibly froze at her announcement, then his eyes narrowed as he slowly responded.

"And?" She looked away from him.

"And, what?" he demanded, "Did you sleep with him?"

She looked him straight in the eye, "Yes.... I did," she said in a matter-of-fact way. The bombshell had landed, and Nathan was now looking like he'd been hit square in the face by David Hay. He went to the sofa and sat down.

He sat looking straight ahead, hands clasped in his lap, a very slight rocking motion in his body as he contemplated what Lexi had just said. Finally, he uttered, "So, what… is this just payback?"

Lexi shook her head.

"No, it was nothing like that," she replied taking the chair opposite him. "In fact, had you not tried to get Eddie onside to call me, the chances are it probably wouldn't have happened at all." (She thought she'd put that one in). "We'd just talked at the spa that morning, nothing more than that. Later I was out walking, Eddie called me in a terrible state," She looked straight at Nathan as she added, "as you knew he would do… and I got terribly upset… as you also knew I would do… and he just happened to drive along at that point in time and see me. He stopped to see if there was anything he could do to help."

"Yeah, I bet he did!" Nathan screeched, his face an absolute picture.

Lexi looked at him, and said, "It's still all about you, isn't it?"

She began to raise her voice, "Poor, poor Nathan, did your little plan backfire? All through this you haven't once put yourself in my position. It's all been about you mending it, you, trying to get your own way; you've just been out for yourself the whole time, that's why you involved Eddie. You've been playing to win, you did it for your own gain, not mine and you didn't care who you upset if it was going to help you get what you wanted."

Nathan sat there with a face like a slapped arse. She was absolutely right; it had backfired on him although he would never have admitted it. He was being manipulative, he had thought that calling Eddie would bring her back straight away, admittedly he had been drunk and in a stew at the time, but yes, that's exactly what he had thought.

"So, where do we go from here?" he said.

Lexi shrugged, "You tell me."

"Well, are you going to see this man again?" he asked clearly perturbed. This was one thing Nathan would never have expected of her. Lexi felt a bolt of pain go through her as she thought of her emotional parting from Conrad. "I don't have any plans to, no." He noticed the ripple of sadness on her face and instantly felt a hot streak of jealousy. Almost spitting, he sneered, "Why's that then? Your knight in shining armour rode away on his horse, did he?"

Quietly, she answered, "No, not at all! I told him I needed to come home and try to work things out," she said in a sad and subdued voice, which immediately deflated his fragile ego.

He looked at her still feeling jealous and hurt but at the same time he was now a little relieved. At least she had now made him aware of her intention; that was one almighty step forward despite the massive bruise she'd made on his pride by dropping her bombshell.

Nathan put his head in his hands and started to cry, more with relief than anything. Lexi sat looking at him; at this point the thing to do would be to sit next to him and make some kind of contact, maybe put her arm round him but she just sat there registering no emotion what-so-ever.

If anything, she felt a twinge of resentment toward him, a little voice in her head saying, "So Nathan does get his way in the end after all, even if it is at a price."

She watched him as he tried to contain himself. To her, he was a mess, and she was still really angry with him. She cast her mind back to Conrad, and as she did so, she felt a sinking feeling as each and every cell in her body reacted to the sadness she felt within and for a split-second, a thought presented itself of just how much she would prefer to be with him right now instead of being faced with this. In that moment, she felt that she had made the wrong decision, her heart yearned for Conrad but the reality of it was that it was her decision to come home and make a go of this.

As she sat there looking at him, she felt now she had to stick by her decision and force herself to make some kind of effort or else there really was no point in being there, she might just as well pack up and leave right now but mentally her head wasn't in that space either. She looked at him for some long moments and eventually she got up, she touched his shoulder as she walked past him and said, "I'll make a cup of tea."

Albeit an extremely small gesture of affection, at that point in time it was all she could bear to do, at least it was a start. She put the kettle on and got two mugs out of the cupboard. As the kettle started to boil, Nathan came into the kitchen still looking glum. He walked towards her and tried to give her a half-smile, Lexi had to muster everything inside of her to give a small smile back. "Thank you for coming back," he almost whispered and put his arms around her.

Lexi started to cry, he hugged her into him and said, "I'm so, so sorry."

She stood with her arms also around him, but her tears weren't of relief for them, her tears were for what she had walked away from to be there with him.

They had a cup of tea, they talked, he asked her about Conrad obviously but wasn't too pushy for which she was grateful. If she'd had to talk about him in any depth, it would have become very, very obvious that she had tremendous feelings for him. They agreed that they would both put this behind them now and draw a line under it, for if they didn't, they would be forever scoring points off one-another. Later, as Lexi cooked a meal, she called Eddie to let him know she was back. He was clearly relieved and as a small consolation, it made her feel a little happier just knowing that he was happy.

As the evening went on, after they'd eaten, Lexi unpacked, did her washing and did some preparation for a class the next day. Nathan went and had a shower and a shave and came back downstairs looking and smelling a lot better than how she had found him. It got to 10pm and time for bed; they both went upstairs. Lexi took off her make up at the bathroom mirror. She looked at her face; she wasn't happy. She tried to convince herself it was because she was only just home and was still unsettled about the whole thing; she was sure she'd feel differently after a couple of days.

By the time she'd finished in the bathroom, Nathan was already in bed. She started wasting time, getting out clothes for the morning and then decided she needed to get a glass of water from downstairs. Eventually there was nothing left to stall over and she succumbed to the idea of getting into bed with Nathan. She removed her bathrobe and hung it on the back of the door, lifted the quilt and climbed naked into bed.

Nathan turned to face her, "I'm so pleased to have you back, I truly am." He reached forward and kissed her; she returned his kiss more on autopilot than with feeling. He stroked her arm and pulled her toward him.

"Nathan," she said quite firmly, her arms stiffening against his pull.

"Not yet, ok? I'm not ready. Sorry, but I'm just not ready for that yet."

He was a little hurt by this but not angry, "Okay, let's just cuddle, yeah?" he replied, and she snuggled into the crook of his arm. This, she could just about manage.

Nathan was so conscious of her naked body touching his; all he wanted was to have her and their relationship, back to normal. He had imagined a movie screen make-up, falling into each other's arms and making passionate love under the covers. He was going to have to settle for softly, softly for now. She lay in his arms and they fell asleep.

17

The alarm went and they both woke up. "You okay?" Nathan said.

"Yes," Lexi replied as she awoke to the realisation that, yes, the dream was indeed over and she was now back to reality. She felt a little more accepting of her decision this morning. Not a lot, but a bit more settled in her mind than yesterday, Nathan kissed her cheek. She just gave him a smile and said, "I'll go and put the coffee on." She leapt out of bed, grabbed her robe and went downstairs. Nathan was a little disappointed at her sharp exit, he had hoped for more. He knew sex was off the menu but felt she could at least have lain with him a while; clearly, he was going to have to be patient for normal relations to resume.

Conrad had two more days of business in the country. He was now in London; he'd woken up in his hotel room and as soon as his eyes were open his first thought was of Lexi. To be honest he hadn't stopped thinking about her, the whole situation of meeting her, becoming so emotionally involved with her and having to say goodbye to her was totally consuming him. He couldn't remember the last time he'd felt like this about anyone. He picked up his phone; there was nothing from her. He was desperate to hear something from her. He pondered over his phone for a few moments, trying to decide whether-or-not to send her a message, just to make sure she was ok. He managed to resist the temptation, thinking it could cause trouble if her husband had intercepted it. He wanted for her to be ok, he wanted for her to be happy but more than anything in the world right now, he wanted her to be happy and back with him. The more he tried to put her out of his mind the more she loomed large in there.

Lexi had made the coffee and while she did, Nathan jumped in the shower. By the time he came down to the kitchen, Lexi was preparing herself a smoothie for breakfast. He felt a sense of relief and reinforced calm as he walked into the kitchen and saw her there, doing her usual thing, in her usual way, back where she belonged. He went up behind Lexi, put his arms round her waist and kissed her on the cheek. Lexi felt herself slightly stiffen at his touch and realised she was going to have to deal with this. She couldn't carry on like this; they would never make a go of it if she wasn't going to try. She picked up both mugs of coffee and turned to face him. Leaning forward and planting a kiss on his lips, she handed Nathan his coffee and said, "I need to get a move on."

With that she disappeared upstairs, smoothie and coffee in hand, to get ready for work. This gesture, however small, signalled to Nathan that things were going in the right direction.

Lexi pulled up in the gym car park for work, she had a full day. She got her kit bag out of the boot, locked the car and ambled into the gym. As she got to reception Paul was behind the desk.

"Hey, how are you doing hun?" he said in his usual, happy manner followed with a more serious.

"How's it all gone at home? Have you managed to sort things out at all?"

"Oh, I'm getting there, I think," Lexi replied in a weary tone, "it's all been a bit emotionally confusing to be honest."

"I can imagine sweetheart," he empathised.

"Oh, you don't know the half of it Paul!" She replied with a look on her face that indicated there was more to come.

"Oh?" he questioned, intrigued by this.

"Seriously! I'll tell you later if you've got a break." She gave him a nod.

"Okay, I'll catch you later."

Lexi disappeared into the changing rooms to put her bag in the locker. She took out her phone and checked it. She opened up her contacts and pressed on Conrad's number, she wanted to let him know she was ok but, in her heart, she didn't really know what to say or how to word it. She could say 'everything's fine and I'm happy' but that wouldn't strictly be true. She still yearned for him, spiritually, emotionally and physically. She still yearned for that amazing connection that they had found in each other and obviously she couldn't put that either. She sat waiting for the right words to come to her for a couple of minutes then gave up and put the phone back in her locker, locked it up and went into the studio for her first class.

Lexi did her work for the morning and then met up with Paul in the café when they both had a break. She told him exactly what had happened.

"Wow, go you!" he said, almost knocked off his chair by what she had told him.

"I can see why you're confused, to walk away from something like that has got to be hard but I'm pleased you had such a nice time, I truly am, you deserve something nice to happen to you after all that," he said looking happy for her.

"It has left me feeling quite unsettled though," Lexi admitted.

Paul could see her inner struggle, "Yeah, I'm sure it has hun."

"Everything was just so right you know?' she said with such passion, then she paused for a moment before she continued, "But then I keep telling myself, of course it was right and amazing and all the rest of it, we were secluded together and almost 'cut off' from the real world. We came together in the most perfect scenario, of course it was perfect; but I have to keep telling myself that in the real world it wouldn't be like that, it would be a long-distance relationship and all the pressures that would put on it. I am a realist; I know our circumstances there were exceptional. I had to decide which way I was going to go, and I decided to come back and at least try to make a go of it with Nathan but I'm finding it very hard though if I'm honest." Her head dropped as a she spoke, "I just can't get Conrad out of my mind."

Paul gently put his hand on hers and patted it supportively, "Give it time Lex, it's really early days yet and a lot of pretty massive stuff has happened to you in a very short period of time. Just try and keep an open mind and give the dust time to settle. You need to give yourself time to process all of this properly and then see how you feel about Nathan, Conrad and where you truly want to be in it all. Stop putting pressure on yourself. Of course, you're not going to be able to push this guy out of your mind if it was so right and so special, especially if being back home with Nathan is still prickly".

"Mmmm," she agreed, as he continued to reaffirm.

"Just give it time hun and then you'll know for sure whether you've made the right choice. If it doesn't work out, then nobody can say you didn't try; this way you'll have nothing to reproach yourself for," he summed up.

"Yeah, you're right, thank you Sweetie." She took her hand out from under his, placed it on top and gave his hand a squeeze. It was time for her next client; she got up, gave Paul a peck on the cheek and went off into the gym.

At the end of her day, Lexi went to her locker took out her phone and again looked at Conrad's contact number. She had promised she'd send him a message; she needed to choose her words carefully.

"Hello sweet man, I'm sorry it's taken me so long to contact you, I'm still feeling very confused if I'm to be totally honest. We are going to try and make a go of it. Nathan does know about you and though he's not happy about it, he has accepted what has happened. I feel this is something I have to do but in truth, the experience of our time together is haunting me and I find myself thinking of you a lot. This is all very hard for me right now, but I just wanted you to know I'm ok. Lexi xXx"

Conrad felt his phone vibrate in his pocket and took it out. He read Lexi's message, the message he'd been checking his phone every 20 minutes for, for the last two days. He sat looking at it, feeling almost sick at her words, that she was thinking of him as much as he was of her and there was nothing he could do about it. He instantly hit 'dial' and called her. Lexi's phone rang; she looked and saw it was Conrad, a strange feeling bolted through her as she answered.

"Hello?"

"Hey... thanks for your message," he said, "it's great to hear from you."

She could feel herself instantly welling-up at the sound of his voice.

"It's lovely to hear your voice," she said, almost in a whisper as she choked her words out.

"It's lovely to hear yours too," he replied and then within an instant asked, "Was he ok with you? I mean, when you told him about me, he wasn't nasty or violent was he?"

She could hear the concern in his voice.

"No, no he was ok, he couldn't very well not be, could he?"

Conrad felt a certain relief at this; his biggest worry had been how her husband would react.

Lexi continued, "I think he was shocked though; I don't think he thought in a million years I'd do something like that." She paused for a moment, "He is trying Conrad, he really is trying and to be honest, he's trying a whole lot more than I am at this point in time," she said truthfully.

Not wanting to steer her, but with an equal glimmer of hope that she might have changed her mind, he asked, "Do you think you've done the right thing?"

"I know I've done the right thing," she answered, "I couldn't not come back and try after twenty years. Yes, I've definitely done the right thing as far as my head is concerned." Then her voice started to crack as she added, "but not necessarily for my heart."

As her words hit him, he felt like his own heart was being torn in two. He'd have done absolutely anything to be able to go to her right then and there. All he could think to say was, "Remember, Lexi, all you have to do is say the word... I mean it."

He said it with such conviction that Lexi simply couldn't cope with it.

"Please don't, please don't," she sobbed. "Oh God, I can't handle this, I have to go."

She cut him off, tears pouring down her face as she thought to herself, she should never have answered.

She sent him a text, "I'm so sorry, I can't handle hearing your voice, it's too much."

A minute or so later she received a message back.

"I understand, it's gut wrenching for me too but I'm so pleased you've contacted me, I can't bear the thought of us not having any contact. I know you're upset but please, please message me again. I promise not to call you again if it's too upsetting but to not hear from you at all would kill me. I fly back tomorrow, so I won't get any messages till I'm back. Please message me again x."

Lexi sat staring at her phone, tears rolling down her face, this had only made her feel worse, making the battle ever more undecided in her head. After a few moments, she put the phone back in her bag. She went into the toilets and splashed cold water on her face; looking at herself in the mirror, her eyes were red and her cheeks blotchy, "Oh God, this is hard!" She said to herself as she thought of how she felt about Nathan and how she was now feeling 'without' Conrad.

Her mind clung onto that beautiful memory of the morning, when they had stared so deeply into each other's eyes as they'd reached such ecstatic heights together. Nothing had ever happened to her like that before. It was such an experience, she would so love to revisit, though she couldn't ever imagine having that experience with Nathan. She figured if it hadn't happened in twenty years, it's unlikely to happen now, and anyway, she wasn't sure she'd it want to.

It had been their moment, hers and Conrad's; she felt deep in her heart that she could only find that total connection with him. It was as if she'd tasted some 'forbidden fruit', she'd had it, she'd felt its overwhelming power and like a drug her heart, body and soul yearned for it.

She stood looking at herself in the mirror; she knew she couldn't leave the gym and go home in her present frame of mind. She stared deep into herself and said, "Whichever way you went you would've had regrets, this way you get to keep your family intact. You HAVE made the right decision," she told herself firmly. "You've done the hardest bit, just give it time, let your head settle down, you have to give this your all, this IS the right choice, you KNOW it is, you HAVE to stick to it."

After some time and having talked herself back into a more positive place she gathered her things and headed for home.

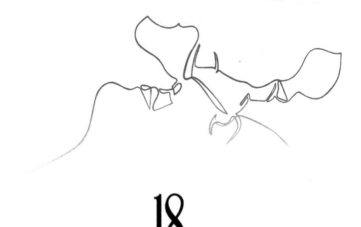

18

Lexi pulled up on the drive to see Nathan's car was already there, this was very early for him, she thought as she went in.

"Hi!" she called out as she walked through the door. Nathan was in the kitchen cooking.

"Oh, you're home early, everything ok?" She asked.

"Yeah, I'd got to a point with something that I either stopped or, if I'd finished it, it would have taken me a couple more hours, so I decided to come home and cook us something nice."

He had bought fillet steak, exotic mushrooms, tender stem broccoli, spinach and avocado and was preparing the veg to sauté in the pan. On the side stood a rather good bottle of organic wine, uncorked and breathing nicely.

Lexi felt herself 'soften' towards him, he really was making an effort, she couldn't just keep pushing him away. She felt that in her head she needed to wipe the slate clean, draw a line under it and get back on with her life.

"Have you showered at the gym?" he asked.

"No, I thought I'd have a bath tonight," she replied.

"You hungry now?" he gestured towards the pan.

"Absolutely ravenous!" she said as she smiled, a little more relaxed now.

"Good job I bought lots then!"

They smiled at each other and then he turned to the job-in-hand and started to place the chopped veg in the ceramic pan. Within ten minutes he was serving up Lexi's most favourite meal.

'Nice move,' she thought to herself.

As they sat and ate their meal, they talked about their day. She spoke about one of her clients that had been worrying her and he told her of his current project; they carefully stayed off the subject of recent events. They ate their dinner and enjoyed a glass of wine together, Lexi felt more settled now than she'd felt since she came back home.

"Mmmmm, that was delicious, thank you," she said, having completely cleared her plate. She stood up, picked up her plate and, as she bent forward to take Nathan's, she gave him a peck on the cheek. He felt himself glow from this and sat there feeling happy that he'd obviously done something right. As Lexi got on with the dishes Nathan took himself upstairs.

He went in the bathroom, put in the plug and started to run the bath for Lexi; he added her salts and lit her candles, then he thought to himself, 'Just the finishing touch'. He went downstairs, Lexi was now in the downstairs toilet, he went in the kitchen, poured her another glass of wine, took it upstairs and placed it on the side of the bath. As he came back into the lounge, she was back in the kitchen putting the last of the dinner stuff away.

"You okay?" he asked.

"Yes, lovely thanks," she said.

"I've run your bath for you," he said, feeling pleased with himself at how the evening was going.

"Oh, thank you, that's sweet of you." She leant in and kissed him on the lips as he added,

"I put your salt in but nothing else."

"Okay, thanks."

Lexi then poured herself half a mug of apple cider vinegar and proceeded to take it upstairs to also put in her bath. When she got up there, she felt quite special as she looked in the candle lit bathroom. She went to her room and got her favourite essential oils, as she came back into the bathroom, she noticed the wine.

"Aw," she said as she poured in her vinegar and added some aluminium free bicarbonate-of-soda and lastly her fragrant essential oils.

'Perfect,' she thought taking off her clothes and then submerging herself in her cleansing and relaxing bath. She took a sip of her wine, washed her face, put on an organic facemask and then slid down in the bath, resting her head on an inflatable bath pillow.

Time drifted blissfully by as she lay there. Feeling completely relaxed, she mindfully emptied her head of all thoughts and just watched the shadowy flicker from the candles rippling around the bathroom while her phone played relaxing meditation music. After about half an hour the water started to chill slightly; she sat up, took another sip of wine then proceeded to take off her face pack. She stood up, showered herself down and got out of the bath. Feeling extremely mellow she popped on her bathrobe and went downstairs; Nathan was watching the television and he looked up as she entered the room. "Hey, feel better for that?"

"Oh yes, much better thank you, just what I needed." She went and sat next to him; they watched a program as they finished off the last of the bottle of wine.

Nathan could detect that Lexi seemed far more chilled now and put his arm around her, she put her head on his shoulder and they sat watching their program just feeling comfortable with one another. When the program had finished, she got up and went in the kitchen for some water. She poured herself a glass and one for him as he came into the kitchen.

"Here," she said, handing him his. "Drink this so you don't have a headache when you get up."

"Ta," he said taking it from her, he leant in and kissed her very gently on the lips; they both downed their water and then Lexi turned to pour two more to take upstairs with them. As she stood with her back to him pouring the water, he touched her shoulder.

"I love you Lexi," he said.

She so wanted to reciprocate but she really didn't feel there yet. She put her hand on his hand and affectionately rubbed it, then, for the sake of not causing any more hurt or bad feeling, she turned around and said, "I love you too."

He put his arms around her waist and pulled her into him kissing her deeply.

As she kissed him back, she kept telling herself it would all be ok, she just needed to relax and go into it with an open mind, they've been together 23 years altogether, it would all be fine. He placed one hand behind her head in her hair and as he did so, he popped his other hand inside her bathrobe gently cupping her breast. Her bathrobe now fell open where the tie had loosened; he looked down at her body and instantly wanted her. He moved forward into her, kissing her deeply and pressing his body into hers; he wanted her so badly. As he pressed himself into her, she could feel his excitement and she knew she was going to have to go through with it. She couldn't hurt him by saying she still wasn't ready or sure of her feelings. At that point he stood back, looked at her longingly, put one hand behind her back and the other behind her legs and picked her up. He took her into the lounge and put her down on the settee; he put his hands inside her robe and flipped it off her shoulders.

"You have no idea how much I missed you and you truly have no idea how much I want this," he said. Lexi unbuttoned his shirt and pulled it off then started to undo his trousers, as she pulled his trousers and pants down his 'manhood' was staring her in the face. She took hold of his penis and placed her mouth over it, sucking and massaging him gently. He groaned with pleasure as she glided him in and out of her mouth sucking firmly. After a short while, she cupped his balls and massaged them with her hands while she kissed up and down the shaft of his penis finishing with quick little licks on the tip.

"Oh, babe that's so nice," shortly followed by, "Oh babe, you're gonna have to stop, for a while!"

He removed himself from her grip, kissed her, then went down and kissed one of her nipples, which became erect as he gave her breast his undivided attention. Stiffening his tongue, he flicked it over her nipple causing her to jump as the feeling became more and more intense, Lexi groaning with the pleasure. He continued until it became too sensitive, then started on the other one, simultaneously putting his hand down between her legs and gently playing his fingers over her clitoris. As she became more aroused, he left her breast and got down between her legs. Softly, he started to lick her, she whimpered as he gave her a delightful blend of licks and kisses to stimulate her, then started to stiffen his tongue making the sensation all the more intense. He could hear how excited she was as her breath began to change; pushing two fingers up inside her he carried on.

As he thrust his fingers into her; her hips were gyrating rhythmically to meet them, gasping now, she was almost there. At that point, he knelt up and penetrated her with his penis, still stimulating her with his fingers; he was kneeling on the floor and her bottom was slightly hanging off the sofa. He then held her by the hips and started to penetrate her harder and harder, until he was thrusting into her desperately, almost as if he were claiming her back as his. He felt like a volcano about to erupt and as she screamed out with pleasure, he had the most powerful and amazing orgasm.

Still kneeling between her legs, he kissed her inner thighs and then crawled up on to the sofa to lay with her. As she lay in his familiar embrace, no words were said. Nathan now felt at peace with himself, feeling that he'd now 'sealed the deal' and that they were now totally back on track. Lexi, however, lay with a conflict of thoughts going through her head. It hadn't been unpleasant, there was absolutely nothing not to enjoy about it. He was a very giving lover, he had always made sure she was satisfied, there really was nothing to take away from it, so what was her problem? Of course, Conrad was her problem. Conrad was still weighing heavily on her mind, she knew it was wrong but hard as she might try to block it out, the 'essence' of Conrad was still with her.

After they had lain for a while, Nathan kissed her shoulder and said, "I love you, I'll never stop loving you, I can't believe I came so close to throwing this all away. I want us to go forward from this and be stronger than we've ever been; I'm just so pleased you're back. We are so gonna make this work." He kissed her shoulder again; Lexi said nothing, she just nuzzled into him. After a while they decided it was time to go up to bed, they both had an early start in the morning. They got up and got their water to take up with them.

"I need a pee," Lexi said as she disappeared into the downstairs toilet, Nathan continued to take himself up to the bedroom.

Lexi sat on the loo with her head in her hands, trying to get a grip of how she felt. Breathing deeply, she kept her thoughts calm and rational. She knew she had to let go, what had been a blessing was now standing in the way of her happiness. It was like a double-edged sword, the experience that had been so sweet and so pleasurable, as if sent from heaven, was now like some kind of cruel twist, haunting her, beckoning her and becoming the biggest hurdle between her and her happiness with Nathan. She got off the toilet and looked at herself in the mirror. Whispering to herself out loud, she said, "You have to let him go, you have to... you can't be here and your heart still be there with him, you have to let him go." She washed her hands and then made her way upstairs, hung her robe on the door and slipped into bed with Nathan.

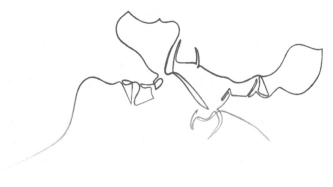

19

The alarm clock went at 6.45, Nathan switched it off, rolled over and faced Lexi.

"Morning," he said feeling relaxed, happy and at peace with the world.

"Morning." She said as he kissed her on the lips and then threw the covers back.

"Coffee?"

"Mmmmmm, lovely," she replied. He got out of bed and went downstairs.

Lexi lay there thinking about where she was in all this. She thought of her call with Conrad, how much it had torn her apart; her heart ached as she recalled the memory. She thought of last night, Nathan had done everything right, he hadn't tried to bulldoze himself back in, in his usual way, he'd been thoughtful and kind. There's no way she could leave him, not when he was being nice and was making such an effort to win her back. That left only one solution, she would have to tell Conrad she could no longer have contact with him.

Nathan came back up with two mugs of coffee, gave Lexi hers, took a sip of his and found it was too hot. "Ouch!" He said, putting his down and went in the shower. Lexi lay there, she would have to write Conrad a message, there's no way she could talk to him again. She tried to think of what she would say, how she would word it, he would be travelling back today, so she had a while to think about it. She knew if she kept in contact, she'd weaken and want to see him again. She just didn't think she was strong enough to resist that pull and the fact that she could recognise that meant she needed to remove herself from the temptation. If they were going to work at their marriage, they would both have to give it one hundred per cent. But that went two ways, it occurred to Lexi, feeling as she did right now, how will Nathan feel when he is back up North, in business with this woman? Would he be tempted? Had he still got feelings for her at all? The more she thought about it, the more she realised this was something that needed addressing.

Nathan came out of the shower, a towel wrapped round his waist, rubbing his hair dry with another. Lexi was sitting up in bed, coffee in hand.

"Nathan, a thought has occurred to me, and I think a very important one."

He looked at her giving her his full attention.

"We had a lovely night last night, our first night back together after both of us sleeping with a different partner for the first time in twenty-three years. I feel that if we're both going to make a go of this, we both must have no contact with that other partner."

Nathan stopped in his tracks and looked at her.

"That's going to be difficult," he answered.

She then continued, "How would you feel if I have contact with my partner?"

"Well, obviously I won't be very happy," he said slightly frowning.

"Well then?" She shrugged with her arms out to the sides; turning her palms up as if to say, 'see my point!'

"Lexi, I work with her!" he tried to reason.

"Can't she work on another project? Did you honestly think I'd be happy for you to stay away on business knowing you'll be working with her again?"

He looked panic stricken. How the hell was he going to explain that one at work? He would have to re organise the whole office, she was a key part in the operation.

"Oh shit! I never thought of that," he said, like the air had just seeped from his balloon.

"Well, I'm sorry Nathan but I don't want you any-where near her again. She knew you were married, and she had no conscience about it," she said trying to get her point across as nicely as the situation would allow, adding, "Is she married by the way?"

"No, she's single," he replied, looking up at Lexi, really not comfortable with where this was going.

"Nice!" Came her backhanded comment.

"Oh, God, I don't know what to say," he said pushing his hair back with his hands.

"Well, clearly any man is fair game to her if she's quite happy to jump into bed with you knowing you're married. Did she genuinely fancy you so much that she couldn't keep her hands off you or is she sleeping her way up the company ladder?" Lexi actually didn't like herself for saying that, but her protective ego was now stepping in slightly.

"I don't know, I mean, no, no, I really don't think it was like that! Without wanting to cause you offence, because I know it's my fault for being weak and I accept full responsibility for my actions, but you are right in as much as she made it very obvious she fancied me, I know it's my fault for acting on it but yes, I did respond to her attention."

The atmosphere was becoming not so comfortable now.

"So, how do you think you would feel working with her again, would you still fancy her?" Lexi was now putting herself in the same situation with Conrad and knowing what her answer would be.

"Lexi don't go there, you know this has been the biggest regret of my life," he said with total conviction.

"Okay then, so how do you think I'll feel if you go back up there and work with her?"

She looked him straight in the eye, eyebrows raised waiting for the response.

"Oh, shit!" He could see where she was coming from.

"Have you heard from her since?" she asked.

"Yes, but I told her what had happened and said that was it!" He was getting worried now.

"Oh, I bet that went down well!"

"Yes, she did throw a few expletives in as it happens!" he confirmed then turned the conversation around to... "Have you heard from him?"

Lexi felt her heart skip a beat as the words left his lips.

"Yes," she said, trying not to sound sad or upset.

It really wasn't going to help if Nathan realised exactly how she was feeling, that would just be cruel.

"He asked me to promise him I'd let him know I was alright," she said almost dismissively.

"Oh, okay, so you're not going to contact him again?"

She surreptitiously avoided answering that one fully.

"Nathan, this is what I've been thinking about. I feel if we are both going to give this one hundred percent, to forgive, forget, draw a line under it and put this whole thing behind us properly, we BOTH have to completely break contact, otherwise there will always be mistrust. You said she made the play for you, what's to say she won't try her luck again?"

"But I'd never do that again!" he protested.

"But I never thought you would in the first place!" She said in an almost 'check mate' fashion.

He looked deep in thought; he knew she was right; he just needed to work out how he was going to get around this.

"Leave it with me, I'll sort it, I promise," he said.

"Okay, well, when you've sorted your situation, and I'm happy you're not going to see her again, I will tell Conrad I can no longer have contact with him."

He looked at her, his head in a spin, he knew full well she was serious and would do nothing until he did, and to be fair, he didn't blame her, as he would hate to think of Lexi keeping in touch with this man.

"Okay, I'll sort it, first thing." He went over to Lexi, touched her cheek, bent forward and kissed her, then continued to get dressed.

Now Nathan had a huge problem on his shoulders. The company merger was just over two weeks away and the lady he had cheated on his wife with, was a key part of the team that was making this happen; how the hell was he going to sort this one out? Nathan called the lady in question; her name was Janet. To begin with, she was extremely 'frosty' toward him. Oh, how situations change. Before they had worked so well together, they were both singing from the same song sheet as far as their work was concerned. They were so compatible in business, why, oh why, had he let this happen? This is obviously why it is always said not to get involved with someone you work with. They would both have to be professional about this and not let their differences get in the way of the final part of such a huge project.

Nathan spent over half an hour on the phone to her. He apologised to her and took responsibility for what happened, he explained to her what had happened since their rendezvous, and how he would never want to undermine her in any way. He told her that he fully respected her as a professional; saying all the right things to avoid any kind of backlash from her. The reality of the situation was that it was impossible to close this deal without working with her again. They had two meetings in the diary, both a week apart, they just needed to get over this hurdle and then they could get back on with their lives.

As Janet calmed to Nathan's extremely careful and respectful approach, she became more accepting of the situation and therefore more understanding and helpful. Nathan had now also convinced himself this most definitely hadn't been a career move or anything so sinister; it was merely a poor choice on both sides. They worked out that the next meeting could be done with him this end on a video call; he would make his excuses why he couldn't travel up. So that was that one sorted, it was just the final meeting before the merger that they would have to be together for. There was no way around it, he would have to go; he resigned himself to the fact that he would have to be honest with Lexi and tell her. This wasn't going to go down well but Nathan decided that honesty was the best policy, especially now.

20

Lexi took her time after Nathan had left for work, her first client had cancelled, and her first class wasn't till 9.30. She started to hand write a message that she would later tap into her phone and send to Conrad.

"By the time you get this you will be back in America on your home turf. It breaks my heart to do this but it's the only way I can move forward. I've been so very confused since I've been home; you have been on my mind so much. You've been the last thing I think of at night and the first thing I think of in the morning, talking to you yesterday made me so sad. I can't carry on like this, I feel it's impossible for us to be in contact if I'm going to try and make this work with my husband because, although our relationship was brief, it's had such a massive impact on me. I feel saddened that something so beautiful has to come to an end but if I can't get you out of my mind then I won't be putting my all into saving my marriage. I hope you can understand. Meeting you was such a wonderful experience; the time we spent together was just so perfect. When I think about it and the effect you've had on me, it tears me apart. I can't carry on trying to make it work here when my heart is still with you. Please understand my decision, I have to do this; I haven't been forced into it by Nathan. We've talked openly and truthfully; we have both agreed that neither of us should have contact with our 'partners' again. I'm so very sorry. You are a special, special person and I will never forget the effect you've had on my life. I truly believe that a small part of my heart will always be with you and I hope you can forgive my decision. Lexi x"

Lexi felt that she'd done the best she could with the message under the circumstances. She folded the piece of paper and tucked it in the pocket of her phone cover for later; she then got her stuff ready to leave for work and headed out the door. As she pulled up in the car park at work her phone rang, it was Nathan and she answered.

"Hi."

"Hi," he replied, a little worried at what her reaction would be to the arrangements he had managed to make.

Lexi, detecting awkwardness in his energy, said, "Everything okay?"

"Er, kind of." He swallowed before starting, "Lexi, I've tried to sort this the best way I can. You know the merger happens in just over two weeks?"

"Yes?" she said slowly, making him squirm a little.

"Oh God, please don't be mad, I've gone through this from every angle, I truly have, okay?" he gabbled.

"Okay," she responded sensing a huge BUT.

"I can get out of going up there this Friday, that's all sorted but the following Friday is a problem... honey, I'm going to have to go and Janet will be there."

There was silence on Lexi's end of the phone.

"Hun, please talk to me, I've called you straight away because I want to be honest with you, there's no way I can get out of next week."

The silence continued while Lexi got her head around what Nathan had just told her. After a few long moments she said, "How many other people are involved in this particular meeting?"

"Eight in all," he chipped in, "the merger team and the directors, I can't 'not' be there." His voice was nervous; "it's impossible as I'm the one who's overseen all of this."

Unconsciously, he was biting his knuckle, as the last word left is lips.

"Well, there's not a lot I can do about it then, is there?" Lexi sighed in a resigned manner.

"Hun, you can trust me, I promise with my whole heart, nothing like that will ever happen again. I won't be alone with her at any point, I promise."

Nerves and sheer desperation were evident in his voice.

Feeling a little deflated she said, "Well if that's the case then it's out of my control, isn't it?"

Nathan all but clasped his hands together to thank the lord, what a relief!

Instantly his voice took on a calmer note, "I promise babe, I will just go up and see the project through. I'll have to go up the day before because it's an early start, but I will leave as soon as it's over and come home that night. Hun, I promise it'll be okay, please trust me. I don't want you to be any more hurt or anxious, but I've been working on this for eighteen months, I can't just bail out at the last part."

Lexi knew she couldn't ask him to do that, even though the thought of him going up there didn't exactly appeal to her either.

"Oh, why does everything have to be so fucking mixed up?" she protested. "We've just managed to get back together, this is a time we should be building and focusing on our relationship, not putting it under more strain. We should be making a new start, now I feel like I have to put all that on hold because I know next week, I'm going to be sitting this end with the problem still at large and worrying about it." She spoke her truth from the heart.

"I swear on my life it'll be ok," he promised. "I'll go up, tie up all the loose ends and see the merger through, that will be it, I promise you with all my heart." There wasn't really anything else she could say, she had to go along with it, she had no choice.

Lexi went into work feeling somewhat deflated. She took her class and afterwards went into the gym, set herself up on the mats and had a breathing and stretching session to try and settle how anxious she was feeling. In her head, it had been all cut-and-dried. He was going off to sort his side and she had prepared her message. When they'd left each other this morning the decisions had been made and they'd both left home feeling positive and knew exactly which direction they were going in. Now it was as if the goal posts had been moved and understandably, this had unsettled her. Should she still send her message, or should she wait? If she waited there's no way she could wait all that time to send it without having any other contact. If she had contact it would create yet more confusion in her mind, no, her mind was made up, she had to go through with this.

Lexi went to the changing rooms and got her phone out of the locker; she took the note out of the pocket and started to copy the message onto her phone, her hands shaking. Did she really want to do this? She sat and looked at the message and read it through; it was so final. She sat for a few minutes, her thumb hovering over the 'send' button.

"Arrrrhhhhh!" she cried out in frustration, the indecision playing through her mind. If she sends it, the contact will be broken on her side, but Nathan's will still be unfinished business. For some reason she couldn't commit herself, she saved the message in 'drafts' and put the phone away again, went and got some lunch and then got on with her afternoon.

Conrad was now on his journey back to the states. Wow! What a difference this one trip had made. He felt like he'd learned a lot about himself from his experience, not only of the weekend but also how he had felt afterwards. It was as if his whole world had changed, Lexi had come into his life and completely turned it upside down. He knew Lexi was set upon making her marriage work, but he had a gut feeling about her, it wasn't often Conrad found himself so fixated by a woman. He felt that this wasn't the end, it couldn't possibly be! His feelings had never been so strong about something. He went into the paper shop at the airport, grabbed a paper and went to the chiller cabinet where all the soda drinks temptingly stared back at him and instantly thought of Lexi. A little, warm smile came over him as he reached forward and picked up a plain bottle of water, went to the checkout, and continued on his way.

He sat in the airport lounge, reading his paper and sipping from the bottle, then, just as his flight was called; he took out his phone to check if there was a message from her but there wasn't. Very soon he would no longer be in the same country as her, they would have thousands of miles separating them. The thought of this noticeably making his energy take a dip. He stared at his phone as if to try and make a message appear. The second call came for his flight;

he switched off his phone, got his hand luggage together and boarded the plane. He sat looking out of the window, the engines roared, he felt the sheer power of the plane's engines as it took off and as he watched the earth disappear from below him, a tear formed in the corner of his eye and rolled down his cheek.

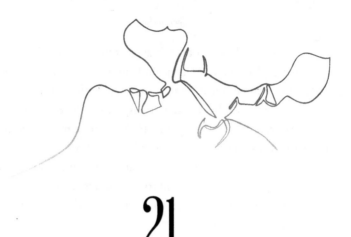

21

Lexi arrived home; she put her kit in the washing machine and sorted out what she needed for the following day, then started to prepare dinner, Nathan came in and walked into the kitchen.

"Hey."

He came up to her and kissed her cheek. He was worried how she might feel about his business arrangements for the next couple of weeks. Everything had been so perfect last night, he really felt like they'd got-it-together. He'd felt relaxed and safe for the first time since the whole sorry situation had started; now he was just worried about the small spanner in the works that was his business trip next week. The one thing he had been relieved about was that Janet and he were on good terms; it would've been so difficult had they not been able to move forward in a positive way.

"Good day?" Lexi asked.

"Yeah, it's all going well, I'm so sorry about next week hun. If there was any other way, you know I'd do it." She looked at him, not in a cross way; she could see that he was just as disappointed.

"We'll just have to take it as it comes and deal with it next week. I don't want to spend the next two weeks in a state worrying about it, that won't serve either of us."

Nathan was relieved at her response; however, he did now wonder if she was going to keep to her side of the bargain. This, he felt, he couldn't be pushy over but the thought of Lexi having any contact with this man at all was playing with his head and totally undermining his self-confidence. He would have to tread carefully; he couldn't have it all his own way.

They had their dinner and cleared the dishes, then sat in the lounge and put the television on; Nathan watched her as she had a look through the channels.

"Have you heard from Conrad at all?" He couldn't control himself.

"No, he's travelling back today, so his phone will be switched off."

"Are you still going to tell him?"

"Yes, I think so, I've drafted a message for him, I just haven't sent it yet," she confirmed.

"Are you still going to send it?" He asked gingerly, now getting a little nervous, as he'd had to change the rules, so might she.

"Yes, I think I have to, it's the only way forward for us. Next week has rattled me though, I'm not going to lie, but I still want to make this work."

The feeling of relief within him was immense.

"When are you going to send it? Not being pushy or anything."

"I'll wait till I think he's landed and has a phone signal. I think the message is too important to run the risk of getting lost across the airwaves," she said.

"Okay."

He kissed her cheek again, he was happy with that, it showed that she was committed, he couldn't ask any more. They snuggled up on the sofa for the rest of the evening and then went to bed.

The alarm went off and both of them jumped out of bed, they both had an early start this morning; Nathan with the project at hand and Lexi had an early PT client. She dived downstairs, made the coffee and put her smoothie together while Nathan was in the shower. As he came down for his coffee, Lexi disappeared upstairs for her shower. In an organised whirlwind they both got themselves ready and departed for work.

After a very busy morning, Lexi went into the changing rooms and took out her phone; she sat for a moment contemplating what she was about to do. The thought of it made her feel sick, she knew she had to do it but there was a part of her that was so very reluctant to. She tried to evaluate what this feeling was, what was it that she felt so reluctant to let go? She very quickly realised that this wasn't helping, she was looking for reasons not to send the message, therefore, keeping Conrad still slightly attached. She couldn't do this, it was all or nothing, she had to send the message. Lexi brought up the drafted message and read it through once more, her finger hovering above the send button. She took a deep breath and pressed send, the tears rolled down her face as she did so.

She kissed her phone and said, "I'm so sorry." She felt ill, "Oh my God, I hope I've done the right thing." At that point, Lexi became aware of other ladies in the changing room. She suddenly felt she needed to remove herself from people's gaze as she felt herself begin to fall apart.

She took herself outside to the tennis court area, there was no one around there at the moment, she sat on the bench quietly thinking about what she had done. That's it now;

job done, no going back, she felt a sad emptiness inside. 'I hope he understands' she thought, 'I hope he's not upset'. Of course, he would understand, but her heart ached at the thought of him being upset for she knew that he would be. Lexi allowed herself ten minutes. She did her best to clear her head of all the mixed-up emotions that had been whirring around inside it, consciously taking slow, deep breaths and as she did, she listened to the birds singing in the trees, using it as a way of mindful meditation, focusing on the bird song, her breathing and letting everything else go. When she felt completely calm, she got up and went back inside.

The rest of the day went by in a blur; it was a long and busy day. Sitting in the car to go home, she checked her phone, nothing yet, 'I wonder if he's got it yet? I wonder if he's alright?'

"Stop this Lexi, it was your decision," she affirmed to herself out loud, she started the car and headed home. Nathan was already there when she arrived; he was in the kitchen preparing some food as she walked in.

"Hiya," she kissed him and said, "How was your day?"

"Yep, all good, it's all going to plan, thank goodness."

"Good."

They had their dinner and then Nathan got his laptop out.

"I just need to send a couple of emails," he said.

"Okay." Lexi went into the kitchen and did the plates, she looked out of the kitchen door at Nathan engrossed in his work, she picked up her phone and there was a message from Conrad.

"I can't put into words how sad I am after reading your message, but I totally understand, I really do. Somehow, I never thought I'd have to say goodbye to you completely, I don't know, I just thought I found something in you that was so special that I thought nothing could stop it. I totally respect your decision and won't pester you. It's gonna take me a while to get my head round this though. When I left you, it felt like the start of something very precious, now, reading your message this just seems so final, I never imagined I'd feel like this. I hope everything works out for you, truly I do but if it doesn't, or, if you get to a point that you feel we could have contact again, I'd love nothing more. You're an amazing woman with a beautiful soul, I can't help but feel it'll be a long time, if ever, before I find someone I can connect with so totally. You have a part of my heart that I will never get back. Good luck to you my beautiful Lexi xXx"

Lexi stood, her eyes glazed over, looking at the message. She hadn't heard Nathan get up; he came in the kitchen; she jumped as he walked in. He instantly noticed she was holding her phone.

"Everything ok?" He said when what he really wanted to do was snatch the phone out of her hand, he felt jealous.

"Yes," she said quietly.

"Is that him?"

"Yes."

"Did you send him your message?"

"Yes."

"Oh, okay, he's good with that then?"

Lexi looked at him, "Yes, he's good with that."

She nodded as she put the phone down, went in the downstairs toilet and blew her nose. She then went and got the washing out of the machine. While she did this Nathan did something unforgivable, he looked at her phone. He saw both her message to Conrad and his reply, he was shocked; he hadn't realised that there had been such a strong connection between them. He thought she'd just had a good old time and let herself go with him, but this was something else. She hadn't told him she'd had feelings for him; mind you, to be fair, he hadn't asked. Just finding out she'd done it was hard enough for him; he put the phone back where Lexi had left it and walked away.

The messages played on Nathan's mind to the point that he was almost driving himself mad. It had never occurred to him that she had feelings for this man and that she had actually had to work out what it was she had wanted, that she'd had to make a decision. As far as Nathan was concerned, she'd gone away for the weekend, mad at him (understandably), met someone, had a bit of a blast and then come back to work things out. The very thought that she had become emotionally involved with him made him feel very insecure. Now what should he do? If he broached the subject, she'd know he'd been into her phone; this discovery had really knocked him for six.

Lexi came in from the utility room; she could instantly see by the look on Nathan's face something was different.

"What's wrong?" She said as her gaze shifted from him to her phone on the worktop and instinctively she knew exactly what was wrong, "Oh, shit, you've been in my phone haven't you?"

He just looked up at her, his eyes slightly 'pinking' up.

"How could you?" She shouted, "I've trusted you to sort things with your 'woman', I haven't interfered, I haven't been through your phone, I've trusted you to deal with it your way, how could you? After everything we've said and been through, I've told you the situation, it was ME that said we should no longer have contact and I have sent a message breaking my contact. It's YOU who will still have contact because you've not managed to keep your side of the deal and despite that, you're the one sneaking around going through my phone!"

She was quite understandably, absolutely livid.

Nathan just stood there like the wind had been knocked right out of him and said, "You never said you had feelings for him."

Lexi, still too cross to show any kind of compassion replied, "You never asked, you were all to consumed by the fact that I'd done it in the first place."

"Well don't you think it would've been fair to tell me?" he said now looking very hurt.

"Nathan, I didn't know how I felt and that's the truth," she explained. "One moment my life's going along nicely, the next I'm receiving a message from you for that was intended for your lover!"

He visibly cringed at this.

"You try to bully me into forgiving you. I take myself away. I met Conrad. He was very understanding and caring. It happened. I don't feel guilty. Yes, I have been confused by my feelings, but I've come home to YOU, I've come home to work this out. I knew if I kept contact with him that it wouldn't be healthy, that's why I said we should both break contact, doesn't that tell you enough?" she tried to reason with him.

This wasn't enough for Nathan, "If you really love me and want this to work, you'll erase those messages and his number."

She stared at him in amazement and replied, "Say's he, who will be shacked up with her next week, the other end of the country where I don't know what's happening!"

"I've told you; I've promised you, I won't be alone with her, nothing will happen," he protested.

"Well, nothing will happen here, you saw the messages, you know I've put a stop to it, he's in bloody America for goodness sake!"

"Please, do it for me, I need to know you're totally committed to me."

Lexi went and got her phone and got the messages up. She could see the last couple of lines of Conrad's message.

"Please, just make that temptation go away, please," he pleaded with her.

She had no choice, she would've done anything to have been able to read his message through again, to have read his words and felt in some way connected to him again, she wasn't quite ready to let that go. Nathan had called her bluff; she was in a corner, and she bit her lip as she deleted the messages.

"They're gone," she said.

"And his number?"

She looked up at him and then resigned herself to hitting the delete button on his contact. She tried not to show how much this meant to her.

"There, are you happy now?" she said showing him the phone.

He got up off the sofa and went to kiss her; she turned her face slightly, so he planted it on her cheek.

"Thank you, that means the world to me."

He hugged her stiffened and unresponsive body into him and then headed off upstairs.

Lexi felt a sick feeling rip right through her. Although it was her that had decided it would be best to have no contact, she hadn't been ready to erase his message and contact details, that had been the 'controlling' Nathan coming out and, in this incidence, he'd won. He knew she had no way back now unless Conrad contacted her, and he'd promised he wouldn't in his message, so, job done, as far as Nathan was concerned, he was now feeling quite happy. As for Lexi, she felt like part of her had been torn out. She probably would have erased them at some point, but she simply hadn't been ready to have that forced upon her. She felt an empty ache, almost despair at what she'd just been forced to do. So, Nathan wins out, he happily goes up to bed and will sleep sound tonight knowing that he's forced her hand for the sake of his insecurities, despite the fact that he would still be seeing Janet next week and keeping Lexi's insecurities very much alive. As much as Lexi had wanted this to work, she felt more than a ripple of resentment toward Nathan for his demands.

She stood still in the lounge for many minutes, her head going over what had just happened. She had a cry, got some tissue, blew her nose again, then poured a glass of water and went upstairs. She washed her face and brushed her teeth in the bathroom, still in a subdued state of almost posttraumatic shock, or regret. She couldn't shake it off, she felt that action should've come from her and only when she was good and ready, Nathan had no right to force it on her in the circumstances. She looked in the mirror, "It's done now and there's no going back." She started to quietly sob, her shoulders shaking with her sobs and thinking to herself, 'what a horrible, sad end to what had been something so wonderful'. It was out of her hands now, nothing she could do about it. She put on her face oils and went into the bedroom where Nathan, now completely chilled out, lay in bed.

Lexi looked at Nathan lying there and felt nothing but anger towards him. Taking off her dressing gown, she hung it on the door and got into bed. Nathan turned on his side to give her a cuddle, which, right now, was the last thing she wanted from him. She lay on her back; keeping her arms to herself as she lay looking at the ceiling until she finally drifted off to sleep.

22

Awaking before the alarm, Nathan looked at Lexi, still asleep. He knew in his heart that she hadn't wanted to erase all of her recent encounter; the very fact that it was so special to her had completely unhinged him and therefore had forced his hand. He couldn't bear the thought of her having feelings for someone else, he felt that now it was all gone she would settle down and forget all about him, he felt his actions were justified and she'd get over it. He stroked her forehead gently with his fingers, then leant forward and kissed it. Lexi stirred and opened her eyes to see Nathan above her.

"Good morning beautiful," he said as if none of last night had happened.

As she came to, the events of last night were looming in her head. The sad emptiness that was the enforced loss of Conrad, the disempowerment she'd felt over the whole situation and ultimately the underlying resentment she now felt toward Nathan for how he had manipulated her. She could see exactly what he was trying to do. He was putting last night behind him and moving on like it never happened, as if it was a bit of business that needed sorting and now he was back on top.

"What's the time," she replied, no 'morning gorgeous' back.

"6.40." He looked at her and before kissing her he asked," We are 'good' aren't we?" with a rather pitiful look on his face.

"As good as we can be in the circumstances," she replied quietly.

This wasn't what he wanted to hear, and he couldn't help but show his disappointment.

"Nathan don't be surprised and don't be the victim, you know what you've done! You've done what you always do, took control and got your way at any cost; don't expect me to pretend to be happy about it," she snapped.

"You were the one who said no contact," he retorted.

"But it would've been nice to have the opportunity to do it on my terms, not yours. You say nothing will happen next week and you won't be alone together, but you WILL see her, you will communicate with her and have whatever closure between the two of you. It will be on your terms and between the two of you, you won't have me standing in the middle stopping anything I don't like the look of or feel uncomfortable with. You haven't allowed me that, I just feel you've been a manipulative bully," she said with honesty.

"I'm sorry, I really am," he said with a look of real concern, trying to smooth the situation over.

"Mmmm," she grunted. "It's easy to say sorry when at the end of the day you've just had everything your own way, and while we're on the subject, I assume you still have Janet's contact number on your phone?" she said with an enquiring expression.

"I will still be working with her on this project until the end of next week," came his quick justification.

She wasn't going to let that one go quite so easily, "In the office, when you're at work; not at home! You have absolutely no reason to still have her contact in your phone, if you need to contact her over work, you can do it in the office via email. Personally, under the circumstances, I think it's only fair that you delete her."

"Lexi you're just being difficult now," he protested.

"I'm not being difficult at all; we start as we mean to go on. I have no intention of being in a relationship with you if there's a different standard for each side, it's straight down the middle, take it or leave it. Last night you felt the need to flex your 'male pride' muscles and dominate the situation, I'm merely stating that it works both ways." There was no way Lexi was going to allow Nathan to keep Janet's number when he'd been so adamant that she deleted Conrad's. Nathan still protesting added, "But I might need to contact her before the merger next week."

"Then write her number down in the office and if the need arises, you will have her number there." For the sake of not starting yet another argument (as he could see Lexi wasn't going to back down on this one), Nathan decided to do as she asked.

"Okay, okay, I'll do it if it makes you happy." He threw back the covers and said, "I'll make the coffee."

With that, he was out of bed and on his way downstairs. Lexi came out of the shower as Nathan returned with the coffees and his phone. He got up Janet's contact details, pressed delete and showed the phone to Lexi. She didn't even bother looking really, she glanced at the phone, looked at him, then went into the spare room to get her clothes and get dressed. She really needed to get her head in a far better place than it currently was; it seemed that no sooner had they taken a positive step forward and felt good and settled for five minutes, they were then taking three negative steps back.

Conrad awoke feeling like shit; tired, jet lagged and emotionally spent. He reached over to his bedside table and picked up his phone, no message back from Lexi. He felt terribly low, how had this happened? And indeed, why had this happened? Why had this amazing person come into his life, just to turn it upside down and to lose her as quickly as he found her? It just didn't make sense and seemed so cruel. Maybe it was to teach him to be more appreciative of the women in his life, not treat them as an afterthought once work was taken care of. The truth of the matter was that no one had ever really been that important to him and now someone was, he couldn't have her.

Friday had come, and Nathan set himself up in the office on Zoom for what was going to be quite a long meeting on the fine details and loose ends of the project in hand. He had given the excuse that his father was in hospital and so he didn't want to be that far away at this point in time. It all went down ok without any raised eyebrows. Nathan, Janet and their fellow co-workers all set to work on their meeting. He looked at Janet, she was very professional, but he could tell something was different with her and he hoped no one else noticed. She looked tired and a little drawn, maybe this had all been stressful to her as well. He felt a little concerned noticing this in her; he wanted to ask her if she was all right but now, he no longer had her number that was no longer an option. The meeting went on for over four hours. They all knew exactly what needed to be done for next week, the meeting closed and they went on their way. Around mid-afternoon Nathan got up and had a walk around the office, sitting for far too long and needing to move about, he went and got a drink and took it back to his desk. He thoughts returned to Janet, she really hadn't looked her usual self, so he opened up email and sent her a message.

Hi Janet, thank you for being so professional and putting our circumstances aside for the sake of our business together. Today was very fruitful and I think it went well. I'm confident we will have everything in place for next week. I couldn't help but notice you looked tired and a little under-the -weather today, I hope you don't mind me saying so; I was just a little concerned about you. I know it's none of my business really but just wanted to make sure you're ok. Regards Nathan.

Within five minutes came Janet's response: Hello Nathan, it's very kind of you to think of me. I'm okay; I'm just feeling a little tired. I've enjoyed working on the merger, but I have to admit I will be very happy for the end of next week to come. It's been very stressful, especially the last twelve weeks. I'm looking forward, obviously, to seeing everything kick off smoothly with the new company and witnessing the fruits of our hard work of the last eighteen months, but equally I'm looking forward to things calming down again for a while. Thank you for thinking of me, I really respect that. Regards Janet.

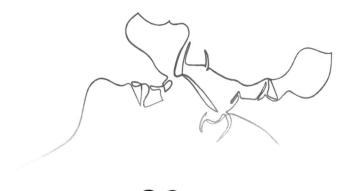

23

Lexi went to work still feeling somewhat confused inside her head. It just seemed that every time she settled, felt positive and felt she had made the right decision, Nathan had this uncanny knack of doing something or behaving in a way that made her question her decision and how she felt about him. She sat with Paul in the gym café and told him what had been happening.

"So, he's video calling with her today then?"

"Yes," she replied, her facial expression not giving much away.

Noticing this he asked, "How do you feel about that?" giving her permission to open the floodgates.

"Oh, Paul, this is all such a fucking mess, I don't know what it is with him sometimes, you know? Right now, I couldn't give a shit! I really couldn't, he's been such an arse!" Lexi said, quite clearly agitated. "That bad eh?" He said frowning sympathetically.

"He just does everything to suit himself, he's such a control freak. He has to be in the driving seat but in his need to do that he sabotages himself. He thinks he's making things better, by controlling the situation, and yes, maybe he did take temptation out of my way but the reality of it is that I resent him for forcing me to do it, I simply wasn't ready." She sat back and folded her arms as she finished. Paul reached over and placed his hand on her arm.

"It's early days yet hun, you're going to have feelings for this guy, probably for a while to come yet. You had a lovely time with him; if it hadn't had been such a wonderful experience you wouldn't be feeling like this. I agree, Nathan's being an arse but give everything time to settle. You walked away from something that seemed perfect, to return to something that will have to be worked on, of course you're going to have reservations." He was right, it was just a state of mind, and she knew that, she just needed to get her head in the right place.

The weekend came and Nathan decided he needed to do something nice for Lexi. He was aware he'd been 'pushy' with her but if he hadn't, he would still be feeling very insecure. As it was, the very fact she couldn't contact Conrad now, made him feel settled in himself. He felt back in control of his life and confident that they could make a go of it; he just needed to think of something really nice to make up for it. Nathan got up on the Saturday morning, went downstairs, made coffee and scrambled eggs and bought breakfast up on a tray.

"Morning babe," he said as he came back into the bedroom with the tray.

Lexi had already stirred and sat up, "Oh, thank you."

He popped the tray on her lap, placed her coffee on her bedside table and took his round to his side of the bed.

"This is a surprise."

"I just wanted to do something nice," he replied.

"Thank you," she said, promptly tucking in.

"There's music in the park this afternoon or there's banger racing, which would you prefer? I've also booked us in to Holbrook Hall for dinner at seven thirty and a room for the night, so we can enjoy a nice bottle of wine and not have to drive home."

"Lovely, thank you," she replied, knowing this was his way of making up for what he'd done but accepting of it all the same.

"I quite fancy the banger racing, we haven't been there for ages," she said, before popping a lovely fork-full of the buttery egg into her mouth.

"Banger racing it is then!" he confirmed, happy that he'd managed to start the day off on a positive note.

Gathering their stuff together in the morning, they had some lunch and left with their evening clothes and over-night case in the boot. They loved banger racing; the atmosphere in the stadium and the roar of the engines, they had a great afternoon together and then left for the posh hotel and restaurant Nathan had booked them into. It was just as well he had booked them in, as they were filthy from the racing. It'd been a hot, dry day and the dust had been thrown up, they were covered in it. The room was impressive, very old and characterful with beams and the massive workings of an old clock, which had originally been a huge clock on the wall outside. Lexi jumped in the shower first washing her hair to get the dust out, as she came out Nathan handed her a glass of wine from a bottle he had packed in the case.

"Mmm, thank you."

"Cheers!" he said, they chinked glasses, had a sip of wine and Nathan went in the shower as Lexi started getting herself ready.

They had both made an effort to dress up for the rather posh restaurant. Lexi had packed a dress she'd had for some time but never got round to wearing. Beautifully fitted in a deep purple, ruched all the way up, it hung on her body just perfectly. She did her make up nicely and wore her hair down, with tiny flower coils in one side to match the colour of her dress. This was something she rarely did, in her job her hair was always 'scragged' up, practical, cool and easy to manage. Lexi enjoyed getting ready to go out. Like any woman she enjoyed feeling a bit special occasionally. Nathan had packed a smart pair of black trousers and a very striking light green shirt with black collar, cuffs and button panel that Lexi had bought for him a few months earlier.

"Lexi, you look stunning." He said.

"Thank you, you don't scrub up so bad yourself!" She responded playfully.

The restaurant was beautiful with extremely attentive waiters; tucking in Lexi's chair behind her as she sat down and draping a heavy cotton napkin over her lap once she was seated.

"Ooh, this is a treat!" She said.

Nathan took her hand over the table, "Nothing more than you deserve."

He looked straight into her eyes and said it with complete honesty. Having had such a fun afternoon and now feeling quite chilled out and happy, Lexi smiled at him. They ordered their food and wine and enjoyed a relaxed meal, managing to keep the conversation light. They talked about the fun they'd had earlier, their children and the possibility of extending the house and how they would do it; there was no mention of recent events or the coming meeting on Friday. They thoroughly enjoyed the meal and for pudding Lexi chose a gluten free chocolate fondant, while Nathan chose cheese and biscuits; to their surprise there was a special cheese waiter! And boy did he know his cheeses! He spoke in a sweet, broken English accent and spent quite some time telling them of all his different cheeses, allowing Nathan to have a small taste in order to make his choice. This amused them and while they both had their rather special cheese board and dessert, they also managed to polish off another bottle of wine.

Finally, they ordered coffees, not something Lexi would usually do at that time of night, but she was all up for the total experience of the place; they were directed to the sitting room for coffee to be served. The magnificent room had beautifully carved, wooden panelled walls, a huge, old fireplace and original leaded windows. The coffee tray arrived, temptingly set out with hand-made chocolates on a doylied plate and a silver cream jug and sugar bowl. What a perfect end to the evening, she thought. As the waiter put the tray down, he said, "It's a beautiful evening, please feel free to take a walk in the grounds, the French doors are over there."

"Ooo, perfect!" She said.

They sat in the grand sitting room, had their coffees and then decided to go for a little walk to round off their evening. It was just getting dusk; the outside area was beautifully landscaped with a big lake. They took a wander around the lake for about half an hour; there was now a chill in the air and a few midges. So as not to get bitten to death they decided to go back inside and retire to their room.

Back in the room Lexi kicked off her sandals and went into the bathroom; Nathan watched the back of her intently as she walked away from him.

"There's a small glass of wine each left in this bottle, if want to finish it off?" he said picking up the bottle.

Lexi poked her head round the bathroom door.

"Why sir, if I didn't know better, I'd say you were trying to get me drunk!" she replied. Smiling to himself he poured the rest of the wine; they were both obviously well-oiled by now! Nathan could hear Lexi in the bathroom, he was now feeling fired up and went to see what she was up to. In her usual autopilot fashion, she had taken off her make-up, brushed her teeth and smoothed her beautifully fragranced organic oils on her face. She looked at him through the mirror as he entered the room.

"I've had a lovely afternoon and evening, thank you, it's been really special," she said.

"Good, I'm pleased you have, so have I. I think you looked amazing tonight," he said as he stepped up behind her and placed his hands on her shoulders.

Lexi was now trying to get the little flower 'coils' out of her hair, he watched her as she struggled a little with them.

"Here, let me help you," he said, and she took her hands away from her hair and watched him as he stepped to her side and gently began 'unscrewing' the individual flowers from her curly hair.

As he got to the last one, he took it out and placed it on the shelf with the others, then kissed her cheek; her eyes hadn't left him. He gently pulled her hair back exposing her neck and kissed her again, as he did so her eyes closed and her head tipped slightly to give him better access. He kissed her again and again and as he did, he slowly unzipped the back of her dress; she felt a warm tingle of excitement as he did so. Nathan gently peeled her dress off her shoulders and let it drop to the floor, as he remained standing behind her.

His eyes scanned her body in the mirror as she stood in front him in her knickers. His hands gently brushed her sides as his arms came around the front of her and cupped her breasts and he started to gently kiss her shoulder. The wine was making her head spin slightly and her breathing began to change as she relaxed into his advances. Nathan leant into her as he continued. She took a sharp intake of breath as her naked skin came into contact with the cold of the ceramic sink.

"Oh, fuck, I want you!" He growled, as he pulled her knickers down and fumbled to undo his trousers as he bent her over the sink. He let his clothes fall to the floor, parted her legs slightly and penetrated her from behind. She gasped as he thrust himself into her, the two of them not really in a fit state to fully appreciate the moment. It was more of a lustful, drunken fuck, but as drunken sex goes, it was most enjoyable all the same. As he thrust into her, she became aware of the hard edge of the sink against her hips.

"This is getting uncomfortable," she said, and with that they both stumbled out of the clothes that were still draped around their ankles, out of the bathroom and into the bedroom where Lexi crawled onto the bed on all fours. Nathan quickly followed behind, he placed his hands on her hips and pulled her back onto him as he guided himself inside her; they thrashed away passionately and uninhibited. They thrust, groaned and panted, changed position a couple of times and eventually, completely shagged out, they passed out on each other.

In the morning, they awoke with dry mouths and sore heads. Lexi reached for the water," Oh, God, I should've had more water before I went to sleep, I hate waking up feeling like this!" Nathan opened his eyes and now also felt the familiar, undesirable effects of dehydration.

"Mmm, worth it though, don't you think?" he grunted with a half-smile on his face as he tried to swallow nothing.

Nathan sat up; Lexi had a large bottle of water on her side of the bed.

"Oh, God, I feel like shit!"

"Pass your glass over," she said, and he did so.

Lexi poured him some water and passed it back.

"Ta," he said. They both downed a glass, then Lexi got up, put the kettle on and went to the over-night bag for some coffee and coconut oil, she made the coffee and handed Nathan his.

"We'll feel better after this."

Nathan took the mug; "You think so?" he didn't look convinced.

"I know so. Cup of coffee and a good run, that'll get it out of your system!" She said in her usual, positive way.

"I'm not sure I've got any running shoes with me," Nathan said trying to make an excuse.

"Wear the trainers you wore with your jeans yesterday!"

Nathan could see he wasn't going to get out of this.

"C'mon then Mrs, let's do it, we'll have a little run, shower and check out and then I think it would be good to find somewhere nice for lunch on the way home, that will round off the weekend nicely." She smiled at him, gave him a big kiss on the lips, got out of bed and went in the bathroom.

They had their run, got back and showered, packed their stuff and checked out. They drove the scenic route back and found a perfect little pub on the way, where they stopped and had an early lunch. The rest of the afternoon passed by harmoniously as they continued their leisurely ride home. Arriving home, they unpacked, put the washing on and selected a good film to watch for the evening. Lexi felt more relaxed and happier in Nathan's company than she had since the whole sorry saga had begun.

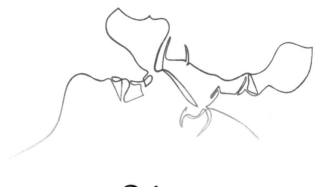

24

Conrad looked at his phone; still nothing! He still felt that he might hear from Lexi or at least hoped he might but would never overstep the mark and call her. He'd promised he wouldn't, it had to come from her. If only she'd just send him a message, anything! She still weighed heavily on his mind. Why is it when you finally find someone who matters, someone who changes your whole thought process, it all goes tits up? He felt so very strongly about her, he just couldn't find it in his heart to accept that it was over; it made him feel very low. He found himself thinking about her, constantly checking his phone in the hope that there would be something from her. Was it simply because he couldn't have her? No, he didn't think so. This was different, everything about it from the moment he set eyes upon her. He kept thinking back over the entire weekend, reliving every moment. Why did it have to end like this? Was it to teach him a lesson? Why was love so cruel?

The week went by uneventfully and Lexi and Nathan seemed ok together. Nathan was working like crazy trying to meet his Friday deadline, tying up loose ends to make sure the project ran smoothly. Lexi had a fully booked week so didn't really have time to get herself in a state over the coming meeting. The week passed in a flash, it was now Thursday afternoon and Nathan had come home early to pack. He planned to leave home around 6pm for the North, stay over-night, and get up fresh for an early start Friday morning; Lexi wouldn't be home before he left. He decided to call her before he set off.

Lexi was between classes, sitting in the café alone and reading details of a course she was interested in. Her phone rang.

"Hi hun, how are you, what sort of a day have you had?"

"Hiya, very busy, just one class to go though, how's your day been?" she replied.

"Yeah, I think everything's ready, or as ready as it will ever be, there might be minor details but that's what tomorrow is all about. I think it's all good though, I'm confident it'll all go smoothly," he said with an air of optimism.

"Good, all your hard work will come together on Monday, and you will see the fruits of your labours," she said encouragingly.

"Yeah, I think so... No, I know so! Oh fuck, I hope so!" He started to falter from overthinking it a little.

"Stop worrying about it!" She cut in, "It won't change anything, you'll just rob yourself of your own peace. You won't sleep tonight and then you won't feel on top of it tomorrow."

Nathan knew she was right, "Yeah, I know, it's just I want it to go well, I've worked so hard on it, this is the biggest project I've ever undertaken."

Of course, he was going to have concerns she thought.

"I know… and I'm sure it will all be fine, let me know when you get there safely, I have to go. Love you."

"Will do, love you too babe."

Lexi did her last class. As she was only going home to an empty house, she went and stretched out in the gym and then had a sauna. Lying there, her mind wandered over Nathan's meeting tomorrow. He would be there with 'her', how would they be together after what happened? Would there still be chemistry between them? How can you go back to just being work colleagues when you'd been intimate with one another? Would they be alone at any time? Would they talk about what has happened? Questions, rolled around in her head until she drove herself mad.

"Oh, stop already!" she exclaimed, telling herself off. Now it was she who was robbing herself of her own peace. All these doubts and questions and 'what if's', were mere speculation. None of it was actually happening, just scenarios in her head. She had to reason with herself, to tell herself that whatever was going through her mind was not helping her right now. She left the sauna, showered, got her stuff together and set off home. Once in, she cooked, got the next day's things ready and did some reading, anything to keep her mind occupied.

At about 9.45pm Nathan called to say he'd got there ok.

"Well, this is it", she thought," it's out of my control now." She made a conscious effort to 'let go' of the negative thoughts that were spinning around her head. She took her water upstairs and read in bed, keeping herself totally focused on the book until it started hitting her in the face where she kept dropping off with it in her hand. After the third time she put the book down, switched off the light and went to sleep.

The alarm went off at 7am. She switched it off, got out of bed and dived in the shower. She went downstairs and put the kettle on, made herself a coffee and some breakfast. At that point her phone rang.

"Good morning!" she answered.

"Hey, morning," Nathan chirped.

"Everything ok?"

"Yes, I just wanted to make sure you're ok, I know this is worrying for you."

Lexi thought this was quite sweet. As much as she had every right to be concerned about Nathan being away in the circumstances, today was a massively important day for him and she hadn't expected him to call; she'd assumed he'd be far too focused to think of her.

"I'm okay," she confirmed, "you've just got to do what you've got to do."

He was relieved at her words, "Everything's going to be fine hun, I promise, and after today we can just get back on with our lives, please trust me?" Lexi's thoughts hung on his words and a little voice inside her head said 'do I trust him?' In all honesty she couldn't say, hand on heart that she did.

"I hope it all goes well, just give it your all I'm sure it'll be fine," she said then added, "Let me know when you're leaving so I know what time to expect you back here," making no reference to the 'trust me' bit.

"Will do, love you," he said and then after a short pause added, "I really do love you Lexi."

"I love you too,"

She pressed the red button on her phone and just stood in the kitchen looking at it for a moment. The sad thing is, once someone has betrayed you in such a way, is it ever possible to totally trust that person again? She cast her mind back to the upbeat and rather matter-of-fact phone call she'd had with Nathan just before that fateful text appeared on her phone; he couldn't have been more normal, there was absolutely no clue in his voice that something was amiss. Though she still felt it was the right thing to do to try and make her marriage work, she also felt that every time he went away this would be going through her mind. She gave a big sigh, looked at her breakfast, forced herself to eat a few mouthfuls and then left for work.

Once at the gym, she totally immersed herself. She had a full morning but finished after lunch; she decided early on that, when she left, she would take herself off into town to occupy her mind. When she had finished, she went into the changing rooms to shower and checked her phone; there was a message from Nathan waiting for her.

"Hope your morning is going well. Just to let you know, Janet isn't here; apparently, she has a tummy bug and is unable to attend the meeting; I thought you'd be happier knowing this, see you later."

Lexi was more than a little relieved to read this.

Lexi left work with a spring in her step, her mood a lot lighter, deciding she'd still go into town and maybe treat herself to something. She looked round all the shops and took her time, something she couldn't do with Nathan because he always got bored. She treated herself to a couple of tops and a pair of jeans. As she was walking along the high street, a voice suddenly shouted out of the crowd,

"Oi, Blondie, nice arse!"

Lexi turned to the familiar sound and sight of Paul coming up behind her.

"Good afternoon most handsome!" she replied playfully, "What are you doing here?"

"Oh, I've had a cancellation and it wasn't worth going home so I thought I'd kill an hour in town. Fancy a cuppa?"

"Yeah, why not?" and they found a teashop in a little walkway and ordered a pot of peppermint tea for them both.

Paul was pleased see Lexi was in a good mood and happy.

"What's up with you then lovely lady, why are you in town?"

"Oh, I had decided I'd come in earlier because Nathan's up north for a meeting that 'She'll' be at!" she pulled a face, "but, as it happens, she's poorly and can't be there. I know it sounds nasty, but I was quite relieved!" she admitted.

"It's not nasty at all, I think it's quite understandable under the circumstances,"

"And so, I came in any way to give myself a treat for my stress!" she said holding up her shopping bags like medals.

"Quite right too, I hope you put it on his credit card?"

She laughed, "Ha, I don't think I'd get away with that somehow!"

"Well, if he hadn't done it, none of this would've happened, would it? Sorry Lex but he owes you big time! He's a very lucky man right now and I hope he appreciates that," he said protectively.

"Oh, I think he does," she said, then added, "Well, I hope he does."

Paul watched her face as she mentally weighed that one up and continued, "You've just told to me that you don't trust him. You did earlier as well when you said you were relieved that she wasn't there today." Paul looked at her with concern. With both elbows on the table, he leaned in and said, "You can't trust him sweetheart. If you had completely trusted him on this, finding out 'what's-her-face' isn't there wouldn't have done anything to your mood at all. The very fact that it did says, despite everything he's told you, you can't one-hundred per cent trust him?"

Lexi looked at Paul and said, "You're right, it hadn't really hit me until today but yes, you're right." They had their tea, the conversation moving on to her purchases and then another course they were both interested in, the time passing quickly. They finished their tea, "Right, I have to be back at the gym in fifteen minutes," said Paul, "lovely to see you." He kissed her cheek as they both rose from the table.

"Remember, I'm here if you need me, if things get tricky, yes?"

"Thank you hun, I really appreciate it," she said.

They hugged, picked up their stuff and went their separate ways.

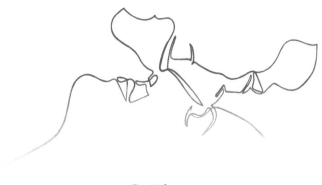

25

As Lexi drove home, Paul's words were ringing around in her head.

"He's absolutely right, if I'd have totally trusted him, it would've made no difference to me whether she was there or not, it simply wouldn't have bothered me but the reality of it all is, I did care. I was worried at what could or might happen and then I was over-the-moon when I got that message to say she wasn't there." This thought stayed with Lexi for a while; she couldn't deny her own gut feelings. As much as she wanted to move on, put it behind her and everything to be perfect again, she couldn't deny the fact that the reason she'd got herself in a state was because, when Nathan wasn't with her, she could no longer trust him.

Lexi got home, sorted out her 'kit', admired her shopping choices all over again and then hung them in the wardrobe. She cooked dinner for both of them, ate hers then, as she wasn't expecting Nathan back for another couple of hours, ran herself a nice magnesium bath. She took up her Ipod and docking station and selected a Tibetan bowl meditation, then lay back in her fragrant, mineral rich, candle lit bath and lost herself. Now, completely 'chilled' she put on her bath robe and went downstairs; rather than put on the television and raise her cortisol levels again, she got some water and went up to read in bed.

She'd been in bed for half an hour when Nathan got home; he came upstairs to find her.

"Hey, how are you?" he said as he entered the bedroom, walked over to her and gave her a kiss.

"You're in bed early!"

"Yes, I've had a bath, I'm feeling quite tired and relaxed, so I thought I'd just read, there's dinner downstairs for you," she said.

"Thank you hun," he said looking very tired from his long day and travelling.

"How did it go today?" She asked.

"It actually went very well, nothing major to change or oversee. It's all going like a well-oiled machine, I'm both excited and relieved, I feel like I can relax a bit now," he said comfortably.

"Good, I'm really pleased for you," she replied.

He kissed her again on the forehead and then said, "I'll go and eat and I'll be back up soon."

Lexi read for a few more minutes; her eyes were tired and her brain was tired. She read a paragraph and then thought to herself, 'I didn't get any of that'. She read it again, no, it wasn't happening, she'd had enough for one day. She put her book down and lay still looking at the ceiling, reflecting on her earlier conversation with Paul. She was well aware that the reason she was so tired was because of the emotional rollercoaster she had been on that day; she was emotionally spent but didn't have the energy or desire to tackle the issue tonight, she closed her eyes. Nathan heated his dinner and ate it, came upstairs to see Lexi fast asleep and quietly got undressed and slipped into bed beside her.

At 5.45am Lexi began to stir as the light entered the room, she felt wide-awake having had what must have been a very deep sleep. She looked at Nathan asleep beside her, her thoughts from yesterday, still on her mind. 'How are we going to tackle this? How am I ever going to trust him again? Or am I just going to have to put up with feeling terribly insecure every time he goes away? She then thought of her own affair; although she was aware that she also had been unfaithful, she was adamant that she would NEVER have done it had she not been in the circumstance she was. Before this had all happened, she would never have worried or suspected anything when Nathan went away, it just wouldn't have crossed her mind. Now, unfortunately it was the first thing on her mind and with the Northern and Southern parts of the company merging, the chances were that Nathan would be spending equal amounts of time at each office from now on. How was she going to cope with this, or even, could she cope with this? She slipped quietly out of bed and went downstairs, ground some coffee and made a nice big pot.

Not wanting to start the day in a negative mood, she looked through her Ipod, chose a playlist of her favourite tunes and popped it on the docking station in the kitchen. She had her coffee and started to prepare her breakfast. Nathan awoke to the sound of music. He turned over; there was no Lexi in the bed, so he got up, then followed the music and the aroma of the coffee downstairs.

"Hey, you're up early babe!"

"Yeah, I think my early night must've done me good, my batteries were recharged early!" she said chirpily, "coffee?" She turned to him holding up a mug.

"Yeah, lovely thanks." He watched her as she poured him coffee from the pot. Although she was consumed with her thoughts of this latest blip in her emotional journey, she chose to say nothing, at least not yet. Despite the fact that this was a real hurdle, she really couldn't face yet another argument and have it ruin the weekend. She kept thinking to herself, maybe this is a temporary state of mind; maybe I'll feel different as time goes on.

They had coffee and breakfast, Lexi deciding she would do the cleaning and then go for a good run after she'd finished. Nathan had been invited to go to a football match in the afternoon with friends and after for a few drinks, so he offered to do the shopping whilst Lexi cleaned, that way she wouldn't spend all day doing chores. Knowing she had the afternoon and most of the evening to herself, she decided she would have one of her holistic, self-pampering days. Exercise followed by detoxing bath, crystal healing, sound bath, ear candles, breath-work and meditation, perfect! She would have no interruptions and no unwanted noise or interruptions in the house. At that point, her phone pinged; it was a message from Paul with a screenshot of some course material they had both been discussing the previous day. She took a quick look and then saved it in her gallery.

Lexi whizzed through the housework with her music spurring her on while Nathan went and did the shopping. He returned just as she was finishing, they unpacked the food together and Nathan had some lunch, he was picked up shortly after by one of his friends. Lexi put her kit on and went for a run, the sun was shining and it was a perfect day for it. She ran along the river wall and up through the fields, loving being outdoors and breathing in the fresh air. Returning from her run to the empty house she went to the kitchen to get a drink of water. Picking up her phone there was another message from Paul regarding a deal on 'block booking' spaces for the course. She went back into her phone to look for the screenshot, as she searched for it she happened upon a separate folder of photos. Her heart gave out an almighty boom as she realised they were the photos she and Conrad had taken on their walk.

'Oh, my goodness, I'd forgotten about these,' she thought to herself, as she looked at the first photo with the folder not yet open. Just that first fleeting image of her with him flooded her with emotion; she sat down, opened the folder and looked through the images.

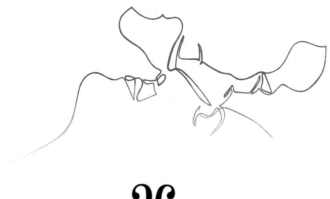

26

The beautiful countryside with the horses, the fun they'd had with the camera and the two of them happy and relaxed with each other. Tears started to roll down her face as the images took her back to that perfect time and place. What a wonderful afternoon they had had. At that point she had no idea just how much that weekend would mean to her. Although she felt terribly emotional looking at the photos, she was so pleased to rediscover them; it was all she had left of him, all she had left of that wonderful experience. She looked through them over and over, she relived every moment, it filled her with a warmth she could never have explained. As she sat there on her own, with her phone and those oh-so-precious memories, her thoughts returned to her current situation.

She looked at Conrad, his happy expression with his arm around her. She remembered thinking during the weekend that he had been a beautiful gift. She was so right; he had been a beautiful gift. The most perfect gift that had been presented to her at the most perfect time; and she had chosen to walk away from it to do 'the right thing'.

She began to think what a fool she had been to do that only to come back to this constant onslaught of emotional insecurity. Her and Nathan's situation was not resolved; she was far from secure and happy. Oh, what she wouldn't give to be in Conrad's arms again, to feel the way he had made her feel. She cuddled her phone close to her chest (usually she wouldn't have a mobile phone anywhere near her!) She so wanted to be near him again, her heart literally ached for him.

"Oh, my God," she said as she hugged her phone," I'm so pleased I have something left of you, you special, special person." Although she did have a little cry, she consoled herself with the fact that at least she still had her memories. No one could take that away from her.

Having found the pictures, Lexi felt slightly happier. Although it'd done nothing to change her situation, the mere fact that she had something physically in front of her to remind her of Conrad made her feel better. She could see his face again; she could see what a lovely time they were having together on that beautiful day. The photos had such a happy and carefree atmosphere about them, she could almost still feel the fun she was having when they were walking and taking them. She could imagine herself back there; it was a beautiful day that was to turn into a wonderful evening and night.

Lexi spent the rest of her afternoon and evening as she had planned; she had some soft and relaxing music playing as she had her mineral bath and practiced her therapies, all of which were very therapeutic and relaxing. It wasn't often she had the chance to really indulge herself in this way. Feeling totally at peace with the world, she cooked herself some dinner and decided to round her evening by opening a good bottle of organic wine. She poured herself a glass; it was now 8.30pm and Nathan shouldn't be long now, he'd help her with it, no doubt. She ate her dinner, cleared up and then decided to read for a while until he got in. She checked the time; it was now 9.30pm. She got up and refilled her glass, she picked up her phone and checked it, there was nothing from Nathan. She knew he was going for a drink, but all his friends had partners to go home to, so they weren't normally this late.

Almost as if pulled by a magnet, Lexi went into the gallery on her phone and opened the folder of pictures of her and Conrad again. She put up a picture of the two of them with the horses; he had a gorgeous smile in that one. She tapped on the image and then 'spread' it with her fingers so that she could see his face close-up. She looked into the image intensely, taking him all in; she looked into his eyes, absolutely lost in him. At that point, she heard the front door go; she quickly came out of the gallery, on her phone, the last thing she wanted was for Nathan to find the images and delete them or insist that she did.

Nathan fell through the front door then misjudged the doorframe as he staggered into the lounge.

"Ouch!" He said, Lexi looked up from her phone.

"I was just going to send you a message to see where you were. You're late, did you have a good time?" What came from his mouth was non comprehensible; he was slaughtered, absolutely slaughtered, which wasn't like him at all! He liked a drink but rarely had she ever seen him in this state. Nathan staggered through to the kitchen.

"You'd better have a big glass of water with some activated charcoal and take a jug up with you," She said, a little annoyed that his rather clumsy entrance had broken her tranquil state; but it was only to get worse.

Lexi was now switching out of 'totally chilled mode' and into 'better take charge of the situation mode'. She got up and went upstairs to the bathroom cabinet for the charcoal and returned to the kitchen with it, Nathan wasn't there, he was in the downstairs toilet throwing up!

"Nice end to the day!" She said to herself. She tried to get in the toilet to make sure he was alright, but it was a tiny room and he was too close to the door for her to open it enough.

"Nathan, are you ok?" she called through the gap in the door.

"Yeah," he slurred back at her.

Starting to feel a little cross she said, "Where have you been to get in that state?"

She couldn't make out the answer he gave her, the door was open by 6 inches and he was half kneeling, slumped over the bowl, he threw up again, then again.

"Oh, joy!" She said, completely unimpressed with it all.

She tried to pass some water into him but in his inebriated state he wasn't receiving it very well or being very helpful. It was so unlike him and equally, she was surprised that whoever bought him home hadn't helped him in. It's not like it was a regular occurrence, this was so out of character for him and by this time, the peace bringing effects of her afternoon and evening were long forgotten. After about an hour of throwing up, she managed to get Nathan out of the way of the door. She squeezed through the gap so she was there with him, at the same time asking him whom he had been with, what he'd been drinking and if all of them had wound up in that state. Of course, she got absolutely no sense out of him whatsoever. Every time she tried to move him, he'd start throwing up again; he ended up passing out, on his knees, hanging over the toilet.

By 3am, Nathan now hadn't been sick for nearly an hour. Lexi decided to try and get him up to bed, "C'mon hun, let's get you upstairs," she said trying to help him up.

He just groaned; he was too heavy for her.

"C'mon, you have to help me hun, I can't do this all by myself," she said struggling with him.

His slurring was now starting to get on her nerves, she was tired and wanted to go to bed but equally felt she couldn't leave him there either.

"Oh, come on, get up! This is getting silly now!" Her voice was now raised in irritation; her change of tone must have awoken something in Nathan. At last he responded, trying to get to his feet but falling forwards and cracking his head on the toilet cistern. As hard as she tried to stop him toppling there was nothing she could do. What a wallop he took on the head, the noise it made went straight through her; she was starting to get worried now.

Finally, she managed to get Nathan out of the toilet. She got him to the settee and got some ice for the now, blue/purple, egg sized lump on his head. He was an absolute mess and by now she wasn't feeling much better. She left him on the settee and took upstairs a big jug of water, a bowl and an old cloth in case he was sick again, then she came down and endeavoured to get him up the stairs. She got him to the stairs and then very carefully pushed him up in front of her with him crawling on all fours. It was a very slow operation, but she managed to get him up. When he got to the top, he stumbled forward and hit his already 'prize egg' on the landing wall, this time it obviously hurt, a lot!

"Oh, for goodness's sake!" She exclaimed, she was now getting to the end of her tether both with worry and tiredness.

"Are you okay?" she asked. Of course, it was a silly question. She helped him up and then proceeded to try and navigate him into the bedroom, at which point he stumbled into her taking her off balance. Lexi went crashing down, hitting her head on the bedside table and taking both the glass and the jug of water down with her. Nathan was completely unaware of what he'd done as he crawled onto the bed and promptly passed out.

Lexi sat on the floor holding her head; the pain was hot and searing. She pulled herself up with the aid of the bedside table and picked up the glass and jug from the soaking wet floor. She looked at Nathan sprawled, face down on the bed; in that moment she felt total disgust for him. It was now just past 4am and she was in an awful lot of pain. She knew she couldn't go to bed without icing her injury. She'd caught the corner of the table right across her eyebrow and temple, her head was nothing short of agony and blood was trickling down her face and neck; she was going to have a lovely shiner in the morning. She went into the downstairs toilet and cleaned herself up, looking at her gaping injury and feeling a certain sense of injustice said to herself, "Why? Why is this happening to me, I thought I was doing the right thing?" She picked up the bag of crushed ice she'd prepared and carefully placed it on her wound to sooth it and stem the bleeding, saying to herself in the mirror,

"I release the pattern within my consciousness that is creating resistance to my own good, I transmute and clear it across all time, space, dimension and reality." She then went back upstairs, put more water in the room for Nathan and took herself into the spare room and shut the door. Feeling tired and very sorry for herself, she finally got to bed just after 4.30am.

27

Sometime around noon the following day, Nathan started to stir and felt suitably hung over from the previous day's alcohol intake, his head felt like he'd been in a boxing ring! He got up to go to the toilet and as he rose, his head literally 'boomed'! He'd never felt quite so ill! He went into the bathroom and as he went to pee, he caught sight of himself in the mirror.

"Jesus!" He said as he saw his reflection, he was literally black and blue, no wonder he felt so bad! He had no recollection of returning home last night, in fact, he had no recollection from about halfway through the evening.

Feeling very sorry for himself but at the same time realising he was probably also in a fair bit of trouble; he went looking for Lexi. He went down to the kitchen, she was no-where to be seen, no music, the kettle hadn't been boiled, maybe she'd got up and gone out early? Nathan made a hot drink and climbed the stairs feeling so poorly he thought he'd take himself back to bed. At that point, he noticed the spare room door closed. He opened the door to find Lexi still asleep.

"Uh, oh!" He said to himself, realising he most definitely must be in a lot of trouble.

He went over to the bed, "Hey hun, you, okay?" he asked rather worriedly.

Lexi woke; her head was splitting but for a very different reason to Nathan's. As she turned over to face him, he saw her injuries from the night before and the bloodstains on the pillow; she literally looked like she'd been hit by a bus!

"Shit, what happened to you?" He asked.

Lexi took one look at the pitiful excuse of a man that stood before her and then turned away from him saying nothing. Nathan felt himself go cold at her reaction to him.

"Did I do that?" he finally asked, "Please tell me I didn't do that…Lexi?"

Lexi just lay with her eyes closed not really wanting to look at him.

"Go away Nathan, just leave me alone," was all she was prepared to reply.

"Babe, what happened? God, seriously? I did that? Hun, please…."

He started to panic; he knew it was definitely something he'd done.

"Nathan, I don't even want to look at you right now." She couldn't even raise her voice her head hurt so much. She had no intention of saving his feelings; she was in so much pain and felt really, quite poorly.

"Shit!" he exclaimed in absolute horror, looking at her face. Clearly, he was responsible, he thought back to his own reflection and injuries, what the hell had happened? At that point, a combination of the pain, worry and dehydration made him 'bolt' for the toilet to be sick. When he'd finished, he looked at himself in the mirror, assessing the damage and trying to recover his memory of the night before. Consumed with worry, he went back into Lexi, who had by now dozed off again.

"Babe, talk to me babe, I have no idea what's happened, I can't remember anything at all," he pleaded.

"Nathan, just leave me alone please," she snapped, her head was literally booming.

Nathan left the room, went downstairs and put the kettle on, thinking that making her a coffee might break the ice enough to find out why they we're both looking like they'd been beaten up. He returned to Lexi with a mug of coffee. As he looked at her head, it was clear she should at least have a butterfly stitch in the rather nasty 'gash' above her eyebrow; he was both terrified and mortified. He couldn't believe that he had been the cause of her injury. As Lexi sat herself up, the world started to 'spin', she felt awfully dizzy and sick, feeling the need to quickly lay herself back down again.

"I think we need to get you to hospital, I'm really worried," he exclaimed.

After a fashion, Lexi told him all that had happened the night before; Nathan felt more awful now than he had before.

"Why did they let you carry on drinking if you were in such a state? They must've known you were absolutely blotto!" she said, still angry at the whole situation.

"I don't know, I don't remember, I honestly don't." His memory was a blank.

After having a coffee and Nathan also taking Lexi something to eat, she was still worryingly ill. Despite the fact he was probably still over the limit, he took her to A&E where they stitched her eyebrow and came to the conclusion that she was suffering a mild concussion. Nathan had never felt so wretched. They returned home, where he tried absolutely everything to make her feel comfortable and better, despite the fact that he himself, still felt like he'd been in a fight with a silver back gorilla!

Nathan tucked Lexi up comfortably on the settee with everything she needed and put a film on, then went upstairs and started to run a bath for himself; he was still feeling very much the worse for wear. Around half an hour later there was a knock at the door; it was one of Nathan's friends returning Nathan's phone that had been left in his car. He was now in the bath, so Lexi had to drag herself up to get the door. She was still very unimpressed with the whole situation. She opened the door.

"Hi," said Jeff. "Jesus, what the hell happened to you?" He asked as he saw her face.

"Nathan 'happened' to me, to be precise," came her un-amused reply. "What happened last night?" she asked. "I don't think I've ever seen him so pissed, I've been up most of the night with him and got this in the process," she said.

"He did that to you?" Jeff said in horror.

"Not intentionally, obviously!" Lexi confirmed.

"Oh shit, what happened?"

Lexi relayed the events of the night.

"Blimey, I'm really sorry," he said, "He was really odd last night. Well, when I say that, he was ok at football and then we went for a drink. He seemed fine at first, then at some point in the evening he went really 'into' himself. I don't know what that was all about, he just seemed as though his mind was elsewhere. Then he started to get his drinking head on and from then on, he just got more and more smashed; it was as if he couldn't get enough down him. We would've come back about nine, but he just seemed to want to stay and get wrecked. After he'd gone to the loo and fell over on the way back, we decided it was time to get him home. Jesus, I'm so sorry Lexi; in hindsight I should've bought him in and got him upstairs for you, I feel really bad now," he apologised.

"It's not your fault Jeff, you're not responsible for his actions!" She said trying to make him feel a little better.

"Yeah, but, look of the state of you, that looks so painful," he said, almost wincing at the sight of her injury.

"You should see him, he cracked his head twice, he's black and blue, only he must have a tougher head than me!" she said as Jeff added,

"Probably because of the alcohol, he was so relaxed he didn't hurt himself so much."

"Yes, you could be right, I'm going to have to sit down, I'm still feeling quite giddy," she said, her head swimming and pounding.

"Yes, of course, sorry, you go and rest. Tell him I've been please," He said.

"Will do."

Lexi shut the door and went back to her settee. She glanced at Nathan's phone; there were twelve missed calls from the same number. 'What's that all about then?' She thought to herself, her instincts telling her this had something to do with the events of last night.

She placed the phone on the coffee table and continued to watch her film. Ten minutes later Nathan's phone rang; Lexi picked it up, it was that number again. She answered it.

"Hello?" There was quiet on the other end, "Who is this?" she asked.

A female voice from the other end said, "Can I speak to Nathan please?"

"Who is this?" Lexi repeated.

"It's Janet."

Lexi froze, 'what the fuck does she want? Blimey is she not content with the trouble they've both already caused? Why is she calling him on the weekend?'

"Nathan's in the bath right now, what do you want Janet? It's Lexi, Nathan's WIFE!" She said in a rather steely tone.

"I realise that and I'm sorry, I wouldn't have called unless it was absolutely necessary."

The voice sounded weak.

"Oh, really!" Lexi almost raised her voice but the pain in her head stopped her from doing so.

"I called him last night and tried to talk to him," Janet continued.

"Oh, did you now?" She replied sounding a bit cynical. At this point, Janet broke into tears on the other end. Lexi, figuring this was some kind of 'other woman obsessive behaviour,' gave out an impatient sigh, just to be completely crushed by Janet's next statement.

"I…. I'm pregnant!"

Lexi felt the bottom of her world drop away as the words fell into place in her head.

"Oh, for fuck's sake, this couldn't get any worse really, could it?" She mumbled.

Janet continued, "I told Nathan last night, he put the phone down on me, I've tried calling him, but he won't answer.

"Yes, I can see that," Lexi replied now feeling a protective streak rip through her.

Lexi, carefully crawled up the stairs on all fours and took the phone into the bathroom. Nathan was relaxing back in the bath with his eyes closed. She broke the silence.

"Phone call for you, its Janet!" His eyes sprung open with a start.

"She's pregnant!" She added as she handed him his phone.

The look on his face was that of sheer horror. Lexi didn't hang around to hear any more, she'd heard quite enough. She carefully got back downstairs on her bottom and as she did, in her heart, she knew her marriage was now officially over; this was now a point of no return. Had she not had a mild concussion, she probably would have stormed out of the house and either driven off somewhere or stormed out on foot. Neither of these was an option in her current state so she just went back down the stairs, shutting the lounge door so she couldn't hear Nathan. She had got to the point where she wasn't the slightest bit interested in his end of the conversation. She didn't want to know or care if he was going to try 'solve' that one. Yes, it seemed a cruel blow after everything, but she took this as her sign to now let go, she'd had enough upset and humiliation, this was her sign to say, enough-is-enough.

Nathan came into the lounge; words couldn't describe the look on his face.

"Babe," he started but Lexi was quick to cut in.

"Don't call me babe please."

His voice was desperate, "Lexi please."

She gave him no room to try and talk her round.

"No Nathan, not this time, just don't, don't waste your breath, I really don't want to hear it. I take it that's what this was all about last night?"

She gestured to his and her bruised faces. He hung his head in remorse.

"I just couldn't believe it, I just couldn't deal with it," he said, almost trying to justify the carnage of the night before.

Lexi replied frankly, "Which lends sense to the saying, 'if you can't do the time, don't do the crime'!"

He looked at her. He could see in her body language and expression that he'd now completely lost her. "If I'd have thought for a moment that ANY of this would happen, I would never have done it. I can't believe how one, really, really, bad decision has affected our lives so negatively and in such a massive way."

As sincere as his words were Lexi replied, "Our lives can never be the same again Nathan, we can never go back to the way we were. I was determined to try and put what happened behind me for the sake of our family, but this changes everything, and you have to understand that. This is your problem, this has absolutely nothing to do with me."

He looked at her face and he could see she was totally serious.

"Oh, my God, this is it, isn't it?... We can get through this, Lexi, I know we can."

She looked at him,"No Nathan, I don't think we can."

"Lexi, don't give up on me now, please, I really need you," he pleaded.

"Don't give up on you? Are you serious? This whole situation just seems to get worse and worse! I'm sorry Nathan…." She corrected herself, "Actually, no, I'm not sorry, I have nothing to be sorry for. I came back to try and make this work and to be totally honest with you, even before this, when you were away on Friday, I knew from my frame of mind on that day that I simply could never trust you again. I knew after Friday that every time you went away in the future, I would have had nagging doubts in my mind about what you might be up to or, whom you were with. Now there's a baby to take into consideration and I have absolutely no desire to play happy families with you and your love child. I take it she's keeping it?" She threw a quick look in his direction as she continued, "No Nathan, I can't do this any-more."

Nathan knew he couldn't argue that one, Janet had already said on the phone that she wouldn't have an abortion.

Nathan's eyes got bigger and bigger as the emotion built up inside him, the bottom rims of his eyes filled with tears as he realised just how enormous the consequence of his actions had been.

Nathan put his head in his hands, his elbows on his lap and stayed there for some moments. After some time, he sat back in the settee, his hands now clasped behind his head, looking forward. Well, he looked like he was looking forward, what he was actually doing was looking inside his head, visualising the massive changes that were now most probably about to happen in his life. If she left him now, he'd have to sell the house and split it. He'd have to start again. What would the kids say about it all, what would they say about the baby? He had assumed his baby days were long behind him, he thought the only babies he'd come into contact with now would be his grandchildren, yet Janet was adamant that she wouldn't have an abortion as she was thirty- five and hadn't any children. He didn't want another baby... but could he walk away from it and have nothing to do with it? Would his conscience allow him to have his child grow up not knowing him? What a bloody mess to get in to!

Nathan looked at Lexi, her bruised face, her stitched eyebrow, he felt sick.

"Oh, my God, what a fucking mess. I love you; I really do love you! I never meant to hurt you, I would never have hurt you intentionally, you know that don't you? I'm so sorry! Sorry I betrayed you, sorry I did this to you." He gestured towards her face, "But more than anything, I'm sorry for humiliating you by punctuating this whole sorry episode with a child. I really can't blame you if you want to leave me, I know I can't, but I want you to know I do love you very much and always will."

His words were clearly of truth and from the heart.

Lexi looked at his face, all bruised and beaten, the massive dark circles under his eyes, he looked a broken man. In that moment, she actually felt sorry for him. Many thoughts went through her head, 'A baby! Bugger that! He'll be getting on for 70 when it goes to uni!' Yes, his life was most certainly going to change, and no one could blame her for not wanting any part of bringing up his child of passion.

"I know you didn't do it intentionally," she said softly, "but at that point in time, you did what your heart wanted. The love you had for me wasn't enough to stop you from doing it and if it didn't stop you then, why should it stop you in the future? Even if you hadn't conceived a child, things wouldn't have been right. I've been married to you for twenty years and I've never felt insecure in my relationship with you before, but Friday proved to me that that had all changed. It just wouldn't have worked, not in the long run, every time you went away it would have become more and more of an issue."

He nodded, "Yeah......... I know."

He bent forward, put his head in his hands again and started to cry. Lexi felt the emotion tugging at her, feeling sorry for him, she shifted over and put her arm around him and with that he turned into a blubbering wreck as she sat gently rubbing his back.

After he'd got it out of his system, he sat back up and turned to her saying, "Thank you, I don't deserve you."

"I don't want us to be enemies Nathan," She said. "I've been with you nearly half my life, we've shared more than twenty years together, we have a beautiful, grown-up family who will probably soon be producing little families of their own. I don't want us to lose the beautiful unit we have built between us, I want us to be able to enjoy it, if we can get through this without falling out, we could still enjoy family events but that's not going to happen if we're at each other's throats, backbiting over who-did-what-with-who. I don't want our children's weddings or graduation ruined because their parents can't be civilised to one another."

At that point, Nathan felt relieved. He gone from thinking he'd lost everything to realising that his wife, the lady he cheated on, put in hospital and then landed a baby on, didn't want to create a divide or use their kids as pawns in a bitter game. He appreciated her compassion; they had always been a very close family and he felt thankful he wasn't going to lose that.

They sat and talked quite calmly about where they were going to go from here; they were both upset but at the same time practical about it. They discussed the house, their finances and came to an agreement over how they would move forward. Nathan's head kept drifting off into his perception of what was in store for him, he hadn't accepted the situation and was reeling at the thought of becoming a father again at this point in his life. Lexi could see that this was really troubling him but still couldn't entertain the thought of being any part of it.

They went to bed in separate bedrooms. Nathan lay looking at the ceiling, the events of the last, few weeks spinning around his head combined with the fear of what was coming and the big question 'WHY'? Why did it have to work out like this? Lexi lay in her bed, she felt sound in her mind, she'd called 'time' at the right time, she knew that they could never have come back from such a massive blow it was just too much. Now she must concentrate on the practical side of getting her life sorted out and getting herself a place that was affordable for her, something she had never imagined she'd be doing at this point in her life.

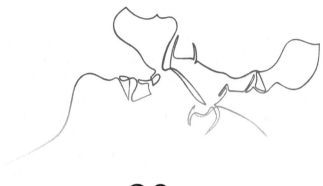

28

It was Monday and Lexi hadn't set her alarm, she considered she deserved a well-earned lie-in after her (to say the least), turbulent weekend. She woke up at 9.10; the first thing she was aware of was a thumping headache. She reached for her glass of water but there were only a couple of sips left. Her head felt 'fuzzy' and as she tried to get up the thumping intensified. "Oh, God!" She exclaimed as she carefully got to her feet. She felt awful; she went very dizzy and could feel herself going all hot and cold, so she sat back down on the bed. After waiting a moment or two, she gave it another go, the thumping increased but she managed to stay up this time; she carefully made her way downstairs, her body felt weak and her legs were shaky as she held on tightly to the bannister. Going into the kitchen she put the kettle on and went to look for some paracetamol, she didn't usually take medicines of any kind but in this case, she was desperate.

She got a glass, poured in some water and added a soluble painkiller, then prepared a strong coffee for the pot to kick-start the paracetamol. Nathan must have got up very quietly as Lexi hadn't heard him shower; today was a big day for him in more ways than one. Today the two companies merged, everything that he had been working on for the last eighteen months was now being set into motion. He also now needed to put the house on the market; they had both said they would get estate agents in to value the house and look for potential places to move into after it had sold. He felt miserable at how fate had dealt him such a blow; this really wasn't what he'd imagined for himself. As he entered the office, there were awkward glances at his bruised face.

"Don't ask!" He said as he walked through to his office and closed the door behind him.

Lexi took her medication, had a coffee and straight away got on the computer to find an estate agent. She booked someone to come around and value the house and then browsed through the many properties for something smaller, but big enough for the kids to stay. She was shocked at the prices; this wasn't going to be easy.

She called the gym, "Hi, yes, it's Lexi, I'm going to have to take at least tomorrow off, maybe the day after. I managed to hurt my head at the weekend, so I have mild concussion; I know I'm not going to be able to drive the car and there's no way I'll be able to jump about with people," she explained. "Oh, ok, sorry to hear that, said the receptionist, "I'll tell Diana."

Lexi went and lay down on the settee; she wasn't feeling at all good. She must've lost herself for a few moments, then suddenly, she came to with a 'start'; her mobile phone was ringing, and she'd left it in the kitchen. She stumbled to get up, her head still banging, she made a lunge to try and steady herself on the kitchen door frame but then everything went black.

Sometime later, she became aware that she felt cold. She was lying on the floor; she'd obviously had a black out, either from the concussion or from standing up too quickly with her injury. She got onto her all fours and crawled into the kitchen scared she might fall again, feeling incredibly weak and shaky. She got to her phone, took it down from the worktop and sat on the kitchen floor.

It had been Nathan, he'd left a text, "Just called to see how you are, you must be having a lie-in, I'll call you later."

She looked at the phone; she felt so poorly and now she'd scared herself by passing out, should she call him back and tell him what's happened? He really could do without it today of all days, she sighed and put the phone on the floor. As she did it rang again; it was Paul.

"Hey Blondie, Kim just told me you cancelled tomorrow and possibly Wednesday, I just wanted to see if you're ok, it's not like you…" but didn't finish his sentence before he could hear Lexi weeping at the other end.

"I'll be round in half an hour!" he said without waiting for her reply, then the phone went dead.

Lexi pulled herself up with the help of the worktop; her head wasn't thumping quite so badly now the paracetamol, aided by the caffeine, was finally kicking in, although she still felt dizzy and sick. Lexi got back to the settee and lay back down again. A while later there was a knock at the door. She called, "Come in!" from where she was and in came Paul.

"Hey, little lady, what's going on with you then?" He said as he came into the lounge and saw the state of her. "Oh, Jesus, what the fuck happened to you?" Shocked at the sight of her stiches and bruises.

"Oh, Nathan came home drunk Saturday. It was an accident, he stumbled and knocked me off balance, but I caught my head on the bedside table as I went down. They said I have mild concussion, I really feel like shit, especially when I stand up," she admitted.

He took a close look at her injury, "That looks really nasty," he said, grimacing in sympathy.

"The really annoying thing is, he smacked his head twice in the process of me trying to get him upstairs. He had the biggest egg you've ever seen in your life, which he then walloped again and, apart from the bruising, he's absolutely fine!" she said ironically.

"Yeah, it's where it is though, isn't it?" he observed, "You've caught it right on the soft bit, no wonder you're not feeling very good!" He took a closer look, "I think you might end up with a scar there."

Lexi's hand unconsciously went up to her stitches, "Yes, I thought that, once it's no longer so sore, I'll rub some oils into it to help it heal."

Paul, concerned, continued, "Looking at you and seeing it for myself, I don't think you should even attempt to come to work for at least four days. You still have concussion; I can see it in your eyes and even after that settles down it's going to hurt when you start jumping around. I think you need to give yourself more time to heal properly if you want my honest opinion."

"Yes, I think you're right."

Trying to lift her spirit he countered playfully, "Of course, I'm right, I'm always right. I thought I was wrong once, but I was mistaken!" He winked at her. "Do you want a cup of tea?"

"Ooh, that would be nice, thank you," she said. Having made them both a cuppa, Lexi told him all about Saturday night and then went on to tell him the events of Sunday. "Sweetheart, you're not having a lot of luck, are you?"

"That's one way of describing it!"

"Well, who would ever have thought it would turn out this way, I bet you wish you hadn't come back now, don't you? What a bloody mess! It's as if there would have been an obstacle there whatever you did," he said in disbelief.

"Yes, that thought had crossed my mind too."

They both sipped their tea.

"And you haven't heard from Conrad at all?" Paul asked.

"No, he did promise that he wouldn't contact me. Nathan, as you know, made me delete his contact number. I've had a look on Facebook for him; you wouldn't believe how many Conrad Edwards there are! I came across these at the weekend."

She got the photos up on her phone and showed Paul.

"Wow, you both look very happy, what a shame eh? I'm sure there must be some way of contacting him, it seems such a shame how it's all worked out."

Lexi agreed then added, "But at least we're working this out without trying to tear each other to shreds, that would just have been awful."

Paul looked at his dear friend, "Well, all I can say is, you're a good woman and he's very lucky, because I don't know many women who would be quite so prepared to be amicable after everything he's done," he said with total respect for her.

"Well, it's not like he planned it is it? It's just circumstance, had she not been at that point in her cycle, we, or he, wouldn't be dealing with this; it's just the way it's worked out and we have to accept it for what it is," she said in a matter-of-fact way.

"Bless ya! Oh, sweetie, I can't think of anyone that deserves this less than you. So, what are you going to do regarding the house?"

Lexi went on to tell him the plan of action. Paul stayed with her for another half hour, as he got up to leave for work, he asked. "Will you be okay here by yourself now?"

"Yes, I'll be fine thank you. Thank you so much for coming over, it's really kind of you." Paul bought a glass of water in and put it on the coffee table for her, making sure she had everything she needed close by, leaving with, "No worries, sweetie, I'll call later and check up on you."

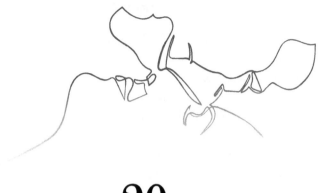

29

Meanwhile, across the pond, Conrad was slowly coming to terms with the likelihood that, with every day that passed without hearing from Lexi, it was less likely that he was going to. He still felt the need to check his phone for messages, but it was becoming less frequent. He still thought about her, still wanted to hear from her; every day he hoped and every day he was disappointed. Her silence was disheartening and being alone with his thoughts was driving him mad. He had absorbed himself in work and when he wasn't at work, he was learning more and more about the subject that had totally driven her and had so intrigued him about her. He'd bought a book that she had recommended and once he'd started reading about the whole holistic experience, it all made so much sense. Now his eyes were opened to it, he was in total agreement that we were never designed to live like this. All the chemicals in our food chain, the fact that people didn't cook anymore, they just opened a packet and heated up 'food like products', but none of it is real food, no wonder the cancer rate was so high! Chemicals are not only in food but also in personal care products, household cleaners and air fresheners and our water. It had never really occurred to him before he met Lexi, but now his attention had been drawn to it, he was almost obsessing over it, checking labels and ingredients, he'd managed to source an organic farm produce company, where he could order his meat and vegetables and they delivered to him. He'd also done as Lexi suggested and created a meal plan for every three-to-four days giving him something to fill the void Lexi had left inside him. He remembered her words, "Everyone comes into your life for a reason, either as a blessing or a lesson..." Maybe that was the purpose of her coming into his life, maybe he was never meant to have her and maybe she was just sent to make him aware of all this? Because now he was aware of it, he felt as passionate about it as she had been.

Now his interest had been sparked he was on a mission. He found it really interesting but at the same time horrifying, just how many chemicals were to be found in day-to-day life that have been proven to have negative effects on human health, yet were government approved to be sprayed on produce, put in processed food, body and household products, drinking water and just about everything else. He could now see why Lexi had been so driven by her pursuit of natural living, reducing her personal exposure to the chemicals in her environment and so very passionate about sharing her knowledge.

Lexi awoke on the settee where she must've nodded off. As she opened her eyes, she didn't feel quite so bad. Sitting up slowly, her head still thumped but she felt better than she had that morning. She went to the computer and started looking again at properties, not a good thing to do with a headache, so she decided to fix herself something to eat. Far from well but a lot more stable now, she fixed herself a smoothie as it was nice and easy but at the same time highly nutritious. She went back to the lounge and lay back down on the settee. It was odd, her body was shattered, she had no strength and just wanted to lie there but her brain wasn't used to the rest of her being so idle, she was bored and restless.

As she lay there her phone rang, it was Nathan.

"Hey, how are you?"

"Oh, I'm okay thanks,"

"How does your head feel now?"

"Not too bad right now, I had a bit if a moment this morning though... Anyway, how's it all going?" keeping the conversation light.

"Yes, good thanks, what do you mean, a moment?" he asked.

"I had a blackout, it unnerved me a bit but I'm okay now,"

"Why didn't you call me?" Nathan said, still feeling full of guilt.

"Because I think you have enough to worry about today, it's ok, I'm fine now, Paul came by and it's all good."

"Sure?"

"Yes, honestly, I'm sure," she tried to convince him, hearing the concern in his voice.

"Okay, I'll see you later."

"Bye." She lay there on her back with the phone in her hand and as if on autopilot, she went into her photo gallery to the pictures of her and Conrad.

She recalled everything about that day, how they'd talked in the car park and then in the sauna, how she'd got so upset when Eddie had called and he just 'happened' along at that point in time. How kind he'd been to her and how he'd done his best to cheer her up. She remembered the coffee shop and the enormous piece of carrot cake and then, suddenly, a thought occurred to her, Conrad had given her one of his business cards when they were in the coffee shop! What had she done with it? She hadn't remembered seeing it since, but she didn't think she'd thrown it away. Which bag did she have with her? Her heart pounded as she tried to remember. Lexi carefully got up and made her way upstairs. She went to her wardrobe, grabbed the handbag that she had taken away with her and opened it, she turned it upside down and shook it until the contents had fallen out on the floor. Nothing! She opened the little inside zipper pocket where she kept her business cards and just as her fingers came into contact with it, she clearly remembered putting it there.

She sat on the bedroom floor with the card in her hand looking at it. At that moment, she couldn't have been happier than if she'd won a million pounds on the lottery!

"Oh, my God, all this time you've been in here!"

She kissed the card and then looked up to the heavens and said, "Thank you!"

In her mission to find the card, she'd left her phone downstairs; she put the other contents that were on the floor back in her handbag, put it away and then carefully returned downstairs. Her hands shook as she picked up her phone, 'What do I do? Do I text or call? What will the time be where he is? More to the point, where is he, he could be anywhere in any time zone, probably better to text'.

She sat and thought about what she wanted to say; it'd been so long; he'd probably be sure she was just settled back into life. She typed him out a text.

"My dearest Conrad. I hope you can forgive me for not contacting you before. The truth is, I have just found your card in my handbag. Things haven't worked out at all well here and I felt very early on that I had made a mistake in coming back. I know I most certainly would've been tempted to call you earlier had my husband not forced me to erase your contact details. I feel very sad and I think about you all the time and how we were together. I constantly look at the photos we took on our walk and my heart sinks at what I've walked away from. I hope you can forgive me; I'd so love to hear from you again. Lexi x."

She read her message through, tears in her eyes, her finger hovered over the send button, 'What if he's moved on? What if he rejects me?' she thought to herself; that was a chance she'd have to take. She pressed send and at the same time felt a rush as if an electric current had gone through her. She got up and went into the toilet, the card still in her hand, she looked at her battered, bruised face, then back down to his card. She placed her hand on her heart, looked into her eyes in the mirror and spoke.

"I am worthy of receiving the very best that love and life have to offer me and I now lovingly allow myself to accept it, to receive it fully and enjoy it completely."

Nathan returned just before 6pm, which was early for him, especially considering how important his day had been. He came in and saw Lexi lying on the settee.

"Hey, how are you now?" he said as he came through the door.

"Yeah, not bad thanks," she replied, "My head still hurts but I don't feel quite so dizzy now."

"Good," he replied, "are you hungry?" he said as he walked toward the kitchen.

"Getting that way, how has it gone today?"

"Yes, it's all gone really well, no 'hitches', it was just a case of overseeing it. I'm really pleased with how it's worked out, at least something's worked out right for me!"

He came back in from the kitchen and sat down with her on the sofa, "I've been having a look at properties."

"Yeah, me too, nightmare!" she said in an unimpressed tone.

He cut in, "Hear me out a moment babe. The mortgage is tiny on this house and only two years left on it. For us to get rid of this and both to get a decent sized house so the kids can stay, for me, it will be manageable because I'm on a good salary. Financially for you, it's going to be a nightmare; to take on a mortgage you would have to up your hours so much to cover it, so I've been thinking…. We both want to be able to keep our family unit together so what would you say if I said, you stay in the house and when we see the kids I come here? Then, if I use my bonus and some of our savings for a deposit, I could get a two-bedroom house to live in, that way there's somewhere for…." he paused,

"Well, you know…." Lexi nodded, knowing what he was referring to.

He continued, "I mean, obviously if you meet someone else, I wouldn't want them in 'our' house the same as you wouldn't want my child in here but for now, I think it could work and if-and-when our situations change further down the line, I'd like to think we can sort it out fairly. We've planned all our married life to travel once the kids have left home, we've put away so much to make that possible, now that's not going to happen. I never imagined that we wouldn't be growing old together; I also never thought that I'd be putting you in this situation. So, for now at least, it would make me feel a bit easier about it, what do you think?"

Lexi felt a huge feeling of relief inside; the financial worry of getting somewhere else had really been troubling her. They needed to sit down and work out what money they did have but for now, what Nathan was suggesting seemed like a far less scary option.

Lexi teared up, "Thank you Nathan, you have no idea what a relief that is to me," she said sincerely.

"Yes, I think I do and I would never want to cause you that kind of stress when you never asked for any of this." He got up and kissed her forehead, then made his way into the kitchen and started to prepare some dinner.

Lexi realised it was now 6.30 and she still hadn't showered, she dragged herself up and went in the kitchen.

"I'm going to grab a shower, I can't believe it's so late!" she said, a little disgusted with herself!

"Why don't you have your dinner and then have a nice bath after?" he suggested.

"Actually, that's a better idea," she agreed. After they'd eaten, he said, "I'll clear up, you go and have a bath." With that he picked up the plates and disappeared into the kitchen. Lexi spotted her phone on the settee; she walked over, picked it up and had a look, nothing on there. Then went into 'settings' and switched off the sound. She didn't want to be underhanded with Nathan, but she also felt the dynamics might change if he knew she'd just sent Conrad a message and equally, she wasn't sure how her message would be received.

It was Monday morning and Conrad had had a very early start; he was still in Los Angeles but had to travel further afield. He'd set off at 5.30am, arrived at his destination by the skin of his teeth and went straight into a meeting. It was now nearly midday and they had broken for lunch; he went and looked for something suitable to eat, found a little Turkish restaurant and ordered some grilled chicken with vegetables and salad. He sat at the table by himself and opened his laptop, quite engrossed in what he was doing, he picked up his phone and there, in all its glory was Lexi's message waiting for him! His heart leapt!

"Oh, my God!" He said, hastily opening the message and unconsciously holding his heart as he read her words. Total elation was the only way to describe how he felt in that moment; straight away he dialled her number. Of course, Lexi had switched her sound off, so she didn't hear it and she was now running her bath. She lay there and relaxed for half an hour, then came back downstairs. Nathan had cleared up and was on his laptop.

As she entered the room, he looked up at her.

"Feel better for that?" he asked.

"Yes, much better thanks, do you want a hot drink?" she said, as she casually picked up her phone and went into the kitchen.

"Yeah, that'd be good thanks." he said momentarily glancing up from his laptop.

"What would you like?"

"Redbush please, you okay to make it?"

"Yes, I can manage." She went into the kitchen and put the kettle on then looked at her phone, there was a missed call and a text message from Conrad. Instantly her entire body was pulsing with adrenaline at both the excitement of hearing back from him and the uncertainty of what the message might say. She looked out of the kitchen at Nathan busily typing away, then returned to her phone and opened the message.

"Lexi, I can't tell you how happy I am to hear from you. I'm not happy that you've been unhappy though. As the days went on, I felt that I would never hear from you again and it was breaking my heart, of course I can forgive you! I said at the time, you had to do what was right for you and I could understand that you needed to break contact and focus on what was in front of you. It broke my heart to lose you, but you've been in my thoughts every day. Although I'd only been in your company for a weekend, I felt like my entire world had changed and I found it terribly hard to accept that it had ended there. I was surprised and equally delighted to see your message, I tried to call you, let me know when you're about, I can't wait to hear your voice again. Conrad xxx."

Lexi quickly typed a message back saying she couldn't talk right now but would be free anytime tomorrow if he wanted to call when it was good for him. She sent the message, kissed her phone, finished making the hot drink and then, with the most warm and happy feeling inside, she took a deep breath, picked up the drinks and took them into the lounge. She watched Nathan tapping away for a couple more minutes. She felt so happy, having read Conrad's message, she was finding it hard to hide. She felt it would really be like rubbing salt in the wound if she told Nathan of her latest developments. Even though she felt like she was going to burst with it, she didn't feel it was appropriate to let him know how happy she was right now when he was full of doom and gloom. So, at that point, she picked up her phone and said she was going to lie on her bed and listen to one of her audio books, as she didn't feel like reading or watching television.

Nathan carried on with his work for a few more minutes and then he took a deep sigh and sat back in the chair, thoughts pricking in his head. He had accepted that it was over with Lexi, he knew there was no going back now, although he still wished it would all go away, and he could get back to how he was before. He had never imagined that night would change his life so completely. A night of high emotion after working for so many months to bring something so important to together, to be followed by a few drinks and what started out to be a bit of flirting. If only it had stopped there. If only he'd had the presence of mind to walk away rather than make that fateful choice. He knew he only had himself to blame but still he felt somewhat sorry for himself for his bad luck. If only she hadn't got pregnant, the outcome might have been very different. But if-only's don't count and clocks don't turn themselves back for our convenience either. He sat quietly contemplating his lot and all that he would need to do regarding his living arrangements. He'd lost the thread now as far as work was concerned; he closed his laptop, locked up and went up to bed.

Lexi lay herself down on her back in the middle of the bed, her phone in her hand, and read Conrad's message again. Just reading his words, she could feel his energy. She felt so happy, so incredibly blessed that she'd managed to find him again and he still felt the same way, how much had her world changed with that one little message? Mind you, how much had her life changed after the first little message? Only this time, instead of going from happy-go-lucky to rock bottom in one big drop, she'd gone from feeling as low as she could ever remember feeling, to feeling on top of the world. She was almost floating she was so happy, thinking back to when she was with him, how she felt when he was close to her, how he smelt, how his arms felt around her, how his skin felt on hers. Dare she allow herself to believe that she was really going to have that beautiful privilege again? She was almost scared to believe it possible after the rollercoaster of emotion she'd been on. Just the thought of being back in his company filled her with joy.

Lexi was almost going crazy wanting to call him but calculated that, if he was in LA, it would be mid-afternoon now and he would be at work, which meant she'd just get his answering service. She decided to send him another message,

"Conrad, I was so relieved to get your message, it's made me so very happy, I feel like my whole world has turned around. Until this afternoon when I found your card, I was as low as I can ever remember being and now, I feel on top of the world. I was devastated that I'd walked away from what we had shared just to end up in a situation that can only be described as some kind of 'soap opera'! Things are still a little complicated at the moment; I'll explain when I talk to you. I'm about all day for the next couple of days; I'll explain that to you too! I'll sleep tonight, being the happiest I've been since our last meal together, I'm so desperate to hear your voice xXx"

She sent her message and lay on the bed now with happy thoughts going around in her head. It was as if the huge emotional burden of recent weeks had just magically been lifted from her. She thought of Nathan downstairs, how his world was about to change in a way he never could have imagined. She certainly didn't envy him; it was almost as if karma had played a part here. At the same time, she felt no animosity toward him. In her head, she tried to work out the best way of going about this. She decided she wouldn't say anything about Conrad now; it might be three or four weeks before she could see him and a lot could happen in that time if the last two weeks were anything to go by. She felt it would be kinder to wait until Nathan was in a better place, figuring that there was bound to be a more suitable time and situation when she would share her news. So, blissfully happy, Lexi drifted off to sleep.

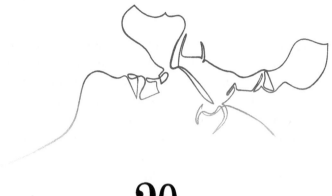

30

The morning had come and Lexi awoke, as always, to the sun streaming through the gaps in the blackout blinds. Looking at the clock, it was only 6.10am. She realised she'd fallen asleep on top of the bed with the phone still in her hand. She never had a phone with her when she slept, it was always switched off and well away from her, that's how relaxed she must have been. She looked at the phone; an instant glow of happiness came over her as she recalled the message from last night. She quietly pulled the blind up and let the sun stream in. She was beaming! Lying back on the bed and letting out a happy sigh, she looked at her phone again; she'd be talking to him today, hearing his voice. She went into her photos and got up the pictures of her and Conrad. More than anything, she wanted to feel like that again. Looking at a selfie of herself and Conrad, she smiled and then enlarged his image with her fingers.

Her eyes searched his handsome face, "Oh my God! This is amazing! I'm going to have you back in my life!" She remembered laughing with him on that walk; casting her mind back to the evening and their meal, she smiled looking deeply into his image, trying to imagine him moving, talking and coming in to kiss her. She'd been lying on the bed in her dressing gown, now she undid it and held the phone with Conrad's image in one hand while her other hand found its way down to her clitoris. Gently, she started to touch herself, feeling incredibly turned on by seeing his image, remembering and reliving his touch, knowing that this beautiful delight was no longer out of her reach. She leaned over, opened her bedside drawer and got out a pot of coconut oil and her little bag of toys. She selected her favourite, then massaged some coconut oil in and began to stimulate herself with it. Her senses already heightened by her exhilarated state of mind. As she relaxed into the delightful, pulsing sensation she imagined she was with him. She journeyed back in her mind to that amazing night; she remembered everything he'd done, every touch and every kiss. She allowed her mind's eye to relive every moment, her body was tingling and her breathing became heavier as she became more and more aroused. She put the phone down with Conrad's image looking out at her, reached in her bag and pulled out a dildo. She massaged coconut oil up the shaft and penetrated herself with it, letting out a gasp of relief as she firmly but gently pushed it inside her. Slow and firm to begin with and then harder and faster as she thought of him and her, how they had been together, small beads of sweat forming on her belly as the magnified heat of the sunlight penetrated her skin through the window. Using a mixture of both toys now, she began to gasp and groan as she reached her first orgasm.

Her orgasm felt like the almightiest release of sexual energy, but no sooner had she come down from it, the sensations that were still rippling through her told her there was more to come. She carried on and in a short space of time she managed to reach that beautiful height once more. With the sun beating down on her she felt like she was on fire; she shifted over to the window and opened it to let some air in, then lie back down, the dildo on the bed by her side. She lay gently stroking herself while the sensitivity died down a little. At that point and quite unexpectedly, Nathan burst through the door with a mug of coffee in his hand! Lexi jumped and let out a little scream.

"Oh God! Sorry..." Nathan said as Lexi covered herself up.

"Shit, I didn't hear you up and about!" she exclaimed.

"Sorry, I should've knocked," he said, "I just wasn't expecting..." He was feeling a little awkward so decided to break the ice with, "Did you need any help with that at all?"

"No thank's, I was doing a pretty good job all by myself!"

Lexi, also feeling a little awkward!

Nathan looked at his wife. Having walked in to see her naked, pleasuring herself on the bed, although he found it hard to get his head round it, he now surrendered to the fact that he would never have her in that way again. He smiled and gave her a joking wink adding, "Just thought I'd ask!" And then added on a more serious note, "Sorry though hun, I'll knock in future, or would you prefer I didn't bring you a drink up any-more?"

"No! Don't be silly, knocking is fine." Nathan was more often than not, up first and there's nothing nicer than a coffee in bed in the morning, of course she wasn't going to say no!

"I'm sorry I hadn't heard you," she continued, "I'd have been more discreet if I'd realised you were up." Nathan carried on getting ready for work and Lexi fell back on the bed giggling to herself, still feeling slightly embarrassed but also bursting with happiness and excitement knowing she would soon be talking to her man. Nothing, but nothing could bother her today.

It was now 6.50 and, despite the fact that she didn't have to go to work, Lexi was far too excited to stay in bed and decided to go downstairs and make another coffee. Getting to her feet, her head gave a short, sharp reminder of why she had the day off; it thumped with the aversion to gravity. Feeling dizzy, she sat back down on the bed and gave herself a moment, then got up a little more slowly and carefully made her way downstairs to the kitchen. Nathan stood at the ironing board ironing a shirt.

"Fancy another coffee?" she said as she put the kettle on.

"Oh, go on then, yes please."

As she put the beans in the grinder, he said, "I was thinking, maybe we should have the kids over at the weekend and tell them what's happening."

"Well, they do need to know but are you going to say anything about the baby yet? I mean it is very early days Nathan."

"I know, I just feel I have to be up front about this, I keep getting messages from Eddie, making sure everything's ok and I don't want to lie to him."

"Yes, I've had lots of messages too," she replied, "I'm quite sure he hasn't said anything to Corrie though, there's been nothing to suggest she knows anything of it in her messages."

"I just hope they don't hate me for it," he said, his tone dropping.

"Of, course they won't hate you for it! They might be a bit upset at first but if we show them that we're okay with each other and not fighting, I'm sure they will be able to accept it," Lexi said, trying to sound optimistic.

"I can't see Corrie accepting a baby, she's always been my baby," he reflected, "Oh God Lexi, I really don't want to be a dad again, why, oh, why did she have to get pregnant? Without the baby there was a chance, a small chance that we, as a family, could have reached some normality again. This is just going to change everything so totally. I've made such a fucking mess of everything." Lexi looked at him sympathetically; there really wasn't anything she could say to counter that.

"I mean," he continued, "I know I've made a huge mistake; I can accept that, I know I've lost you because of it and it breaks my heart, but I can accept that too... but a baby?" He shook his head.

"Have you discussed this with Janet yet?" Lexi asked.

"Only in as much as I've said I'll support the child," he replied.

"Well, don't you think it would be a good idea to talk it out with her properly and find out from her what she hopes for or expects from you? She might not want you to have anything to do with it. At least discuss it with her first and find out where you stand, we can deal with the kids from there," she said trying to be positive and practical.

"Yeah, you're right, I'll contact her today and see how the land lies."

"I think it's best Nathan," she confirmed, "find out exactly where you are in all this."

Nathan knocked his coffee back, went over to Lexi, kissed her on the cheek and said, "Yes, I will, thank you hun."

He picked up his case and keys and shouted, "Bye," as he walked out the door.

Lexi started to prepare herself a smoothie. She popped her ipod in the docking station and found a playlist with her favourite 80's bands. She sang happily along with 'The

Lightening Seeds' as she chopped her avocado, asparagus, green beans and spinach, stuck it all in the blender with a handful of blueberries, some bone broth and whizzed it all up. The blender whirred away noisily. Upon turning it off, her heart jumped as she suddenly recognised her ring tone singing out, she dived on her phone and answered it.

"Hello?" She answered.

"Hello baby," came Conrad's soft voice, she filled with emotion and with a faint sob said, "Oh my God, it's so, so lovely to hear your voice again!"

"Yeah, it's lovely to hear yours too," he said softly, "I didn't think I'd ever hear from you again."

Lexi started to weep happily, "I know, I thought I'd never find you again."

"I'm so glad you have, there hasn't been a day that you haven't been on my mind. You've been the first thing I think of in the morning and the last thing I think of at night and in the hours between, just a feeling of loss, no-one has ever left a mark on my heart in the way that you have Lexi," he said with such conviction.

"I feel the same, I knew I had to come back and try but you never left my heart for a moment; my head said I had to do the right thing, but my heart ached for you."

"I've got your email address here from your business card, I've just sent you a contact request on Skype. Get yourself on there honey, I want to see you, so we can talk properly," he said, now desperate to see her in the flesh.

"Okay."

Lexi went over to her computer and did the necessary.

Straight away the computer started 'singing' at her as Conrad's call came through. She clicked on the phone and the camera, a couple of anxious moments went by and then at last they were connected. There he was, the man who had made such a timely appearance in her life and turned her world around; she felt the frequency of every cell in her body flourish as her eyes finally fell upon him.

"Oh, Conrad," she sobbed happily, "It's so lovely to see your face again."

"Jesus!" he exclaimed a little shocked, as Lexi's face filled his screen exhibiting her stitches, the bruising now turning multi-coloured and pooling down her face. "What the hell happened to you?"

Lexi told him how it had happened and of everything that had happened since she'd returned home. They talked for over an hour completely wrapped up in each another.

"What's the time there?" She asked.

He looked at his watch, "Nearly midnight,"

"You're going to be knackered in the morning,"

"I think you're worth it!" he said teasingly.

Her eyes searched his handsome face, "I can't wait to see you again," she whispered.

He looked into her eyes and replied, "I can't wait to see you either," adding, "I'm back in England in three weeks' time; I arrive on the Tuesday evening and finish up near the Peak District again on the Friday. Then I'm in London the following week, flying back on the Thursday afternoon. Can you meet me?"

Bubbling with delight, Lexi didn't even have to think about her answer! "Of course I can! Try keeping me away!"

"We could see if our little barn is free," he added, "It would be great to go back there again, we can enjoy it all over again knowing that this time, we don't end when the weekend finishes." Lexi felt herself positively glowing at the mere thought of it. "Oh, that would be lovely," she beamed.

"It would, wouldn't it? A fresh beginning for us both," he said, "leave it with me, I'll take care of the bookings." He looked at her and gave a happy sigh, "Lexi, I'm so pleased we've found each other again, now I have you back in my life I'm never going to let you go again."

Lexi melted at his words, "Me too, just the thought of being with you again is filling me such joy and hopefully, by then I won't be wearing the Dulux colour chart on my face!" Conrad laughed at this, "I want to see you whether it's there or not, you wear it well!"

They both laughed and then cooed at each other for a little while longer, Conrad, realising the time said, "I really don't want to go but I've now been up twenty hours so I'm going to have to get some sleep."

He leaned forward and touched her face on the screen.

"Ok honey, you go and get some rest," she said feeling incredibly happy and settled for the first time in weeks.

"And you take care and look after that head,"

"I will, good night sweet man."

She kissed her fingers and blew the kiss into the screen.

"Good night beautiful."

He blew her a kiss back and with that they closed down. Lexi sat back in her chair, with a big smile on her face feeling totally elated.

Conrad closed his laptop and placed it on the coffee table in front of him. He let out a large exhale saying, "I knew it couldn't be the end, I just knew it." He felt like he could run a marathon; he felt so alive. He picked up his phone, got Lexi's number up and texted, 'Hello beautiful, can you send me the pictures please? I'm so happy I have you back in my life xxx.'

Lexi received the message, by now in the lounge on the sofa with her feet up watching 'The Wright Stuff'. She beamed as she read it and went straight to her album and sent them to him.

Conrad got ready for bed, brushed his teeth, picked up his phone and took it to bed with him. No sooner had he got in there the first photo arrived. He opened it up and looked at it. As his eyes hit their image standing with the horse, (she'd sent her favourite one first), his heart swelled. His mind flew back to that day, the fun they'd had on their walk back from the village. He smiled to himself; it was such a happy image; he pressed the menu on the side of the photo and saved it as his wallpaper. As he did, another image came through; he opened it and there was another happy shot of them together. He lost himself in that one for a few moments and then, realising he had to be up in five hours, switched his phone off and placed it on the bedside table. He lay on his back with the happiest smile on his face and in no time at all, he drifted off into a deep sleep.

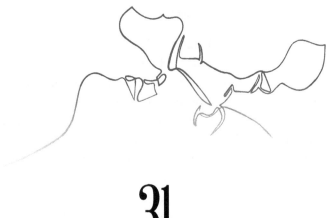

31

Nathan arrived at work with a rather large grey cloud above his head. Upon arrival, he responded to emails and had a brief meeting with his team. At around 10.30 he got himself another coffee, took it back to his office and then psyched himself up before calling Janet. When Janet answered, it was clear straight away that she wasn't very well at all. She'd been so sick she couldn't get herself out of bed and being a singleton, she had no one to fall back on, so it wasn't long before she was weeping down the phone to Nathan.

"I'd expect to be sick, you know, morning sickness and the rest of it but I wasn't expecting this, I just don't seem to be keeping anything down," she wailed as Nathan listened with concern.

Janet had been ill from the very start; the reason she did a pregnancy test wasn't because her period was late but because she had started being so sick. She welcomed Nathan's support; she'd been sick most of the day, every day for twelve days now. She was feeling very 'out of control' of her situation, frightened and understandably quite sorry for herself.

Nathan had started saying, "We need to get straight in our heads where we're going with this, whether you want me involved and if you do, how much, so we both know where we stand and how we are going to move forwards," but after the second time of Janet having to clear down to be sick, Nathan was cutting it fine for a conference call and had to go, saying he would call her again tomorrow.

Later on in the day, he sent out a text message to both kids saying, "Hey guys, mum and I were wondering if you would both be free this weekend to come home? Xx".

As he drafted the text and added their contact names, he sat with his thumb over the send button.

'This is it' he thought to himself as he reluctantly pressed send.

Lexi spent a blissful, lazy morning on the settee watching television. Around lunch time there was a knock at the door. She started to get up, as she got to her feet, the door opened and Paul stuck his head round.

"Koo-ie! You ok Blondie? Can I come in?"

"Hello you! Yes of course you can!" She called back.

Paul entered the lounge, "Hey, how are you? You look a bit better in yourself and if I might say so, you really suit that colour!" he joked as he gestured towards her face, which was now turning all manner of colours.

"I thought so," she replied, "It's actually quite pretty when you look at it up close!"

Sensing a total difference in her mood from the day before, he went up to her, took her head in his hands, scrutinised her face for a few seconds and then added, "Maybe you could've gone with a bit more purple and less yellow!"

Lexi laughed, "Do you think so?"

"Just giving my opinion!" He said, as they both laughed.

"You seem a lot better today hun, I was really worried about you yesterday."

Lexi chirped happily, "Yes, I'm feeling a lot better, thank you. Obviously, it still hurts but I'm in a much better place and you won't believe what happened after you left yesterday."

"Go on?" he said intrigued as Lexi bubbled over with excitement, telling him everything that had happened, up to the Skype she'd had with Conrad this morning.

"Wow, I'm really pleased for you, that's great news; so, when are you seeing each other again?"

Lexi beamed happily, telling him of Conrad's next visit. "I can't wait," she said, "I'm almost frightened to believe that this is really happening."

Paul, absolutely delighted for her, interrupted with, "Don't doubt it, you've more than earned this, just enjoy the ride now my darling and embrace every moment of it."

He stayed for a bit of lunch and they discussed the course they intended booking, then Paul returned to work leaving an extremely happy and completely different Lexi to the one he'd left the day before, on the settee.

Lexi drifted through the afternoon, her newfound happiness affording her a very tranquil state of mind and with this came a desire to nurture and do the very best for herself. She practiced her chakra energy healing with crystals and tuning forks followed by a 'mindful' healing practice and rounding it off with some breath-work.

The alarm rang and Conrad was wide-awake; considering how little sleep he'd had he was feeling fine and dandy. He switched on his phone and went and put the kettle on while it fired up. He came back into his bedroom with a coffee, picked up his phone and went straight to his messages, finding the rest of the photos Lexi had sent through to him. He smiled as he looked at them sipping his coffee and feeling like the happiest man alive. What a difference a day makes! He was fired up and full of energy, he showered and made himself a smoothie for breakfast. He'd embraced pretty much everything he'd picked up from Lexi during their encounter. Albeit a brief introduction by her, the books he'd bought had expanded on this knowledge and in true 'Conrad style' he was on a roll. He was now all organic, mostly cooking from scratch and also beginning to clear out his bathroom cabinet replacing his chemical filled products with chemical free products he'd found online. Step-by-step, he was taking it all on.

He picked up his phone, switched the camera on and took a 'selfie' holding up his smoothie, messaging her, "Thank you baby, let me know when you're free again for a chat. I'm off to work shortly but not before getting on the outside of a highly nutritious green smoothie. You see, I did listen! XX"

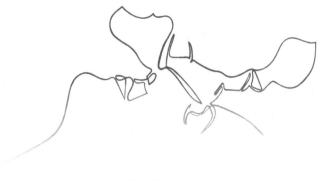

32

Having spent the afternoon indulging herself, Lexi's energy was upbeat. By late afternoon she felt hungry and decided to fix some dinner for both her and Nathan. In the kitchen she checked her phone and saw the message from Conrad, she opened it and there he was with his smoothie. She laughed at his expression, holding up the glass like a trophy. She felt quite chuffed that he'd taken in what she'd told him and was making the effort to do it.

Selecting another of her favourite playlists she chopped, sautéed and marinated happily as she sang along to the music. Nathan had returned from work; he came through the house following her voice, singing along to 'Love shack' he leaned against the kitchen doorframe, smiling and watching her quietly for a few moments, she seemed like a different person.

"Hi!" he said,

"Oh!" Lexi jumped and turned around, "I didn't hear you come in!"

"Evidently!" He laughed, "You sound a lot better,"

"Yes, I feel a lot better thank you."

"Good, it's nice to see,"

"Have you had a good day?" she asked.

"Er, yes and no, the kids are coming over on Saturday but I'm a bit concerned there might be complications with Janet." He explained Janet's 'sickness' situation to Lexi.

"Oh dear, I've heard of this before," she said, "let's hope it calms down for her; that was something I never really suffered with, with ours."

"I couldn't even hold a conversation with her," he continued, "she had to disappear twice! I'm back up there for Thursday and Friday, so, travelling up Wednesday evening. I'm going to go and visit her while I'm there, so we can talk properly."

Lexi smiled and agreed, "It makes sense to while you're up there." Her brain was also ticking, thinking how much more freedom she would have to talk to Conrad, as this thought went through her mind it made her tingle inside.

Lexi finished cooking and dished up the meal, as they ate, Nathan told her the content of his earlier conversation with Janet. Although he seemed a bit more on board and accepting of what was happening, he still felt very weighed down by it all. Whilst talking, he noticed there seemed to be a massive change in Lexi, as if her very spirit had lifted. She seemed much happier, the hurt victim in her had all but disappeared; it was nice to see, he could only assume that having a bit of time to herself was doing her good. After clearing up, Nathan showed Lexi three different houses he intended viewing.

"It's just a thought," she said, "but don't you think you might be better off renting initially? You might decide once the baby comes that you want to live closer."

"Mmm, I didn't think about that. Oi! Are you trying to get rid of me?" he jested.

"Ha, no!" She laughed shaking her head, "I'm just trying to think practically. To be honest, you're up there that much I don't think it matters which end you base yourself at the moment. But if you buy down here and things are going well, you might wish you hadn't. It's just going to avoid the hassle and expense of having to sell again within a short space of time."

Nathan mulled that one over in his head for a moment; he still wasn't completely there with the 'baby' thing.

"Nathan, there's no rush," she said, "you don't have to make any rash decision, I'm not in a hurry to get rid of you, providing we can continue as we are now, I'd rather you take your time and work out exactly what's going to work best for you."

He smiled, "Thanks babe."

For the rest of the evening Lexi curled up on the settee watching a film whilst Nathan sat with his laptop, looking for flats to rent short term.

The next morning Nathan's alarm went off, he needed to be up and out for an early meeting. Just before leaving, he came upstairs with a cup of coffee for Lexi and tapped on her door. Lexi stirred; she'd been sound asleep.

"Hey, morning, thought I'd bring you up a cuppa before I go," he said putting it down on her bedside table.

Lexi yawned, "Oh, thank you."

"No worries, I'll be home early afternoon to pack and have something to eat before I travel," he said.

"Okay, I'll see you later." She rolled onto her back, she could hear Nathan putting on his shoes, picking up his keys and eventually the 'click' of the front door as he closed it behind him. She sat up in bed; her head was feeling much better now. She went down to the kitchen, grabbed her phone and took it back upstairs with her.

She rolled up the blind and sat up in bed drinking her coffee. With the mug in one hand and her phone in the other she switched it on. There was a message from Conrad.

"Night, night, beautiful. I've had the most amazing day; the world seems a better place all of a sudden XX."

"Oh, that's so sweet!" She cooed as she read it.

She replied, "And my world is a much happier one too, I wake up 'happy' now xXx."

She sent her message and then, rather predictably went into her gallery to look at her pictures again. At that point her phone pinged, it was Conrad, "Fancy a Skype?"

Excitedly, Lexi texted back, "Yes!" she got out of bed, took her coffee downstairs and put the computer on. While it booted up she refilled her coffee and quickly checked herself out in the mirror.

"Oh dear!" She said as she caught her reflection looking back at her, her hair in a very floppy pineapple on top of her head where she put it before she went to bed last night. By now, half of it was hanging down and of course her bruise was now all kinds of colours as it changed daily. She didn't have time to worry about that; the computer was obviously ready as she could hear the call come through. She dived in front of the computer and answered his call. As he appeared in front of her, she felt a happy ripple of excitement go through her.

"Hello," she said, positively beaming.

"Hey, ah, it's so nice to see you again, I haven't been able to get you out of my mind. I've been so high since we spoke, I can't tell you. Everything seems to have been great, you know? Like the world's a different place all of a sudden!" He said with a very happy heart.

"Yes, I've felt the same, a really special, happy feeling," she glowed back at him.

"That's because you are special," he said beaming at her. "You look lovely!"

Lexi laughed, knowing she probably couldn't look a lot worse.

"Now I happen to know that is not the case!" She joked.

"It is as far as I'm concerned." He beamed again as she cooed back at him. They were totally lost in each other. They talked for about ten minutes and then Lexi said,

"What time is it there?"

"11.45am," he replied.

"Shouldn't you be asleep?" she said in a caring way.

"Yes, but I'm not! I have been to sleep though; I went to bed at ten; I woke up because I heard your message come through."

"You don't sleep with your phone in your room, do you?" she asked, "You mustn't do that, it's bad for you! You shouldn't have anything electrical in your room apart from your light!"

"Ha ha, the lectures begin!" He laughed. "I haven't been, I did listen to what you said; ever since I got back it's stayed in the kitchen apart from the other night. It's just I've been on such a high ever since I received that first message from you, I keep checking my phone cos I don't want to miss anything. Also, I was hoping you'd message me when you woke up, so I could talk to you while Nathan's out of the house."

"Aw, that's so nice but you also need to sleep and be up for work tomorrow. Anyway, Nathan's going up North this evening and comes back Friday so we will have much more freedom for the next couple of days; I don't want to keep you up all night to talk to me," she said, as she always taught her clients the importance of getting to bed on time and of getting enough quality sleep.

"You could keep me up all night, every night my darling," he said, then added, "And you can take that anyway you like as well!"

They laughed and talked a while longer, then Lexi told Conrad to get some sleep and to call or message her any time he was up and free to chat.

The day went by, Nathan came home around 2.30 as he had planned. He packed for his trip and Lexi cooked a main meal, which they both sat down to before he left. With his case and laptop in the hall he was ready to go.

"I'll see you Friday evening then," he said.

"Ok, hope it all goes well, both with work and with Janet," Lexi replied.

"Yeah, thanks, well, at least when I get back, I'll have a better picture of what I have in front of me." He grimaced as he said it.

Lexi, noticing this, replied, "I'm sure you will and don't worry, it'll all be ok."

"Thank you, see you Friday then."

"See you Friday, drive carefully."

With that he was on his way and Lexi had the house to herself.

Over the next couple of days Lexi and Conrad sent messages freely to each other and fitted in a couple more video calls. They were now getting fully reacquainted with each other, making plans for their meeting, talking, laughing, reliving some of their special moments and planning new ones. Lexi went back to work on the Thursday afternoon and again Friday morning for personal training clients only. With the enforced rest and her romance now positively blossoming she was happier than she could ever have imagined.

33

It was now Friday evening and Lexi was home, fed and bathed; it was just after 7pm when Nathan walked through the door.

"Hiya!" Lexi chirped.

"Hey, you ok?" He replied.

"Yes, thanks and you? How did it go?"

"Work was great, no problem there, it's all going very well. Janet, on the other hand isn't so great though!" He said, his tone dipping.

"Oh dear, things not good there?" she said, concerned.

"Not in that sense. We're okay but she's so sick! And I mean really sick! I've never seen anything like it, it's getting a bit worrying actually," he admitted.

"Well, what does the midwife say?" she asked.

"Well, everything with the pregnancy seems ok, blood pressure, heartbeat etc but they're getting concerned that she'll get dehydrated," he explained.

"Mmm, nasty." she frowned.

Nathan went in the kitchen and got the meal Lexi had prepared for him when she had eaten earlier. Having finished he unpacked, showered and then went back downstairs. Lexi was pottering around in the kitchen, he appeared in the doorway with a bottle of wine.

"Do you fancy one? I think I could do with one right now,"

"Ooh, yes, go on then, thank you," she replied. He poured two glasses and then they sat and talked.

He told her about Janet's condition in more detail. Although he still wasn't enamoured with the idea of becoming a father again, he seemed to be far more accepting of his lot. It was also apparent he was genuinely concerned for Janet. The conversation then turned to their kids coming home the following day. They brushed over how they were going to break the news to them and at this point Nathan went very quiet for a few moments.

Lexi, noticing he'd seemed to go deep inside himself, asked, "Are you okay?"

"God Lexi, the kids are going to think I'm such a let-down, I've un-done everything that constituted our marriage, how will they have any respect for me ever again?"

Lexi could see the worry this held for him and said, trying to be of some support, "Nathan, I've broken the rules too remember?"

"Yeah, but you wouldn't have if I hadn't done what I'd done... How many years have you worked around gyms? How many men have come on to you in that time? And don't say none cos I'd know you would be lying. It would never have even crossed your mind before. The only reason you went with him was because I'd hurt you, otherwise you wouldn't have been there in the first place!" He said, he clearly hadn't made peace with himself over this.

"But I've still been unfaithful, the only difference is your 'fling' produced a love child; it was a fifty-fifty chance, it's just the way it's worked out," she tried to console him.

Nathan took a long sip of his wine and turned to Lexi.

"I'm so sorry I hurt you,"

"I know you are."

"You know I would never have put you through this intentionally, don't you? Honestly, if I could turn the clock back, I'd give anything to have that evening again and end it differently."

"I know you would, I've seen you beat yourself up over it enough," she paused and then continued.

"Nathan, I believe everything happens for a reason. I wasn't going to say anything, but now we are being honest with each other I feel I need to tell you, I'm in contact with Conrad again."

"Yes, I did wonder," he replied.

"Oh, did you?"

"Yes, you just seem happier all of a sudden, you know, singing and masturbating and stuff!"

He looked at Lexi in a playful manner; she gave him a bashful smile.

"And you're alright with that?"

"Lexi, I love you and, even though we are parting, I still feel you are my best friend. I hate the fact that I've hurt my best friend so badly and I would do anything to try and mend that. Just to see you with a bit of a glow has been a relief to me, especially after that awful weekend." He shook his head reflecting, "I just want you to be happy and if he makes you happy, then I'm happy.

"Thank you, that means a lot to me," she said, placing an affectionate hand on his forearm.

He looked at it and continued, "On the Sunday night, when you'd found out about the baby and I caved in, you still cared about me even after everything I'd done. I'd cheated on you, put you in A&E and given you concussion but you still showed compassion for me when I didn't deserve it from anyone, least of all you. Most wives in your situation would have taken great delight in celebrating my dilemma, I really appreciated both what I got and what I'd lost, if that makes sense?"

"Yeah," She nodded, I am still pleased I came back though, despite everything that's happened. Had I not, I might have wondered at some point down the line whether he was worth walking away from my family for. As it turns out I don't have to make any such sacrifice. We can make this work Nathan; tomorrow we will sit down and tell the kids the whole story. We can explain that we want to keep the family in harmony and how it's going to work. I honestly think if they see we're ok with each other, once they get their heads round it, they'll be ok. It's only if we're bickering and arguing that the kids would feel the need to take sides."

"I hope so," he said.

"I'm sure so," she said, "They'll adjust to it."

They sat and finished their wine and then made their way upstairs to their separate bedrooms.

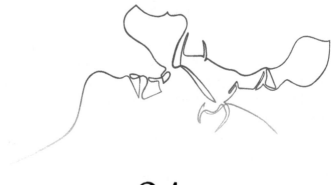

34

It was Saturday morning and Lexi awoke bright and happy. She made the spare beds up and went food shopping. When she'd put the food away, she made herself a cup of green tea and sat down to drink it. At that point, the front door opened and in walked Nathan with Corrie; he'd picked her up from the station.

"Hi mum," Corrie gushed as she bounded in and gave her mum a big hug.

"Hello my lovely," said Lexi, as she enjoyed her daughter's familiar, warm embrace. "Ooh, I've missed you," she said wrapping her arms around her and giving her a big squeeze.

Nathan took Corrie's case upstairs while Lexi made her a cup of tea and heard all about what she'd been up to. About half an hour later Eddie rolled up and joined everyone in the kitchen.

Lexi made lunch and they all sat and talked generally about what they'd been up to and how life was treating them. As the conversation was going on, Nathan was contributing, but at the same time trying to think of how he was going to put into words the news his two grown up children were about to hear. As he endured this multi-task, he could feel the anxiety pulsing through him.

This didn't go unnoticed by Corrie, "Are you okay dad?"

Nathan looked at Lexi, their exchange was one of 'now is as good a time as any'.

"Guys, we've got some news for you," Nathan started.

The kids looked on, awaiting his next contribution. Nathan looked nervously at Lexi again.

"God, I don't know how to begin," he said as his confidence took as massive dip.

"What's up dad, what's the problem?" Corrie asked concerned.

At this point, Eddie started to shift uncomfortably, feeling this must have something to do with what had happened earlier in the month.

"Ok, here it is," Nathan finally piped up, "your mum and I are breaking up!"

Eddie's head went straight in his hands.

Corrie instantly screeched, "No! Why? You can't be!"

Eddie looked up and fired at Nathan, "You said everything was fine now!"

"You knew about this?" Corrie shouted, "So why am I the last person to find out?"

"Sweetie, hear us out," added Lexi, trying to bring some calm the moment.

Then, between them, Lexi and Nathan started to try and explain everything.

Corrie cried at her father, after Nathan had finally managed to utter the words he was dreading to speak and the response that he knew would come from them, "I cheated on your mum."

"How could you dad, how could you?" she cried.

At this point it all got too much for him to contain, he put his head in his hands and started to cry.

"I told you! I told you she'd hate me for it!" he cried as Lexi jumped in, trying to limit the damage.

"Nathan, she doesn't hate you, she's shocked! Let her have time to digest what she's hearing."

Lexi took over for a while as Nathan tried to detach himself from how wretched he felt so that he could actually take part in the family discussion and not sit there feeling sorry for himself.

The discussion went on for quite some time as Lexi managed to calm Corrie a little. As she did so, she told them of how she had taken herself away and how she had met someone there; she then admitted it had gone further than a friendship.

"Oh, for fuck's sake! Seriously? It didn't take you long then, did it?" Corrie snapped at Lexi.

"Hey!" shouted Nathan. "Don't you dare talk to your mother like that! That's out of order! You can't judge your mother; you have no idea of how she felt at that point in time. I've accepted that and so should you. She wouldn't have been there if I hadn't been unfaithful. We both decided to try and put this behind us and make a go of it for your sakes," he finished.

Lexi and Nathan looked at each other; a little voice inside Nathan's head said, 'here we go!'

As the penny dropped Corrie said, "So why are you splitting up then?"

Nathan took a deep breath as he stood up and started to walk about, his hands clasped behind his head and flapping his elbows like wings.

"Oo-oo-k-ay," Nathan thought, shit or bust here!

"Well… here it is, Janet… the lady I had the fling with… she's, well, she's pregnant!"

He screwed his eyes up tight as the word 'pregnant' left his mouth and squeezed his wings tightly shut waiting for the bomb to drop! And boy did it drop! It came down on him like a ton of bricks! Corrie went absolutely, berserk and had what could only be described as a little girl's temper tantrum.

After a minute or so of this, Corrie calmed slightly and looked up with tearful eyes saying, "She's not keeping it right?"

"Yes, she is keeping it honey." Nathan looked straight into Corrie's gobsmacked face, "I'm so sorry honey, it's just the way it's worked out, I would've done anything to have got back with your mum and built our relationship but as you can understand, that's too much for mum to bear; I truly don't blame her, and neither can you."

Corrie started to cry again, "But you're not going to have anything to do with it right?" she pleaded.

"Wrong Corrie, I am, sweetheart, you have to understand, I have a responsibility."

"Only to support her financially, I mean, you don't have to have anything to do with it do you?"

Nathan sighed and then softly tried to explain, "But I don't want to know I have a child out there somewhere that I know nothing about, I just couldn't do that. I mean, look at the two of you, you are amazing people, I love you both to bits, I love the young adults you've become, I just couldn't bear to always be wondering what the child was like. It won't change anything about my relationship with either of you, I promise, but I can't just walk away from it."

Nathan sat with his arm around Corrie as he convinced her that she wasn't about to be knocked off her throne; the storm gradually passed and after a while they started to talk the practical side of it. Once the kids had established that the family home was staying, things calmed more and by the end of the afternoon both kids, although still somewhat shocked by the events of the afternoon, were now much calmer and okay-ish with it.

Just after 5.30 Nathan's phone rang. He picked it up from the table and looked, it wasn't a number he recognised so he hit the red button and put it back down. After a couple of minutes, it rang again, the same number, he picked it up and answered. There was a quizzical expression on his face as he listened to the person on the other end and as he realised the seriousness of what he was hearing he got up and took the phone out into the kitchen.

By the time Nathan returned they had retired from the dining table to the lounge. Corrie sat huddled up with her mum, they were choosing a film to watch. Nathan came back in the room quite flustered.

"Everything ok?" asked Lexi.

"No, that was Janet's mum, she's been admitted into hospital. She's just so sick they've had to take her in, she's badly dehydrated, she's on drips and all sorts apparently; her mum says she's very upset and worried." He was full of concern.

"Oh dear, that's not good," Lexi added, "but better she's in there and getting the right care. Are you going to go up there?" she asked.

"Well, I am worried for her, and it can't be nice coping with this on her own," he replied.

"It's not something I'd want to go through on my own," said Lexi. "I think you should go Nathan to be honest."

Nathan turned to Corrie, the words he'd uttered no more than ten minutes ago trickling back through his head,

"It won't change my relationship with you, nothing will change." And now, for the first time of seeing his daughter in five weeks, he was about to bail out on her; fortunately, she didn't seem to take it that way as he asked,

"Do you mind if I go pumpkin?"

"It's ok dad, you go, I don't mind," she said.

"Honestly?"

"Honestly, it wouldn't be right if you didn't go."

Thank you, pumpkin," he said as he kissed her on the head and then left the room to go and throw an overnight bag together.

By the time he came back down, Eddie had joined the girls to watch the film arriving in the lounge with a bottle of wine, some glasses and a couple of bowls of nibbles containing pistachio nuts, dates, figs and dried wild bilberries (all organic of course)!

Nathan came in the lounge. "Okay, I'll be off then."

Lexi got up and froze the television as the opening credits of the film had begun.

"Let me know you get there alright," she said.

"Will do, the roads shouldn't be that bad!"

As he sat on the stairs to put his shoes on, he looked back into the lounge from the hallway. Lexi and Corrie got back on the settee and were spooning, Eddie had pulled his massive bean bag into the middle of the floor and opened the wine; he poured it and gave glasses to the girls along with a bowl of nibbles. Nathan felt a sinking feeling as he watched them all getting cozied in for the film while he would be making his way up the country to look after the mother of his love child. He so didn't want to leave them, not tonight of all nights. Could he stay? Have the evening with them and then go early in the morning? As it was, he wouldn't get there before at least 10pm and there would be nothing he could do at that time of night, equally, the chances were they wouldn't let him in the hospital at that time of night to visit her either.

After arguing that one over with himself for a few moments, Nathan came back in the lounge and shared his thoughts with Lexi, Eddie and Corrie.

"Well, to be honest, now you put it like that, maybe it would make more sense to go in the morning," Lexi agreed.

"If I get up at 6.30, get out of the house and on the road quickly, I could be up there by 11.30- 12pm." Now he'd got everybody on board with his idea, it was easier for Nathan to both convince himself and give himself permission to stay and be part of the evening. At that point, he sent a message to Janet to say he would be there the next morning. He then went into the kitchen, got himself a beer and joined his soon to be, ex-wife and his children in the lounge, where he dived on his favourite bean bag and 'cozied' down, all set to enjoy both the film and the company of his family.

As the evening went on, Nathan intermittently removed his gaze from the film to his family; his beer sat untouched. He watched Eddie as his hand moved unconsciously from the nibbles bowl to his mouth. He looked up at Lexi and Corrie on the couch, chilled out and absorbed in the film. He thought to himself how lucky he was not to have lost this familiar comfort. They weren't living it up, they weren't partying, nothing amazing was happening, they were simply spending an evening as they had thousands of times before. Nathan inwardly enjoyed a feeling of relief that there was calm and yes, just maybe things could still be as 'normal' as possible in their little world.

The family enjoyed their evening and Nathan went to bed feeling a lot happier than he had the night before. As he lay in bed, his attention moved to Janet. His conscience started to prick at him now, making him feel a little selfish for lounging and watching a film, when her world was falling down around her. How must she be feeling right now? He hoped she was all right; surely, they'd have contacted him if there had been any change. He consoled himself that he'd followed his heart and done what he'd had to do for his own mental and emotional security. Now, having satisfied his own emotional needs, he felt he could focus on Janet and what was needed there; he could now go up in the morning with his head in the right place. He dropped off and slept surprisingly well, waking just after 5am, feeling fresh and positive in his mind, his focus now intent on getting to Janet and doing the right thing, whatever that might be. Quietly he got ready, picked up his bags that were still in the hall where he had dropped them the night before and crept out of the door.

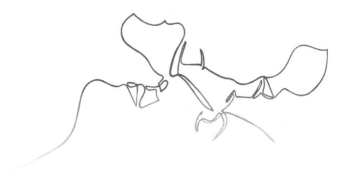

35

Lexi and the kids didn't surface until about 9am and by this time Nathan was long gone. They came down to the kitchen for some breakfast and spent most of the morning ambling from one thing to another. Then, late morning, Lexi took Corrie to the station to get back for Uni the following day. As they drove along Lexi said," You ok hun?"

"Yeah, it's still hard to take in that dad and you aren't going to be together any more though, it all seems a bit like I'm going to wake up and it will all have been a weird dream."

"Yes," Lexi sighed, "I'm sure you do, it's a lot to take in but really there was no other way of letting both of you know other than being totally straight with you," she said as she manoeuvred through the traffic.

Corrie watched her mum for a moment, talking and driving as if it were a regular visit; she was still struggling to come to terms with the news and how her family, as she knew it, would change.

"How do you feel about it mum, I mean really?" she asked.

"Darling, I'm a strong believer in fate, you know that" Lexi replied. "When I first found out I was very upset; obviously I was, that's why I took myself off the way I did. I didn't have any designs on meeting anyone; it's just how it happened. Had I not met Conrad there I would've come back and tried to make a go of it, just as I have but quite frankly, whether I'd met someone or not, I wouldn't have stayed with your dad once I had found out about the baby. Meeting Conrad didn't sway it in any way; in fact, I wasn't in contact with him at all when I found out about the baby."

Corrie looked straight ahead, "Yeah, the baby," she said in a low key, "I can't imagine dad having another child. It's like, well, I'll be a twenty-year-old with a newborn half-sister or brother. It's just weird, I can't get my head round it and I know it might seem selfish but I'm struggling to see where I will fit in to all this," she said with honesty.

Lexi knew it would trouble her, she'd always been such a daddy's girl, she knew this would be the hardest part for her.

"It's early days yet poppet," she reasoned, "you've only just found out about all this. Let it sink in and try not to overthink it. Of course, there will be some changes, but dad and I love you and Eddie, you two are the most important thing to us. We've tried to do this as amicably as possible because we don't want the two of you to be affected or feel caught up in the middle of it all, can you understand that?" She gave a sideways glance to Corrie as she finished her sentence.

"Well, yes I can but, God mum, there aren't many women out there that would accept this in the way you have, most women would've cut all the sleeves out of his shirts by now or put chilli powder in his underpants!"

Lexi laughed out loud at this, "Yes, I know and maybe, had things worked out differently, I might well not have been so accepting of the situation. But this is where I feel that fate has played a part. Had I not met Conrad, right now I would be looking at making a start again on my own because, like it or not, there IS a baby on its way, and yes, I would have been sad; probably angry and resentful, very insecure with zero self-esteem after such a blow. But in meeting Conrad, I honestly feel as though the universe sent him to me knowing this was going to happen; I know you think I'm 'odd' when I talk about things like that, but I truly believe it. He was my gift, Conrad came to me when I couldn't have been any lower and I couldn't have been less interested in meeting someone, but he's made me so incredibly happy. He's so warm, kind-hearted and affectionate; we communicate so beautifully together; I truly feel like, out of such a disaster, I've found my soul mate. That's not to say that your dad wasn't my soul mate once, but obviously something was lost somewhere along the way, otherwise none of this would have happened."

"And the baby? I mean… whoa!" Corrie said shaking her head slowly.

"Sweetheart, the baby is a by-product of their 'fling' or whatever it was, or still is. It's not going to make you any less special or less important to your dad, he loves you to bits and always will. What you also have to understand is that this child didn't ask to be born into this mess, its innocent, it hasn't come along purposely to hurt you or push you out, it has simply come along. All children deserve to feel loved and wanted and this child is no exception."

Corrie looked at her mum as she manoeuvred the car into a parking space outside the station and then turned back to her daughter.

"I don't have any resentment toward this child, it's not its fault. I know it's a terrible shock for you but if you can put yourself in its position; the child needs love and security not people wishing it hadn't happened."

Corrie nodded trying not to cry, Lexi could see she was holding it back and put her arm around her gently stroking her shoulder.

"Give it time hun, give it time."

Corrie hugged her mum as she had a little weep.

"We both love you and nothing will ever change that."

They sat for a few minutes as Lexi held and coaxed her daughter, reinforcing her love and worthiness until she was calm and it was time for Corrie to catch her train. They hugged and kissed goodbye and Corrie got out of the car.

"Let me know you get back ok," said Lexi.

"Will do," Corrie replied as she got her bags out of the back of the car and went on her way.

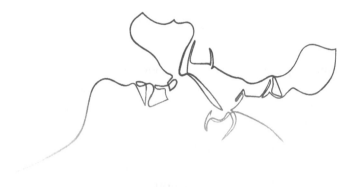

36

When Lexi arrived back home, Eddie was in the kitchen getting himself some lunch.

"You ok hun?" Lexi said as she walked in.

"Yeah, you?"

Yeah, Corrie's gone off ok, we had a few tears before she went though." Eddie looked up, "Oh?"

"Mmm, she's a little bit unsettled about the baby,"

"Well to be fair it does take a bit of getting your head around, I can't imagine dad with a baby, it's just not something I find easy to visualise," he admitted.

"Mmm, I know but like I said to Corrie, try not to overthink it, it will just give you fears that hold no truth. None of us really know how this is going to pan out yet. Try to keep an open mind and when the baby comes along things will eventually find their place."

Eddie looked at his mum as she went to the fridge, got some salad stuff out and took it over to the chopping board. He cast his mind back to the day he'd called his mum, as a direct result of his dad saying she'd disappeared after a row, purposely omitting to tell him what the row was about. He remembered how terribly upset she had been and how adamant she'd been about standing her ground after suffering such a hurtful betrayal. Now she stood before him discussing this love-child calm and seemingly accepting of the situation. Was this real? Was she really ok with it or putting on a brave front? The questions were there in his head but as he observed her, he could see she was at peace with it all. She wasn't agitated or angry, she wasn't crashing pans about in the kitchen to let everyone know how hard done by she was feeling, she wasn't reeling at the injustice of it all. Surprising as it was, Eddie could see for himself that his mother was absolutely fine and simply getting on with it.

They sat and had lunch, followed by a cuppa and by mid-afternoon Eddie was packed up and ready to go. Having got his stuff together in the hall, Lexi gave him a hug and told him to drive carefully and added the usual, "Let me know you get home ok."

He hugged his mum and as they broke their embrace, just to satisfy his piece of mind, he said," You are ok aren't you mum?"

"Yes, I am hun. Please don't worry, it'll all be fine," she said reassuringly, giving him another big hug, "I Love you."

"I love you too, mum." Lexi waved him off as he left the drive.

She walked back inside, closed the door, went back into the kitchen and put the kettle on. Okay, so the weekend hadn't been without its emotional moments but considering the reason for the visit, she felt it had gone as well as it possibly could have. Now the not-so-nice bit was out of the way, she could focus on her life, where it was going and, most importantly, meeting up with Conrad again. It seemed like a lifetime ago that they had found each other again! They were sending each other numerous messages throughout the day and having video chats whenever their time difference and work schedule would allow them to. They still had an agonising 10 days to wait before they would be together again. Every minute they weren't at work and were both awake, they were in constant contact, sending messages, blissfully happy and very eager to be back in each other's lives.

37

To Lexi, each day that passed was another day out of the way and a step closer to being reunited with the man who had changed her world. She was positive and happy, and this happy state of mind simply radiated out of her. She was at peace with everyone and everything. Even situations that would usually provoke her to retaliate or feel the need to state her grievances just simply went over her head, it simply didn't matter; love most certainly is a wonderful thing! She'd moved events in her diary so that she could be with Conrad, not only for the weekend back at their cosy retreat, but also cancelling work the following Wednesday afternoon and Thursday, so she could spend Conrad's last few hours in the country with him. She was now completely focused on making their stay back at the retreat, absolutely perfect; she was already planning what food she would take to cook for their romantic reunion.

Conrad's world had been affected in much the same way as Lexi's; the normally immovable, focussed and shrewd director was appearing particularly mellow and laid back to his colleagues. The truth of the matter was that, for the first time ever, something, or someone, was now more important to him than work. He was far more open to other people's ideas and suggestions. His head was no longer full of business matters but full of thoughts of Lexi, imagining what it would be like to be with her again. The time couldn't go quickly enough for him; he kept trying to immerse himself in a project just to realise he was sitting there, back up in his head daydreaming! All he could think about was that he would soon be back in England with this amazing woman who had made him feel so differently about everything. Not only had she stolen his heart, but she had also introduced him to a completely different way of life and attitude to living. His interest in the subject was ever-growing as he'd now finished his second, rather comprehensive book on the subject and had just taken delivery of his third. This was typical of Conrad; everything he did was with 100% of his focus and effort providing he was driven by it. In this case he was not only driven by it but had become passionate about it to the point of being quite obsessive and the more he read and learned, the more important it was becoming to him.

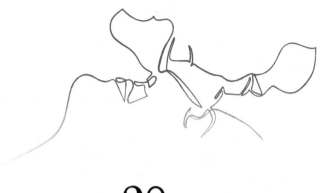

38

It was Wednesday evening and Lexi had returned home from work. She prepared a meal for both herself and Nathan as he had called to say he would be home this evening from up north, she dished hers up and left Nathan's for when he got back. After she'd eaten, she went for a shower and as she got out and dried herself off, she heard Nathan come in the door. By the time she was dried off, in her comfy clothes and making her way downstairs, Nathan was sitting eating his meal.

"Hey, how are you? How did it go? Is she any better?" Lexi asked, as she walked through to the kitchen.

"Hey," he said, finishing a mouthful, "well, no, not really. She's still in hospital, she's so dehydrated they need to keep her on a drip, but she isn't so scared now. At least we know everything's fine with the baby, it's just this awful sickness.

"Mmm, nasty," she empathised.

Nathan continued, "I honestly would never have believed being pregnant could make someone so ill; it's completely alien to the experience of our two pregnancies.

She's so poorly, I even found myself apologising to her at one point."

"Apologising?" Lexi quizzed.

"Yeah." He looked up at her for a moment and then his eyes dropped to his lap.

"I feel like I've given her this, like it's some sort of karma. I don't know... it feels it's like a punishment, a massive punishment at that and I feel it shouldn't just be hers to bear," he said truthfully. "We were both in it; we are both equally to blame. I just feel I should be there for her; she has no-one."

This statement worried Lexi.

"But in your heart of hearts, do you WANT to be there for her, or do you just feel duty bound to be there?" she asked.

"No, it's not just out of duty," he replied, "I want to be there. Like I said before, planned or not, this is my child and I want to do the best for it and as for Janet... Mmm, I don't know really, it's all so odd." his voice tailed off.

"Well, no, it's not odd at all, you obviously care for her. I'm pleased you care for her, really, I am, this means that it wasn't all for nothing. I'd hate to think that it has ended our marriage and you couldn't stand the sight of her, that really would be a shame! To be quite honest Nathan, I'd be happier if you did end up having some kind of relationship with her, it would help to justify the destruction this whole episode has caused," she said with total honesty but without attitude.

"I suppose that's one way of looking at it; I just hope she gets over this sickness and soon, it's just crippling her." he said shaking his head.

"I think, once she settles into the idea that you're there for her, she'll be less stressed, and it'll calm down on its own. This is a completely different situation to when we had our babies. We were settled and happy and it was all planned and part of a bigger picture; don't forget, her situation is very different. She's single and there is, or was, no security for her. I think if she can manage her stress levels, her hormones will settle down; her adrenal glands have probably been doing summersaults ever since the day she conceived this baby because of the situation she was in. Of course, it's going to have a negative impact on her pregnancy," she explained.

"I hope you're right." Nathan said not sounding convinced.

"Of, course I'm right," she said, "I'm always right, I thought I was wrong once, but I was mistaken!" She winked at him, stealing Paul's, well-used saying; this brought a welcome break to the seriousness of the conversation.

They spent the rest of the evening together and talked of their individual plans; Nathan was now aware of Lexi's plans to meet Conrad and Lexi was supportive in Nathan's decision to base himself up north with Janet, at least until she was out of hospital. The following day, Nathan headed off and Lexi carried on with her day-to-day life, ticking off the days until she would be with Conrad again.

39

At last, the time had come, it was Monday and Lexi and Conrad were having their last video call before he was to travel to England. They were both so excited they could barely contain themselves.

"The next time we see each-other we'll be together, properly, not halfway across the world from one-another talking into a screen," Conrad said in both a relieved and excited manner.

"I know! I really can't wait," Lexi squealed.

"Neither can I," He beamed into the screen longingly.

"I just want to be in your arms again," she said breathily.

"And I want you to be in my arms again, I can't think of anything I want more, I can't remember a time that I ever wanted anything this much," he said with complete devotion, his eyes penetrating into the screen at her.

"Me too," her eyes searching his. "The wait has been agony but the thought of being in your arms again is making it so worth it!" She said, imagining the moment in her mind's eye. Then she went on to tell him of the preparations she was making for their weekend and the lovely food she would be taking. As keen as he now was on the matter of food, all he wanted was to simply be with her again. All he could imagine in his head was to finally take her in his arms and hold her again, inhale her and feel her embrace, these were the thoughts that were constantly flooding his brain and leaving little room for anything else.

As the next few days passed, knowing her man was well and truly on his way and that this was really happening, Lexi was like a little girl who'd managed to pick out and eat all the blue 'Smarties' from the tube! On Tuesday night, Conrad let her know he was now in England and in his hotel ready for his business for the next couple of days. They excitedly made their plans to meet on Friday at the retreat. Lexi would be leaving after work around lunchtime and Conrad was expecting to arrive there after a conference around mid-afternoon. They eagerly talked of their now imminent reunion, both of them experiencing butterflies in their tummies as their happy brain waves radiated those beautiful emotions out into the body to be felt.

On the Thursday, Lexi had an hour's break in the afternoon in which she got her food shopping for the weekend and when she got home, she packed her case ready to take with her in the morning. Her meats, fish, bone broths and vegetables were uniformly lined up in the fridge to be pulled out at the last minute and put in the cool box before she left for work. Her list was checked and double-checked. Sleep wasn't going to come easy; she was so fired up she felt like she had an electric current running through her, thinking of everything and anything. She settled herself down to her evening meditation but her 'monkey mind' would not stop reminding her that tomorrow was gearing up to be one of the most special days in her life. As that wasn't working, she started some deep breathing exercises and by 1am she had finally nodded off.

Lexi awoke two minutes before her alarm clock went off, as if someone had flicked her 'ON' switch. She leapt out of bed and set to getting herself ready. She showered and had some breakfast and then she started emptying the fridge of all her prepared food, putting it into the cool box ready to roll. At that point her phone rang, it was Conrad.

"Hey beautiful!" he chirped. "I'm just calling to make sure you haven't changed your mind!" he said jovially.

Lexi was so excited, "Hey! Nothing would keep me away, nothing!"

"Good. Because nothing would keep me away either, I'll see you later, message me when you leave." He was aware of his heart pounding at the very thought of being with her again.

"Okay, will do. I'll see you later, I can't tell you how I feel right now because I can't put it into words," she said, happily flustered.

"I'm pretty sure I feel the same, hurry up and get your arse up here!"

They said their goodbyes. Lexi finished her packing, got her kit together and sung happily to herself as she packed up the car. Once she was loaded, she had a quick check of the house, locked up and left for work a very happy and excited bunny.

40

Conrad arrived at his conference with a fire in his belly; the deal to buy his software offered by this company was worth a huge amount to his company. He felt on top of the world, full of energy and confidence and had the company directors eating out of his hand. After a successful and fruitful, morning's business, Conrad jumped in his hire car and set off for the retreat. He stopped along the way and bought some organic strawberries, chocolate and wine with which to treat his lovely lady. Conrad's phone had bleeped at 1.30 to say that Lexi was on her way, his heart pulsed as he read it, not long now, he thought. He made his way there, checked in, got the key to the lovely old barn that they had stayed in before and unpacked for the weekend. He'd bought his shopping in and put it in the fridge, then gone out to the little out-house and bought in some wood to make a fire in the evening as the day had been overcast and felt a little chilly. Around 3.30pm Lexi sent another message to say that she was stuck on the motorway in a queue of traffic due to an accident and nothing was moving. Conrad sighed anxiously disappointed; he'd hoped she'd be here by now.

A few minutes later she called, "Hiya."

"Hey, what's happening?" he asked.

"Nothing right now, I'm just sitting here. Ooo, hang on, there's some movement up ahead as people are taking the slip road off, I'll try to get over to the inside lane so I can get off the road and find another way."

She started to try and manoeuvre the car as she spoke (hands free of course.)

"Okay, let me know how you get on," he said, eager to know she was on her way to him.

"Will do," she said, trying to edge her way into the inside lane.

"Uh! This is so unfair; I just want to be with you!" he said with sheer frustration!

"You will be soon," Lexi said calmly and finished the call. As she made her way off the jammed road, her trusty sat nav reset itself and she quickly called Conrad back.

"I'm off the road and the sat nav says about fifty minutes so I reckon I'll be at least half hour on top of that as everyone else is also leaving the motorway and it's manic but at least I'm moving now," she said relieved.

Conrad relaxed at this news, "Okay, that's great, see you soon".

With that she plodded slowly forward with her journey.

Now, with an hour or so on his hands, Conrad was feeling restless; they should've been together by now, instead the torment was to last a while longer. He went in the kitchen and opened the fridge, the strawberries and chocolate sat there on the top shelf. Remembering something he'd seen on a cookery channel some time back, he decided to indulge Lexi a little more. He took the strawberries and chocolate out of the fridge, got a pan of boiling water and started to melt the chocolate. Once it was a thick, melted, warm mess he dipped the individual strawberries in the chocolate, coating them, and placed them on a plate. Pleased with his effort, he smiled as he put the plate of coated strawberries in the fridge to cool. He washed the pan and bowl and put them away, as he did, he thought he heard a car door closing. He went to the window and looked out and there was Lexi taking her suitcase out of the boot. His heart began to pound; he opened the little wooden door and strode towards her.

Hearing the door open she turned round and saw him. Their eyes connected and Conrad's stride turned into a run. Lexi dropped her bag and dashed towards him, opening her arms as they launched themselves at each other.

They held each other tightly as their lips came together for the first time. Conrad held her head with both hands and kissed her deeply, tears of joy starting to roll down Lexi's cheeks.

"Oh, God, you feel so good, it felt like I was never going to get here," Lexi cried.

They wrapped their arms around each other again and stood holding each other for a good minute or so, their hearts beating so hard against each other. As they stood in this blissful embrace, both of them felt an inner calm at their awareness of each-others touch; the anxiety of separation was now behind them.

After some moments, they finally managed to let go enough to look each other in the face; they positively beamed at each other as they took each other in.

"Oh, God, it's so lovely to see you again, it's seemed like such a long time coming," Lexi murmured.

"I know, all I've been able to do for the last couple of weeks is imagine this moment, it felt like it was never going to come," Conrad pulled her into him again and kissed her head. They held each other again for a while longer and then Conrad reached for the handle of her case, Lexi picked up her bag and they walked to the barn arm in arm.

As she stepped through the door Lexi said, "Ooh, it smells lovely in here!"

"Ah, I thought I'd make you a little treat as I had some time on my hands." He opened the fridge and showed her the plate of strawberries.

"Ooh, lovely!" She chirped.

"All organic!" He added with pride.

"Well done you! They look good enough to eat!" She said looking at them, taking in the sweet aroma.

"Could I interest you in one of my strawberries madam?" He offered the plate to her, "They're not quite cold yet, they'll be better later but I think you deserve one after your journey." He offered her the plate to choose.

"Mmm, don't mind if I do!" Lexi said taking one from the plate. He smiled, watching her as she popped the strawberry in her mouth, awaiting her reaction.

"Mmm, that's delicious! What a lovely thought, thank you." She leant forward and kissed him. "Nothing but the best for you, my dear," he said as he put the plate down and then pulled her in for another kiss, which turned into another kiss and another, which then turned into another long, affectionate embrace as Conrad enveloped her in his arms.

"I knew it would be wonderful to be back with you, but I honestly can't put into words how I feel right now," said Lexi, nuzzling into Conrad's chest.

Conrad stroked her hair and said, "I know exactly what you mean, I don't think there are words for it, it's just the most amazing feeling."

As she snuggled into him, feeling every bit of anxiety slip away, she said," I was almost frightened to believe that I could be this happy again, it all seemed too good to be true. I kept thinking something would happen to stand in our way, I can't believe we're finally here. It feels so good; I've never been happier and now I'm here with you, I'm beginning to trust the process that the universe has mapped out for me, I want to enjoy every moment I have with you."

"We can both enjoy every moment now," Conrad replied. "Now I have you in my arms, I feel like I'm 'home' and I never want to let you go. All of this, despite being emotionally turbulent, was all meant to happen, we were meant to be in each–others' lives."

After yet another cuddle Lexi said, "Boy, I need a wee, I've needed to go for over an hour!" He kissed her on the cheek as she pulled away in the direction of the bathroom.

"You go to the loo and I'll put the kettle on

"Damn fine idea!"

"Is there anything else to come in from the car?" He called out, feeling he may as well make himself useful.

"Yes, there's the cool box still in the boot and a large holdall in the back of the car with kitchen stuff in," she called back, relieved to be able to dive in the loo!

"Okay, I'll go and get that, you sort yourself out and then we can chill properly." Conrad put the strawberries back in the fridge, switched the kettle on and went out to the car.

Washing her hands, Lexi caught sight of herself in the mirror; her hair had started to loosen and fall down a little, something she would usually attend to straight away. She looked herself straight in the eye, feeling more comfortable in her own skin than she'd ever been and had no desire or need to change or fix anything. She smiled to herself a happy, fulfilled smile.

"At last," she said, "This is the start of my 'happily ever after', I'm ready to welcome happiness into my life." With that she dried her hands and went back into the kitchen where Conrad had just walked in with the cool box and holdall.

"Okay hun?"

"Absolutely!"

"Right, what have we got in here then?" He took the top off and had a look inside. "Wow! How many more are joining us?" he joked.

"Well, I can't have you going hungry! Like I said before, it's better to have too much than too little!" she laughed.

"I've never seen so much food for two people!" Conrad said as his eyes eagerly took in the sight of all the delicious, fresh food. "This is going to be great! You'll be really pleased with me though, I've been mostly organic for the last couple of weeks and cooking from scratch, even when I've been away, I've been on the ball."

"Oh, excellent, that's good to hear, it'll make a difference to you, I promise," she said with conviction, very impressed.

"It already has, my tummy seems to have calmed right down; it used to gurgle like a drain after I'd eaten before and that hasn't been happening at all lately."

They sorted through the food together, Lexi telling him what meal she was going to cook with each thing as they put it all in the fridge. After all was put away, they sat and had a cup of tea, still taking each other in, almost in disbelief that they were finally reunited.

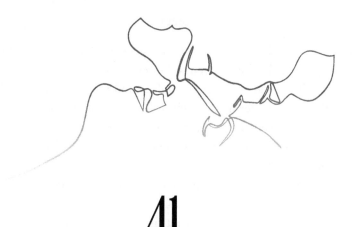

41

"God, I can't believe we're finally here together," He sat back and looked at her.

"I know, it feels almost like it's a dream, doesn't it? I feel like I've been waiting for this for so long... So much has happened since getting back in touch with you, my head's been in a whirlwind. Now I'm with you, it seems like time has slowed right down and I can enjoy the moment, as if I've been stuck on a runaway train that's finally slowing and allowing me to enjoy the scenery.

She smiled at him; he put his cup down, took hers from her and placed it on the coffee table then put his arms around her and pulled her in towards him.

"Oh, baby, you've rocked my world," he said, "after I'd spent that weekend with you, I was so hung up on you, the things that had really spun my world before that weekend were suddenly not important to me anymore. No one's ever been this important to me. But you are Lexi, you have literally changed how I feel about everything." He kissed her, looked deep into her eyes and said, "I'm absolutely fucking crazy about you."

"And I'm absolutely fucking crazy about you!" She replied, as his kiss moved to her cheek and then her neck.

She could feel herself tingling and warm from the feel of his lips on her skin, a feeling she had thought she'd never have the privilege of feeling again. As his lips touched her, it sent the most delightful sensations rippling through her, making her murmur gently.

"You ok?" He whispered as he glanced up, dragging his lip gently across her skin.

"Your touch, it's so beautiful; I've imagined it so many times since we parted, it's haunted me, I've yearned for it," she whispered back to him.

As the words were still leaving her lips, he 'cupped' her head in his hand and carefully let it fall back, as he started to kiss down the front of her neck with beautiful little kisses and gently stroked her skin with his tongue between them. His kisses returned to her lips as he changed his position slightly, he gently supported her back as he laid her back on the settee and lay down with her, still kissing her. Lexi ran her hands down his firm muscular back, feeling an incredible heat coming from him. She took hold of his shirt and pulled it from his trousers, now with her hands on his back under his shirt, she sank deeper into a wonderful state of bliss at the feel of her hands in contact with his skin. His arousal now all-the-more heightened at the feel of her touch, he unbuttoned her shirt and let it fall away to her sides, he gently stroked his fingers over her torso, filling her with beautiful shivers and sensations.

Lexi unbuttoned his shirt, peeled it back off his shoulders and he let it drop to the floor. Her eyes took him in; she slowly exhaled as she touched his chest, running her fingertips lightly over his skin, his nipple stiffened as she traced her fingers gently over it. Conrad watched her pupils dilate with desire as her eyes scanned his torso; he put his finger under her bra strap and let it drop off her shoulder, which he then kissed as he took down the other strap. Carefully, almost tickling her with his kisses, he removed her bra and cupped her breasts with his hands kissing one of her nipples. Gradually the clothes came off until they were both just in their undies, his erection almost forcing its way through his boxers as if it was trying to set itself free. He sat her straddling him, facing him. They both kissed slowly and deeply whilst their hands and fingertips still explored each-others skin. He stroked and caressed her back and then pulled her in firmly to him, she murmured as she felt his erection pressing into her. Supporting her back, he lay her back in his arms and gently and slowly swept her from one side to the other in a big sweeping circle then pulled her back up to him to meet his kiss. He kissed her lips and then her cheek, then he let her head fall back again as he gently kissed her neck allowing her to drop back further, supported by his hands, taking her again into this sensual, sweeping circular motion. She was completely lost in the moment, lost in the sensations whilst at the same time, aware that his beautiful, erect penis was so, so close to her, separated only by their undergarments. He swept her around again and again; there was no sense of urgency. They were enjoying becoming reacquainted with each other's bodies, kissing, stroking, moving together and giving each other the most amazingly pleasurable feelings and as they continued their tantric dance. Conrad then lowered her back down to the settee and as she slipped off his lap, he held on to her leg. He turned his face and kissed her ankle as he massaged her skin, his touch was amazing as he massaged towards her knee and then above it, the movement of his fingers made her flutter inside and gasp. He moved his hands higher up her inner thigh until he was almost, but not quite touching her; the slightest hint of his hand came into contact with her through her knickers. Then, as if to tease her, he made his way back down her leg with his sensual touch, kissing, stroking and massaging; she felt like she was going to burst, she could feel herself getting more and more aroused. At that point, he took her big toe in his mouth and gave it a playful suck; the sensation of it almost sent her through the roof.

"Oh, God, that's so nice!" She cried out.

"You like that?" he said watching her whole-body writhing with pleasure.

"I love everything you do to me. Oh God, I want you so badly," she said breathily.

"Yeah?"

"Yes, I want you, I want you now."

Still on his knees he came forward and took hold of her knickers and gently pulled them down. Now riding a blissful wave of passion Lexi was desperate to get his boxers off. He looked at her intensely as she almost tore them off him; he loved her uninhibited passion.

"I wanna give you everything Lexi… everything you want," he said as he pulled her legs back as far towards him as he could and then knelt in between them.

With her bum slightly raised he entered her; as she felt that beautiful sharp pain of his 'rock-hard' penis, she cried out in ecstasy, the penetration felt amazing. Both of them gasped and groaned at the immense pleasure of their oneness, each of them totally consumed by the other, each of them thrusting as if they simply couldn't get enough of each other.

"I love you," Conrad said, "I absolutely fucking love you."

Tears started to fall down Lexi's face as she cried, "I love you too. Oh God, I love you so much."

Conrad lowered himself onto her and their lips met as they both reached a crescendo of emotional and sexual release, both saying 'I love you' over and over to each other until they became a breathless heap.

They held each other, suspended in their moment, nuzzling one another for some time just lying together and stroking each other's skin, neither of them with the slightest desire to let go.

"I could stay here like this forever," said Lexi dreamily.

"Mmm, me too," said Conrad, his fingers playing with her now, very floppy topknot. She lay with her head on his chest and hand on his belly, the two of them emotionally, physically, and sexually spent in the most delightful way; they lay there for another twenty minutes or so just 'being' with each other.

"God, I'm hungry now!" Conrad suddenly exclaimed as his belly started to make noises.

"Yes it sounds as though you are! I'm quite hungry too now actually," Lexi agreed, "what do you fancy out of that little lot then?" She gestured toward the fridge.

"Well, the steak looked good, and I think we could do with topping up our iron levels after our exertion!"

He winked at her and she giggled, "Steak it is then, I have boc choi, mushrooms, avocado and okra to go with the steaks, how does that sound?

"It sounds awesome," he said and kissed her head. "I need the loo and then you can give me a demonstration of your fine cuisine!"

Pushing himself up he went to the bathroom. Lexi lay there for a couple of moments, hugging one of the settee cushions with a huge, relaxed smile on her face, she was in absolute heaven.

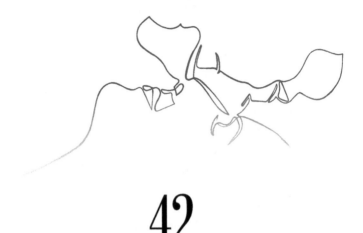

42

Finally getting up from the settee, she picked up Conrad's shirt, put it on, rolled up the sleeves and went to the kitchen area. She started to get out the organic fillet steak and the vegetables, coconut oil, butter, salt, pepper and garlic ready on the worktop. She went to her handbag and got her Ipod out, then searched in the holdall for her little docking station, found a playlist of slower, relaxing songs and put it on. Conrad came back from the bathroom as Lexi was looking in the fridge for something.

He tapped her bum lightly as he passed and said, "I seem to remember you pinching my shirt before." She looked up and smiled a sweet, 'yeah but I can get away with it' smile as he picked up his boxers and put them back on. He came up behind her, put his arms round her and added "But you wear it well, you look extremely cute in it, and I can't think of a better look when you're making a romantic meal for two!"

He watched Lexi as she easily threw together their meal, adding herbs and rattling off their nutritional benefits as she went. He'd taken a tremendous interest in the subject of nutrition over the last few weeks and had picked up a huge amount of knowledge in comparison to what he had known beforehand, but he was blown away by Lexi's knowledge of the nutritional values of everything she picked up. He opened the bottle of wine and set up the little breakfast bar ready for them to eat; within ten minutes it was on the plates.

"This looks amazing! God, I'm famished!"

"Mmm, tuck in,"

"Wine?" he gestured with the bottle.

"Oh, go on then, it'd be rude not to wouldn't it!" She winked at him.

He poured them both a glass, handed Lexi hers and said, "Here's to us."

"To us," she repeated, as they chinked glasses and took a sip. Then he gave her another little peck on the cheek for good measure and started to tuck into his meal.

"Oh, man, that is so nice!" He said as he finished his first mouthful.

"Good," she said as she poured a glass of water and took her supplements.

"So, what are these for?" He asked and then listened intently as Lexi talked him through her supplements, explaining what they were and the role they played in the body.

Their dinner was leisurely, as the conversation rolled from supplements to a whole host of other things but all to do with the lifestyle and principals that Conrad had become so interested in, he was totally absorbed in it. Dinner had been finished a good half hour ago and still they chatted away intently, Conrad totally on a roll with it and Lexi more than happy to talk about her favourite subject. With still half a bottle of wine left, Conrad suggested the strawberries would now be cold and go well with it.

"Ooh, lovely, I'd forgotten about those, I'm just gonna clear this up and we can sit comfy and have them," she added as she got up and took the plates. Conrad dried and put away the things as Lexi washed them.

As they finished the clearing, Ed Sheeran's 'Thinking out loud' came on the ipod.

"Oh, I love this one!" Lexi said, Conrad put down the cloth and faced her, put her arms round his neck, took her by the waist and they started to slowly sway to the music; looking into each other's eyes.

"This is so perfect," he said and kissed her.

"Mmmmm." She melted into his chest, and they swayed to the music comfortably wrapped up in each other. They stayed there in the kitchen for another two songs and then the playlist finished. At that point, they decided it was time for the strawberries; they got them out of the fridge and took the wine and glasses over to the settee.

"D'you know what would make this perfect?" Conrad said.

"Go on?" said Lexi.

"A nice log fire."

"Ooh, yes, that'd be nice." With that, he went over to the wood burner where he'd already set up the fire and started to light it.

"Right, keep your fingers crossed, this isn't something I've done much of." But within only a few minutes, he'd managed to get it started, shut the little door on the burner and returned to the settee where Lexi handed him a glass of wine.

"Thank you beautiful." Then he reached for the plate of strawberries on the coffee table, picked one off the plate and fed it to her.

"Oh, delicious!" She said, taking one herself and popping it into his mouth; the chocolate, now cold and hard, made a cracking sound as he bit into it.

"Mmm, they've come out well," he said, pleased with his effort.

"Bloody lovely!" Lexi agreed.

Conrad went back over to the fire, prodded it, added another piece of wood, closed the door and opened the vent a little, at which point it really started to burn nicely. He returned to the settee, pulled the coffee table a bit closer and they both lay up one end of the settee cosily, where they cuddled, talked, fed each other strawberries, drank wine and loved again and again before retiring to the bedroom, where they fell asleep in each other's arms.

43

Daybreak was upon them, Conrad awoke as the sun found its way in, sending laser-like rods of light across the room. Still wrapped around each other, Conrad felt the need to move to let some blood back into his arm, which had gone dead from the position he had fallen asleep in.

Lexi stirred, "Morning handsome, are you okay?"

"Yeah, I've got a dead arm, it feels like rubber, like it doesn't belong to me!" He replied.

"Here," she said, sitting up and massaging some life back into it; rubbing it briskly and lightly slapping it, the blood now pulsed back into it with a 'booming' sensation.

"Ooo, that feels horrible!" he said as the life started to come back and he felt pin and needles.

"Keep squeezing your fist and moving your arm, it'll soon go off," she assured him.

"Is there no end to your talent's I ask myself?"

"Handy to have around, aren't I?"

"You most certainly are!" They giggled and he gave her a playful kiss.

"I can't remember EVER feeling like this, I want this weekend to last forever," he kissed her again. "Me too," she replied nuzzling into him.

After a good while of more cuddling and smooching, Lexi got up, firstly, she went in the kitchen and put the kettle on and then went into the bathroom, she looked at her reflection in the mirror and gave herself a big smile, no words were needed.

The couple enjoyed their coffee in bed, after which they decided to have a workout before a hearty brunch.

"What would you prefer, outside on the grass or in the gym?" asked Lexi.

"Well, as it's such a nice day shall we take it outside?"

"Outside it is!" she chirped as she began to pull her kit out of the case.

"You haven't even unpacked properly."

"I know, I had more important things to attend to yesterday!" She winked as he gave her a knowing smile.

"I'll never forget watching you outside that first morning," he remembered, "I'd never seen anything quite like it! I've always exercised but mainly running and yoga so this will be a new experience for me."

"It's great," she chirped in her usual enthusiastic way, "uses your whole body, strengthens you in a functional way and helps you to burn fat."

"Well, I'm up for it," he said enthusiastically, punctuating it with, "Be gentle with me though!"

"Of course, I will! It's enjoyable and it'll leave you full of energy!" She said convincingly, as she put her trainers on.

"Okay, I'll have to trust you on that."

They left the little barn and went to Lexi's car where, in the boot, was an assortment of weights and balls. She picked out what she thought he would need and then went to the rear seat of the car and got out a big black holdall on wheels.

"Blimey, what's in there?"

"A battle rope!"

He watched her take it round to the grassed area, pull it from the holdall and feed it through the bottom, upright post of a fence, leaving two, equal lengths of rope.

"Right, we'll do a little warm up and then I'll take you through a HIIT training session."

She was already in her element, Lexi liked nothing more than working out; outside on a sunny day, in fact, just working out outside, it didn't really matter what the weather was like, it always felt good to her, but sunshine was a bonus. They skipped, sprinted, threw heavy balls forwards and backwards, did squat jumps, burpees, lunges and numerous exercises with the battle rope.

"This is one of my favourite pieces of equipment," she beamed as she finished a demonstration of what she wanted him to do and then coached him to do the same.

She took Conrad through two sets of each exercise with rest intervals, careful not to overdo it, as she didn't want him to have sore muscles for the rest of the weekend. After about forty minutes, they'd finished the two circuits. Lexi then took the rope from where it was hooked around the fence and laid it out straight on the grass.

"Fancy a little tug-of-war then?" She asked. "I know you'll be much stronger than me in this but it's good to get that pulling exercise."

They started square on facing each other as she got a decent hold and went down into a very strong squat. They laughed and played around; despite the fact he did manage to pull her over, he was impressed by her technique and how strong (for a petite lady) she was. At that point, along came Charlie from the gym.

"Hello again, I thought it must be you!" He said as he approached them.

"Hello Charlie, how are you?" they both said,

"I'm good thank you," he replied, "Lexi, isn't it?"

"Yes, and Conrad. We've come back for the weekend; thought we'd make the most of it out here today."

"I think we'd only just refurbished when I saw you last, hadn't we?" He enquired.

"Yes, that's right, how's it all going?"

"Yes, it's all good. We've got lots of members from surrounding villages now as well as the hotel guests, just the right amount; there seems to be a constant 'happy hum' in the gym. I'm really pleased with it," he said happily.

"Good, I'm pleased it's worked out well for you, you've put a lot of work into it," Lexi congratulated him.

Charlie added, "You'll have to pay another visit while you're here."

"Oh, we most certainly will, the sunshine was too tempting today," Lexi gestured with her palms up the heavens.

"I don't blame you, perfect isn't it," he agreed then said to Conrad, "Is she putting you through your paces today then?"

"She is indeed!" Conrad replied, "It's good though, I've really enjoyed it, this is something completely new to me."

"Excellent!" Charlie smiled, "I'll let you get on then but do come and pay me a visit."

"We'll probably go in the 'wet side' later; but are you working tomorrow morning?" Lexi asked.

"Yes, I'm there until 1pm tomorrow."

"Okay, we'll come and use the gym tomorrow."

They said their goodbyes and Lexi and Conrad started to clear away the equipment from the grass, Conrad feeling quite radiant and energised from his first ever HIIT experience. They packed everything away and returned to the little barn.

"FOOD!" Lexi exclaimed.

"Absolutely, I'm starving now!" Conrad said, feeling very much in need of refuelling!

"Me too, what do you fancy? I'm going to have a green smoothie, but I also have eggs, bacon, mushrooms and tomatoes if you would prefer that?"

"Why don't you make a large smoothie we can share and then we can have a cooked breakfast after." Lexi laughed, "I take it from that you're very hungry!"

"You could say that!"

"Ok, sounds like a plan to me," Lexi went to the fridge and pulled out bone broth, avocado, blueberries, asparagus and spinach and started to go to work on fixing the smoothie.

While she did that, Conrad got out a pan and started to prepare the cooked breakfast. Lexi put the smoothie together, added some turmeric, black pepper and chlorella and whizzed it all up, she opened it and shared it between two mugs and passed one to Conrad.

"Thank you," he said, "Cheers," Lexi said as she knocked hers straight back. She cuffed her lips with the back of her wrist and turned to the hob where the cooked breakfast was shaping up nicely.

Having breakfasted, they decided they would go for a walk and then visit the spa later when they got back to unwind. Lexi went to her case and finally took out her clothes and hung them up. On the bed, she set out something to wear, along with a bikini and flip-flops for later and then went into the bathroom where Conrad was having a shave.

She watched him intently as he tidied up one side of his face; his chiselled features suited his neatly trimmed 'goatee'. She popped herself up on the worktop space next to the sink. He looked at her and then at himself in the mirror.

"Do you like it, or do you want it off?" he asked.

"Oh, no, I like it, I think it suits you." She carried on watching him as he carefully took the razor down his face leaving the precise outline of the goatee. "It's like a little work of art," she said, and with that he gave her the razor.

"Want to put your mark on it?" He said.

"Blimey! You're very trusting," she said, "I might mess it up!"

"You won't mess it up, even if you do it'll grow again. Go on, I trust you!"

He stepped in front of her, so she could see him face on. She looked at his stunning features, put some shaving oil on his skin, wrapped her legs around his waist as he stood in front of her and carefully, she did the other side. He amused himself with the concentration on her face as she did it.

"Not bad at all!" He said, checking out both sides in the mirror, impressed with her effort. Lexi was now feeling a little pleased with herself.

She got in the bath and pulled the shower curtain across, pulled out her 'top knot' and threw her hair scrunchie out from behind the curtain. She got the water to the right temperature and started washing her hair. Conrad rinsed the sink and brushed his teeth; he could see Lexi behind the curtain, he took off his shorts and climbed in behind her. As the shampoo lathered up, he put his hands in her hair and took on the job of washing it. She felt instantly relaxed at his touch and he watched the calm expression on her face as he massaged her head, her eyes shut, enjoying being pampered by him. He rinsed off the shampoo and put the conditioner on, which he also massaged through with his fingers. She turned to him, pulled him under the powerful jets of water and returned the favour by washing his hair for him. They then washed each other, cuddled and held each other under the falling water, their bodies slippery and warm against each other. Conrad got out, grabbed a towel, roughly dried his hair and then put it round his waist as Lexi bent forwards and wrapped a small towel round her head in a turban. He then picked up another big bath towel and went to her. As she stepped out of the bath, he wrapped her up in it, picked her up, took her into the bedroom and lay her on the bed, where they made, sweet love all over again.

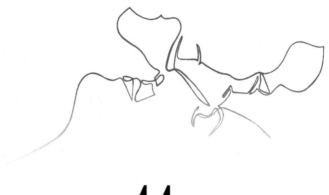

44

After they had lain there for a while, Lexi got up and went in the bathroom to sort out her hair before it dried too much. She put her leave-in-conditioner and serum and left it to dry naturally while she put on a little mascara.

Conrad came in with a cuppa for her, put it on the worktop, kissed her cheek and said, "It looks pretty like that, why don't you leave it down for a change."

"Okay." She smiled, she finished her make-up, got dressed and then they set off for a walk in the opposite direction to the way they had gone the last time they were there. They had picked up a local footpath map from the reception on their way out, worked out the direction they were going in and decided to take a walk away from the road. The scenery was absolutely amazing; everywhere they looked the hills seemed to roll forever.

"I love it here, it's absolutely stunning," she said, her eyes scanning the rolling hills with green grass and rough, rocky edges.

"It's just so 'captivating'," he added, "I can't take my eyes off it."

"I've fallen in love with it," she said, her eyes soaking it up as if she couldn't get enough of it. Conrad looked at her expression as she took in the beautiful surroundings, just standing there in awe. He felt totally on the same page as her, it was indeed, some kind of heaven.

"Yes, so have I," he agreed and as they walked arm-in-arm, the sun soared high in the sky with hardly any clouds. They took a footpath that led them up and over a hill. As they walked along the bottom looking up, there was a small waterfall coming down the hill, it was only about two feet across and it poured down through the rocky surface with pretty grasses and heather either side of it. "Oh, look at that," she chirped, "Shall we find the source?"

"Absolutely, I like an adventure!"

Lexi took a few pictures of the waterfall and then put her phone away safely. They left the footpath and made their way through the overgrown land to the waterfall, climbing up the side of the waterfall on the rocky surface; up and up they went until they reached the top. Once up there, they sat by the little stream that forked at the top, part of it was feeding the small fall and the other fork rolled down towards the village they could see in the distance. They sat for a while and took in the scenery.

"Amazing!" she said.

"Absolutely!" He agreed. Their eyes scanned the countryside, they could see for miles so out came the camera again to capture it all. They took a couple of 'selfies', also capturing the views behind them. They could see the little village that they were intending to reach, with its quaint stone-built houses and more secluded properties in the hills.

They carefully made their way back down the huge hill and finally connected with the footpath again. Once on the footpath, they made their way through the pretty countryside to the village. The characteristic stone cottages came into view as they entered the village; it was almost as if they were stepping back in time.

"Oh, this is just lovely!" said Lexi, as they walked along the little road with all the pretty cottages framing it.

In the heart of the village, there were two pubs, an art gallery, a bakery, a well-stocked general store, an off licence and a little gift shop. They went into the gallery; the paintings unsurprisingly were mostly of the surrounding area. After that they went into the gift shop; it seemed to sell everything from walking boots to binoculars, to beautiful pieces of jewellery and trinkets of all sorts. Lexi picked up a little dish, just big enough to put maybe a couple of pairs of earrings in; it was intricately fashioned out of 'Blue John' crystal.

"Oh, that's pretty!" she said, turning it over to see it was nearly £100! "Blimey! Seriously? That can't be right surely?" She put it back down and carried on looking at the other wares. They looked all around the shop, then Lexi said, "Actually, I'm beginning to get a bit peckish, shall we take a look at the menus in the pubs?"

"Sounds good to me," said Conrad and they left the little shop and made their way to the first of the two pubs, then on to the second.

Having seen both menus, they decided they would prefer to eat at the first pub; they went in and up to the bar.

"What would you like to drink?" Conrad asked.

"I think I'll just have some still water please."

"Two still mineral waters please and can we order some food?" Said Conrad.

"Yes, of course," replied the barman, "The menus are here and there's the 'specials' board."

They took their drinks and put them down, then went to look at the specials board. All of it looked good, boasting home cooked food with locally sourced produce.

"It all looks nice," said Conrad. "Mind you, we did have a good breakfast and going by what we have in our fridge we're not going to need a massive meal."

"Let's just have something light," she said as her eyes scanned the board, "they've got a slow cooked, pulled pork salad on here."

"Ooh, yeah, that sounds nice," he said. He picked up the menus, went to the bar and ordered the two salads. When they came out, they were enormous! A lovely, big, juicy helping of pulled pork with crispy crackling on the side, beautifully presented on a large plate of leafy salad consisting of different leaves, herbs and even flower petals!

"It's a good job we only went for the light meal!" Conrad winked at Lexi.

"Mmm, it's lovely though and by the time we've walked back over that hill and been to the spa and had a swim, I'm sure we'll be hungry enough again later."

They ate and drank sitting, talking for about an hour, then decided to head back to the retreat and chill out in the spa. They worked out a different route on the map that would get them back and set upon their way. As they made their way along the footpath, it took them past a charming, converted barn with stone buildings around it.

"Oh, wow! That is just heavenly." She said.

"Yeah, amazing isn't it!" He agreed.

"Imagine that, every direction you look out from it, there's a stunning view, it must be wonderful!"

They stood and admired it for a while and then carried on their way, back up over the hill, through the gorgeous countryside back to the retreat. They had a cup of tea, got their swim stuff and went over to the spa. The cool water of the pool was welcome after their trek. They swam a little, messed about and then retired to the edge of the pool where they sat on the little shelf around the edge with the jacuzzi bubbles floating up. Resting their heads on the side of the pool so the bubbles were lightly tickling their backs, they held hands as they sat there. After a while they decided they would go in the sauna. Lexi laid her towel down on the wooden bench and lay down; Conrad sat on the bench next to her.

"Mmm, this is the life!" Lexi exclaimed.

"Mmm, tell me about it," Conrad agreed, "It's a lifestyle I could get very used to!"

"Mmm, me too!" She said. "Mind you, I have it all where I work. That has a spa, nothing as posh as this but I do use the sauna two or three times a week; so, although the work can be physically challenging, I always make time to rest and chill after."

"How long have you worked there?"

"About five years now,"

"If you had the means, would you like to own something like this?" He asked, really fishing now.

Lexi thought for a moment and then replied, "No, not really… at least nothing of this scale, it would just be too much, but I have always dreamed of having my own holistic retreat on a much smaller, more personal scale."

This intrigued Conrad, "Tell me more, what would be your dream?" He said turning to her and giving her his full attention.

"My dream," she replied, "if I had the money, would be to own a lovely old building on a bit of land, an old farmhouse or something like that, somewhere with land and outbuildings. I'd have the main house as my home and then convert any outbuildings into a gym, sauna/steam room and hot tub, salt or fresh water of course!"

She winked at him and he winked back, "Of course!"

"Then depending what kind of out buildings there were, I'd like a separate treatment room and an indoor 'open space' for teaching groups, exercise classes and meditation; just a room that anything could be held in it. And any other out-buildings that were left, I'd convert them into accommodation for people to stay and if there weren't any, I'd put log cabins on the land for the guests, not too many, maybe six or eight clients at any one time; I wouldn't want any more than that, that way each individual would get the most out of it. She rolled out her obviously, much thought about dream.

"What, like a B&B and then they can use the facilities?" He asked.

"Erm, more structured than that. I regularly work with people who really need to make big, big changes in their lifestyles. They've either had a nasty health scare, or they've been in stressful jobs for so long they've 'burned out' and been made to realise it's affecting their health and they need to make huge changes.

"I'd quite like to do a structured 'reset' week. Firstly, get them to fill in an extensive questionnaire on all aspects of their lifestyle before they arrive so that I know as much about them as I can before I meet them. Once I have the questionnaire back, I'd have a one-to-one video call with each of them to determine the areas they need to work on the most and then plan the week's time-table around that with scheduled sessions for the group as a whole and then the individual input. I'd most definitely do a scheduled day on nutrition that included practical cookery, you'd be surprised how many people have never really cooked for themselves," she said.

Conrad instantly added, "Well, me being one of them until a few weeks ago!"

"Exactly! Quite often when I talk to clients about the nutrition side, they often don't have a clue how to cook from scratch because they've always bought shop prepared food. I would teach them just a few basic things, like making a bone broth, and then everything you can do with that bone broth base like sauces, curries, smoothies and soups using lots of different vegetables and fresh herbs; just showing them how to put it all together, because it really isn't that hard. I feel it would just give the clients that extra bit of confidence when they're trying to make such big changes to support their health; bearing in mind many people's idea of cooking is to open a packet of fresh pasta, stick it in a pan and pour boiling water over it! I would also do a one-day whistle stop talk on the principals of health and wellbeing and then each day there would be a different exercise session and also a stress reduction practice of some kind."

Conrad listened intently.

"Most people are obviously aware of the importance of diet and exercise when it comes to health and wellbeing whether they put it into practice or not, but not many pay attention to reducing their stress levels. People don't realise how damaging stress is on the body. In fact, most think of and treat the mind and the body as two very separate things, when in reality our bodies are a physical manifestation of our thoughts and feelings; you can't have a healthy body without a healthy mind. Emotional wellbeing is just as important as physical wellbeing, whether it's dealing with toxic relationships in the present day or being unable to let go of a trauma suffered in childhood. If these things aren't addressed, the negative emotional energy will be having a negative impact on the physical body, so it's important to treat the person as a whole, mind, body and spirit, that's why it's called 'Holistic'.

"Mmm" Conrad pondered, "That makes sense, I've never really thought about it like that."

Lexi continued. "Obviously clients with specific problems in this area would have to be seen on a one-to-one basis because it would need to be private and it wouldn't all be done and dusted in one week but the foundation of treatment can be set in place with a plan for going forwards when they leave. This is why I like to find out as much about people beforehand because it makes such a difference to people's lives. I would also cover mindfulness and meditation, breath work, Qigong, functional exercise and maybe a couple of more specialised workshops for individuals with other specific health problems." She was now on a roll!

"Like?" he said, encouraging her to continue.

"Like one on maintaining a healthy digestive system. Most people I talk to have digestive issues of some kind. Also, hormone and menopause, these are issues that I frequently come across. By finding out all about them before they arrive, if there are issues that are coming up in one or more areas, with one or more guests, I could schedule in that specific topic. Say, if I had three females with hormone issues, I would schedule that topic into the week for them, or if all six or eight of them had indicated digestive issues I would schedule that in."

"Yeah, I can see how that would work. So, what you're doing is taking them through a whole journey to health that's tailor-made for them. I really like the idea of that," he said nodding thoughtfully.

The idea of the week's course is to really push the reset button, to come and learn what they need to do to create a better state of wellbeing from every angle. They would be removed from their familiar, day-to-day routine for just long enough to absorb it, adopt it, put it into practice and also to recognise just how different they feel for 'living' the whole experience. It's to educate people that it's not just about diet and exercise and that real health goes far, far deeper than that! A week would be sufficient to learn the basic practice and set-in place a new lifestyle and routine for themselves, which will give them the foundation for continuing and building upon. When they leave, they will know what they're working towards, have a good head start with new, healthful habits set in place and then they will be able to build on that knowledge and the changes they've already adopted."

Conrad listened to Lexi's, clearly well thought out ideas. Yes, she may have never been in a position to do anything like that, but she had obviously spent a great deal of time thinking about it. She had all the ideas; she had a huge amount of knowledge, and she taught many different disciplines of exercise and practiced many different holistic therapies. This, to Conrad was something well worth thinking about.

They left the sauna, had a quick rinse off and got in the hot tub, where they continued chatting, Conrad encouraging Lexi to share more of her ideas as he quietly took it all in, at the same time his brain started turning like a hamster on a wheel. They got out when they were too hot and lay down on two recliners near the pool; they pushed them closer together and lay on their towels facing each other, holding hands across the gap while their bodies cooled down. After their morning workout, a good five-mile country walk and the heat of the spa, they were now quite tired and comfortably relaxed. Sometime later, they made the two-minute walk back to their little barn where Lexi threw together another small culinary delight for them both while Conrad lit the fire. Having eaten they cuddled up on the sofa watching the flames 'dance' in the wood burner. They were both well and truly shattered. With full tummies, they lay contentedly, Lexi with her head on his chest, getting lost in the flames while Conrad unconsciously played with her hair and mulled his thoughts over in his head.

Conrad stroked Lexi's cheek, "Hun, it's 1am, we've fallen asleep!"

Lexi was well and truly zonked.

"Come on baby, let's go to bed, you'll get stiff lying here."

He sat up and Lexi's head 'lolloped' wearily as he sat her up, he looked at her half asleep.

"Bless," he said as he stood up in front of her, helped her up and then picked her up and carried her to the bedroom. He gently lowered her onto the bed, took off her outer clothes, popped her under the quilt and got in beside her; she was instantly asleep again. He looked at her, stroked her face, kissed her forehead and fell asleep himself.

45

Morning broke and Lexi woke up not quite knowing where she was; she'd slept so deeply; she had no recollection of Conrad moving her. She opened her eyes and with daylight breaking through the curtains just enough, she took in the familiar flowery curtains. She turned her head to see Conrad still happily in the land of 'nod', lying on his back, head facing her, and his arm and hand draped across her body. She instantly felt the surge of feel-good, happy hormones, as her brain became present and recognised Conrad's head next to hers on the pillow. She stayed quiet and watched him sleep for many minutes, feeling happy, peaceful, content, whole and above all grateful; grateful that she'd been given this opportunity to find such happiness. As Conrad began to stir, he opened his eyes to see Lexi lying there looking at him.

He breathed in a deep morning breath," Morning beautiful, how long have you been awake?"

"Oh, not long," He reached forward and kissed her. "I was watching you sleep, you looked so peaceful."

"That's because I feel peaceful when I'm with you," he said as he pulled her toward him for a cuddle. "My whole world is a better place with you in it."

"I was just thinking the same. I honestly can't remember the last time I felt this happy."

"Your children being born?" he suggested.

"Well, yes of course," she replied, "they were the two happiest days of my life, but I don't mean in that way. I mean I can't remember ever being so happy to simply 'be' with someone, in their company, I'm so happy you're in my life."

He pulled her on top of him and said, "And I'm so happy you're in my life, I never want this to change, I never want it to end, I want you in my life forever."

Lexi positively glowed at his words. "Me too. I want you in my life always. Always and always."

All 'loved up' and happy, Lexi went into the kitchen and put the kettle on, she ground some coffee, filled the pot and returned to the bedroom with two mugs.

"Pour vous!" She placed the coffee on the bedside table and jumped back in bed. Whilst drinking their coffee, they planned what they would do that day, starting with the promised visit to the gym.

Once up they ventured off to the gym, although Conrad kept himself fit, lifting weights was something he hadn't got in to. The gym was quiet; Charlie was over the other side with a PT client, he waved and acknowledged them as they came in. They waved back and then Lexi took Conrad over to the squat rack and talked him through a squat pattern, teaching him position and technique. They happily got on with that, taking turns and then going on to different sets of exercises until she'd taken them through a decent, full body workout; Conrad thoroughly enjoyed it.

"You know, I tried weightlifting a few years ago and just didn't really get into it, it just didn't 'do it' for me then, but I enjoyed that," he said.

Lexi replied, "Good! I'm pleased you did; I'd hate to think you'd suffered it just to be polite!"

"Ha, don't be silly, I don't think any activity spent with you would be suffered! That's probably why I didn't get into it before, I just didn't have the right motivation!" He winked as they made their way over to sit on the mats, at which point Charlie came over for a chat, pulling up a ball to sit on. They chatted and exchanged experiences and techniques, which turned into a bit of horseplay, showing off their core-stability skills on the ball, kneeling, squatting and all manner of core exercises. Conrad had a go at each and did well at some of them and not so well at others! He tried to master kneeling on the ball and fell off twice. They all laughed but Conrad being Conrad refused to be beaten by it and eventually managed to stay up convincingly with a big, triumphant grin on his face to a round of applause from Lexi and Charlie. When they'd finished chatting, the couple went back to the barn to shower, dress and have a hearty brunch consisting of wild caught salmon, field mushrooms, avocado, green beans and spinach sautéed in garlic butter with grated lemon rind. Lexi had precooked a beef curry for them to have in the evening. They decided to walk to the little village they had walked to when they first met. Having had such a big brunch, they considered maybe tea and cake in the little teashop would be just enough for a treat mid-walk to tide them over until they ate later in the evening.

They set off through the delightful countryside, map in hand eager to try a different route to the village; the area was so picturesque they wanted to explore as much of it as they could. Wandering through a pretty wooded area, the sun was glistening through the leaves, the birds were singing and the two of them held hands and chatted away as they walked.

"I absolutely love it here," Lexi said, "It's weird isn't it. I've never been here before; it was simply what came up when I typed in a rough area looking for accommodation. It's so beautiful around here, just everywhere you go, every direction you look in, it's just keeps giving."

"Yeah, isn't it?" Conrad agreed, "I've stayed here a few times now; usually when my trip spans over two weeks with the weekend in the middle. A couple of years ago, I had business in three locations in England, over an eight-day period. I found this on the Internet and thought it'd be a nice stopover for the weekend. I liked it so much, it was like having real time-out, it's a bit of a novelty for me as I live right in the city at home."

"Do you prefer it in the city?" She asked.

"I never really thought about it, it's practical for work. I've been with the same company since I left uni; I've always worked long hours and I mean long, long hours! It's just how my lifestyle has been due to circumstance, no lengthy commute home; I'm just ten minutes away. I have a nice apartment though. It's a penthouse, with an amazing, skyline view of the city; it's just how it all worked out with my life. Since I've come here, I've felt it's a different world altogether, I love it, it's like a fairy tale land, I always feel good when I've had some time-out here, it breaks the trip up nicely!"

They carried on through the woods until they came out near a field.

"I know where we are, weren't those horses down there somewhere?" Lexi said.

"Yes, I think you're right, once we pass that hedge, we'll be at the bottom where that pond was, then the horses should be a bit further up." They carried on along the footpath past the pond and sure enough, there were the horses as they started to make their way back up again. They beckoned the horses over and made a fuss of them.

"Do you think they remember us?" she said.

"They might do, we spent enough time with them last time, fussing them and taking pictures; they probably think, 'there's those two-mad people again!'"

They laughed and stayed with the horses for a little while, stroking and patting them, the horses enjoying the attention. The horses kept putting their heads through the fence to get the longer grass, so Lexi and Conrad tore up a couple of handfuls and fed it to them. After they were satisfied with their re-acquaintance, they carried on along the footpath, up over the hill and back down the other side. Once they were in the village, they walked down the pretty little streets, admiring how lovely they looked. There was a church that they hadn't noticed the last time, so they went in and had a look then headed for the teashop.

Conrad went straight for the carrot cake again; Lexi had a gluten free chocolate brownie, and they had a pot of tea.

"Mmm," Conrad enthused savouring a mouthful of the cake.

"Nice?"

"Bloody lovely!" he mumbled with his mouth half full, "Yours?"

"Mmm, excellent," they munched contently while the tea brewed in the little china pot.

"What time have you got to leave in the morning?"

"It's actually not that bad," he replied, "I need to be in the London office for midday, then it's pretty much back-to-back meetings after that."

"Oh, great, at least you don't have to be up at the crack of dawn. We can take our time then, so long as you leave by about nine or nine-thirty," Lexi said practically.

Conrad's voice dipped slightly at the thought of being separated again, "Yeah, it won't be the same without you though."

"I know, it'll be horrible leaving separately but I'll be back with you Wednesday evening and I'm not working Thursday so I can be with you right up until you leave to catch your flight."

As the words left her mouth, she could see Conrad's expression change.

"God, I hate the thought of leaving you and going back," Lexi could almost read his mind, as her own thoughts turned to the fact that, despite them being back in each other's lives and so devoted to each other, they would soon be separated again.

Trying to be positive for both of them, she said, "I know it's going to be difficult, but let's try not to think about it otherwise it'll spoil the time we do have left together."

She poured the tea and Conrad tried to turn himself around but the underlying thought of being separated from Lexi again played on his mind. They were holding hands and talking when an older chap came and sat at the table next to them.

"You're staying at the hotel up the road, aren't you?" He asked.

"Yes," replied Lexi.

"I thought I recognised you," he continued, "I watched you out on the grass yesterday morning and you were in the spa when I was there in the afternoon."

"It's lovely isn't it, have you been here before?" Lexi asked.

"No, I haven't but I'm thoroughly enjoying my stay, it's a lovely area,"

"Indeed, it is,"

They chatted with the man for a little while, then the loved-up couple stood up to leave. As they stepped out of the teashop, clouds were starting to form, big and dark in the sky.

"That doesn't look so good, it looks like it's going to pour down." Said Conrad.

"If we go back through the woods, we'll be more sheltered," Lexi suggested.

They made their way with no great urgency, back up the footpath, over the hill, said hello to the horses again and then the rain started.

"Oh, well, we're gonna get wet, it's not the end of the world," said Conrad putting his arm around Lexi.

"I like the rain, it doesn't bother me," she affirmed.

"I'll never forget the first time I saw you, soaking wet from that storm!" he reminisced.

Lexi laughed, "I couldn't have been any wetter, could I?"

"Ha, I don't think so! I thought you looked sexy though."

He gave her a cheeky smile, "Seriously? I think I looked like a drowned rat!"

"A sexy drowned rat!" Conrad added, not for a moment would he allow her to put herself down. They laughed and carried on walking as the rain got heavier. They made their way through the woods, which didn't really give much cover as it was now raining very hard; their hair and clothes were getting wet. They stopped and looked at each other, he pulled her towards him and kissed her as the rain fell down their faces.

Through the wood and out onto the road they walked, it felt like the sky was literally falling down! The harder it rained the more they laughed; they started jumping in the puddles like a couple of children. They were like a pair of free spirits, nothing mattered, despite now being soaked through to the skin; they were oblivious to any discomfort. At that point, a car came up behind them and came to a stop beside them; it was the old man from the teashop. He wound down the window.

"Do you two love birds want a lift and get in the dry?" He asked as he peered through the crack in the window.

"Why, is it raining?" Conrad answered jokingly as he pulled his soaking wet girlfriend into his arms.

Lexi politely added, "No thank you my lovely, we're ok." The man smiled an understanding smile, "Loves young dream! I remember it well." Still smiling he wound the window back up and waved as he drove off, the two of them blissfully untroubled by any of it.

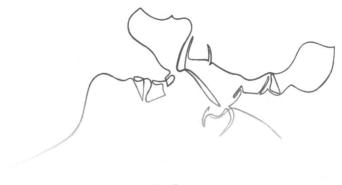

46

They finally got back to the barn, opened the door and stripped off on the doorstep. Lexi got the bowl from the kitchen and put the clothes in it, to take them to the bathroom where she wrung them out and hung them on the bathroom radiator. They both got in the shower and warmed themselves under the hot jets of water.

"What do you fancy doing now, did you want to go over to the spa again?" asked Lexi.

"I really don't mind, as long as I'm with you," he replied. "I tell you what I would like though," he added as a thought entered his head.

"What's that?"

"I would quite fancy some rice with the curry tonight and we don't have any wine left, shall we take a quick drive to the village and get them now and then go to the spa and take our time?"

"Sounds like a plan to me," said Lexi. So, in clean, dry clothes they made a dash to the car and headed off.

As they got to the big gates Conrad turned right saying, "I think we're more likely to get a decent bottle from the off licence in the village we went to yesterday to be honest." The rain started to slow down and within a couple of minutes it fizzled out and, as it did, the sun came streaming out powerfully.

"Wow! It's like it never happened!" Joked Lexi.

They made their way along the winding, three-or-so-mile road to the village. As they approached the outskirts of the village, they saw a 'For Sale' sign at the side of the road; they both peered through the gap in the tall-tree hedge at the property as they went past.

"Oh, wow, look at that!" said Lexi, "I think that's the place we could see from the footpath yesterday."

Conrad stopped the car and they peered down the drive towards the lovely stone building.

"God, that's awesome," said Conrad. They admired it for some moments and then continued on into the village. Having got what they wanted, they started to drive back. Again, Conrad stopped at the property and positioned the car so they could see the building in all its glory.

"My God, it's absolutely stunning isn't it, I wonder how much it is," he said.

"Mmm, mega bucks I should imagine, the sort of place you just dream of," she replied dismissively.

"Not necessarily, don't forget I have an apartment to sell."

Lexi looked at him, shocked at his comment, "You wouldn't do that would you?"

He looked at the property and then back at Lexi, "I could be tempted!"

"I should imagine it's a hell of a lot of money Conrad," she said, still sounding somewhat dismissive.

"I'd be interested to see how much it is," he said, getting out his mobile and dialling the estate agent's number on the for-sale board. The call went straight through to an answering service.

"It is Sunday evening, they're not likely to be open really," said Lexi.

Conrad looked deep in thought, "Have you got a pen hun?"

Lexi looked in her bag and produced one. He took a scrap of paper from his pocket and wrote down the name of the estate agent.

"I've got my laptop in the boot; I'll look it up when we get back and see how much it is." Having parked up at the barn, Conrad collected his laptop and they made their way inside.

"Right, I'll just 'prep' the veg, put some rice on for you and the curry on the hob to heat up slowly and then we can eat whenever." She started to get her food out of the fridge as Conrad placed the laptop on the breakfast bar and 'booted' it up.

"Are you going to have some vegetables as well or do you just want rice with yours?" She asked.

"Oh, yes please, I loved the way you did it last time, I just fancied some rice with it as well, old habits die hard, and all this exercise is really giving me an appetite!" He rubbed his tummy.

"Your wish is my command," she joked as she started washing the vegetables.

Conrad tapped in the estate agent's details and area name. "It's £895,000!" he said, "Come and have a look at it, it's amazing!"

Lexi came around the breakfast bar and looked at the photos of the property over his shoulder. "Mmm, I said it wouldn't be cheap," she replied.

"Do-able though," Conrad added, his eyes not leaving the screen.

"Really?" She looked at him.

"Yeah, I'd get well over a million for my apartment now, easily! The last time I had it valued it was one-point-two-mill."

Lexi was gobsmacked, "Seriously?" Her voice, almost 'shrill', "Blimey!" She looked at him in disbelief.

"Yeah, it's a penthouse apartment right in the city centre," he replied, still admiring the photos.

"Oh," she said, still shocked by his statement but then added, "Would you really want to sell it though? I mean... you might not like it here," she pointed out.

"So long as I'm with you I'd be happy wherever I was," he replied without even having to think about it, then he looked up at her and added "and anyway, I couldn't expect you to come and live in America when your kids live here."

"Well, no, I wouldn't want to be too far away from them," she admitted.

"Well then?" was his conclusion as he turned to her and shrugged his shoulders.

Lexi was finding it hard to believe that he was making such a huge, impulsive decision.

"No, seriously Conrad... that's a massive leap, I mean, don't get me wrong, I don't doubt 'us' for one moment. I love you and want to be with you beyond any shadow of doubt but honestly, what if you moved here and then didn't like it?" She tried to reason. "I'd feel awful, I just feel it would be too much to give up for a venture into the unknown. I'm just saying think carefully about it. Would you really be happy to change your whole life? To move to a different country and leave behind your roots?" She looked at him, she could see his brain 'ticking' and she could almost hear it!

"But that's exactly it, Lexi," he explained, "I don't HAVE any roots! The only commitment I've ever had is my work! I've always been shy of commitment when it came to relationships because of my mum and dad. Equally, I've never wanted children, so, whenever I've been in a relationship that my work didn't manage to ruin, as soon as they started making noises about marriage and babies, to me it was a deal-breaker. It's just never been on my agenda and having always been in that mind-set, I've never really laid down any roots."

Before Lexi could say anything, he continued, "Nothing has ever meant this much to me before. All I had was my work and I thrived on it, it was my world and everything else came second. It took me meeting you, losing you and finding you again to make me realise just how much I want this. Honestly babe, every time the thought pops into my mind that I have to go back on Thursday, I feel sick to my stomach. In the weeks that I'd lost you, I knew I'd lost something really BIG, and I felt it tremendously. This whole experience has taught me so much about myself. I've had many, many moments when I've found myself evaluating my life lately. Everything I've ever achieved is in that company, but outside of it I have precious little. I have an amazing apartment, a fast car and company shares but that's the extent of it, there is nothing outside of what I've gained from my career. I've been so busy being a success I've forgotten to have a life, quite frankly. You've shown me a way of life that didn't exist to me before; you've made me look at life differently. I really feel now that I do want to lay down my roots, and I truly feel that I belong with you, so as long as I'm with you, it doesn't matter where I am. The lifestyle you've introduced me to really appeals to me. The more I think about it the more I want to get away from the fast life, my heart just hasn't been in recently. I don't want to be gadding around the world chasing deals and going home to an empty apartment, I want to build a life with you, make a proper home and lead a life that's both desirable and fulfilling. When I'm here with you I feel like I'm where I should be; this place drew us together, I think it would be quite fitting if we set-up home here."

Lexi hugged him, "Wow, I'm completely bowled over by that, it's just not what I was expecting to hear," she said. "I honestly had visions of us having a long-distance romance for the foreseeable future and I was fully prepared for it knowing how you felt about your work, you were very honest with me from the word go! I still feel that this is going to be an enormous change for you," she said, concerned.

"It's going to be an enormous change for both of us," he said, "think about it, I'm not moving into your world and you're not moving into mine, we're creating a new world between us. You have an abundance of knowledge and training in your field, and I have the business acumen, the obsessive nature to give whatever I'm involved with 100% and I'm completely on the same page as you with 'all things holistic'. I can honestly see myself loving it and I think it'd be great. This has the potential to become the retreat you've dreamed of; this venture will be equally new to both of us. I can really see it working."

Lexi was completely taken aback by all this. She stood there looking into the computer screen with this dream property right there before her and thought, 'dare I think that this could actually happen?' Then another thought dawned on her.

"The only problem is, Nathan and I have agreed that we're not going to sell the house, we've even promised the kids. We told them that nothing would change, that when they come home, their home would still be there, at least for the foreseeable future anyway."

Conrad sensed she was flapping a bit, "Well, that's ok, we'd be able to afford the house with what I'd get from my apartment."

Lexi's brain was also now ticking away, "But we could've done with the money from the house to spend on the outbuildings, that kind of thing isn't going to come cheap."

Seeing the obvious doubt in her face he continued, "Don't forget I've never married or had kids, I've only had myself to cater for, I have other investments babe; I'm doing ok, trust me, I'm quite sure we'll manage," he said enthusiastically.

Lexi went to the bottle of wine and opened it, her hand shaking slightly as she poured two glasses and pushed Conrad's across the breakfast bar toward him saying, "I can't believe this is happening. Really, honestly, would you give all that up for me?"

"In my head I think I'd given it up as soon as we were back in contact. From the moment I got that first message from you, I have never been in any doubt that this would be for keeps. I associate you with being here, in this little place far away from the crazy business world that has been my life. I have never imagined, nor would I ever want to imagine for that matter, you, in my apartment, in the thick of the city, while I work 18-hour days! When I heard from you again, I just knew this was going to be a completely new chapter in my life and I was, and am, totally ready for it."

His words were so sincere. She reached forward and placed her hand on his; he looked at her, stood up from his stool, leaned across the breakfast bar, touched the side of her face with his hand, pulled her to him and gently kissed her. Lexi stood up and came round the breakfast bar, they took their wine and the laptop and sat on the settee, looking excitedly at the pictures of the property, the out-buildings and all the land that went with it. Lexi still felt that this was all too good to be true, whereas, as for Conrad, it was 'in the bag'.

"I still can't believe it," she said, shaking her head and looking at the screen.

"Well believe it baby, cos it's happening, and if this one falls through, we will simply find another, what is meant to be, will be, though I do have a very good feeling about this." He smiled; it was perfect, he could just imagine them in this place. They didn't go over to the spa, they had dinner, the laptop was never further than a foot away from them and excitedly they talked about what might be about to happen for them.

"There's a nice bit of land with it, part of that wood that we went through also belongs to it; that footpath that we walked along was pretty-much the boundary of the property," he pointed out on the screen.

"Wow, plenty to keep you busy then!" she said excitedly.

"Yes. I don't think you need to worry about me being bored! Aside from getting all the work done on the out-buildings, which I'd be very keen to be hands-on with, the land will take a lot of time to maintain," he observed.

"Would you be happy with that?" she asked.

"Absolutely! I can imagine it now; I'll be working on our own personal haven, making it perfect for us and our needs. I'm learning all the time and I'll be able to put that knowledge into our paradise. I feel it would be an amazing journey for me. My pace of life will be very different, but my days will be both full and fulfilling. I bet you must already have loads of ideas for the outside, don't you?"

"Oh, yes! Don't worry about that, I've got it all up here." She said tapping the side of her head.

"Go on then, what would you like to do with it?"

"Well, it already has a lovely patio looking out over the land, but I'd like an open covered area, with seats, a table and a patio heater; somewhere to sit when the weather's not so nice, so we could still have barbeques even in mid-winter if we wanted. I'd like the area beyond the patio to be a pretty garden area, kept but not 'clipped', I don't want it perfect, just full of colour and maybe a water feature of some kind, something to sit and lose yourself in. Beyond that a wildflower area with plants and grasses, I want it to be a haven for wildlife and have bird feeders up and nesting boxes in the woods. Our holistic retreat would also be a beautiful nature reserve. We can have benches placed in secluded spots in different areas; what an amazing place it would be to practice mindfulness with all the colours, sounds and fragrances to heighten your senses. We could also have an organic allotment and grow our own veggies and herbs, imagine that!"

Conrad was bowled over by her ideas. "Wow, you really have been thinking about this haven't you, I don't think there's any detail you haven't covered!" This was all really appealing to Conrad; he could totally imagine it.

"It's been a fantasy for a long, long time," she said passionately, "I've always known what I'd do given the chance, but I honestly never thought it would become a reality, this would be a dream come true for me." She was positively beaming at the thought of it.

"It would be amazing for me too," he said feeling really fired up about it; then he asked, "What time do you need to leave by in the morning?"

"Doesn't really matter, I'm not working tomorrow," she replied.

"Ok, if we get up early, get ready, breakfasted and packed, I'd quite like to take a chance and call the estate agent at 8.30 on the dot and see if we could view it, even if it's very briefly, before we leave, just to get a feel for it and start the ball rolling in some small way. That way I won't be so gutted going back because I'll have that to think about." Conrad was on a mission now.

"Okay, that sounds good to me,"

"Providing I'm on the road for 9.20-9.30 I should make it there in time," he calculated.

"Let's do that then!" Lexi felt a streak of excitement going through her. When she had set off for her weekend, she had never envisaged this turn of events and in a small way, she still couldn't believe it.

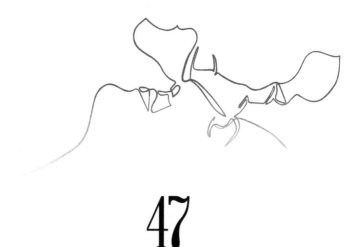

47

The morning came, both of them were awake at 6.30am, still incredibly excited. They got showered and ready, had breakfast and started to pack. It was now 8am and Lexi had packed away her kitchen stuff and took the holdall out to her car. Conrad being Conrad tried the estate agent despite the answerphone message previously saying they opened at 8.30. There was just the answerphone still; he left a message, briefly explaining the situation and left his mobile number. At 8.20 his mobile rang, he answered. The estate agent explained that the owners were away, but he held the keys, he would be happy to meet them there and it would take him 15 minutes to get there. The two of them instantly jumped into action, they'd never moved so quickly. Within five minutes everything was packed in the cars, and they had a last check of the little barn to make sure they hadn't left anything behind. Lexi had never felt so excited.

They arrived at the property in their separate cars. As they pulled into the driveway, both of them had an instant feeling of 'this feels right'. They parked up outside the delightful building; Lexi got out of her car and into Conrad's and they sat waiting for the agent.

"Wow, it's even better close up," said Lexi, "what do you think?"

Conrad's eyes scanned the amazing property, "Yeah, I really like it, let's have a look around while we wait for him."

They got out of the car, went up to the house and peeped through the windows. Lexi's tummy was turning somersaults as she peeped into the characterful lounge.

"Oh, my goodness!" she exclaimed as she spotted the massive open stone fireplace and an exposed stone wall, "That is absolutely fabulous!"

"I'll say," added Conrad, "It's like a scene from a film set, it's the perfect picture of cosy!" At that point they both turned as they heard a car pull into the driveway and up to the house and a young man got out and walked towards them.

"Mr Edwards!" he walked toward Conrad with his hand extended.

"Yes!" Conrad replied enthusiastically.

"Pleased to meet you, my name's Greg."

Conrad shook him by the hand and then he turned to Lexi and shook her hand.

"So, you're leaving today?" He asked.

"Yes!" They both replied at the same time.

"Thank you for fitting us in at such short notice but I travel to London today and fly back to the states on Thursday," Conrad explained.

"Not a problem, that's what I'm here for, let's not waste any time then and get you inside."

He unlocked the door and opened it revealing an ample hallway with flagstone floor and wooden bannisters leading to the upstairs. Lexi could feel her heart beating fast; she was in love with it already. First, he took them into the lounge they had just seen through the window. It felt so homely, the rawness of the exposed stone, the huge fireplace and beamed ceiling, the windows on both sides of the room affording it plenty of light. Out of that room into another reception room, then a dining room, which led into a rather admirable conservatory. Lexi's jaw almost hung open the entire time finding it harder to close it with every room they entered. Conrad squeezed her hand tightly; he instantly loved it and was experiencing a 'this is it' feeling. From the dining room they were then led into the kitchen.

As they walked in Lexi exclaimed, "Oh, my God!"

She cast her eyes around what was surely a kitchen that she thought she could only ever have dreamed of. It had rustic hand-made wooden doors with more flagstone flooring; more exposed stonewalls and beams, with a range cooker, an island in the middle with a stone top and again, the hand-made wooden doors. There was a breakfast area and patio doors that looked out into the vast garden. Lexi was speechless. Conrad's smile now went from ear to ear, he looked at Lexi's expression and could see she was completely bowled over by it. Yes, he would do anything to get this place for them, anything.

At that point Greg said, "And through this door is a utility room, with a rather handy shower cubicle should you have dogs and want to wash their paws before they get into the house.

Conrad digested that comment, "Dogs, that'd be nice!" Lexi was unable to say anything, she could feel herself welling-up with emotion at the very thought of this ever becoming her home.

Conrad could see the tears in her eyes, "You ok hun?"

Lexi nodded, "It's just so perfect," she said, as a tear dropped down her cheek. He turned to Greg,

"We're very interested, this is absolutely what we're looking for."

"You haven't seen upstairs yet!" said Greg.

"I don't think we need to!" Conrad replied instantly.

"Let me just take you up there," he said and led the way as the pleasantly gobsmacked couple followed. There were four double rooms and a bathroom; the main bedroom had a spacious en-suite and superb wooden built-in wardrobes. There was nothing not to like, they were both absolutely smitten by the place.

"Do you have time to look outside?" Greg asked.

Conrad looked at his watch, "I really need to be on the road in ten minutes but yes, let's just have a quick look." They went back down the stairs, through the kitchen and out onto the patio.

"So, you have four out-buildings with this property situated over there. Two of them have been converted for the business purpose of the owner, and a third has had work done but not finished; the other one would need to be totally renovated."

Conrad and Lexi looked at each other, no words could describe their expression.

"This is the land, it goes all the way down to that hedge-row, right down the bottom there and you would own all of this wood to the side, right down to where you can just about make out the 'stile' at the bottom there.

Conrad said, "Perfect, we're very, very interested."

He explained his situation, the apartment to sell and the shares that could probably be got at more quickly should the apartment take time to sell.

"Let's just say, we want it, we have the funds for it, it's merely a case of what money becomes available first."

The estate agent smiled a triumphant smile at his effortless, big sale. "Excellent, I'll let the owners know the situation and we can take it from there."

"Is there anyone else after it?" Conrad added.

"No, not yet it's only been on the market for a week. Properties in this bracket tend to take a while longer to sell," he replied.

"Great, can you take it off then please, I'd be gutted if someone came along after I'd gone back and took it from under our noses. There's no if's or but's about it, we definitely want it, it's just a case of organising the finances," Conrad repeated.

"I will let the seller know, I'm sure it'll be fine. I should imagine he'll be delighted to sell it so quickly; they've bought a bankrupt farm about five miles away and are currently in the process of setting up their business over at the new property, so it has the potential to go through quite quickly."

Conrad and Lexi grinned at each other, Conrad hooked his arm around her neck, kissed her cheek and then said, "I'd best be making a move." They thanked the estate agent for everything and made their way back to the cars.

Lexi's head was in a whirl, "I still can't believe it!"

"Believe it hun, this was meant to be, we were meant to see it, it has everything we would need for what we want to do, like it was tailor-made for us." He put his hands either side of her face, kissed her on the lips then looked deep into her eyes and stated, "Don't question it or doubt it now, just enjoy it."

The estate agent waved as he drove off, they waved back then Conrad turned to Lexi.

"I really need to get on the road now, beautiful," he said, far happier to be leaving now than he would've been had this development not happened.

"Yes, I know," she said, adding, "drive carefully and don't lose concentration dreaming all about this!"

"I won't babe, just relax, it's all going to be good from here on." He kissed her, pulled her in and kissed her again. "Right, I really must go."

He got his keys out of his pocket as she said, "Just message me when you get there, please."

"I will and you do the same." They both pulled an excited 'grin' at each other at their exciting change of events, then pulled in for one last hug as Conrad said, "I will, see you Wednesday."

One last kiss and then both got in their cars and pulled out of the driveway. Lexi followed Conrad through the lanes back to the 'B' road, until Conrad's sat nav sent him en route to London. They waved to each other as the two cars separated, Lexi still thinking to herself 'did that really just happen?' She felt like the luckiest girl alive.

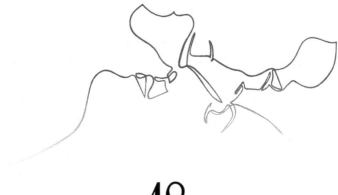

48

Lexi made it home in just over three hours; with her head blissfully in the clouds, she didn't find it necessary to swear or give hand gestures to even one other driver all the way back! About twenty minutes before she got home, she heard her phone bleep, conscious that it would be Conrad letting her know he'd reached his destination safely. She smiled, trying to imagine them in that breath-taking house; more than anything, she tried to imagine them being together full-time. She warmed at the thought of never having to say goodbye to him again, it was all she yearned for.

Conrad made good time on his journey, reaching the underground parking of the offices he was attending. He parked up, got out his phone and sent Lexi a message. Taking a deep breath and exhaling a huge, happy sigh, he was buzzing, his head in a whirl from the events of the morning. Instead of being in work mode, his head was full of what he needed to do when he got back, putting his apartment on the market, giving his notice at work, trying to work out just how long he'd actually have to work after subtracting his owed holiday; the thought of that gave him a shiver of excitement. Never before had he made a decision he'd been so sure of and in true, 'Conrad' style, he wanted it yesterday! He thought about them both making that lovely house their home, all he could think about was them, there, together and happy. He was on top-of-the-world and now itching to get the ball rolling, to sell his apartment and have something concrete set-in place to secure this massive life-change he now yearned for with every fibre of his being.

Lexi parked up on the drive, then got out her phone to check that it was indeed Conrad's message she'd heard. She smiled at her phone; her world was a lovely place right now. She gathered her stuff off the front seat, got out of the car and walked towards her house. As she approached the front door, she thought to herself, 'I wonder how many more times I will enter this door as my home', a wave of excitement pulsing through her at the very thought. She opened the door and put her stuff inside the hall and then went back to get her case and other bags from the weekend. With everything now out of the car, she made the third trip up the path with her final load. Pepys spotted her and trotted towards her, meowing for attention.

"Hello handsome!" She said, stopping to pick him up and make a fuss of him, he purred loudly as she rubbed his ears. When he started to dribble, she put him back on the ground, picked up her bags and went inside. She walked into the empty house and looked around; she had lived there for many years, her children had grown up there, the house held a lifetime of memories for her. She thought back to the night she came home after receiving Nathan's fateful text, how devastated she'd been, worried at what the future might hold for her. Then she bought herself back into the present moment, here she was, so happy, happier than she'd been in a long time and about to start a whole new, exciting chapter in her life. The next step was to tell Nathan of the developments in her new relationship and of course Corrie and Eddie. In her heart she hoped her news would be received happily. Yes, it would mean she would be over three hours away, but she still fully intended to make time for family days. With Corrie at uni, her visits were every six weeks at the most, and would be for the next two years, Lexi's brain was now ticking over how this was going to work out. Would they accept Conrad? Would the kids accept Janet and the baby? Is there a chance they might all get along in time? She shook her head; she didn't want to stress herself by over-thinking it. She decided the best approach was to tell them of hers and Conrad's plans, make it very clear she'd be back at regular intervals and that the kids would always be welcome in hers and Conrad's new home. She went into the kitchen, put the kettle on and started to unpack her kitchen stuff while it boiled.

Once she'd unpacked, she sat and had a cuppa with her laptop on her lap, open at the pictures of the superb property; she went through all the pictures of the rooms, happily thinking of how she would like to have them. Then she went over the outside space, "Wow!" She said to herself as she went through the different areas and outbuildings, it really was perfect. She'd earmarked one of the outbuildings for the studio or place where she would teach; it was a good size and currently just an open space, they wouldn't have to do anything to it other than decorate it, it was perfect. Another of the outbuildings was being used as offices. It was a large building and had two ample sized rooms downstairs as well as an upstairs that was just open space. Lexi felt this would make a good gym with a sauna, jacuzzi and relaxation area. Oh, how exciting to think she could amble on out to the gym, have a workout and then shower and sit in a relaxing sauna or bubble tub after; it was her wildest dreams coming into fruition. Once Conrad had finished in his meetings, he called her and they chatted, excited about their plans.

49

On the Tuesday, Lexi was fully booked all day with classes and clients right through till the evening. The day went by in a whirl until she had a break in the evening before her last class. She went into the café for her much-needed break and spotted Paul also having a break; she went over and joined him.

"Hello Blondie, how's things with you, how did your weekend go?" He said as she sat down.

"I'm good thank you…well, better than good actually!" She said beaming at him.

"Go on then, spill it, I can see you're gagging to tell me!" He said, eager to hear her news.

"I so am! I'm so excited!"

"Come on then, don't keep me in suspenders!" He screeched!

She told him what a lovely time she'd had and all about the house, how they'd seen it and admired it before they realised it was on the market. She told him how Conrad had blown her mind, by making it very clear he wanted to commit to her so soon in their relationship, that he was prepared to leave his life and career in America to run a holistic retreat with her.

"Oh my God, Lex, that's great news! Wow! That's amazing, I'm really happy for you. I'll miss you though, what am I going to do without my buddy?" he said jokingly.

"You can come and stay, there'll be plenty of room… and anyway I'll still need to study, I'll still be going on courses, so we'll still see each other."

This bought a smile to his face, "I'll take you up on that and I will most definitely be coming to stay!"

They chatted excitedly, Lexi got him to bring the property up on his laptop showing him the gorgeous house and talking him through the ideas she had for it as the different pictures came up until it was time to go and take her last class of the day. Once she'd finished at work and got home, she busily began packing again for her overnight stay with Conrad. She prepared a small amount of food for their breakfast to go in the cool box, as they had already decided they would go to China Town to have their dinner that evening.

With everything ready, she just had the morning to work and a lunch time class to do, then she'd get showered and be on her way to see him again. Her heart fluttered at the thought of it, she simply couldn't wait to be in his arms again but equally she was now getting the inward 'awareness' that they would only have a few precious hours together before he would have to fly back to the States, for how long, she didn't know. She tried to push that thought right to the back of her mind.

Conrad had been in back-to-back meetings since he got to London. This was nothing new to him, this was the pace of life he was used to and had been living for many, many years. Only now, in his head, he was saying to himself, 'I'm not going to miss all this,' and, 'I'm so ready for a change… and 'Just a couple of months tops and I'll be living a completely different life.' The thought of it had a calming effect on him, slowing down his habitually high flow of adrenaline. He was aware now that he'd been living in a constantly 'wound up' state from as far back as he could remember. He recalled how he felt at the retreat with Lexi, relaxed and happy, he'd liked how that had felt. The only time his adrenaline had kicked in was when he saw that the property he had admired the previous day was for sale. He knew he wanted a change and as soon as he saw the 'for sale' sign, he felt it was a sign for him to act upon, as if it had purposefully been sent to him. It had provoked his impulsive decision, he felt it was going to give him the change, he so craved. He was aware there would be a lot of work to do but he yearned to be settled, for the tranquillity of not jetting off all over the world and living half his life in hotels, not being in back-to-back meetings; he now yearned for the time when all his productivity and effort was being spent on his own surroundings, their business and their home.

Lexi finished work, had a quick shower at the gym and then set off for London with a change of clothes in her case. As she left the gym, Paul was at the reception.

"Have a nice time Lex," he said.

"Thank you, I intend to," she replied with excitement rippling inside her tummy. "I'm not looking forward to him going back though." She sighed.

"No, I'm sure you're not, but just think, soon you won't ever have to be apart again."

"Yes, I'm looking forward to those days," she said, as she picked up her bag and went on her way.

Once in the car, she tapped in the postcode Conrad had given her, for the one bedroomed flat he had hired for his stay in London. She made her way to it with the trusty guidance of her sat nav. She pulled up outside what appeared to be an old Victorian house and then sent Conrad a message to let him know she was there. Collecting her case and cool box from the car, she walked into the front porch, inside which, there were four small boxes on the wall that contained the keys to the flats. Conrad had sent her the flat number and code number for the box; she put the numbers in and opened it, took out the key and took her baggage into the hallway where she found the door to their flat. The flat was basic but quite pleasant; she had decided to surprise him with the romantic gesture of sprinkling red rose petals over the bed. She also put a bottle of organic wine on the bedside table, with two glasses and a box of chocolates. She got changed, went into the bathroom, touched up her make-up, let her hair down and made it look pretty; she wanted their last evening together to be perfect. She heard her phone go and picked it up. It was Conrad.

"Hey, how's your day going?"

"Yeah, good thanks," he replied. "We're just winding things up now." He gave her directions to the tube station and where to meet. Lexi checked herself in the mirror, opened the bedroom door, looked at the rose petals awaiting their return and smiled to herself. She closed the door, grabbed her bag and left.

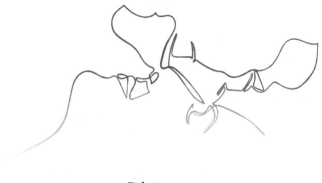

50

They had arranged to meet at Covent Garden to go for a drink and then they would venture on to China Town. As she came up the escalator, she could see Conrad waiting there for her, looking all business-like in his suit. Her heart did a little somersault as her eyes fell upon him; she thought he looked smart and sexy. Equally, as Conrad saw Lexi step off the escalator, his heart skipped a beat. He walked towards her, enveloped her in his arms and kissed her, then they walked arm in arm to a little bar that he knew of. They stayed for a drink and then made their way to Gerrard Street to eat. Walking up and down the busy street of restaurants, they looked at the different menus; finally deciding on one they liked the look of and went inside.

"I'm starving!" He said.

"Mmm, me too, it smells amazing in here," she replied.

"Doesn't it?" He agreed looking around at the other tables and said, "Man, that looks nice, I have a feeling I will be over-ordering!"

They studied the menu and chose a set meal for two that had the duck and pancakes. Lexi asked the waitress if she could have iceberg lettuce leaves instead of the pancakes, yes, that was possible.

"I would never have thought of that!" said Conrad. "It actually sounds quite nice, could I have mine that way as well please?" he asked the waitress. They placed their order and then talked, holding hands over the table as they waited.

"You look amazing!"

"You look rather tasty yourself!" she replied, "You look really 'dapper' in your suit."

He briefly looked down at himself and then replied, "Something I won't be wearing for that much longer!"

"I know, you'll look like a lumberjack instead!" she said, and they laughed.

"I can't wait, I really can't," he said enthusiastically. "I just want to get the ball rolling now, I feel like we're in limbo. I can't wait for it to be just 'us', no long-distance relationship, no having to leave you again. Our offer has been accepted, so it's just a case of winding things up over there now. If I've worked it out right, I might get away with only working for about six weeks. I will obviously have to give notice like anyone else, but I haven't used any of my holidays for this year and I carried over two weeks from the last. It'll be a case of me making an agreement on a finish date, finalising deals and delegating new projects so I don't leave them in a mess. He held her hand tightly, "In one way I can't wait to get back and get things started but in another, I'm not looking forward to leaving you again, I just hate to even think of it, it's making me feel quite anxious," he admitted.

"I know, I can't bear the thought of you going back either, the time has just whizzed by, but it won't be for long, hopefully. We just have to think of the bigger picture now, soon we'll never have to be apart again," she said longingly.

They were both quiet for a moment, contemplating being thousands of miles apart, yet again, uncertain of how long that might be.

At that point the starter turned up, "Ooh, lovely!" Lexi chirped, breaking the slightly solemn moment. They tucked into their starters, which did an excellent job of raising the mood again. Next came the duck, the waitress shredded it at the side of the table, both of them looking on hungrily. The moment of truth came, Conrad had taken his lettuce leaf, put some plum sauce on it, added his duck, onion and cucumber, wrapped it all up and took a big bite. Lexi watched him as he bit into the lettuce, the sauce dripping down his hand.

"Mmm, that's lovely, I really like that, I think I prefer it to the pancakes actually," he said picking up a napkin.

"Good," said Lexi, also taking a big bite; this was her favourite Chinese food.

The food kept coming and they enjoyed every mouthful, feeling quite stuffed by the end and having to leave some. When the waitress came, Lexi asked her to box the leftover food; they paid the bill, picked up the 'doggie bag' and left.

Once outside Conrad said, "I'm so full I think I could do with a little walk."

"Yes, me too, I'm absolutely stuffed!" She agreed, and they walked for about twenty minutes in the general direction of where they needed to go.

As they walked arm-in-arm, they passed a homeless man in a shop doorway.

"Have you got any spare change?" Asked the man.

"No but I can give you some dinner," was Lexi's reply as she handed over the bag with the box of food in it.

Conrad smiled, "That was sweet."

"Well, I'm happy to give him food, it's not like we need it!" she said, and they carried on their way. Sometime later, they decided to look around for a tube station as it had started to rain. Conrad looked around as Lexi got out her phone.

"It's okay, I'll find it on here," she said, but at that point Conrad spotted a black cab approaching them and stuck out his hand.

"Don't worry we'll jump in here," he said as the cab pulled over for them. Conrad gave the address and the cab set off on its way.

It was most welcome to get into the dry and warmth of the cab; they snuggled up in the back. Conrad put his arm around Lexi and hugged her into him, smelling her hair and the subtle perfume of essential oils. As he inhaled her scent, he could feel his desire rising up inside, he kissed her cheek; she tenderly returned the kiss to his cheek. They looked at each other, he took hold of her face and kissed her deeply, the journey home couldn't go quickly enough now. Lexi was wearing a smart mid-thigh length jersey dress with hold-up stockings and knee-high boots. Conrad ran his hand up from where it had been placed on her knee, up her leg under her dress. As he felt her lacy stocking tops, the mere thought of what she would look like when the dress came off, filled him with desire as he touched the naked flesh above her stocking. The two of them lost in each other as if rest of the world didn't exist; that was until Conrad 'clocked' the cabbie looking at them in his rear-view-mirror! He took his hand out from under her dress and remained with his arm around her kissing her until they reached their address.

"Cheers, mate!" said Conrad, handing the cabbie a ten-pound note, "Keep the change."

"Thanks," replied the cabbie, giving them a knowing look as they exited the cab. Still raining, Conrad guided

Lexi briskly with his hand in the small of her back, to the front door. They went through the porch and into the unlit hallway; Lexi fumbled for the key as Conrad embraced her again, kissing her deeply, crazy with desire, they kissed passionately, Conrad's hand going straight up her dress to where he had left off in the cab. He was hungry for her. He felt the top of her stocking and the bare flesh above, he pulled her knickers to one-side and penetrated her with his finger, as he did so she let out a small gasp.

"Let's get inside," she panted.

Fumbling again with the key, eventually, she found the keyhole and they we're inside. The door closed behind them as he passionately caressed her, desperate for her. Kissing her deeply, his hands then traced down to the hem of her dress. Taking hold of it, he pulled it up over her head and let it drop to the floor; there she stood in her stockings, knickers and knee-high boots.

With sheer desire he said, "Oh, fuck, I really want you right now!" as he led her to the breakfast table that separated the kitchenette from the lounge.

He sat her on it, kissed her and then said," Lay back."

As she did, he started to take her knickers down; although the room was unlit, the curtains were open letting in the streetlight.

"You're really doing it for me!" he growled.

Lexi felt hugely turned on by this, the romantic surprise she had organised for their return would have to wait; she was enjoying the spontaneity of the moment.

On the table, naked apart from her stockings and boots she said, "Take your shirt off."

He obliged as he took in every inch of her erotic image, lying back, naked on the table. He clumsily unbuttoned his shirt and threw it on the floor behind him, his animal instinct roaring up inside. Lexi sat up wanting to touch him as he dropped his shirt, just to have him gently push her back, open her legs and kiss her clitoris setting her senses on fire. In no time at all, those beautiful nerve endings had her dancing inside, crying out his name and becoming too sensitive for him to touch her. Shaking with the passion rising inside of him, Conrad undid his trousers and let them and his boxer's fall to the floor. He pulled her to the edge of the table and entered her hard, both crying out as he penetrated her, relishing the ultimate connection they so desired from each other.

After a couple of moments, he took hold of her hips pulling her a little more towards him saying, "Oh babe, you're gonna have to come this way a little, I'm hitting my nuts on the table!"

Shifting herself forward they resumed, it was less of an emotional, spiritual encounter and more of a 'frantic fuck', the moment entirely consuming them, hungry for each other.

"Oh, God, this isn't going to last long," he said as he could feel his orgasm approaching fast and had absolutely no desire to stop it. He pushed into her harder and harder, then let out an almighty, "Oh, Jesus!" as he came.

He put his hands under her back and sat her up. He kissed her lips and wrapped his arms around her, holding her tightly, both panting heavily and neither of them saying anything for a few moments. As their heartbeats began to calm, Lexi said, "Well that wasn't quite what I had planned for our return but most enjoyable all the same!"

"Why, what did you have planned for our return?" he asked.

"Ah, you'll see." He looked at her quizzically as she slipped off the edge of the table, both of them standing naked in the street lit room.

"I think it might be an idea to close the drapes!" he said.

"I think it's a bit late for that isn't it!" she laughed.

Conrad went over to the window and drew the curtains. As he walked back over to her, she took him by the hand and led him to the bedroom. She went to the window, drew the curtains and turned to him as he put the light on.

"Aw! Oh babe, that's lovely! I kind of ruined that one then, didn't I?" he said as he took in the sight of the red rose petals scattered everywhere.

"Hardly!" she replied, "I don't think I've ever been on the receiving end of such unbridled passion! It was just as it should've been in that moment, I can honestly say I've never spent a moment with you that I would've wished to be any other way than it was."

He took her by the hand, "Come here."

He lay on the bed and pulled her down beside him. "This is lovely, perfect, like you, just perfect." They lay cuddling for a while. "Is that an organic Shiraz I see?" he asked,

To which she replied, "It most certainly is!"

He loved her effort, "What a perfect way to spend our last evening."

As she pointed out, "Choccies too!"

"Like we need them after all we've just eaten, but hey!" he winked at her, "It'd be rude not to, wouldn't it?" He got up and opened the wine, poured it and opened the chocolates. As they sipped their wine they talked and cuddled, fed each other chocolates, cuddled some more and made love again in amongst the rose petals. Some-time later Conrad looked at his watch.

"What's the time?" Lexi asked.

"Twenty-to-one," he sighed, "I really don't want tonight to end, I don't want to leave you again, I really can't bear the thought of it."

She hugged him tight, "I know, I can't bear the thought of it either."

"It's going to be horrible going back to my apartment and being there on my own knowing you're so far away." She propped herself up on her elbow looking at him and ran her finger gently under his eye tracing a small line.

"What are your lost loves?" she asked.

"Excuse me?" he asked not knowing what she meant.

"Your lost loves, these lines here", she traced it with her finger again, "indicate lost loves…. It doesn't have to mean 'l-o-v-e-r-s' necessarily but things you used to love or loved to do. What did you used to love doing that you no longer do?"

He searched inside himself for a few moments and then said. "I used to play the guitar; my dad got me it, he used to play as well. I played a lot as a teenager, then it just stood in the corner of the room, I don't know why I stopped really, I just got out of the habit," he pondered.

"Do you still have the guitar?"

"I'm not sure, I don't ever remember getting rid of it, but I don't remember seeing it since I moved into the apartment either. I can't think that I would've gotten rid of it though cos dad got it for me," he said searching his memory.

"Why don't you search your storage space and see if it's there and if it's not, get yourself another one and start to play again? You'll probably really enjoy it, you'll be able to lose yourself in it and the time will pass more quickly," Lexi said positively.

"Yeah, I'll have a look when I get back," he said as she lay in the crook of his arm. They talked into the small hours, held each other and then fell asleep.

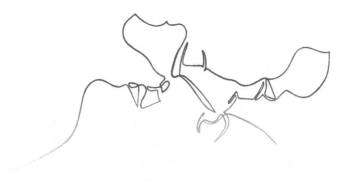

51

They woke about eight. "Morning beautiful," he said, as he looked at her.

"Good morning handsome," she replied, "God, my mouth's dry!"

"Yeah, me too, I'll get us something to drink."

He jumped out of bed and went into the kitchenette, where there stood two large bottles of water that Lexi had bought with her. He went over to the kettle and filled it, then poured two glasses of water and took them into the bedroom. Lexi thanked him as she took the glass and drank thirstily.

"God, I needed that!" she exclaimed.

"Yeah, red wine does leave you a bit dry doesn't it! I've put the kettle on, do you want a coffee?"

"Ooh, yes please." He went back out of the bedroom to the kitchenette where he rummaged in Lexi's bag for the coffee and made a pot. As she listened to him 'chinking' mugs and getting the coffee ready, she shouted cheekily from the bedroom, "I could get used to this!"

Conrad smiled at this replying, "You will be soon, I'll be able to bring you coffee in bed every morning."

She lay back on the pillow visualising it, she couldn't wait. Conrad poured the coffee, his heart sinking as the thought crossed his mind that he would be at the airport in just under four hours. Taking the coffee into the bedroom, Lexi sat up and took hers from him and he sat on the bed.

"Thank-you." She took a sip.

"God, I'm dreading, going back, I have to be at the airport soon," he said solemnly.

"I know, it's going to be hard. I feel so complete when I'm with you." She said as he leant forward and kissed her.

"That's exactly how I feel… When I'm not with you, I feel like a part of me is missing."

Lexi could feel herself getting sad inside, but in her usual, positive way she said, "But just think, the sooner you get back and give your notice, the sooner we can be together for keeps." They put their coffee down and cuddled, staying in bed until they had just enough time to get showered, dressed and breakfasted, before Conrad's car arrived to take him to the airport.

As they sat and had their breakfast the mood got quieter, both of them feeling a bit emotional at the thought of having to part, neither of them saying anything because they knew if they did, they would cry. She looked at him, he looked at her.

"Not long to go now," he said looking at his watch.

Lexi felt her stomach drop and her chest sink, the thought of saying goodbye and going back home without him made her feel downhearted. It was as if, when their two energies were combined their cells 'flourished' but at the very thought of his energy leaving hers, her frequency was already faltering.

"Have you checked you have everything, checked all the drawers, got your passport and everything?" she asked, trying to sound positive.

"Yeah, everything's packed, it's just us now, for ten more minutes."

They faced each other and held hands, "I love you, "he said.

"I love you too, more than you could ever know," she said from the bottom of her heart.

"Oh baby, I do know, trust me. Fuck, I don't want to be without you."

The tears started to roll down Lexi's face and Conrad's tears were soon to follow. He pulled her into him and held her tight; he kissed her head and enveloped her in his arms. She immersed herself in that 'perfect fit', being so mindful of how he felt and making the most of every second, feeling his touch and breathing him in. All of a sudden, a thought occurred to her.

"Can I have one of your worn T shirts out of your case please?"

They went to the packed cases, and both exchanged a worn item of clothing, so they would have something to cuddle up to in bed. At that point his mobile phone rang; it was the car company; his airport car was outside. Both of them felt their hearts drop; he put his phone back in his pocket and held her, the tears starting again as they kissed tenderly.

"Oh God, this is awful!" he said. Lexi's jaw just quivered; she couldn't get any words out. They held each other then kissed, it was time to go. He picked up his case, they went to the door and she walked with him out to the car. The driver got out, took Conrad's case and put it in the boot.

Conrad turned to Lexi, "I love you." He kissed her.

"I love you too," she said tearfully.

"Message me to let me know you get home ok, I'll probably still be in the airport, just," he said sadly.

"Ok, and you message me when you land,"

"I will," he promised.

One last heart wrenching embrace and then he got in the car, he looked at her from the back window as the car pulled away. Lexi stood at the side of the road, tears rolling down her face, as the car disappeared out of sight. She walked back inside, sat back down at the breakfast table, put her head in her hands and had a little cry. Once she'd got it out of her system, she gathered herself and cleaned away the kitchen things. She packed her stuff, loaded the car and had one last check around the flat to make sure they hadn't left anything, then came out and closed the door. She deposited the key back in the little box on the wall, got in her car; set up the sat nav and set off.

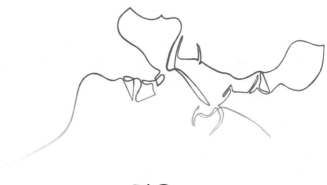

52

The journey home passed in a haze; Lexi's mind full of everything 'Conrad'. She felt sad that he was, yet again, going to be virtually on the other side of the world from her. Her insecurities started setting in, not that he'd change his mind, but that something might go wrong; her destiny and future happiness was now in the hands of the Gods. After she'd spent a good portion of her journey thinking of all the worst possible scenarios, she decided to stop for a toilet break. She pulled into the services and had a well-earned break from all her over-thinking.

"Why am I thinking like this? She asked herself. "Why am I putting all this negativity out there when my life is potentially about to become something, I could only have dreamed of a couple of months ago?" As she washed her hands, she looked at herself in the mirror; the basin area was buzzing with other people also taking a break from their journeys.

She looked into her eyes and said mentally to herself, "Stop torturing yourself and trust the process, this is your turn to be happy, you deserve this, embrace it and welcome it." She smiled a small smile to herself as her insecurities now started to fall away, she threw her handbag over her shoulder and returned to her car, now, a far more positive version of herself.

The rest of the journey went well, and she made it home in good time. As soon as she pulled up on the drive, she got out her phone and rang Conrad in the hope he would still be able to answer his phone, though she was cutting it a bit fine, he'd be about to board any time now.

"Hi hun, I've just arrived home," she confirmed. He was pleased to hear her voice again before he flew.

"Hey baby, you've made good time."

"Yes, the roads were good," she said, adding, "I miss you already."

"Me too, I'm sitting here feeling like one side of me is missing."

"Yes, me too, but we have think positively and console ourselves that it's only for a short time, let's just think ahead to all the good things that are in store for us. We will have the rest of our lives together soon," she said, projecting her thoughts forward.

"Yeah, I know, that's what I do keep thinking every time I start to feel low, it's like this is the last 'hoop' to jump through."

At that point she could hear Conrad's flight boarding being announced. "I have to go now babe," he said, standing up and picking up his hand luggage, the phone still to his ear.

"Let me know when you get your end, no matter what time it is." She asked.

"Of course, I will, love you babe."

"I love you too," she said. With that he closed down and went to board his plane, slightly more relaxed and happier for hearing her voice.

As soon as Conrad touched down, he sent Lexi a message. Tired from his journey and the stress of separation, he abandoned his case just inside the entrance to his bedroom and fell on the bed. He woke up five hours later, still on top of the bed, fully clothed and not knowing where he was or what time zone he was in. As he came to, so came a surge of purpose and energy. All of a sudden it was 'all systems go', his head in a whirl with what he had to do to get the ball rolling; he wanted to be back in England with Lexi as quickly as possible. He contacted the real estate office to come and value his apartment and made an appointment for the Saturday morning. He had the rest of that day off to adjust back into his time zone, but not wanting to wait until Monday, he called the CEO and asked for a meeting with him. He went to the office and told him of his plans. It hadn't crossed his mind how the news would be received. He'd worked for the company for so many years, of course he would be a great loss to them, but as sad as the CEO was to see him go, he was equally delighted for him. He could see in Conrad's face that he was different; he was happy and almost glowing. Having known him from when he was a university leaver and knowing him very well personally, this was something he'd never witnessed in Conrad before. He could tell this was the 'real deal' and agreed that they would make it as painless for Conrad as possible. Feeling, positive and on top of the world, he got back to his apartment feeling he'd moved mountains in just a couple of hours and couldn't wait to tell Lexi all about it.

It was mid-afternoon, he sent Lexi a message, "Are you still up?"

Lexi was upstairs brushing her teeth before bed when she just about heard her phone vibrate on the kitchen worktop; she went downstairs to see if it was Conrad.

"Yes, I'm up," she replied.

"I know it's late but fancy a quick Skype?"

She was hardly going to say no, was she? She quickly went to her computer and booted it up, then sat there looking every-bit-gorgeous in her Amber tinted glasses that she wore at night to protect her from the 'blue light 'of the screen raising her cortisol levels. He told her excitedly of his achievements of the last three hours, both of them feeling waves of excitement that 'this was really happening'! They talked excitedly for twenty minutes and then Lexi went to her bed a very happy girl. She lay there feeling grateful for the happiness she was being afforded.

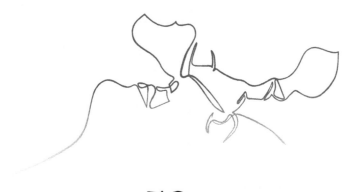

53

On the Saturday morning as planned, the real estate person arrived at Conrad's apartment; viewed and valued it and the details were on the Internet by the afternoon. Conrad felt good, both he and the estate agent knew that such a sought-after prime location wouldn't be on the market for very long and sure enough by the Saturday evening there were two potential buyers booked to view it for the following afternoon.

On the Saturday evening however, he was feeling lonely; he'd eaten and cleared up, he'd looked on the television, but nothing took his fancy. He sighed as he walked around his apartment, it had always been his pride and joy, spacious, superbly finished with every mod-con and an amazing skyline view of the city; now, it was just lonely walls. He felt like he wanted to wave a magic wand and fast-forward to his life in England. He kept casting his mind to the awesome stone house that was hopefully to become their home, he had a warm feeling at the very thought of it. He could picture himself and Lexi there and imagined them making their new life together. He could almost feel it. God, how was he going to get through the next few weeks? At that moment a thought occurred to him.

"Guitar!" he said out loud, where would it be? He knew he wouldn't have parted with it. He went into the storage space of one of his spare rooms where most of his unused clobber lived and started looking. Sure enough, up on the top shelf of the massive built-in wardrobe, lay the guitar; he reached up and got it down.

"Yay, buddy, long time!" he said to it as he sat on the spare bed and strummed the strings, "A bit of tuning and you'll be fine."

He started to tune the strings, one of them 'twanged' noisily as it snapped. He got up and took the guitar in the kitchen, got a cloth and fished about in one of the cupboards, pulling out some cleaning wax, deciding to give it a bit of tender loving care. He started polishing off and livening up the dusty wood; spending the rest of the evening working on it, bringing the beautiful wood back to its original glory and before he knew it, the hours had passed. Still tired from his journey, he decided to go to bed and get up early to find a music shop and buy a new set of strings; he set the guitar down and lovingly stroked the wood, pleased with his work. Just then he had a thought, he got his phone and took a photo of it, he sent it to Lexi with a message saying, "Look what I've found!"

Lexi was slow to get up on Sunday morning; she had slept very heavily. She looked at the clock; it was 9.10. "Blimey!" she said to herself, it was very unusual for her to sleep in that late, she considered she must have needed it. She sat up and drank her glass of water, went to the bathroom then made her way downstairs. She put the kettle on and ground some coffee; waiting for the kettle to boil, she checked her phone.

"Aw, bless!" she said as she opened the picture of his guitar. With a happy heart she went over to her ipod and put on some music, made her coffee and took her time reflecting on everything that was happening in her life while she drank it.

The day passed uneventfully, she did some housework and food shopping and had a video call with Conrad in the evening. He had now re-strung his guitar and was waiting for the strings to settle; he showed her his handy-work, very pleased with his achievements. He told Lexi of the pending appointments for the afternoon and by this time there was now also a third viewer booked in.

"I've got a good feeling about today," he said confidently.

"As long as you're absolutely sure you want to sell it," replied Lexi.

"I already told you, I've never been so sure of anything in my life," he said with conviction. She knew that really, she just needed to hear it again.

By the end of Conrad's day, two of the viewers had made an offer; one of them had made their offer there and then while he was at the apartment. This young man was also a bachelor, a highflyer type; Conrad could see his former self in this man. He accepted his offer, feeling the apartment suited him; it was as if the apartment was going full-circle and he was handing over the baton to another 'young gun'. Nothing was going to stop him now, the pieces of the puzzle were falling into place nicely, indeed, this was all getting very exciting. Knowing Lexi would be asleep; he sent her a message to let her know for when she got up the next morning.

On the Monday morning Lexi woke up to her alarm, she didn't usually work on a Monday but had agreed to cover two classes for someone at the gym. She got out of bed and went downstairs to make her habitual coffee and checked her phone while the kettle boiled. She felt a wave of excitement at reading Conrad's message; she had never dared to think it would be that easy. She left him a message knowing that he would be asleep, letting him know what time she would be home so that they could have a much-needed call later in the day. She took her class in the morning then had two hours before the next one. She went into town for a while and then texted Paul to see if he was free for a cuppa.

"Always free for you Blondie!" came his reply and they met up back at the gym for a catch up before her second class. She told him of the developments excitedly.

"Wow, it's all happening then! That's great, it proves it was meant to be, if it wasn't meant to be it wouldn't all be going so smoothly," he affirmed. "So, do you have any idea of when he'll be over then?"

"No, I don't know how long it'll take to tie all the loose ends up out there. As soon as I get a firm date, I'll be giving my notice here," she beamed. He looked at her bright, happy expression; he was really pleased for her.

"God, you must be so excited! You are literally going to start a whole new life!" he said, excited for her as she chirped,

"You're not wrong, I can barely contain myself!!"

"What does Nathan say?" he asked.

"Ah, there's the thing," she said, "he doesn't know yet, neither do the kids but I'm sure it'll be fine. It's not like I'll be going back on my word and insisting on selling the house, we'll work things out. As far as Corrie and Eddie are concerned, the house will still be their 'family' home, at least for the foreseeable future and I fully intend continuing to visit when the kids come home. Maybe things will change when Corrie moves out and makes a life with her boyfriend but until then it will remain as it is. It was never going to be without some kind of change, the most important thing was that the kids didn't suffer as a result of it." They finished their drinks then Lexi took her last class and headed off home.

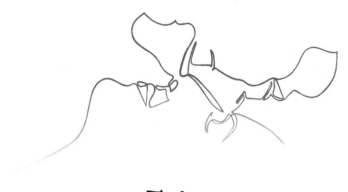

54

As she sat at the dinner table, she heard the front door go and Nathan came in.

"Hiya!" he said as he dropped his bags in the hallway and walked through to the lounge.

"Hi, how's things, how's Janet doing?" she asked.

"Yeah, she's getting there, thanks," he replied as he came through the lounge to the dining room. "The drips came out today, she's still being sick but not quite as bad now. There's a possibility she'll be coming out tomorrow or the day after if she carries on like this, they just want to make sure she doesn't get dehydrated again but it's much better than it was thank goodness."

"Good, that's good news," Lexi said, quite relieved to hear Nathan with something positive to report.

"Well, yes and no...." he continued, "Obviously, she won't be going back to work yet, at least not until the sickness gets to a manageable level and we're nowhere near there yet. Because her situation is fragile and this project has only just gone live, they've had to appoint someone to take on her role. The problem with that is they're in the

London office, which means I now have something like fifteen meetings in London over the next four weeks and only one up North, It's just what I don't need right now.'"'" Nathan said looking glum.

Lexi sat back from her meal and thought for a moment, he wasn't exactly having a lot of luck. She then said, "I never thought I'd hear myself say this but why don't you ask her if she wants to come here, at least that way you'll see her every evening and if anything's amiss, you're close by to help."

Nathan was quite taken back by this. "Blimey, that, I wasn't expecting! Are you sure?" he asked in disbelief. At this point Lexi thought it as good time as any to tell Nathan of her news.

"Nathan, I have something to tell you, well, quite a lot really and I hope you will be happy for me." Lexi explained about her weekend with Conrad, the house and everything that had happened since. He pulled out a chair and sat next to her.

"Wow! I'm really pleased for you, what an opportunity, this is what you've always dreamed of. Of course, I'm happy for you! I told you before, to see you come out happy after all of this is really important to me. I honestly, hope this works out for you... I'm just still gob-smacked you've suggested for Janet to come here!" He realised she'd probably said it to soften the blow of her news but appreciated it all the same.

"Look, I can't say we'll be bosom buddies but I'm moving on and I bear no grudge. The two of you are also trying to make a go of this in less-than-ideal circumstances and I want it to work for you. It isn't going to be easy, if she comes out of hospital to be on her own and you're only able to get up there for a day at the weekend having spent most of your time there the last couple of weeks; it's going to put more pressure on you both straight away. I will be fine with it, but you will have to run it past the kids, especially Corrie," she added.

"Have you told them you're moving yet?" he asked.

"No, it's all happened so quickly," she said in all honesty, "and Conrad only sold his apartment this morning."

Nathan sat and thought it through for a moment.

"Right, as long as you're sure you're ok with Janet coming here, maybe we could arrange a call with the kids and just explain everything to them," he suggested.

"It's going to be a bit of a double whammy, isn't it?" she said feeling a little concerned, "I'm just thinking of how fragile Corrie still is with it all."

"What else would you suggest? There really is no easier way of doing it that I can see," he reasoned. "I mean, not wanting to bulldoze in now I've been given the go ahead but, if Janet comes out of hospital tomorrow or the day after, it'd be nice if I could go up Friday straight from London and bring her back. I can't see any way of us doing it face-to-face with the kids before then, can you?"

Lexi pondered, "It's just the thought of them sitting in front of their computers and being 'hit' with it from both sides that's worrying me, they've had a lot to process lately. God, I don't know, this is a bit difficult isn't it." Her words tailed off as she tried to think the situation through.

"Okay then. Why don't you call Corrie and tell her your news first. At the end of the day, she knew you'd move on with your life some time and quite honestly, where you're going sounds totally amazing and the sort of place she'd love. I honestly think once she gets over the fact that you'll be three hours away, she'll be ok and let's face it, she's further than that from us right now and has been for nearly a year; when you put it like that, it's just logistics isn't it?" Said Nathan with his 'practical' head on, though Lexi was still unsure.

Knowing how sensitive Corrie was, she muttered, "Mmm, we are talking about Corrie here!"

"Hey! If she'd been here all the time and this was happening, I could understand her being upset but she's only been home every six weeks or so since she's been there. In fact, she's closer to where you're moving to than here, chances are, by the time she finishes uni, she'll have been to stay with you numerous times and it won't be an issue. I'm sure she'll quickly come around to the idea," he said convincingly, closely followed by a far less confident, "Not sure how she'll feel about Janet being here though!"

"Mmm, good luck with that one!" Lexi said, kind of jokingly but knowing that somehow, she felt that Corrie wasn't going to make this easy for him. After much thought Lexi decided she'd call both kids to give them her news and leave Nathan to give his separately, somehow, she felt it would just be kinder to them that way and equally, she didn't really want to be there when the shit hit the fan with Corrie over Janet!

Lexi called Corrie the following evening. Explaining how the whole thing had come about, she told her all about the picturesque area, the house and surrounding land and of their plans for the whole holistic experience. To her absolute surprise Corrie took it surprisingly well. Lexi gave Corrie the details of the property, to look at it and see for herself then explained, how much easier it would be for her to visit from uni, what a lovely place it would be for her to unwind on her breaks and how both Corrie and Eddie would always be welcome, this left Corrie quite excited and accepting of the situation.

The next task was to call Eddie. Again, she told him how it had all come about and gave him the details of the place. Eddie took in the amazing house with its stunning views on his tablet while he talked to his mother on the laptop.

"Yes, I can imagine you here!" he said," It's everything you've ever described when you've talked of your dream. I can see why you've fallen in love with it." Cheekily adding, "So which room is my room then?"

Lexi laughed, "Oh, don't you worry, we have lots of rooms, I will set one up especially for when you come to stay, obviously, the two of you are always, always welcome."

They chatted about what was going to happen and hopefully when it was going to happen. Lexi carefully stayed off the subject of dad and Janet; that was his news to tell. She felt relieved that this had been received so well by her children and finished her evening at peace with herself, knowing that she hadn't caused either of them any further upset. She just hoped now that Nathan would give them a couple of days before he hit them with his news. They might be fine with it, only time would tell.

In the meantime, Nathan had talked to Janet of his wife's unexpected offer, should she come out of hospital later in the week. Janet, though very appreciative of the gesture, declined for fear that it would create bad feeling with the children and that she wouldn't really be accepted or wanted there. For this reason, he saw little point in broaching it with the kids, so this now left Nathan with the task of overseeing his massive business venture as well as going up north at weekends to spend time with his sickly, pregnant girlfriend.

"I can't believe she's said no, it'd make things so much easier if she came here," Nathan said despondently.

"Yes, I know it would, but I can see it from her side as well, "said Lexi. "Even though it was me that suggested it, I can imagine it would feel like she was entering the lion's den, coming into what is our family home. Of course, she's going to have reservations; maybe once she's been at home for a couple of weeks by herself, she might change her mind? Or, maybe she'll be happier once I've gone? Just go with the flow for now, don't put her under any pressure but make her aware that the offer is still there. She might come around if she can see the travelling is doing you in, see how it plays out," she said trying to keep Nathan positive.

"Mmm, it's a case of having to really, isn't it? When do you think you'll be on the move then?" he asked.

"Well, I'm not sure. The sellers have already bought another property apparently and are in the process of moving as they run a business from there."

"Blimey! They must have some dosh!" he said with surprise.

Lexi continued, "Mmm, apparently they've bought a bankrupt farm, so they now have masses of land, not sure what it is they do though."

"Well, yours doesn't look exactly small!" he observed.

"I suppose it's whatever you want, I'm not complaining," she beamed, "this is my dream come true." Of course, it was! He could see it literally radiating out of her.

"I know, you've always dreamed of something like this haven't you? I'm really made up for you," she could tell he truly meant it. "Thank you, that means a lot."

"I suppose I'm going to have to make a decision as to where Janet and I are going to live. I can't see the kids being very impressed with me going all the way up there, it will create too much of a divide." The thought worried him, but Lexi was more positive.

"I have a feeling she'll come around; I honestly do. She's in 'protection' mode right now; she's frightened of what she might be letting herself in for. Incidentally, while I think of it, would you have a problem with Conrad staying here should he end up in the UK before the sale goes through?" she quickly put in.

"No, not at all," he replied.

"Great, thank you, we don't have a game plan yet. It's all going ahead and that's as much as I know. It would just be nice to make it as stress free as possible… and I mean that from both sides, I just want us to all get along and move forwards from this. You have told her that haven't you?" she asked.

"Yes, I have but I think she's a bit insecure," he explained, "she still thinks the blame will sit with her, from both yours and the kid's point of view."

"It took both of you to make it happen Nathan, not just her," she said, Nathan appreciated that.

"Yes, I know, I think she's just worried how she would truly be received, both by you and Corrie."

"Well, she's going to have to leap that fence one day if the two of you are going to be together. There will come a point where the two families will overlap for whatever reason, Corrie's graduation, one of the kid's weddings or whatever," Lexi reasoned.

"Yeah, I know." Said Nathan as she added, "And she really doesn't have to worry about me, I would never have invited her into my home just to make her feel uncomfortable, that's not who I am."

"I know that, we'll see what happens," he said.

"We shall indeed, it'll all be fine, you'll see, everything will fall into place eventually," she said positively.

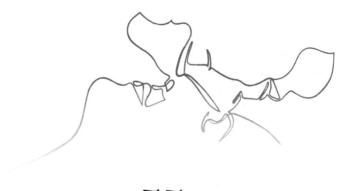

55

The next two weeks passed with Lexi in regular calls to Conrad; everything was going ahead without a hitch. They were both dying to get back together again but also very excited and happy as they plodded forwards through the diary day-by-day, ticking the days off in celebration. Conrad was now exhibiting quite a talent with his guitar playing. Ever since he had restored it, he had played it every evening and had fallen back in love with how relaxed it made him feel to sit and jam for the evening. Lexi had been absolutely right; he would sit down to play and before he knew it a couple of hours would have passed; it had been a most welcome distraction for him. He sat and played to her over their call.

"Wow! That's brilliant! Have you had any refresher sessions?" she asked.

"No, just from memory," he said, strumming away gently.

Lexi was really impressed, "Wow, you play really nicely, it's hard to believe you haven't played in years." He smiled at this, "Well, I have spent a good, few hours strumming away here over the last couple of weeks, I've had plenty of time to become reacquainted with it thanks to you, it was a good call!" Which made Lexi quite pleased for suggesting it.

Conrad had just over three weeks to go in his job, with two final trips away. He was now finishing deals, handing over big projects and delegating the things he wouldn't be there to see through to fruition. His financial advisor had overseen the sale of his company shares and now it was just a case of waiting for the legalities of the apartment sale to finalise. This was all going to plan and due to exchange within the next couple of weeks. With everything ticking along nicely and a guaranteed sum of money to be in the bank within a month, he suggested that Lexi give in her notice at work so she would be free when he finally arrived in the country.

With a month's notice to work, Lexi drifted from day-to-day and week-to-week in a blissful haze of getting up happy every morning, knowing that she was another day closer to being with the man who had stolen her heart and living her dream with him. She excitedly told her work friends and clients why she was leaving and where she was going, proudly showing them the photos of herself and Conrad on her phone. She was on top of the world, her days passed happily and the two of them talked at every given opportunity.

Nathan was backwards and forwards between home, London and up North like a 'fiddler's elbow' as three more weeks passed. Janet was doing well, though still being sick daily, so she still hadn't yet returned to work. The travelling was really starting to get to Nathan, so he dared to bring the subject back up of Janet moving down to be with him. Expecting her to respond in the same way, she surprised him by not needing much persuasion at all. Having been at home alone now, only seeing Nathan at weekends, seeing how tired and stressed he was despite his attempts to cover it up, she realised that she would be far better off facing her fears and moving to be with him. She would see him every day, he would be far less stressed, and they could get to know each other properly and build a good relationship before their baby was to arrive.

Now that she had agreed to come, Nathan had the task of telling his kids. This was made easier by Lexi, who on her weekly calls had informed them both it had been her suggestion because of how negatively the situation was affecting their father. At the end of the day, the children loved their parents, neither of them liked what had happened to their family but equally, both knew that no matter how much they protested, things would never go back to being as they once were.

Corrie had matured a great deal over the last couple of months. Many of her friends were the produce of 'broken' relationships. Equally, many of her friends expressed their emotional trauma at how their parents were constantly at each other's throats and that they were always caught up in the middle of their parents, anger, jealousy and power struggles. Corrie felt grateful that she was being spared all this; not once had her parents argued in front of her, nor had she been made to feel she had to take anyone's side. She felt, as sad as it was, she was being spared from all of this drama and anxiety which seemed to be the norm for a handful of her friends. As far as the baby was concerned, her mother's words kept ringing through her head, "All children deserved to feel loved and wanted and this child is no exception." Though she did secretly hope it would be a boy, she had always been 'daddy's princess' and wanted to remain that way!

56

The following Saturday, Nathan bought Janet to the house. He had a full diary for that week, ending back up north, so the plan was that if she wasn't happy, he could take her back then if she so desired. It was getting on for lunchtime and Lexi was in the kitchen fixing some lunch for when they arrived. She was happily singing away as she chopped and prepared an extensive salad to go with some lovely wild caught salmon fillets she was marinating in fresh herbs and oil in the fridge. She was so absorbed in her culinary mission; she didn't hear the front door open. Nathan appeared at the kitchen door with Janet almost 'sheepishly' tucked behind him.

"Hi!" he said.

"Oh! I didn't hear you come in!" she said as she went and turned the music down, returning to offer her hand to Janet to shake.

"Hi," Janet said, as Nathan announced,

"This is my wife, Lexi, Lexi, this is Janet."

"Hello there," Lexi said, shaking Janet's hand. Although Janet had been assured that this truly was going to be okay, she'd still felt anxious upon entering the house but with first impressions of Lexi smiling and shaking her hand, her anxiety quickly began to subside.

"Hi, it's nice to meet you, I really appreciate you welcoming me into your home," said Janet.

"Well, I thought it made sense really, poor Nathan has been shattered! How was your journey?" she said trying to put Janet at ease.

"Yes, good, thanks," she replied as Nathan added, "Only one sick stop!"

"Oh dear, that all still happening then?" Lexi replied.

"Nothing like as bad as it was but yes, still two or three times a day; we didn't even make it to a lay-by, he had to pull up and I was sick as the side of the road!" Janet added.

"Ooo, classy!" Lexi joked, making Janet feel more relaxed by the moment. "I'll put the kettle on, I'm sure you'd welcome a cuppa and a chance to get yourself together before lunch."

Lexi made some drinks and they sat at the kitchen table and broke the ice together. Maybe Lexi would have been different toward Janet, had she not been in the wonderful place she was now, who knows? But for Janet, this was so much easier than she'd ever imagined it would have been, Lexi was very easy to talk to, both working with the public and one-to-one clients, it was in her nature to be very approachable. They finished their cuppa and then Nathan took Janet upstairs with her case while Lexi put the lunch together.

They sat over lunch, Lexi told Janet about Conrad and where they were going, adding, "So, in a couple of weeks' time there will be all four of us here for a short while! That should get the neighbours talking!" she joked.

"I bet you can't wait!" said Janet.

"You could say that! I'm so excited, I just want him to be here."

"I'm sure you do," said Janet. She looked at Nathan and he smiled at her as if to say, "You see, I told you it would be ok."

The lunch was pleasant and after clearing away, Lexi went into town for the afternoon leaving Nathan and Janet to it; she felt it would be a good idea to give them a bit of space.

The weekend passed uneventfully, and Nathan went off to work on the Monday morning. Although Lexi didn't usually work on Mondays, she had clients booked in for the afternoon. She needed to fit everyone in, give them programmes and day-to day advice; she also needed to 'suit' her clients to other professionals before she was to leave. Having built such a personal rapport with her clients, she cared about them a great deal; it was important to her to not leave any of them high and dry. She was pleasantly surprised that quite a few of them had expressed a desire to come and stay at her retreat once it was up and running, this meant the world to her.

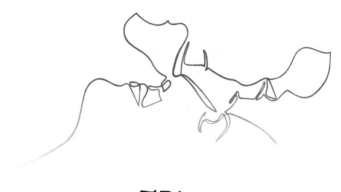

57

The week passed and Lexi was 'buzzing' with excitement; every day for her was a good day, her goal getting ever closer. On the Friday, Nathan was up and out of the house by 6.30am. Lexi hadn't set her alarm; her class wasn't until 11.30. So far, her week had been jam-packed, she had been on a roll organising her busy clientele but by Thursday night she was shattered and quite relieved to have a slow start in the morning. She awoke to the sound of Janet throwing up in the bathroom, not the most pleasant way to start the day! She lay there for a few minutes listening to the sound of Janet 'barfing' into the loo, thinking it would soon stop and she could nod back off, but the retching went on for some considerable time. In the end she decided to get up and put the kettle on.

As she passed the bathroom she called, "Are you alright in there?"

A muffled voice came back from the bathroom, "I'll be ok in a minute, thanks."

Lexi went downstairs thinking to herself how horrible it must be to be that sick, she'd never had any sickness with either of her pregnancies, it all sounded so violent, like it was coming up from her boots! And to think this had been going on from the very start, she felt quite sorry for her. She put the kettle on, ground some coffee and then searched the fridge and got out some ingredients. She made a hot drink using fresh ginger and a slice of lemon for Janet in the hope of settling her stomach. Lexi sat at the table going through some pages on her laptop from an auction that was to take place the next day not far from her. She thought this might be an opportunity to pick up some bits for the house. She also felt she should start keeping an eye out for potential furniture for either the house or the accommodation. She had a 'look' in mind; she felt a rustic, bohemian look would suit the place well, with colourful throws, old wooden furniture and dressers for the many nick-knacks, shells and crystals she liked to display. She loved natural things and had an amazing collection of crystals and fossils. As she sat there Janet came into the kitchen.

"Are you ok? That sounded quite unpleasant. I've made you a ginger drink, though I'm not sure if you'll even get it down you but I thought if you can, it might settle you," she said gesturing towards a hot drink on the worktop.

"Oh, thank you, that's very kind," Janet said, picking it up and carefully sniffing it to make sure it didn't make her retch.

"Not a problem, you really sounded like you were struggling up there," Lexi said, still scrolling through the auction pages.

"Yes, it's not the best feeling in the world I have to admit, but having said that, I'm nowhere near as bad as I was."

"It can't be nice," Lexi said, empathetically.

Janet took her drink and sat at the table making polite conversation by enquiring what Lexi was doing. Lexi showed her the website.

"I've been looking for auctions and antique dealers, we have quite a few in the area. Conrad and I will be going to a lot of them once he's here, we're going to need furniture for both the house and the outbuildings and modern stuff won't suit where we're going. I've also found this website and I quite like the look of that little table; I think it has character," she said turning the laptop to show Janet.

"Oh, that's sweet!" she agreed. Janet looked at Lexi as she turned the laptop back and began to read the description.

"I really do appreciate you having me here Lexi," she said, "I just want you to know that… I'd like to thank you for making me so welcome, especially in the circumstances, I would never have expected it from you."

Lexi looked up at her and smiled. "Janet, I'm happy, I honestly couldn't be happier. I'm also happy the two of you are making a go of it, really, I am. My biggest concern was my children, I wanted it to have as little, negative impact on them as possible and we seem to have managed that. Now, hopefully, your child will also grow up in a loving and harmonious environment and THAT is what's important. Honestly, let's leave it at that and all move forwards."

Both women felt all the better for getting that out of the way and Lexi left for work leaving Janet a lot more confident than she had been feeling with the proverbial 'elephant-in-the-room'!

In her break, Lexi went into town to see the little table; it was every bit as enchanting as it had looked on the website and she happily made the purchase of her, 'first of many' pieces of furniture. She proudly showed Conrad her purchase on their call to one another late that evening. He was impressed with her choice. Then, out of the blue, he proudly announced, "Another seventeen days and we'll be able to go to all the auctions and antique shops you want together! My apartment has exchanged today, my work schedule finishes Friday week and…wait for it…I've booked my ticket to fly over on the following Tuesday," he said excitedly.

"Oh, my God! That's great! It's 'really' happening, at last!" She squealed with delight.

"Yep!" he grinned excitedly. "I can't wait!"

"Me neither." They beamed eagerly at each other through their laptops.

"Oh, my God, just seventeen days and we'll be together, forever. That's the best news ever! Seventeen more days and our lives will completely change, no more Skypes, no more sleeping in an empty bed; just you and me together making our new life and setting up our new home. Wow! That makes my table rather insignificant news now!"

"Your table is lovely!" He laughed.

"I wasn't going to get anything until you were here," she chirped, "I was going to wait for you to come before I did anything. I was only looking to see what auctions and antique shops were around this way. But once I'd seen the table I had to go and get it, it just looked perfect," she rambled happily.

"It is perfect, I can totally see it in there," he agreed. "Not long now babe, just a couple more weeks," he said, feeling relief at his own words.

"It can't come quick enough," she said longingly into the screen. "Oh, I'm so happy, I can't tell you…"

"Tell me about it! I couldn't wait to tell you, finally, we're on our way," he said excitedly. As always, the call ended with the two of them full of enthusiasm, completely caught up in each other and their dream, separated only by eight hours of time and a few thousand miles of ocean.

58

The next couple of weeks flew past; Lexi seemed to be extra busy with her one-to-ones, her clients getting extra sessions in before she left. Her classes were packed and there was an all-round happy atmosphere at work as Lexi seemingly floated along on a tide of joy. At home things seemed settled, though Janet had still been throwing up daily. After a week or so, Lexi suggested a program to nurture her adrenals and set her some calming meditations. This couldn't be far more removed from Janet's familiar world of work, drive and office politics but as her extreme pregnancy symptoms had removed her from the office environment, she decided she had nothing to lose by giving it a try, despite the fact that she'd always been very 'closed-minded' in the past about this sort of approach and deemed it all a waste of time and a load of rubbish!

"You just seem permanently wound up like a coil, you need to get yourself out of this constant state of fight or flight, everything about you feels uptight and stressy, you even walk and talk fast!" Lexi observed, "You need to allow yourself to come down, you're so used to being stressed, you're addicted to the feeling and don't know how to be any other way," She tried to explain.

"I know, you're absolutely right. It just feels so unnatural to me to relax, I've always lived life at a certain pace, I thrive on stress, it makes me more productive," Janet said as if to justify it.

"But you're not thriving on it right now, are you?" Lexi kindly pointed out.

When Janet thought about it, from recollection, the only time she'd ever felt truly relaxed was when she was on holiday, and explained that, even then, it had usually taken her at least five days to really let go. She'd always been aware that just as she was getting used to being relaxed, it was time to go home and rev back up again.

"Think of it this way, you don't have to rev back up, at least not right now, so why don't you try to embrace the idea of a different experience of life?" Lexi tried to reason. "If you can train your mind to slow down a bit and get control of that constant 'chatter' in your head, I'm sure you'll feel a lot better, and the chances are you'll probably have a far more laid-back baby if you can master calm within yourself."

Janet could see Lexi's point, she was well-aware she was up-tight, even when watching a film, she'd become aware that she'd be sitting there, quite stiff with her fists clenched tight; she'd relax her hands and arms and carry on watching her film just to notice she'd be in the same, clenched position only five minutes later. Reflecting on this, she decided to give the meditations a go, she also took on board other tips and approaches that Lexi suggested she might try doing.

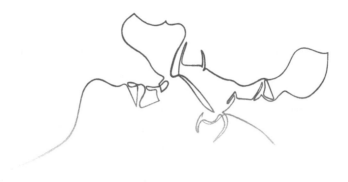

59

It was Sunday afternoon; the day of Conrad's arrival was getting close now. He was due to arrive in England early Wednesday morning and Lexi was due to finish work on the Friday. With all her chores, preparations and diary changes done to accommodate this, Lexi cozied up on the settee to watch a film; it didn't take her long for her to recognise that not a lot of the film was going in! Her thoughts kept drifting forwards in time to Conrad's arrival. After a failed but concentrated effort to keep herself focused on the film, she realised her brain was simply on a roll with all things 'Conrad'. Her imagination of meeting him at the airport was totally running away with her, her tummy doing somersaults at the thought of it. So, with a restless but happy mind she gave up on the film, went into the kitchen and put the kettle on; she wasn't particularly thirsty but needed something to do.

Nathan came in, "You, ok?" he asked.

"Yeah, just restless," Lexi replied.

"Not long now," he added.

"I know, I can't wait, I'm finding it hard to think of anything else!"

"I'm sure you are!" he laughed.

At that point Lexi's phone bleeped, she opened a text message, "What you up to Blondie?" It was Paul.

"Oh, not a lot, just trying to keep my mind occupied," she replied.

"Fancy doing something?" he asked, "Cuppa, walk?"

"Yes, that'd be most welcome right now, thank you, want to meet me somewhere?" she asked.

"No, I'll come pick you up and then we can decide, see you in fifteen."

So, Lexi went upstairs, changed out of her comfy, pants and into some jeans, tidied her hair up and was ready to go. A few minutes later Paul arrived and tooted his horn outside. Lexi left the house and got in the car.

"Hey! How are you doing?" he said.

"Driving myself crazy!" came her honest reply.

"Thought you might be. I also thought we won't be getting the opportunity to do this much more, well, not on the spur of the moment anyway...What do you fancy doing?" He said as he started the car up.

"Oh, I really don't mind, I'm pleased you called when you did, I just needed to get out and stop my brain going at ten thousand miles an hour!" she laughed.

"You spend a great deal of your time teaching other people how to do that!" He pointed out as if to say, 'why aren't you doing it'?

"I know, and to be fair, I hadn't done it because I'd only just realised, I was on a 'roll' when you messaged me. Let's go up to the creek and walk along the foreshore," she suggested; she hadn't been there in a while.

"Sounds like a plan."

Off they went on a scenic route that started in a small creek on the shore. They walked a mile or so along the shoreline, then up through the woods and over the fields until they came 'full circle' and ended up, nearly two hours later, back at the little creek car park. It was now just after 5pm and they decided to drive to a little local pub they knew and order a pot of tea.

"I really enjoyed that, thank you," she said.

"My pleasure," he replied, "the next time we get to do this, I'll be visiting you in your holistic heaven!"

Lexi felt her heart pound at his words

"I know… Oh Paul, I really can't believe this is all really happening. I feel like my bubble is going to burst at any moment!" she said almost anxiously.

"I keep telling you, believe it baby!" he said, "I know you'll make a go of it at there, you'll smash it. Right back from when I first met you, you've always had a vision of your perfect retreat and how you would run it, you've been living it in your head for so long, now's your time to make that fantasy a reality. I just know you'll do a great job of it. My only 'downer' is that I won't be part of it; we've worked and studied together for such a long time now, I always thought you'd be there," he said with honesty, his tone dropping slightly.

"You could always move up if it takes off," she suggested.

"I'll hold you to that!" he said enthusiastically.

They had their pot of tea and with so much still to talk about, they decided to stay there and order some food.

"So, when does he get here?" Paul asked.

"Wednesday, 5am, providing there are no delays," she said with a happy sigh.

"Heathrow?"

"Yes."

At this information, Paul picked up his phone and went into his diary.

"I'll take you if you like," he offered.

"Seriously?" She turned to him, "You won't get any sleep though!" she protested.

"Nah, it'll take about two and a half hours to get there that time of night. I'm just on the gym floor in the morning, it won't matter too much if I'm a bit late, Andy can cover. I have a two-hour break in the afternoon so, if need be, I can get my head down then before I come back for the evening; it's fine and it'll be less stressful for you," he said convincingly, wanting to help.

"That's really kind, thank you," Lexi was really chuffed at this.

"I know, I'm a kind person!" He winked, then on a more serious note said, "I want to do it for you Lex and I'm really looking forward to meeting him."

"Thank you," she said, really appreciating the gesture.

So, with that settled, they had their meal and Paul returned Lexi back home. She felt blessed to have such beautiful people in her life that genuinely cared for her.

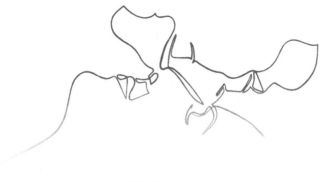

60

Lexi had moved her diary around to work Monday and take Wednesday off for Conrad's arrival. Then all she had left to do was three clients Thursday afternoon and her final class at 11.30am on Friday, then she was done. Conrad Skyped for the last time on Monday evening before he was due to leave for England.

"The next time I talk to you we'll be together."

"Together, forever," she replied, "I never want us to be apart again."

"There will be no reason for us to be apart again..." he said. "I can't wait to be with you, I can't wait to hold you in my arms and know that this time it's for good; no more packing up and leaving, no more, lonely apartment, just you and me and an amazing new life together."

"And I can't wait to be in your arms knowing it's for good this time." She leant forward and touched the screen, as did he.

"See you on Wednesday morning beautiful," he said softly.

"See you when you get here, beautiful man." Her voice cracked with emotion as she tried to get her words out.

Monday and Tuesday went by in a whirl; it was a welcome distraction for Lexi having to focus on her classes and clients. Tuesday evening, she got home around 6pm, prepared and ate her evening meal and decided she'd get her head down really early to be up for 2am. Nathan was away overnight on business. As Lexi washed the dishes Janet came in the kitchen.

"Hi, how are you?" She asked.

"Incredibly excited!" she replied, hardly able to contain herself!

"I bet you are!" replied Janet.

"How are you?" Lexi asked.

"Yes, good thank you, I've been doing some mindfulness daily, I still find it hard, my mind wanders very easily but I'm giving it a good go!"

"Good. Your brain is like a muscle, persevere with it and you'll find you can stay focused for longer. Don't forget, your brain is used to thinking quickly and finding solutions; it's always in 5th gear and it won't feel natural to be in 1st or 2nd gear. The more you make your brain go to that pace, the less 'unnatural' it'll feel and the happier it'll be to be there. Actually… I was planning on doing a guided meditation to empty my mind before I get an early night tonight, you're more than welcome to join me," suggested Lexi.

Janet appreciated the invitation, "Yes, if you don't mind," she said.

"I know it's going to be really early, but I want to get my head down as soon after 8.30 as possible, I'm getting up at 2am," Lexi explained.

"Well, I'm tired anyway so I'm game for it," Janet replied, welcoming the opportunity for some guided relaxation.

"I'll go and get a quick shower and brush my teeth then, so all I've got to do is fall into bed afterwards," said Lexi.

About 20 minutes later, with them both ready for bed, Lexi chose one of her favourite-guided meditations. Janet lay on the settee and Lexi lay on her back on the floor with just a salt lamp to light the room and the meditation coming out through the surround sound. The meditation focused both ladies on their bodies, concentrating on their breathing and sensations in the body followed by a journey through their imaginations, as the orator took them on a beautiful, orally illustrated woodland walk. The meditation lasted 45 minutes and by the end, both ladies were completely relaxed. Once it had finished Lexi went straight up to bed saying only "goodnight" so she wouldn't wake herself back up.

61

At 1.50, Lexi's alarm went off; surprisingly enough, she had slept. It took only a couple of moments to realise 'This is it! The time has finally come!' She dived out of bed and into the bathroom, had a quick wash, brushed her teeth and put a tiny bit of mascara on. She then went downstairs, put the kettle on and made a big pot of coffee. She transferred it into two large thermos mugs, went to the fridge and grabbed a large glass-lidded dish filled with chicken, carrot and celery sticks, chopped avocado and fermented vegetables. She put the dish in a 'cool bag' with some kitchen roll and cutlery in case any of them needed food and finally grabbed a big bottle of water. In the hall she quietly put on her boots. At that point she saw the lights from Paul's car through the opaque glass of the front door. Grabbing her coat, she picked everything up and quietly left the house.

"Morning Blondie!" Paul said as she opened the car door.

"Good morning!" Lexi said, positively beaming.

"What have we here?" he enquired, gesturing toward the bag.

"I've made us a healthy breakfast, should we be hungry, not sure if Conrad will eat the food on the plane now that his eyes have been opened!" she winked.

"Well, we can always rely on you for food, can't we?" he joked.

"And… fresh coffee for you sir!" she said passing him the mug. "It's not boiling, so you won't burn your mouth, just thought it'd wake us both up a bit."

Paul took the mug, "Ah, excellent! Thanks," he said as he wedged it between his legs and they set off.

The journey went without a problem, although Lexi was surprised by just how many cars were on the road at that time in the morning. They got to the airport and Paul dropped her off outside.

"Just call me and I'll come back to this point and pick you both up," he said.

"Thank you, sweetie, I really appreciate this," she said as she got out of the car. Her tummy turning somersaults with the excitement.

"No worries, it's worth it just to see the look on your face, you look so happy, I swear the closer we got, I could feel the excitement coming off you! It's a nice thing to witness and be a part of," he said, "See you in a little while."

"Thank you," she said as she shut the door and then turned and walked into the building to look for the flight information on the boards.

Conrad's flight was arriving on time; he should land in 20 minutes. This was the longest 20 minutes of Lexi's life! She was like a cat on hot bricks! She watched the information boards eagerly; eventually she went and got herself another coffee as the suspense was driving her insane! Finally, his plane had landed; her whole body was 'aglow' as she waited in the greeting area. Mentally, she was thinking, 'he'll be getting off the plane now…. he'll be waiting for his cases now'. She watched the arrival gate intently as a stream of people poured through. She was aware of happy people all around her greeting each other. Her eyes fixed like cement on the entrance willing him to walk through and then, like a 'golden moment' there he was. She instantly felt her tears brim up as their eyes met across the sea of people. He pushed forwards with his four, large cases on the trolley, the only stuff he deemed important enough to bring with him from his forty-one years of life! The two of them patiently strived to get to each other through the crowd of people. When he was only a few feet away from her, Lexi spotted a hole in the wall of bodies and made a dash for him, he let go of the trolley and swept her up in his arms kissing her as he did so. They held each other tightly, kissed each other and cried with joy. They were together at last, this moment was to be the start of the rest of their lives together and it felt truly, truly wonderful.

Once they finally managed to release from their embrace, they moved out of the way of the many other people, who were also trying to reunite with their loved ones. They moved to the side of the terminal, out of the sea of people and fell into each other's arms again.

"Oh, God, at last, you're here," she murmured into his chest.

He kissed her head, "It felt like forever babe! Oh man, it feels so good to hold you."

They had a few moments to satisfy the intensity of their reunion and then Lexi called Paul.

"I'll be there in ten!" he said, so they both went and grabbed coffees for themselves and Paul and started to make their way outside. Within a couple of minutes, Paul rolled up and got out. Lexi introduced him and Conrad, they shook hands and then Paul helped to arrange the cases in the car; two in the boot, one behind the passenger seat and one on the back seat.

"Only just!" Paul exclaimed as he managed to slam the boot shut.

"Well, it'd have to stay here if it didn't go in, I've got all I need right here!" Conrad said as they beamed at each other; Paul smiled an 'Aw' smile to himself as he walked back round to the driver's side.

"Do you want to go front or back?" asked Lexi.

"Back is fine," he replied getting in.

As she got in Lexi handed Paul his coffee.

"Aw, thank you, Blondie," he said taking the lid off and pouring it into his mug; he shoved it between his legs, and they took off.

On the way, Lexi said, "Let me know if you're hungry, both of you, I've bought food for us."

"A banquet, knowing her!" said Paul.

"I wouldn't expect anything less!" added Conrad.

"They say the way to a man's heart is through his stomach!" Said Paul.

"Something like that," Conrad replied looking at Lexi with total desire, adding, "I really appreciate this, Paul."

"No, worries mate, it's a pleasure," the two men exchanged.

Then all three went on to talk about where Lexi and Paul worked, how long they'd known each other and the different courses and subjects they'd studied.

"You'll have to come in on Friday when she leaves, it'd be nice for them to see who's whisking their favourite girl away!" Paul said.

"Sure, I will do, I'm intrigued to see the place," Conrad replied.

Paul added, "And then she'll be all yours."

Conrad looked straight at Lexi, "She so will," he said, their eyes connected lovingly as he did so.

Conrad started to tell them about the books he'd now read and how well he was doing with his eating habits and personal care products, before they all went on to discuss cookware, food storage and chlorinated water.

"It's just something I never even thought about before I met Lexi, now I'm obsessed with it and I'm learning more by the day! It's a minefield! There are chemicals everywhere that people simply aren't aware of and the more I've learned, the more important I realise it is to do something about it, for us and for the health of the planet. Lexi and Paul looked at each other, smiled and simultaneously added,

"And the more people that become informed and start to make healthier choices, the healthier both the population and the planet will become." Paul said smiling back at Conrad in the rear-view mirror. "An informed public will vote with their wallets. If they stop buying all this, unnatural stuff, conventionally farmed meats, fish, vegetables, processed foods, GMO's, personal care products and other chemically laden products and start buying more organic foods, cleaner products and biodegradable packaging, they will create a greater demand for them, which will firstly, bring the price of it all down and secondly, the cleaner trend will naturally have a positive impact on both the health of the population and the planet. Companies can only sell their products if people want to buy them, they have to go with the consumer." Paul continued, "But in my opinion, the biggest issue that needs addressing right now is the use of glyphosate in agriculture to grow crops".

"Yes, I've just been reading a bit about that, the book I'm currently on has been really informative on glyphosate and the harm it's doing to human health." Conrad 'chipped' in as Paul continued.

Good, because that must be the evillest, most widely used chemical on the planet, both for the planet and for mankind, I've been looking into this a lot. Did you know glyphosate was never developed as a weed killer? Originally it was patented as an antibiotic. The reason it's so harmful is because it blocks something called the 'shikimate pathway'. This where the natural enzymes in the soil biosynthesize the essential amino acids in the plant, and those amino acids are essential to build a healthy and functioning human body, the science is there to back it up.

There are some really informative interviews on YouTube, "The Nuntucket Project' has to be about the most informative thing I've listened to on glyphosate. It states in this interview that in 1975, the year before glyphosate was used, autism presented in one in 5000 children, but today autism presents in one in 35 children. And it's not only autism, by the late 80's and early 90's, the health service began to see an epidemic of diseases in the population such as MS, Parkinson, Alzheimer's, auto immune disease, and cancers.

In tests on lab rats injected with glyphosate, initially, there didn't seem to be any ill effects until the next generation were born. Then the rats presented with immune and metabolic dysfunction, and obesity. Then, by the third generation there was a high percentage of still born pups, severe birth defects and cancers. So, from the mid 70s when glyphosate was first used to the present day, we are now seeing the very same decline in three generations of humans as was observed in the three generations of the lab rats."

"It's just sick isn't" said Conrad shaking his head.

Paul continued. "The other important fact about this poison is that it's water soluble, so once it's out there, it not only penetrates the crops, but it evaporates into the air that we breath and rains down on us from the clouds, it simply should never have been used in agriculture in the first place. There are fungi and bacteria in the earth that can reverse these effects over time, but it's estimated even if we stopped using glyphosate tomorrow it would still take fifty years to reverse the toxic effects that farming with this poison has created. People just don't realise, we only have a small window of time in which we need to make major changes in agriculture, otherwise our food chain will see a predictable and steady decline in human health and ultimately the inability to build a healthy and functioning human body".

"Mmm", Conrad pondered, "It's just criminal, it really does make you wonder how it was ever allowed to be used in the first place, despite the science."

"Money and greed!" Lexi and Paul countered simultaneously. "And then there's the massive concern with our bees." Lexi continued, "It has been proved beyond any shadow of doubt that the pesticides they have been using in agriculture is killing the bees. Many, many countries seemed to get on board with this and ban these pesticides but now it appears they've done a U-turn and are using them again! I mean, what's all that about? It's a known fact that we can't survive without bees, so how has this been overturned and why? It just doesn't make sense... We need to be working with nature, not against it. I mean why, oh why, aren't we growing and utilising more hemp? There's nothing you can make from plastic or wood that can't be made from hemp... paper, clothing, bottles, bags, even houses, fuel for cars and of course lifesaving medicines. Hemp produces four times the pulp per acre that trees produce, it only takes five months to grow and it also consumes four times as much CO_2 as trees, giving it massive potential to reverse climate change. It's naturally repellent giving no need for fertilizers or pesticides to grow it and it also has the ability to break down the toxins in the earth, so it would help to reverse the damage done to our soil by the use of glyphosate. It's a no-brainer, the more I look into it the more I realise how wrong it all is that we stopped using it.

We always assume that the people who run our countries and the councils that control entire continents are well read, intelligent and are doing their best for the health and wellbeing of mankind but it's not the case. It can't possibly be, otherwise they wouldn't be pressing forward with nuclear or fossil fuels, using bee-killing pesticides and working against Mother Nature and making her struggle, instead, they treat this planet as if they have another one to go to. In an ideal world, as we move forward, I feel that anything not recyclable or sustainable or indeed takes thousands of years to break down, should be banned.

"Absolutely!' The boys agreed simultaneously.

She continued, "Imagine if we switched to farming a high percentage of hemp and then built our economy around it by growing businesses from all the different trades that turn it into the desired forms. I always say, we need to take a step back in order to move forwards, but that doesn't mean we have to live like cavemen, with hemp we can still have our creature comforts because it can provide them, in doing so we will be reversing the damage to our planet providing there are strict rules covering the use of chemicals in the processing of it, obviously."

Again, the boys agreed with her. Paul laughed and said, "She's got it all worked out, save the world if you could, wouldn't you Lex." he said affectionately. Conrad took a deep look at her and felt a massive surge in his chest.

She carried on, "I was taught, as human beings we are designed to adapt and quite frankly, it is the level of 'how quickly' we can adapt as to whether we survive as a race or not. They either find a way to do it that is in harmony with Mother Nature, or the human race will start to die out, it's as simple as that and there's massive evidence to support this already.

"Yes we have a very small window indeed," said Conrad as Paul 'Hmmmmmm'ed and nodded his head.

All went quiet for a few moments as each of them sat with that thought.

At that point Paul pulled over at a service station and they sat in the car eating their breakfast courtesy of Lexi. They had a quick toilet break, stretched their legs and then continued on their way.

62

With the busy morning traffic, they made it back to Lexi's house just before 9am. Paul pulled up outside; they had talked incessantly all the way home and it seemed that, had the journey gone on for another couple of hours, they wouldn't have had any trouble filling it with things to talk about. Lexi was pleased that Paul and Conrad genuinely seemed to like each other, not that there was anything not to like, but as Paul was such a close friend and someone she felt she would always keep her friendship going with, it pleased her that they hit-it-off so well. They all got out of the car and Paul helped Conrad with the cases.

"Did you want to come in for a quick cuppa?" Lexi asked Paul.

"No thanks Lex, I need to get to work really, someone is covering for me…. It was nice to meet you though Conrad," he said turning to him and shaking his hand.

"Yes, likewise," said Conrad, "thanks again for the lift I really appreciate it; we'll have to go out for a meal before we leave, my treat." Then he added, "Although I'm sure you'll be coming to visit us, yes?" This pleased Paul somewhat,

"Try keeping me away, it just looks amazing, I'm really looking forward to seeing it and spending some 'chill-out' time there."

"I'll make a room up especially for you!" Lexi said as she kissed his cheek.

"Thank you hun, I'll see you tomorrow, I'm not in till the afternoon," she finished.

"Okay, see you tomorrow… and see YOU Friday!" he addressed Conrad.

"Yep, cheers mate!" Conrad replied.

Paul got back in the car, gave a quick wave and drove off. Lexi smiled at Conrad, as he looked up at the house.

"Right, let's get you and this lot into my humble abode, shall we?" she said, taking the handles of two wheelie cases and walking towards the door as Conrad followed her up the path.

She stopped outside the door and said, "Welcome to, what will be your slightly crazy home for the next couple of weeks!" To which he replied, "I'm looking forward to the experience, all of it, it's all part of us starting our lives together."

She opened the door and heaved one of the cases over the step as Conrad picked up the other one for her and handed it over, then he passed the others in. Lexi wheeled them to the side of the hall, where they stood all lined up. Conrad gestured toward them.

"Not much to show for forty-one years, is there?" he said.

"Have you got more to follow?" Lexi asked.

"No, I just packed the stuff that was important to me and the rest I either sold or got rid of. I managed to do a deal with the guy who bought the apartment; he had all the furniture. To be fair, there wasn't that much; the apartment was very modern and minimalist and none of it would have suited our place. I sold my car to a mate at work, settled on a deal a couple of weeks ago and he had it the day before I left! These two cases I won't need until we get to our place, it's just stuff I didn't want to leave. Oh, apart from..."

He went to one of the rather large cases, placed it on its side and opened it. Lying diagonally across the top with everything carefully packed in around it was his guitar in its zip case. He took it out, closed the case and said," I don't know what I'd have done without this these last few weeks, it's been a godsend."

Lexi smiled, "I'll look forward to you playing it to me when we're chilling out, there's nothing more relaxing. Let me show you around, then we can get your stuff upstairs and get you unpacked, I've made space for your clothes in the wardrobe."

The pair of them went into the lounge, where Lexi gave Conrad's guitar pride-of-place, standing up beside a large armchair, ready for him to serenade her later. They went through to the kitchen, just as Janet came in from the utility room.

"Oh, hello!" she said, Lexi introduced them to each other.

"Hi! Pleased to meet you." Conrad shook her hand.

"How was your journey?"

"Yes, it was fine thanks, no delays, anyway,"

"Oh, well that's a promising start, you must be tired though?" Janet continued making polite conversation.

"I'm ok, I'm used to it, it's been a regular part of my life doing long flights and adjusting to different time zones," he explained. "Mind you, I'm now looking forward to it 'not' being a part of my life! I'm welcoming a complete change of pace now."

"I bet you are, you must be really excited?" He looked at Lexi and squeezed her hand, "Yeah, I am, can't wait for it to all go through now." Lexi beamed back at him, the two of them just happy to be finally together.

"Did you want to get your head down at all?" Lexi asked.

"I managed to get a few hours on the plane, so, to be honest I'll be better off trying to stay up till this evening and then getting my head down early; mind you, you've been up half the night, did you need to?"

"I know I should be tired but to be honest, I've been that excited about meeting you and getting you back here, I don't think I could sleep now! Let's just get you unpacked and then we can chill out, then you can play your guitar to me."

"Sounds like a plan, although, I think I'm gonna need one of your super-duper coffees, the airport coffee wasn't a patch on yours, I'd feel a bit cheated if that was my only coffee for the day!"

Lexi laughed. "Of course, you can! Do you want a bullet proof one?" she said as she went to put the kettle on.

"Whatever you're making," he replied.

"I'm gonna have to pass, I've already had three, which is another reason I wouldn't be able to sleep! But I'll make you one and have something else."

Lexi set to making the drinks as Conrad took in his new surroundings and got a feel for being part of it as she happily buzzed around him.

They sat and had their drinks, then Lexi took Conrad upstairs, showed him everywhere and then they unpacked his clothes and other belongings. They lay on the bed chatting and cuddling, still both excited at the novelty of knowing that this was for good. Later, they put the other two cases in the garage and sat in the lounge, where Conrad got his guitar out, gave it a little tuning and started gently strumming away to her as they sat together on the settee. At around 3pm, Lexi decided to put some dinner on, Conrad went into the kitchen with her. She put an enormous chicken in a glass roasting dish, filled it halfway with water and put it in the oven on a low temperature. She always cooked a large chicken every week and made bone broth from the bones.

"What do you fancy with that then? I'm going to cook it and take all the meat off, so it's your call, whatever you fancy, stir-fry? Curry? Or do you fancy a roast?" she asked.

"Ooh, now you're talking, I can't remember the last time I had a roast." he replied enthusiastically.

"Ah, roast it is then! Actually... I'm wondering if it might be an idea to do it for all of us, I just think it'd be a nice way to kick things off now we're all here under the same roof, what do you think?" she said. "Yeah, I'm happy with that, I think it's a nice idea," he said as she smiled at him and then called up the stairs to Janet to make sure she was ok with it, which she was.

She then messaged Nathan to see what time he'd be getting home and asked him to bring a bottle of wine in with him. Lexi got potatoes, parsnips and carrots out and started peeling them to roast; she also got out a big bag of kale. Conrad came up behind her, slipped his arms around her waist and kissed her cheek.

"Let me help." he said.

She gave him a small knife and chopping board, then got a big pan out and boiled the kettle. As they stood side-by-side preparing the vegetables Conrad said, "You're one in a million, you know that?"

"I try to be," she looked at him earnestly.

"You don't have to try, it comes naturally to you, that's why I love you so much." He leaned over and kissed her and then kissed her again; he put down his knife, took hers from her hand, placed it on the worktop and embraced her, wrapping her up in his arms.

"God, it feels so good to be here with you." She melted into his chest, and they stood just holding each other for many, many moments.

Once the veg was prepped and ready to roast; they went into the lounge and cozied down in front of the telly for a while, both starting to feel a little punch-drunk from tiredness now. They chilled out for an hour or so and then started to bring the meal together as Nathan came through the door. Lexi introduced the two men to each other.

"Hey, how you going?" Conrad said as he put his hand out to shake Nathan's.

"I'm good mate, pleased to meet you at last." Nathan said.

'Good start', Lexi thought to herself, then said, "Go, get yourself out of your suit and I'll dish up, I think Janet's having a lie down."

"Ok," he said, disappearing upstairs while Lexi and Conrad began to set the table and dish up the roast. Just as they'd put it all on the table, Nathan and Janet reappeared from upstairs.

"This is a treat, having a roast mid-week!" Said Nathan.

"Mmm, I just thought it'd be nice," said Lexi.

"Very nice, thank you," said Janet.

"You're welcome," Lexi replied.

Nathan opened the wine and poured for three of them. They gave a toast to welcome Conrad, closely followed by a rather sweet gesture from Nathan wishing them all the best for their future together.

"Thank you…and the very same to you," Lexi replied and Conrad agreed. They tucked into their meal and made pleasant conversation. Their introduction went very well. With both Lexi and Conrad now having been up for so many hours they were visibly flagging.

"Well, this has been a lovely introduction thank you, Lexi, I'm sure I speak for both of us that this is really appreciated," said Janet.

Lexi could tell she really meant it and replied, "You're most welcome."

"Yes, thank you hun," said Nathan finishing up his plate.

"You two look absolutely shattered!" added Janet.

"You'd be absolutely right there!" Lexi replied.

"Well, I suggest you two get yourselves off to bed and I'll clear away the dishes."

Lexi and Conrad thanked her and as they got up from the table, Nathan added, "You know what else might be good? I think it'd be nice to get the kids over before you leave. I feel, if they experience how we can all be around each other it can only help them with moving on."

"Yes, I'd be fine with that if we can organise it," said Lexi. So they verbally planned to arrange for the kids to visit the following weekend.

Exhausted, Lexi and Conrad got ready for bed, crawled under the quilt, snuggled up to each other and drifted off in each other's arms for the first time safe in the knowledge that they need never be apart again.

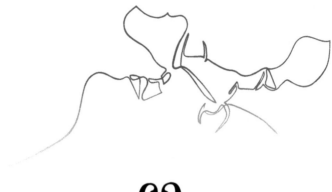

63

Morning had broken, and Conrad awoke to sounds of Nathan getting up for work. He lay, looking around the room getting a sense of the newness of his surroundings. He felt relaxed and tranquil; gone was the instant adrenaline surge of his familiar morning routine... alarm going off, diving out of bed and instantly switching to work mode. He lay feeling the warmth of Lexi still nuzzled into him and was instantly at peace that, all that was now part of his past. He looked at Lexi, her head on his chest, her hair covering most of her face; he gently pushed her curls back and looked at her with total adoration unconsciously letting out a warm and happy sigh. Lexi, sensing his energy opened her eyes.

"Good morning beautiful," he said.

"Good morning handsome!" came her automatic reply. He kissed her forehead and she hugged him tight.

"Mmm, this feels nice," she said... "To wake up next to you, knowing I'm not going to have to say goodbye to you ever again."

"Doesn't it just?" he replied, "I feel like a completely different person in a completely different world!"

"We're in 'our' world now," she added happily.

"We so are!" he replied as he kissed her again, she tilted her head and he kissed her lips and whispered, "Just us, now, forever."

They kissed more passionately, the awareness of their skin-on-skin embrace provoking a mutual, sensual desire. He pulled her on top of him, his hands feeling her warm skin. Every cell in his body came to life in response to the feel of her body upon his. She started instinctively moving her hips, rubbing herself slowly up and down on his erect penis. His hands moved down to her bottom as she did so, caressing her, taking hold of her buttocks and pulling her deeper onto him; both of them, totally captured in their spontaneous act of desire. The more she writhed, the firmer he pulled her to him, assisting the movement until she moved herself slightly higher up his body and then slid herself back down him, enabling him to enter her without guidance. Both of them letting out a little groan at the pleasure of his penetration.

"Oh, God, I love you," he said as she continued to take him into her, deeper with every stroke.

"I love you too.... So, so much..." She cried out with pleasure as they began to thrust together, deeper, harder, faster. He guided her with his hands firmly back-and-forth until she placed her hands on his chest and sat herself up on him, bearing down hard on him, feeling his maximum penetration. Both of them beginning to cry out with the impact of every stroke, she leant forwards again pressing herself into him, allowing the firm brushing action of his pubic hair against her clitoris, stimulating herself to a point of no return. As she 'came' her muscles contracted firmly around him, bringing him to a powerful orgasm; the two of them, looking into each other's eyes and treasuring the unity of their combined being.

They lay in each other's arms feeling content in their world. Conrad gently stroking her back as Lexi lay, projecting her thoughts forward to all the good things that were now to come for them, building their new life together in their wonderful new home, surrounded by nature.

Out of the blue Lexi broke the silence, "I'm really excited about having a wood, we will have to find the perfect spot and put a log cabin in, it would be a great place to do my full and new moon rituals," she said, adding, "I haven't told you what I do on the moons yet have I?"

Conrad looked quizzically at her, "Go on?" He said, as she had a little chuckle to herself and added playfully, "You didn't know you were shacking up with a hippy, did you?" Conrad's expression was a fusion of both intrigue and amusement as he waited for Lexi to reveal yet another of her little quirks to him. "Go on then, spill it!" He said as she continued, "I believe in the power of the conscious mind and intent, I believe it's possible to create positive energy, both for myself and to send it out to the universe. I also believe that there is such a thing as the 'collective consciousness', so I use the energy of the full and new moons to create this energy. It's a very positive experience and I feel it constantly reinforces a positive mind-set and I also believe it helps to raise the vibration of the collective consciousness.

"Okay..." Conrad said digesting what she had just explained, "So what is this then? Like... Witchcraft?" He asked. "Oh, no, just the power of intention, from the heart with love. People honestly don't know just how powerful their thoughts and words are. If they did, they would choose them far more carefully!" she said earnestly.

Conrad, although not quite convinced by this concept, felt that it was quite a sweet notion and very fitting of Lexi and how she did things, "You're just full of little surprises aren't you!" He said, "I knew the moment I clapped eyes on you that there was something unique about you. I think it's a lovely notion and now I'm intrigued to know how you're going to create this energy!"

"Ah, well, you'll have to wait and see, I can't go giving all my secrets away," she winked, "and anyway, it'll make it all the more of an experience for you. It's the new moon on Saturday so I will introduce you to this beautiful practice then." She said, as he replied, "And I will very much look forward to it."

Lexi and Conrad made a slow start to the day, with Lexi not due in at the gym till 1pm. They spent a contented morning, sitting in dressing gowns with coffee, going through the internet looking at furniture, finding auction houses and antique shops in the hope they would be able to accumulate some suitable furniture for when they completed on the purchase of their new home. Conrad was getting quite into it and liking the style of furniture Lexi was attracted to.

Lexi went off to the gym to work while Conrad carried on the search, making a list of places and auctions to go to and possible, random pieces of furniture for her to look at when she got back. He sat and made a note of all the things he thought they would need immediately they moved in, from kitchen equipment to bedroom and bathroom, putting 'markers' on items and saving it all for when Lexi got home. Before he knew it, it was just after 6pm and Lexi walked through the door. "Hey!" he said in surprise.

"Hello you! Have you even moved since I left?" Lexi observed.

"It would appear not!" he replied, "I've got loads done though, I think you'll be very pleased with my productive afternoon."

He showed Lexi his lists and tabs, asking her if there was anything else she could think of to add. He showed her all the things he'd managed to source over the Internet.

"Oh, wow! You have done well, haven't you"! He'd even managed to find a reverse osmosis company so that they would have clean, filtered, chemical free water once they were in.

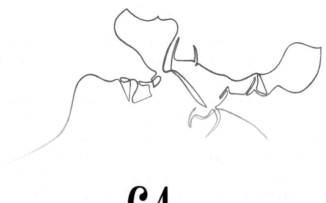

64

With one more morning to work, Lexi floated along happily to the gym. She'd loved working there; she'd loved both the staff and clients but felt no sadness at leaving. Her time there had been a positive experience and had served her well, but it was now time for her to move on to this exciting new chapter in her life. Conrad dropped her off in the morning, then used Lexi's car for a solicitor's appointment, arranging to be back at the gym before she finished, to officially whisk her away to her new life.

Lexi walked into the building and stopped at the reception desk, she had two 'PT' clients booked in and her regular class last thing before lunch.

"Morning! Last day then?" Said the girl on reception, "Currently your class is full and there are eight people waiting on the cancellation list! I think they're all keen to make the most of your last day!"

"Aw, bless, I've made a point of putting all the favourite routines on the playlist for my last class with them, I think they'll enjoy it," she replied happily and went on through to the changing rooms.

She put her stuff in her locker; her first client was in fifteen minutes which was just as well because it took her that long to peel herself back out of the changing room, away from the members who were in there chatting to her and giving her best wishes for the future. She went into the gym and found her first client; she had a lovely last day booked. Although there weren't any clients, she particularly disliked, she had a very, very good relationship with the two clients she had this morning. Both had said they would come to her retreat once it was running, and Lexi knew their intentions were genuine.

Each of them said things like..." Oh, God, I'm really going to miss you!" And... "It's not going to seem the same around here without you!"

But at the same time, all of them expressed how pleased and excited they were for her, and not one of them tried to make her feel bad about her decision in any way, she felt truly blessed and bursting with happiness.

Her morning spun by and before she knew it, it was time for her class. She dived into the studio and plugged in her ipod as her ladies all piled in the door. There was an excited 'ripple' amongst them as the music started and Lexi, of course, didn't fail to please. She gave it her absolute all; all their much-loved routines came out one by one. Lexi, as usual, was motivating them with her unique, high energy; only today, her level was through the roof, lifted by the amazing energy that filled the room. She savoured and enjoyed every moment of what was to be her last class in the gym environment. The hour flew by in a happy buzz and as Lexi came to the end of her cool-down the studio door opened and a handful of ladies who had been on the waiting list came in.

One of the clients yelled out, "Three cheers for Lexi!"

They all yelled out, "Hip, hip hooray!" three times. Two of the ladies carried a card and a huge bouquet of flowers, which they presented to Lexi on behalf of them all; unbeknown to Lexi they'd had a whip-round before the class.

At this point, taken aback by this show of appreciation, Lexi burst into tears and thanked them very much, adding that she'd had the best time teaching them all. She came out of the studio to see Conrad standing by the reception desk chatting to Paul. She went straight to him and as they kissed, one of her ladies said,

"Is this the young man who's taking our instructor away?"

"Yes, he is!" replied Lexi, introducing her clients to him.

They all said hello, a few of them playfully nudging her and giving her their approval. Conrad then also enjoyed a happy exchange of well wishes from them. He watched Lexi proudly, still holding her beautiful bouquet as her clients started to say their goodbyes.

"Here, let me take that for you," he said, taking the bouquet so she could give hugs and say goodbye to them properly. Suddenly, as if from no-where, Lexi was whipped up into the air by Paul and another male member of staff. She didn't struggle; having worked at the gym for so long, she knew exactly what was coming!

They walked over to the pool, holding her arms and legs, then swung her high shouting, "ONE. TWO. THREE!" And as they shouted "THREE!" they let her go and she flew out of their hands and splashed into the water.

Everyone roared with laughter as a soaking wet, fully clothed Lexi climbed back out of the pool and took a bow.

Once the excitement had died down and the little crowd of people had dispersed, Lexi went to get showered.

Knowing this was on the cards, she had put a change of clothes in her kit bag. Paul was now on a break in his schedule and sat chatting with Conrad in the café while Lexi got showered and washed her hair. She emerged from the changing room a short while later, in dry clothes, her hair still wet and carrying a very full kit bag where she'd emptied her locker for the last time. She went to the reception desk and handed over her key. As Paul saw her through the glass, he and Conrad got up from the table and went over to her. Paul gestured to the girl behind the reception desk, who produced a massive card and another beautiful bunch of flowers, he took the card from her and gave it to Lexi.

"Here you are Lexi! That's from all of us!"

She opened the card he had just handed her and sure enough, everyone who worked there had signed it and put lovely little notes for her inside; then he presented her with the flowers. She felt her cheeks go hot and then her jaw started to quiver.

"Thank you," she said in a slightly cracked voice, her eyes filled with tears.

"Aw, bless ya!" Paul said, pulling her into him and giving her a hug, "You're making me start now! ... No, seriously..." He continued, "You're a little star and we're all going to miss you here, but I know in my heart you're both going to have great success with your retreat because I know how passionate you are and what you're capable of."

"Yes, absolutely!" added the girl behind the desk, "We all believe you're going to do great things with that place. I think you'll have each and every one of us come and visit you once you're set up!"

"And you'd all be more than welcome!" said Lexi sincerely.

"Well, I for one will be coming as soon as I get my invite!" said Paul.

"You don't need an invite; you'll always be welcome, you know that!" Lexi responded before he even had time to finish his sentence, she then added with a wink, "But you might be required to do a bit of gardening to earn your keep!"

"Hey! That's fine by me!... What are you two doing for the rest of the day?" he asked.

"Well, we're going to have some lunch at the farm-shop restaurant. Then, there's an antique shop I'd like to take Lexi to, where I've seen a fantastic, old wooden French dresser I think she might like for our kitchen," said Conrad.

"Ooh, check you out! You're really in the 'zone' now!" said Paul jokingly.

"Totally, mate! I met with the solicitors this morning; and by the way," he interrupted himself, "It looks like we'll be completing next Friday week." He smiled and nodded to Lexi, whose face broke into the biggest smile, as she started to jump up and down on the spot with excitement like a little girl.

He continued, "Yeah, I saw the shop on my way back to the car, thought I'd have a quick look inside and noticed the dresser as soon as I got in the door, it was as if it'd called me in!"

"Well, I hope you like it then," Paul said to Lexi.

"I'm sure I will!" she replied, then added, "We have the kids and their other halves visiting next weekend, apart from that we're pretty much free apart from Thursday, it'd be nice if we could all go out for a meal before that following Friday, what do you think?"

"Yeah, lovely!" Paul agreed.

"Well, we're 'free agents' now, so you have a look at your diary and let us know when suits you best," said Lexi.

"Will do," he replied and with that Lexi picked up her cards and flowers and Conrad picked up her kit bag.

She said, "Good-bye," to the girl on the desk, gave Paul a massive hug and another two members of staff who were still in reception, then they turned to leave. Conrad threw her bag over his shoulder and put his arm around her as they walked towards the big glass doors.

"You, ok?" Conrad said.

"Yes, I'm more than ok thank you, in fact I'm bloody marvellous!" They laughed as left the building.

65

Over lunch, they talked of their plan of action for the next two weeks, the stuff they needed straight away and the stuff that could wait until they got a proper 'feel' for the place. They had an auction to go to the next day and another one the following Thursday.

"God, this is exciting, isn't it?" said Lexi, "It all seems to be happening at once now!"

Conrad replied, "Well, it seems as if it's been a long time coming!"

"Just think, in exactly two weeks we'll have the keys!" she squealed with delight.

"I know, I can't wait, I just want to get in there and start our new life now; I'm itching to get on with it, our house, the set-up of the out-houses, everything. My head's full of what can be done and needs to be done, I'm on a roll."

"Well, you're allowed to be enthusiastic about it but when we're there we will start as we mean to go on. Knowing how you've been in the past; I think I need to set out some ground rules; otherwise, you'll slip back into your old patterns. There's a time to work, a time to exercise, but equally, a time to rest, repair and enjoy our surroundings. It's important not to let how much there is to do run away with you, otherwise you'll end up in the same mental space as you were in before, just in a different place and setting and nothing will have changed for you."

Conrad nodded, "Yeah," he agreed, he knew what she was getting at, he also knew she was right.

"There has to be a balance," she continued," One of my biggest principals when running my holistic business is that I walk my talk; I wouldn't dream of telling other people what they need to do to create their optimal health and wellbeing if I'm not doing it for myself. If we don't look after ourselves, we won't be a very good advert for it! People will be coming there to learn how to reset themselves, to learn the principles of health and wellbeing, to live in that environment and then take that experience home with them."

"Yeah, I know, you're absolutely right and I know I do tend to let things completely consume me. We have the means to take our time on this and get everything done that needs to be done. I honestly am looking forward to living that whole experience with you. I'm so aware of how much better I've felt since I've known you and made the changes I have done so far. I'm looking forward to building our lives around it, learning more and it becoming a habitual practice. I feel with that combination of work and lifestyle it's going to be awesome, so yeah, if I am galloping ahead, just pull the reigns back and tell me. I don't want to fuck it all up again; the reason my relationships failed in the past was because work just took over, I never want that to happen with you, I definitely want to break that pattern."

Lexi was relieved to hear this response. They enjoyed their lunch and then Conrad took Lexi to the antique shop.

As soon as she walked in the door, her eyes were drawn to the huge, wooden dresser.

"Oh, wow! That's perfect!" she said.

"Isn't it?" he smiled, "As soon as I saw it, I could just visualise it in our kitchen." They walked over to it.

"It's just perfect," she repeated as she admired it, stroking her fingers over the grain of the wood.

Conrad asked, "Is there anything else you like the look of while we're here?"

They wandered through the shop; Lexi chose a rather nice set for the fire. In the end they bought the dresser, a table, a chest of drawers and quite a few other bits and pieces. As Conrad staked his claim on all the things they wanted, the owner thought all his Christmases had come at once as it felt like they'd bought half the shop! They got chatting and told him of their imminent move, the shop owner then kindly offered to store their purchases until the completion date and arranged to deliver the pieces in the company lorry for a small fee. Conrad paid for everything, and they went away chuffed that they had made a good start.

On the Saturday they both attended an auction; neither of them had been to one before. There were lots of things they liked the look of. They decided between them what they would be prepared to pay for each individual piece, put their top price next to each one on the program and then had a rather enjoyable and entertaining afternoon bidding on 'lots' they were interested in. They were hugely successful; although, having not really thought about how they would transport their purchases back to the house, quickly they organised a courier. Then, when everything arrived, they didn't know where they were going to put it all!

"I really enjoyed that!" Conrad said.

"Me too!" replied Lexi as they made their way back in the car.

"It's a good job we're going to beat the van back to ours, I hope Nathan and Janet don't mind the house turning in to a furniture storage unit for a couple of weeks!"

"I'm sure they'll be ok with it; it's not like it's going to be for long is it?" he said.

They got back home and squared it with the others; all was well and when the furniture arrived, they stuffed it literally anywhere it would fit.

It was now late in the afternoon and as promised, Lexi got set up for Conrad's introduction to her new moon practice. Lexi got together her 'trug', some clippers and a notebook and pen. "Right, are you ready for this?" she said, almost teasingly. "I'm more than ready, I'm very intrigued." Conrad replied.

They set off on a walk down a footpath close to Lexi's house, which led them onto fields. Every so often Lexi got her little clippers out and clipped off leaves and flowers and as she did so, she explained herself. "I both clip and pick up, things that resonate with me for whatever reason and I write it down. Almost everything you pick; you can look up the metaphysical or spiritual meaning of but firstly I tend to go from my own intuition of it. So, for instance, these brambles to me signify strength, ability, endurance, tenacity and being unstoppable, because they grow at such a rate and are almost impossible to get rid of. They also symbolize to me protection from the sharp thorns, nourishment from the berries and little pink flowers to me represent love."

Conrad watched as she carefully clipped some of the bramble and put it in her trug, she jotted down what she had clipped and why and she then continued on her way. As she walked along the footpath, she saw a feather, "Ooo, lovely!" She chirped as she bent down to pick it up, "This is a dove or pigeons feather and these represent love, I consider that you can never generate too much of that!" Conrad smiled, "Oh, I agree with you there." he felt like he was being privy to something quite special as she continued on her way, wrapped up in her mission, her belief in what she was doing was clearly so real, he felt like he was stepping into another world, he'd never seen or heard anything like it, yet he felt completely open to what she was explaining as she went along.

They wandered further, collecting Lexi's trug of goodies for about an hour and once she had satisfied herself that she had what she wanted they returned home.

"So, what are you going to do with that lot now then?" Conrad asked eager to know what was coming next.

"I'm going to make a Dispacho." She replied, Conrad's expression remained blank, "Ever heard of a Dispacho?" she asked, continuing "Clearly not by the look on your face! It's a lovely practice, very therapeutic and positive." She said convincingly.

She placed the trug on the patio table and then disappeared into the kitchen, returning with a large square of brown paper. Conrad looked on as she laid it out on the table and then went back inside again returning with a bottle of Florida water. "What's all this then?" he asked.

"Right, well this is a cologne, I use for cleansing and purifying." She undid the bottle and tipped a small amount in the palm of her hand, then, with her finger she drew a cross in the middle of the paper with it and a small dot in each corner. She then focused on her trug and picked up some fern leaves and laid them neatly down on the paper, speaking her intention aloud as she did so.

"Fern leaves represent eternal youth, new life and new beginnings, they also symbolize hope for the future, which is quite appropriate for us right now." She said as she laid them down on the paper, this bought a smile to Conrad's face but he said nothing, curious to see what was coming next. Lexi, in her own little world continued to lay down the different items, verbally giving they're meaning as she went and making an elegant assembly of the things she had collected.

Laying down the different leaves first, fanned out in an eye-catching circle, she continued.

"A large, variegated leaf to symbolize variety in life."

"A dock leaf, to take the sting out of life!"

"Horseradish leaf, to add flavour to life."

"A few little dead leaves to symbolize letting go of that which no longer serves us." She cut the long piece of bramble into smaller pieces and laid them around the outside and added some holly leaves, "Thorns and prickles for protection from all negative energy."

"Red leaves to strengthen the root chakra for a sense of safety and security."

"Dandelions, the first food for the bees in springtime, every part of the dandelion is both edible and highly nutritious. They are also used in medicine, good for cleansing the liver, their yellow flowers stimulate the solar plexus chakra, nurturing a good sense of 'self', self-belief, self-worth and courage, so they are a lovely one to add."

"White petals for crystal clear intuition, purity and honesty."

"Daisies and Buttercups to nurture the child within and bring joy into life."

"Ivy, because it's tenacious and unstoppable, symbolizing strength and drive."

"Pink petals to symbolize God's love at work, gratitude and peace."

"Seeds to symbolize abundance, new growth and new beginnings."

As she laid the feathers down in the centre of her creation, she finished with "And of course the feathers to symbolize love because you can never have too much of that."

"That's quite beautiful." Conrad said in awe of her, "I have never seen anything like that in my life." He picked up his phone and took a picture of it. "What will you do with it now?"

"I'll leave it there until it gets dark and enjoy its beauty for a few hours, then I will fold it into a package and give it to one of the elements to create the energy from the intentions held within." She replied adding, "You can burn them, bury them, simply let them go in the wind or scatter them in a river to create the energy, I usually burn them or bury them though.

Darkness came and the moon rose in the sky. It was a pleasant evening, so Lexi decided to light the fire pit in the garden to burn the Despacho. By this time Janet had also seen Lexi's little creation and learned of the reason behind it.

When the time came to package it up, Lexi went over to it, picked up the two opposite the corners and lifted them tossing the pretty masterpiece into a pile in the middle of the paper.

"It seems a shame to spoil it really." Conrad said as he looked on. "Ah, it's all part of the process, we'll get to do another one in a couple of weeks!" Lexi smiled as she continued neatly folding the Dispacho and packed it into a tidy square, they then went over to the fire pit where the flames were dancing nicely.

Lexi stood holding the package to her heart with her eyes closed for a few long moments mentally connecting to it, visualizing all the positive intentions that were held within. She then drew a deep breath held the package before her and blew 'life-force' into the package. "This is to give strength to the intentions inside." she explained before continuing, "Once this energy is created it doesn't stop, energy keeps moving, so at this point my intention for this package is to create the energy I've made inside it for myself and us, then to send it out to my family, my friends and out as far as it can travel in to the community so that everyone will benefit from it, so now I'm visualizing just that.

"That's beautiful." Conrad said spellbound as she finished her visualization and then placed the Despacho in the fire. They stood and watched the flames turn all different colours as they engulfed the package. "Wow! Conrad commented not wanting to take his eyes off it, he felt he was witnessing something quite special, "I will enjoy doing this every couple of weeks, it feels almost magical."

"That's good." Said Lexi, "I'd hate to think you just suffered it to please me!"

"Absolutely not! I've never heard or seen anything like this but the whole thing is really resonating with me. Imagine how much positive energy could be created if everybody did it!" He pondered. "Exactly!" She replied as they both stood arm in arm watching the Despacho burn in the flames.

"I do a Despacho for both the full and new moons," she continued, "the energy of the new moon is very good for creating positive energy and setting your intention to bring that which you desire into your life every month. For this I also write down on paper all that I'd like to bring in and use water and intention to do it. I also do this on the full moon, but first I consciously focus on 'releasing' any negativity from the month that I feel I need to let go of. So, it's a bit like having a New Year's Eve mind-set at the end of every month, that's why I think it's so powerful."

"That sounds equally promising, I can definitely see why you do it, it does have a very positive feel about it. So, I have a couple of weeks to wait before I get to witness that one then." Conrad was beginning to feel like he'd stepped into another world. "We can do the water one tonight if you haven't had too much of the woo-woo stuff for one day!"

"Yeah, I'm game!" He said enthusiastically, "Great, let's go then!" And with that they headed back to the house.

Once inside, Lexi handed him a piece of paper and a pen and got one for herself, she then left the room and returned with a tray containing two small glass lidded bowls filled with mineral water. "Right," she said, "you don't have to show me, it's personal to you. You can write down anything you would like to bring in, it can be anything, physical, spiritual or emotional and as many as you like." Conrad sat; his pen poised above the paper for a few long moments. "I honestly can't really think of anything I want; I feel like I've got all I want right now!

"Yes, I have to admit I feel the same, but it could simply be something like our move going smoothly and the retreat coming to fruition with relative ease."

"Yeah, let's do that then." He said, starting to write. Lexi also wrote on her paper and then said, "Right, this is what I want you to do... You've written down what you would like to bring in, then I want you to sit and imagine the move going smoothly in as much detail as possible and with that thought in mind, I want you to imagine how you will 'feel' at that point and be present with this feeling, take a deep breath and then blow it into the water, like this." She demonstrated and Conrad then followed her example. "Then just imagine the retreat taking shape, being completed and coming to fruition, imagine how you will feel once we've achieved this, be really 'present' with this feeling of how you will feel and again, blow it into the water." His smile was from ear to ear as he did so; though this was a far cry from Conrad's previous life he was accepting of her notions and felt a child-like enthusiasm at the idea of it.

Once they were both done Lexi then gave him the lid, "So, put the lid on and then we will put the bowls outside under the moon so that the energy of the moon will pass over them." "Okay." Having done so, they went out in the garden and placed the bowls on the patio table. "And in the morning, we will drink our intentions!" she concluded quite happily.

"Well, thank you for the insight into your practice; I had absolutely no idea people did stuff like this! I can totally see why you do it though, and I can understand how it could help to make and keep anyone positive, especially if you practice it regularly." He said as he hugged her into him under the moonlight and kissed her on the lips. "You're most welcome, I'm pleased you enjoyed it, imagine how special it will feel in our new place surrounded by nature."

"Yeah, absolutely." He agreed. "Our wood will be perfect for it." she said confidently and with that they returned inside, got themselves two glasses of water and retired to bed.

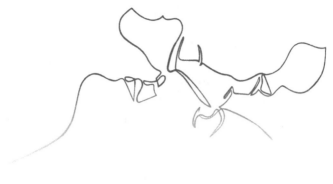

66

On the Friday evening, they arranged to go for a meal with Paul. They booked a table at quite a posh Thai restaurant in the town and decided to get a taxi in so that they could both enjoy a glass of wine with their meal. When they arrived, Paul was already there having a drink at the bar. He greeted them and got them both a drink, they sat in the bar chatting until their table was ready.

Paul raised his glass, "Here's to you two, I wish you all the best for your future, home and business together." They chinked glasses.

"Aw, thank you, and here's to you as well, and whatever your future holds for you!"

Paul had always been quite keen on doing something similar to what Lexi and Conrad were doing; only he enjoyed the gym side of it more. He also practiced and preached that 'lifestyle was key' and most certainly walked his talk. In the years that he'd known Lexi, despite her being twice his age, they'd shared a very similar mind-set and had complemented each other well in the gym. In the back of his mind, he had always assumed that Lexi would be a permanent thing in his life. Many times, at the gym when things had been done a certain way by the management, they would've had the conversation…" If this we're our place…" They both had a definite 'ideal' of how they would run things totally on the same wavelength. It saddened Paul to lose Lexi but at the same time, he was pleased to see her happy, especially after witnessing her recent, traumatic events. He was totally made up for her that she was about to live her dream and what's more, he really liked Conrad.

They had a lovely meal, talked over their plans for the new place, told Paul of their fun and games at the auctions and about how you could barely move in the house for furniture and other stuff now accumulating, all ready for the big move.

"God, it's going to be so strange without you, you're the only one that really 'gets me' at work," said Paul.

"Yeah, I must admit, they do seem more about 'what makes money' rather than what's right. What do you think you'll do; will you stay there?" Lexi asked.

"Not sure really, I'll see how it shapes up after you've gone, I do enjoy working in the gym and I've got a massive clientele now," he said.

"Wouldn't you like to try to branch out on your own, your clients will follow you?" she suggested.

"I've always thought I would, if not out-right own somewhere, maybe run a place with someone else. We'll have to see what comes up, thing is, I need to meet someone who's on the same wavelength as me, I need to meet another you!" He said jokingly, only there was truth in his jesting and Lexi knew that.

"We have always worked well together, haven't we? Mind you, you never know who might take my place there, you could end up with another colleague that you get on with and you just never know where it might lead," she said in a positive manner.

"We'll see," he replied, "I'll keep an open mind, if not you might find me on your doorstep!"

"That wouldn't be a problem, I'm sure we'd find plenty for you to do!" she winked.

"Watch this space!" he winked back at them both and raised his glass. They finished their drinks and ordered the taxi back home. The taxi driver popped his head in the door and they all stood up, having arranged to drop Paul off first. Once outside Paul's place, he jumped out and Lexi and Conrad quickly got out to say goodbye. Paul shook Conrad's hand, a good, hearty shake and hugged him into him with the other arm at the same time.

"Look after her won't you mate," he said starting to feel a touch emotional.

Conrad could see just how much this meant to him and promised, "I sure will, trust me, she is my world!"

"I know she is; I can see that and I honestly couldn't be happier for you both," He said with total conviction. Then turned to Lexi and said, "Bye, bye Blondie," and hugged her tight.

"Bye, bye sweetie, thank you for being the 'best-est' friend to me," she said as she hugged him back.

"It's worked both ways over the years, hasn't it? We've had many-a-late night in your kitchen when you've tried to console me for one reason or another!"

They hugged and both had a little cry, then Lexi, trying to break the sadness of it, said "Well, check your diary and let me know when you can book some time off to come and stay."

"Yes, I will do that," he hugged her again and then re-shook Conrad's hand and walked to his front door, as they got back in the cab. He turned back and waved to them as the cab drove off, he watched the taillights go down the road and gave a sigh of mixed feelings as he turned to go inside.

67

Saturday morning came, and Lexi and Conrad got up early to get food for the family get-together. Down in the kitchen, just as the coffee beans were being ground, they were joined by Nathan. "Coffee?" Lexi asked.

"Ooh, lovely, yes please; you're up early." He said.

"Yes, we thought we'd make an early start. I rang the butcher and ordered some juicy steaks for tonight and a chicken for tomorrow; we just need to get the veg, some wine and some beers for Eddie. We wanted to go over the field for a session first and I don't want to run out of time," Lexi explained.

"Well, I can get the wine and beers for you, that'll save you some time," Nathan offered.

"Oh, that's great, thank you," she said, as she poured the coffee into three mugs; the rich aroma filled the air. Time stood still for ten seconds as they all immersed themselves silently in that heavenly, first couple of sips.

"Mmm, hits the spot, doesn't it?" said Conrad.

"Absolutely" Nathan agreed, adding, "Actually, if you give me a list, I can pick up the other stuff as well, that way you can take your time. I might as well get it all while I'm out and let's face it, you'll be the one busy in the kitchen later because you're the one who does it best!" He winked.

"I'll drink to that!" said Conrad raising his mug, "She's an awesome cook…. Mind you, I'm getting more of a 'handle' on it now!" He looked to Lexi for confirmation.

"You most certainly are." Lexi agreed.

Conrad added, "And I'll help you with the veggies later anyway, I enjoy doing that."

Lexi smiled and then turned to Nathan saying, "Well, if you don't mind Nathan, that would be great."

"No, not at all," He replied, "write a list for me and I'll get everything." With that sorted, they finished their coffees and went their separate ways.

No longer in a rush, Lexi and Conrad had a super workout at their leisure, then ambled on home, got showered and ready and came downstairs just as Nathan was coming back through the front door with a couple of carrier bags. They took the shopping from him and through to the kitchen while Nathan went back to the car for the rest; Janet was in the kitchen and had just put the kettle on.

Once it was put away the four sat round the table and had a cuppa. Janet seemed a little stressed.

"Are you ok Janet?" Lexi asked.

"I'm feeling a bit apprehensive to be honest," she replied.

"Well, that's understandable but just think, if they were that against it, neither of them would have entertained the idea of coming, would they?" she tried to reason, "Just try and relax a bit."

Janet tried to force a half smile and then said, "I'm feeling a bit sick."

"That's because you're stressed, you've been so much better these last two weeks, try your breathing exercises."

But the advice came a little late; Janet got up and rushed to the downstairs toilet, the sounds of her retching obvious to all. Lexi looked at Conrad, they exchanged an 'oh dear' kind of face.

Nathan stated, "She's been getting herself in a state over this for the last couple of days."

"Mmm, tricky one, it's the unknown isn't it," Lexi said, "She'll be fine once the initial meeting is over and done with." After about five minutes Janet reappeared.

"You ok hun?" said Nathan, followed by the other two.

"Yes, I think so. I know I've got to meet them some time, it's just this initial meeting, I can feel my adrenaline pumping through me," she said looking very pale and shaky.

"I'm sure it'll be fine Janet," and as the words left her mouth, they heard the front door go and Eddie's voice ring out.

"Hiya!" As he and his girlfriend came through the door. Janet looked like a rabbit caught in the headlights! Nathan got up and shouted, "In the kitchen!" and stood behind Janet rubbing her shoulder in a supportive way.

Lexi reached out, gently placed her hand on Janet's arm and said, "He'll be fine, honestly," while in her head she was thinking, 'It's Corrie you need to worry about!"

But even then, in her heart, she truly felt that the kids wouldn't come with the intention of giving her a hard time; in her chats with the kids, they had both seemed far more accepting of the situation now they had had a while for it to all sink in.

As Eddie and his girlfriend, Sophie, entered the kitchen, Lexi and Conrad got up from the table. "Hello love," Lexi said as she walked over to him with open arms, giving first him a big hug and kiss, and then Sophie; she then turned to Conrad and introduced him to them.

Eddie and Conrad shook hands exchanging, "Hi!" And "Pleased to meet you!"

Lexi smiled, sensing an easy and comfortable energy between them. Janet got up from the table, Nathan, with his arm around her, encouraged her over to them, greeting them and introducing Janet. They both said hello politely and without the slightest suggestion of negative feeling. Janet, although incredibly pale as she stood there, felt a certain relief as soon as the moment was over. "Do you both want a drink? We've only just sat down to a cuppa," said Lexi, as she refilled the kettle and took two mugs down from the cupboard.

Then they all heard a "Hi!", then a bump and "Blimey!" from the furniture-packed hall, as Corrie and her boyfriend Alfie were now navigating their way through it.

"In the kitchen!" Lexi called, taking another two mugs down from the cupboard.

They entered the kitchen and again, Lexi went over, gave her a hug and kiss, kissed Alfie on the cheek and again turned and introduced Conrad to them both. Corrie smiled at her mum giving her a certain 'look', which said she approved of Conrad. Conrad was completely comfortable and at ease with the whole thing, happy to finally meet these two strapping young adults that Lexi always talked of so proudly. Nathan then greeted the two of them and introduced Janet. They all shook hands and everything seemed fine although, Lexi knew her daughter inside-out and was extremely perceptive of the energy she gave out. She could detect that Corrie wasn't quite so relaxed with Janet but was being polite all the same.

In a bid to diffuse any awkwardness she said, "I just got you a couple of mugs out, what would you like to drink?" They replied, and Lexi made the drinks, lightening the conversation with, "You managed to climb over all the furniture in the hall then!"

"Only just! Blimey, there's a lot of it isn't there?" Corrie replied.

"That's not the half of it!" Nathan added, "It's in the garage, the shed, your bedrooms..."

Then Conrad contributed, "And a lorry full at the antique shop waiting to be delivered! We were thinking if the retreat doesn't work out, we'll go into the second-hand furniture trade; your mum is the absolute business at the auctions!" He winked at Lexi, and they all laughed, it was a nice icebreaker.

"It must be a nightmare constantly climbing over that lot!" said Eddie.

"Well, to be fair it's only been this cluttered for the last two days and it's not for long, we complete on Friday." Lexi beamed, feeling a streak of excitement rip through her as she said it, Conrad squeezed her hand, equally feeling the tingle of excitement at her words.

They stayed at the kitchen table, from the cup of tea onto a light lunch and beyond. Though, maybe a little 'careful' to begin with, the ice was well and truly broken between them, all of them contributing to the conversation. Firstly, it was just pleasantries, followed on by some of the more practical topics, raised by Eddie. Obviously, the kids were concerned as to what would be happening with regards to their family home, now that things had changed so dramatically since their last visit. The parents assured both of them that the house wouldn't be sold for the foreseeable future. The kids were also made aware by both parents that they were to treat both homes as their own and were welcome to either house whenever they wanted. With all that out of the way, they spent a harmonious afternoon.

In the kitchen Lexi made a healthy sweet while Conrad prepared the vegetables for the meal. Once that was done, they all went out for a country walk, an activity Lexi and Nathan had done with the kids from a very young age, finishing up at the local pub, for a drink and then heading back home.

Lexi and Conrad started cooking the meal and between the rest of them the table was set, wine glasses put out, wine opened, and Corrie appeared from upstairs with some board games and a pack of cards to play after dinner. As Lexi stood in front of the cooker doing the steaks, Conrad came up behind her, put his arms around her waist nuzzled into her neck and gave her a kiss, Lexi smiling to herself as she glowed in his affection.

"It's all going very well I think," he said.

"Yes, it couldn't have gone any better really, could it? I did have my doubts, but I'm really pleased we've done it now," Lexi replied.

"Yes, so am I and I'm really pleased to meet your kids, they're lovely young people, you must be very proud of them."

Lexi 'cooed' "Thank you, I am very proud of them, I think they've both handled this with such maturity, it makes everything so much easier."

"Totally, it's all good… it'll always be good from now."

He kissed her again, then Lexi said, "Right, tell everyone to sit down at the table, I'm about ready to dish up!"

Conrad went through and Corrie went into the kitchen to give her mum a hand dishing up, getting the food out hot onto the plates and they all enjoyed a delicious, well-deserved feast after their walk. They stayed around the table well into the evening playing games and getting a little bit silly as the wine flowed. Around 10pm, Janet excused herself as she was now well and truly exhausted and went to bed. Nathan and Eddie sat in the lounge playing on the x-box and the rest of them stayed at the table playing cards for a while longer.

Eventually, they all decided it was time to go to bed; happy and tired they said goodnight and made their way upstairs. Lexi, being Lexi cleared the glasses from the table and took them into the kitchen before going up, while Conrad tidied up the games. As Lexi pottered in the kitchen, Conrad saw Corrie go back through into the kitchen; deciding to give them some space, he went upstairs and got ready for bed. As Lexi loaded the dishwasher, she noticed Corrie.

"You, ok hun?" she said.

"Yes, I've just come down for some water," Corrie replied.

"Mmm, I think we'll all be needing plenty of that, don't you? I hope the others thought to take some up!" Lexi added, Corrie hovered as her mum was tidying the last bits.

"Thank you for today mum, it's been really enjoyable, better than I imagined it would be."

Lexi felt relieved to hear this, saying, "Good. I'm really pleased you've had a nice day. I just wanted to get everyone off on the right foot. A clean and positive start, it's important to both your dad and me that you're both ok and still feel that you matter in all of this."

"I know we do mum," she replied. "Obviously, I would have been happier if it'd never happened in the first place, but it has happened. It's taken me a while to get my head round it but I'm there now and I am truly happy that you've found someone who clearly makes you so happy," she said, Lexi could tell she really meant it.

"Thank you darling," she said, giving Corrie a hug. "And your dad and Janet, are you ok with that now?"

Corrie looked at her mum, "I'll get there, I'm not quite there yet if I'm honest."

"I didn't think you were, but I appreciate how you've handled it," Lexi said, still in their embrace, rubbing her daughter's back. "You'll get there, it's all going to be alright."

"I know I will. I mean, I don't dislike what I've seen of her... it's just the baby thing," she said with honesty.

"I know it is sweetheart, but don't forget, you will always be his princess, nothing will change that... ever." She hugged Corrie tight in her arms.

"Thank you, mum, I love you," she said.

"I love you too darling." The two girls got their water and Lexi grabbed a couple more bottles of water and clean glasses, "I'll leave these on the landing table in case anyone else needs water in the night." Finally they went upstairs.

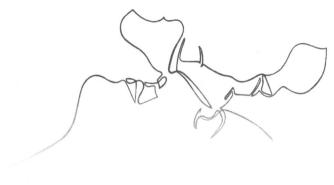

68

In the morning they all surfaced between 8.30 and 9am. Nathan was the first out of bed and down to the kitchen; he put the kettle on and ground some coffee. The rest of them gradually migrated towards the kitchen once the aroma of the coffee had travelled upstairs and got their attention, along with the smell of the bacon Nathan was now cooking under the grill. Lexi and Conrad were the next to appear, closely followed by the others.

Sitting around the table, Lexi started the conversation, "Did you all sleep ok?"

"Yes, great thanks," said Eddie, backed up first by Sophie, then a chorus from the rest of the table. Lexi then added jovially, "You all managed to get through the night without falling over the furniture then?"

"Just about!" said Eddie.

Corrie piped up, "Mum, I love that little grey bed-side table that's in my room."

"Lovely, isn't it?" agreed Lexi.

Corrie nodded, mid-sip of coffee, "I think it's really pretty and so unusual."

"Well, I'll make sure I earmark that one for your bedroom then!" Lexi, affectionately placed her hand on Corrie's and patted it. This instantly bought a smile to Corrie's face.

They all enjoyed the much-needed cooked breakfast, then, one-by-one they disappeared upstairs to shower and dress while Lexi put a chicken in the oven to roast slowly and prepared the vegetables to accompany it. They had planned on going to a massive park on the other side of town with a big lake to take a walk and feed the ducks, something both the kids had never grown out of; then they would all return home for a roast mid-afternoon, after which the kids intended to be on their way.

They spent a pleasant afternoon out despite the fact it had turned a little chilly. They had all wrapped up warm and spent a couple of hours out, finally returning home, eight of them in two cars, with the car windows steamed up and runny noses. They opened the front door and stepped into the homely smell of the roast cooking.

"Mmm, I love that 'Sunday' smell!" said Eddie.

"That's what Sundays are all about!" said Nathan.

For Lexi, Nathan, Corrie and Eddie, this was the regular Sunday experience, when they had all been at home. Every weekend, Lexi would put dinner in to cook slowly and they would spend the afternoon out; it seemed both fitting and enjoyable that they should now share this family tradition. The house was warm and inviting, within an hour, the 'roasties' were ready, and Lexi was dishing up the meal while Conrad happily carved the chicken, totally enjoying being part of this family experience.

Everyone enjoyed their meal and with full bellies and happy hearts the kids packed all their stuff together, ready to head back to their individual homes. They all said goodbye with hugs and kisses all round; the introduction weekend had been a success, no bad atmospheres or expressions of bad feeling. Both Lexi and Nathan were relieved that it'd gone so well, and both felt very proud of their children and how they had represented themselves.

After waving the kids off, the four adults flopped in the sitting room.

"Well, that couldn't have gone any better, could it?" said Lexi happily.

"No, not at all, it was lovely to meet them both and their other halves. I have to say, your children are a credit to you both," said Janet.

"Totally," agreed Conrad.

"See, I told you not to worry, didn't I?" said Lexi.

"I know, but it's easier said than done when you feel that you've been the catalyst in something so huge," Janet replied

"Shush now! Put it in a box and move on, let's just all live in harmony now," said Lexi.

"I second that!" said Conrad.

"Yes, totally," added Nathan.

"Let's just all move forward now and enjoy what life has to offer us," Lexi finished. At that point Janet went for a lie down and the rest of them watched a film to finish the day.

The next few days were spent finalising everything ready to move on the Friday, Lexi and Conrad getting so excited they could barely contain themselves.

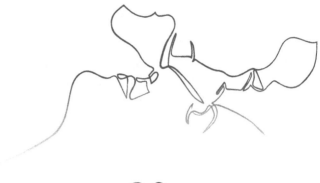

69

The big day came, Lexi and Conrad instantly aware of what the day was. With everything packed apart from what they would need that morning, they were good-to-go. They both dived out of bed and went excitedly downstairs to make the coffee, their excitement on-a-par with that of two small four-year-olds at around 5am on Christmas morning! They decided to have a massive breakfast and Lexi also packed up a well-prepared cool box of at least two day's of food to be transferred to the fridge once it was installed and running. By the time they were showered and ready, the lorry had arrived to move their belongings and the almighty stash of furniture. Their instructions were that they could pick up the key any time after 12pm.

With everything packed, the lorry set off on its way with Lexi and Conrad all set to follow on in the car. Nathan and Janet came to see them off in the now, seemingly, enormous hall without all the furniture in it!

"Wow! It seems bigger than I remember!" said Nathan jokingly, "Have you got absolutely everything?" he asked.

"Yes, I think so," said Lexi, so excited she could barely get her words out.

"Well, if you haven't, I can always send it to you," he confirmed. He gave Lexi a hug and shook Conrad's hand.

Janet faced Lexi, held both of her hands and said, "Thank you Lexi," they exchanged a kiss on the cheek and Conrad shook her hand.

"Right!" Conrad said, addressing Lexi, "Let's go start our new life, shall we?"

"Yes!" Lexi squealed, clapping her hands together and doing a little dance on-the-spot. They took the bags left for the journey out to the car.

"Good luck with it all," said Nathan.

"Yes, best of luck, I hope it's everything you've dreamed of," said Janet.

"Thank you," they both replied and got into the car, with Conrad in the driver's seat.

He started the car and they both waved as he drove off. Lexi looked back at the house with no sadness, her last weekend spent in her family home had been a pleasurable experience and, in her heart, she was now bound for new beginnings.

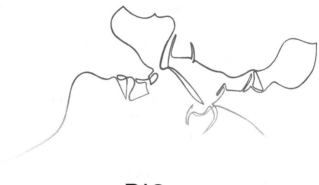

70

When they arrived at the house, the lorry was already parked there. Turning in to the driveway both of them felt as though their hearts were going to come out of their chest.

"Welcome, to our wonderful new home," said Conrad. Lexi just looked at the beautiful stone house in awe, tears in her eyes that it was now theirs.

They went to the heavy wooden door; Conrad took her hand so both their hands were placed on the key and together they turned it and opened the door. Lexi felt like she was riding on a cloud; apart from when her children were born, she could never recall being so blissfully happy. At that point Conrad snatched her up and carried her inside. The removal men looked at each other and exchanged an "Aw!" as they went around the back of the lorry and opened it.

They all started moving in boxes and furniture. The removals men deposited the bed in the master bedroom and all the bedroom-type furniture was distributed around the upstairs of the house for them to sort out once they'd got a feel for the place. Then all the tables, a bookshelf and other, downstairs-type furniture was bought in and shared between the rooms for them to position while Lexi and Conrad got on with the most important job of unpacking and putting in place all the kitchen equipment. Within an hour, the lorry arrived from the antique shop with their enormous wooden dresser that took pride-of-place in the kitchen. It looked like it had been made for it. Over the next couple of hours, the white goods arrived and were set up; now their home started to really take shape. All they now needed was their lounge furniture, which was due to arrive before 6pm.

Once they'd finished the kitchen, they both went around the house deciding which room was best for what furniture. The television and hi fi were installed and as arranged, the settee and two armchairs arrived shortly before 6pm. By the end of the day, although still a bit empty, the house was looking more like a home. They didn't yet have a dining room table, but the kitchen had an island that they could eat from. Lexi prepared them some dinner while Conrad lit the wood burner using some of the chopped wood the previous owners had left stacked next to the fireplace. As he did so, he discovered an envelope left for them and took it into Lexi in the kitchen. They opened it, it was a little card wishing them luck and happiness in their new home.

"Aw, how sweet of them!" Lexi said, really appreciating the gesture; Conrad put it in on the centrepiece of the kitchen, the beautiful dresser. Both of them were feeling 'blessed' and their home felt instinctively right, like it was simply meant to be.

They had their meal and then sat in the lounge in front of the cosy wood burner, both feeling absolutely shattered from the day's events. They tried out the new television but by 9.30, tiredness got the better of them and they went upstairs to bed. Finally cuddled up, Conrad asked. "Are you happy, baby?"

"God, yes, I feel I'm the luckiest girl alive! I thought I was when I managed to contact you again; that in-itself would've been enough for me, it wouldn't have mattered where we ended up, just having you back in my life was wonderful. I could never have imagined in a million years that in just over three months we would be here; it's like the happily-ever-after in a fairy tale and I feel like the princess!" she said in a state of bliss.

"You are the princess. My princess!" He kissed her and then, despite how tired they were, they made love for the first time, in their lovely new bedroom in their wonderful new home, where they would be spending the rest of their lives together.

71

Getting up the next morning, they decided the first thing they should do was go and have a look at one of the out houses, to Lexi, the next most important place to get 'functional' besides the kitchen, was the gym. Then, they needed to go food shopping and source a decent, organic butcher and a farm shop, so these were the tasks they had set themselves for the day.

Lexi had already bought a lot of gym equipment with her that she'd accumulated over her many years in the industry. They had everything they needed for an outside workout, plus some weights and barbells, a physio ball and some other bits for inside. As they mentally put their gym together, they sourced, enquired about and ordered everything online. Firstly, some proper gym flooring, a squat rack, cable machine, more weights, another ball, kettlebells, mats, the list was quite extensive. Conrad found it highly entertaining listening to Lexi as she visually made the gym come to life in this blank, open space with her experience and logic. She was as excited about kitting the gym out as she was about the house.

"Oh, wow! It's going to be great in here, a totally functional gym and no silly machines! It's such a lovely space too, light and airy, absolutely perfect," she said enthusiastically.

Together they set out how it would work and where equipment would be situated. It was a substantially sized building; the entire upper floor was currently one big open room. This, they were planning to be the gym with the changing rooms and a separate treatment room to one end. The downstairs was divided into two rooms, one considerably larger than the other. They took measurements for installing an infrared sauna, jacuzzi and tiled shower area, leaving the smaller room for somewhere to lie on spa-style couches and chill out; this would work nicely as there were large, glass doors in this room that looked out onto the glorious setting. With everything that they wanted and needed to make the space work, either ordered or at least sourced, including local tradesmen, Lexi began to think about the colour scheme she would like in the rooms to create the right mood for each. She was in her element as she could see her dreams coming to life. Outside, there was an expanse of grass that ran behind two of the outhouses; they both felt this was perfect, left for outside activities and workouts.

They went back to the house for some lunch. Lexi put together something from their stash in the fridge. Outside was a small stone wall in keeping with the walls of the house situated at the end of the patio area. Being a warm day, Lexi suggested, "Let's take it outside and get a real feel for our new surroundings." They sat on the wall eating and looking out over the land. "Oh, it's heavenly out here, isn't it, I still can't believe it's ours, it's an absolute paradise."

"I know what you mean," Conrad replied with the most contented smile on his face, "I keep pinching myself and thinking I'm going to wake up in a minute! We were so lucky seeing this when we did, it was so meant to be. I literally feel like I never want set foot out of here again!"

"I can see us having many breakfasts and morning coffees out on this patio," Lexi said, unconsciously patting the wall she was sitting on and taking in the fresh air. "In fact, I can see us being out here at every given opportunity!"

"Yeah, it's such a lovely outlook and what a fantastic way to start the day. One of the next most important things on the list needs to be a patio table," Conrad said.

"Absolutely! I'd also like a covered area, possibly there," she pointed, "with another table, a heater and barbeque so we can enjoy the outside in all weathers. We can store a few extra loungers under there for laying out in the sun or star gazing on a clear night.

He turned and looked at her and said, "I love the way your mind works Lexi, that's something I would never have thought of!"

"All food for the soul hun," she replied, "that's what it's all about; I've had this vision in my head for such a long time. It's all geared about finding that 'peace' within and with all that's around."

"I already feel I've slowed down by about a hundred miles an hour just being here. Despite everything we plan to do, inside I feel like I've taken my foot right off the gas, you know?" He said.

"Yeah, I know, nice, isn't it? I don't think either of us will miss the pressure we'd associated with our previous lives; it's not till it drops away that you realise just how stressed you were on a day-to-day basis," Lexi observed, and Conrad agreed.

"Yeah, you're right there." They sat casting their eyes out over the landscape. "Listen to the birds…" she said, both sat taking in the chatter of the bird song, after a few moments Conrad said "I think it would be good to spend tomorrow morning exploring the land"

"Mmm, yes," Lexi agreed.

"We need to explore every 'nook and cranny'. As lovely as it is sitting here, we need to become properly acquainted with it, to know exactly what we've got out there and get some idea of what we might like to do with the different areas within it. We can have an exciting day exploring it and exchanging ideas, then come back and have a hearty dinner to round the day off, ready to start work 'proper' on Monday when the gym flooring arrives," Lexi said getting her business head on.

"Sounds like a plan to me," he agreed, "we can get that flooring down. I should imagine some, if not all of the equipment will have arrived by mid-week. Once the gym is sorted, we can pick off the other jobs one by one."

"Absolutely, I was thinking, it would be good to complete the gym and spa so that we can make use of them straight away. I want to show you the true benefit of balancing hard work with rest and pleasure."

Conrad smiled at her words, "I'm up for that and then we can get the garden how we want it."

"Yes and start a vegetable patch!" She added enthusiastically.

"Yep, vegetable patch… poly tunnel if you want?" he suggested.

"Ooh, now there's a thought!" She chirped," I think it would be an idea to get a gardener to help us initially. I love the thought of growing our own vegetables, but I don't know much about gardening at all, ours was always for the kids" she admitted.

"That's not a problem, I'm sure there are plenty of gardeners around here! Let's get it all done and set up for us, get ourselves in a good routine and last of all sort out the accommodation; while that's being done, you can get your 'retreat head' on and put together a plan of how you want it to run. Work out what you're going to need, how you'd run your day-to-day schedule, how many days you feel each 'intake' should run for to get across all the information and practical activities you have in mind. It's your dream, Lexi and I want you to take your time working out exactly how you want it all to run."

Lexi felt a massive surge of excitement at his words; it was going to be absolutely superb!

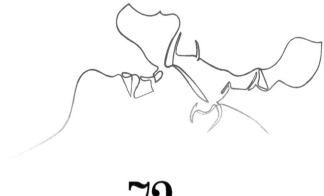

72

The next morning, they got up and had their coffee out, sitting on the stone wall in their fleecy dressing gowns; it was a slightly chilly but pleasant and sunny day.

"I'm looking forward to this today," said Lexi.

"Yeah, me too," he agreed, "a bit like a magical mystery tour, we never know what we might find! I'm hoping there's a pond, I'd quite like a pond."

"Well, if there isn't, that can be a project for you further down the line!"

Conrad liked the sound of this, "Yeah, that can be my project once the buildings are done."

"Are you thinking of a pond with fish as well?"

"Not sure, hadn't really thought that far ahead, there's just something I find peaceful about sitting by a pond," he said as they finished their coffees. After a substantial breakfast, they got themselves ready and headed out for a day of exploring.

They walked beyond the patio, both already in agreement about where the vegetable patch would go and the poly-tunnel, if they decided to take it that far. Just beyond the patio was a 'kept' area of garden that was enclosed by a neat hedge, with a gate through to an area of fruit trees; not enormous, about fifteen different trees with apples, pears, cherries and Victoria plumb, all nicely in fruit.

"Well, I think there's an opportunity for some jam making here!" said Conrad.

"It's fabulous, isn't it, and an absolute haven for wildlife," she added.

"Do you know how to make jam?"

"No! It's not something I've ever been into, not eating bread; besides, it's too high in sugar… though we could pick a lot of it and make our own cider and Perry; or we could have a go at making some organic wine and fermented juices from it, there's no end of stuff you can do with it really; maybe down the line we could have a little hatch out on the drive selling the fruit as well and then leave the rest for the wildlife."

They carried on making their way towards the boundary across an unkempt field that was rich with different grasses and wildflowers and as they made their way through, they could see a little wooden bridge. Approaching it, they realised there was a stream going through the land and the little bridge went over it.

"Oh, wow! This is a nice surprise!" She exclaimed

Conrad's eyes traced its path, "If you look, this is the stream from the waterfall we found that day."

"How odd is that… and it's going right through our garden!" Lexi felt this a very positive omen. The stream busily babbled past, the birds chirped happily in the hedges beyond the stream and the sun beamed down on them.

"Wow! What a lovely spot!" They were both in awe as they approached the stream and sitting down on the grass for a while, they soaked up the sun on their faces and lost themselves in the sounds of the trickling water and the birdsong.

"Oh… this is divine!" She sighed happily.

"Isn't it?" He agreed.

"We need to put a bench here, it's a perfect place to come and sit. God, I feel so privileged!" said Lexi.

"It's a very tranquil setting," he agreed, adding," I think a picnic table would also be a good idea here."

"Mmm, definitely." They enjoyed this spot for quite some time, finally stepping onto the little wooden bridge and watching the water run underneath them.

"Who would have thought that the day we found the source of the waterfall, and saw this stream rolling down toward the village, it would become a permanent feature in our lives? This gives me another idea for my releasing ritual for the full moon and the stream would become a significant part of it," she said, her brain enthusiastically ticking away. "I'd better earmark this place for a log cabin then?" Conrad offered. "Absolutely, or a yurt!" Lexi countered with a big grin on her face, really on a roll now as her surroundings were inspiring her. "Wow, I can just imagine it, this is so exciting." She chirped happily. "I'll do this with you on the next full moon, though right now I can't think of anything I'd like to release!

"I'll second that," he agreed," there isn't a single thing in my life right now that I'd need to release. I honestly feel at the moment like the world has been rigged in my favour, I'm so happy." He said earnestly. "Yes, I have to admit I feel exactly the same." Lexi agreed.

They stood on the bridge and watched the water for a few more minutes, then had a game of 'Pooh sticks', and at last carried on their way to the wild, overgrown area beyond that took them down towards the boundary.

They followed the boundary through the long grass walking in the direction of their little wood.

"I never dreamed I'd have my own wood," said Lexi as they carefully made their way through the trees.

All at once, they spotted a small deer; they stopped completely still and watched it going about its business, oblivious to their presence. "Oh, my God!" she whispered, squeezing Conrad's hand as they exchanged an excited glance.

The creature carried on ambling through the trees and then suddenly spotted them stopping dead in its tracks, startled by its unexpected audience, it then darted off into the wood out of sight. They were both filled with wonderment.

"Oh wow! There must be so much wildlife here," said Conrad.

"Absolutely! I definitely want to install some cameras, different ones so that we could watch the wildlife by day and night; I bet we have badgers and all sorts in here!" She said enthusiastically.

"Yes, we'll definitely do that, "Conrad agreed. "The more I encounter our new surroundings, the more in love with it I am!" Conrad said caught up in the whole experience.

"Me too, I could happily become a hermit!" she agreed, as they laughed. "We also need to put up nesting boxes with cameras in, it would be a real point of interest for us and our guests, it would be lovely to be able to watch the new life that's being created in our own wood, to watch the birds nesting and the chicks hatching. We could have an observation room with the different screens on a wall, or one big screen split into sections. We could even have a Youtube channel; people could subscribe and have access to however many cameras we install 24/7 and do our own version of 'Nature watch'!" She added excitedly.

"Now I really like the idea of that!" He replied enthusiastically, being the one with the head for technology, "Most definitely another project for me there, that's right up my street!"

Then she continued, "And I think we need to add a few benches, not many, just a few, carefully placed so there are places to sit quietly and just take it all in." They carried on walking through the wood, the birds singing, undisturbed by their presence and squirrels effortlessly jumping from tree to tree as they walked through their domain. Approaching a circular clearing in the trees, Lexi said, "Look at that. I think this would be the perfect spot for a log cabin, for that total, outdoor experience. Imagine one there," she pointed, "with a nice fire pit and wooden loungers as well to lie out and watch the night sky."

"Now you're talking! That would be pretty awesome, wouldn't it?" Conrad's eyes were scanning the area visualizing it.

As they continued to walk through the wood, they noticed that some of the leaves were beginning to take on their autumn colours. "This is going to look so pretty in a couple of weeks," said Lexi.

"Yeah, I was just thinking that," Conrad agreed, "It's all just starting to turn, isn't it?"

They walked along hand-in-hand, taking in the textures and colours, when they came upon another large opening in the trees, where a big, old tree trunk lay on the ground. Lexi climbed up and sat on it and Conrad joined her. "This would be another perfect spot for a cabin I think." She observed. They looked around themselves taking in the beauty of the wood and the birdsong.

"Yep, I'll just add it to my list." Conrad said jokingly elbowing her in the side.

"I'm just so happy here," Lexi sighed.

"Me too," Conrad put his arm around her pulling her into him and planted a kiss on her cheek. Lexi turned her head and returned the kiss, which turned into another and another.

Conrad jumped down from the trunk and stood between her legs as she sat there, put his hands inside her coat and caressed her waist and then moved his hands up to her breasts.

As he carried on kissing her, he whispered in her ear, "I want you naked!" Lexi shivered with excitement as he slipped her coat off.

"What, completely naked?" she asked.

"Yeah, why not? It's not as if anyone is going to come along, is it? It's our wood, I think we need to christen it!"

Lexi didn't need any more convincing, "Well, if you put it like that..."

She started to undress him, as he did her. Although the air was quite 'crisp', both were feeling turned on by the freedom of being able to make love, naked in broad daylight surrounded by nature in their own, private paradise. Lexi popped her coat under her to make the tree trunk a little more comfortable. This wasn't going to be a marathon, once unclothed it was apparent just how chilly the air was. Lexi leant back against the tree and Conrad got between her legs and entered her, she gasped and leaned back on her elbows on the trunk as he thrust into her. Cold as it was, it seemed to intensify the sensation, their skin, tight and covered in goose bumps, their nipples hard and erect from the chilly air mingled with sexual arousal. Her muscles, slightly rigid from the cold, amplified the force of his penetration, both groaning with the excitement of their spontaneous nature 'romp'. He picked up her legs under the knees and pushed them gently back towards her chest as she remained on her back, the penetration was phenomenal, making her groan with pleasure.

After a while he stopped, smiled a knowing smile and said, "Turn over."

Lexi turned belly down over the trunk; it was the perfect height to support her while Conrad, delivering the perfect grand-finale, taking her from behind, galloped for the finishing line. Needless to say, in the chilly air there was no lying, caressing and cuddling for half an hour, once their mission was complete, Conrad smacked her bum and they quickly got back into their warm clothes. As Lexi was doing up her coat, Conrad stepped toward her, kissed her tenderly and said, "We'll have to do that again in the summer!"

"We most certainly will, in fact, I think there will be many places we will be christening!"

They laughed and then Conrad added, "As long as we're not in view of the footpath the other side of the boundary!"

"And not when we've got clients staying here!" Lexi added.

They laughed, then continued on their way, walking and exploring every inch of this nature's paradise. By the time they returned to the house, they had a clear picture of what they would like to do and where they would like certain things to be. Over dinner they made a list of the things they would need to make the outside space exactly as they'd envisaged it, to take their time with once the buildings were sorted.

By the end of the first week, the gym was all set up and usable. Next, they focused on the sauna and jacuzzi, Lexi had fallen in love with some beautiful, bohemian style aqua colour tiles for this area. By the end of week three, the tiling was finished, and the sauna and a shower were installed. This was done mainly by Conrad as Lexi focused on the relaxation room, which she'd decorated in rich purples and golds, with a comfy couch, two spa beds, vibrant, colourful throws, and 'peaceful' relaxing pictures on the walls; it really was a pleasant space to lie and relax.

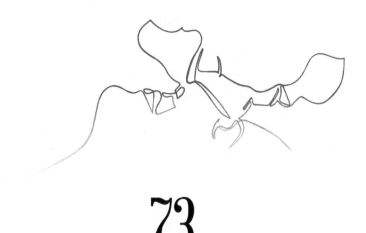

73

At the beginning of the fourth week, the jacuzzi was installed. They both now set out to include a certain amount of structured exercise, breath work, meditation or mindfulness daily. They made sure they spent time out in nature every day, especially when working on the outbuildings. They enjoyed relaxing in the sauna, jacuzzi and relaxation room at the end of their working day, which now had a sound system installed to play relaxing music to add to the ambiance. The relaxation areas were filled with wonderful aromas from organic essential oil diffusers and soft lighting was provided by the warm glow of both salt and crystal lamps.

Every day they plodded contently on, gradually bringing the place to meet their vision and every evening they went to bed, happy with their achievements of the day. The studio now finished was a tranquil, open space that could be used for any kind of teaching or gathering.

They hired a gardener to show them the ropes for setting up a vegetable and herb garden. Lexi loved being out there; it was something she'd never been into before, never having had a big enough garden, nor the time; this was a whole new, fulfilling project for her, to grow her own food organically. Conrad started work on the accommodation with the help of outside builders. He was pleasantly surprised that, despite the fact they were getting a tremendous amount of work done, he wasn't the slightest bit stressed or letting things run away with him, he retained those feelings he always associated with Lexi. He totally respected and enjoyed the way of life she was introducing to him; he had never been more aware that he could work hard and be productive without becoming that familiar, hamster-on-a-wheel he had been, pretty much all of his life.

With most of the building work done, it was now a case of furnishing the accommodation. They were going out to more auctions and finding characterful pieces for both the accommodation and to add finishing touches to their home. Lexi was now putting together a plan-of-action for how she would run the retreat, taking into consideration every little aspect that had ever crossed her mind since this venture had been a mere dream.

One evening after dinner they sat and discussed Lexi's plans. She explained she would need a week set aside before every intake to become properly acquainted with her clients and their individual needs, which would start with their questionnaires. Once she had gone through them and had a good overall picture of her clients and their habits, she would then follow up with a video call, so by the time they came to the retreat, they could focus on what changes were needed in order of importance and fit those disciplines and advice sessions in around the 'general' schedule of the weeks course. Obviously, there would be on-going help and advice available afterwards should they need it.

Conrad listened intently and then said, "Can I suggest something?"

"Yes, of course, you can!"

"I had a call today from one of the 'CEO's of a company I've done a lot of business with over the years. I've always got on really well with him. He's just had a minor heart attack at the age of 46. He's always been a workaholic but now he's literally driven himself to a point where he can no longer function. I'd told him about this place and what we were planning to do with it during our final meeting and he thought I was crazy! When I spoke to him today though, he was playing a very different tune. He said it sounds like just what he could do with right now, he's very aware he needs to make some big lifestyle changes. I can really imagine what this place could do for someone like him but in my opinion, he's gonna need way more than a week! He needs to remove himself completely from the life he knows in order to adjust and that's not going to happen in such a short space of time. This is going to be like 'rehab' for him."

"Mmm, yes, you're right, I think he would most definitely need longer." She agreed

"Don't get me wrong, I think the week's course for many, would be a great introduction to get the basic principles of the holistic lifestyle across. But I've worked with and provided software for some of the biggest and most powerful companies that exist over my career and I think there's a big opportunity here for us to get some clients that really, need this kind of place. However, these individuals are in such a conditioned 'mind set', I feel beyond any shadow of doubt, they will need much longer than that scheduled week."

This concept really interested Lexi. Of course, Conrad had lots of connections, they would have no shortage of visitors to the retreat, but he was right, for these people, a week really wouldn't be enough. They put their heads together and started to talk over the different ways they could make it work with people from different walks of life, staying different amounts of time according to their needs and desires.

"I just want to add at this point that I've never felt so 'balanced' with my work and life, despite how much we've got done in the last couple of months, which is one-hell-of-a-lot, and that's because right from the start you enforced the principles and we stuck to it. I honestly, never want to go back to how I used to feel, I never want to lose this way of 'being' now that I've lived it.

"I'm really pleased to hear that, the whole point for us now is to live the life and share that experience," Lexi confirmed.

"Good..." He continued, "So, here are my thoughts based upon your vision. I'm thinking you should advertise for an intake all to start on the same week, with an option to stay for different amounts of time to suit the individual depending on what it is they want or need to get out of it, and how far they have travelled to be here. So, you do your week of groundwork before they arrive like you've said, and run your initial week's schedule as you've planned to that everyone would take part in. At the end of that week's course, some would leave with the basic principles set in place. Then the individuals remaining after the initial week could expand on their previous week with more personal, individual help and therapies specific to them; that way you won't be trying to cater for everyone's needs in one week. Then I feel, if they have the option of staying on for longer, you could still make further individual appointments for those who have more challenging issues. They can take proper time out and put into practice their new way of life while they still have support here from you, doing daily practices and therapies and having the surroundings to completely unwind and settle into their new way of living. They could even get 'hands on' and help outside with the vegetables, gardening and other maintenance. That in itself would be therapeutic and also a way to keep the cost down of both of staying after the course and for us running the place."

"Oh, wow! Yes, I love the idea of that!" Lexi, totally on board with what Conrad was suggesting as he continued, "So, by the time they leave, they've had the input they need and exactly the right amount of time to adjust, hopefully it will give them lasting results whatever their job."

They beamed at each other instinctively knowing they'd found the perfect plan and then Conrad concluded, "But most importantly, we need the place to ourselves again for at least a week before you start to do your groundwork all over again. This is our haven, I've never felt so relaxed and happy, and I want it to stay that way," he said with conviction.

"That sounds perfect." Lexi sighed in agreement.

Another three weeks passed, and the accommodation was now finished. They had managed to turn the large old barn into a living space with eight en-suite bedrooms, a communal lounge and a large, fully functional kitchen. Lexi had found someone to provide breakfast, lunch and dinner for the visitors, who would also help with the day-to-day running of the accommodation, cleaning and laundry. All was going to plan, Conrad had put out 'feelers' to every contact he'd ever had, which had created a huge amount interest. Lexi had also sent pictures and details of 'The Retreat' back to her old gym and invited Paul to come and stay with them at the house for their opening week. She was eager for him to take part and experience the weeks planned activities and give her any kind of constructive feed-back on his experience there. She valued his opinion and knew if he noticed anything she'd missed, or could be improved, he'd say so. The excitement was building up.

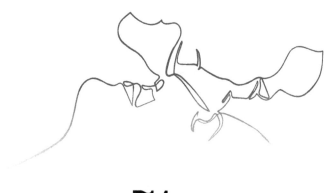

74

The full moon was upon them again and Lexi was gathering her Dispacho from her surroundings, as always, she was selecting leaves, flowers, seeds, thistle down and anything she associated with bringing in success for their venture, grace and ease, good health, protection from all negativities, abundance, joy and of course love. Conrad joined her as she put her small work of art and intention together. "Have you thought of anything you'd like to release at all?" She asked.

"I have actually," Conrad replied, "It's nothing current though. I remember you saying when we were staying at the barn about emotional wellbeing and childhood trauma... and it took me back, it was something that I overheard my mother say in a moment of anger to my father when I was quite young, and it has never left me. I feel that her words and how they made me feel at that point in time had a lasting effect on me and how I saw myself, although I like to think it hasn't harmed me, I still remember it like it was yesterday; so I do think it's something I would like to rid myself of, I take that it would work for something like that?"

"Oh yes, absolutely, if it's something your subconscious mind has held on to, then it could have a negative impact on you. The point of this is to release ALL that no longer serves you, whatever it may be, past, present or indeed fears of the future. If you feel you need to, write it down, everything you remember and how it made you feel, you don't have to tell me, it's just so you don't leave anything out."

Conrad sat in the kitchen with a pen and paper and reflected on this small moment in his life that he had found necessary to carry with him. As he sat there and gave it his attention, he could feel the emotions he'd experienced at that point in time and was surprised at just how much it changed his mood and how he felt once he had become totally present with it. "Yep, I definitely need rid of that!" he said to himself, really beginning to understand Lexi's philosophy on this; although he had been around 9 years old when this had happened, these words had stayed with him and as he recalled the memory, he could feel this obvious 'dip' in his energy and a sensation in his torso as he did so. He realised in no uncertain terms that this was indeed something he needed to let go of.

So far, they had only put a bench by the stream, but they wrapped up warm and walked down to it with lanterns. It was a crisp, cold evening and their warm breath was visible in the air as they made their way through the autumnal night.

Once there, they sat on the wooden bench. "Right, are you ready for this?" Lexi said as she reached into her pocket and pulled out a black stone. "Yes, I surely am," he replied, "what is this then?" He asked as he faced her. "This is what I use to release negative beliefs, energy or experiences and I find it quite powerful. Remember, this is the 'tool' that is combined with the power of your own intention to achieve this." She reinforced. Conrad nodded. "Ok, let's go!"

Lexi handed him the stone, "So now, what I'd like you to do is think about what it is you want to release,"

"Ok," he sat holding the stone with his eyes closed, "Be very present with what it is."

"It's a feeling, "he instantly replied, "It's weird, I've always remembered this quite vividly but until tonight when I really sat and thought about it for a while, I never noticed before that when I recall it, I get this 'feeling' inside."

"Okay, how would you describe this feeling?"

"Well, that I'm not good enough." His tone of voice lowered slightly as he said the words.

"Okay," she said softly, "where do you feel it, Conrad?"

"Kind of around here." He said, placing his hand on his lower ribs, below his chest.

Gently she touched his arm as she did, softly saying. "So, can you see how this may well have had an impact upon you in your adult life? Your need to be the great 'achiever' at work, this innate need to always be achieving and proving to yourself and others that you ARE in fact, good enough?"

"Yes, I can see that now, most definitely." He replied.

"Okay, so, this is 'unworthiness' that you need to release. I'm quite sure your mother never intended to make you feel this way, her words were a projection of what was going on inside her head and how she felt inside; it was really nothing to do with you at all, but you have taken it on and carried it. So, I know it doesn't feel nice but I'd like you to sit and recall this memory and be very present with the feeling it gives you inside, understand it in the 'here and now' for what it is and then with the intention of ridding yourself of it, I would like you to take a deep breath, focusing on that feeling and spit it with all your might into the stone, and if you feel it hasn't all gone, then do it again until you feel completely satisfied that you have purged all of this unworthiness out into the stone. This is a very personal thing, so I'm going to just go over there to give you space to do this." She said as she went to stand up.

"No, don't go, I'd rather you stay." Conrad said, feeling a little emotional, "Okay, however you prefer." She said softly. He sat with the stone in his hand, his thoughts turned deep inside himself, as Lexi sat quietly beside him. He remembered the moment so vividly, he felt the deep feeling in his solar plexus where this emotion had manifested itself, it was unmistakable, and as he recognised it, he consciously and adamantly focused on ridding himself of it. He took a deep, deep breath and then spat with all his might, the negative energy he was feeling into the stone, small tears forming in the corners of his eyes as he did so, from both exertion and emotion.

He sat for a moment, "Is that it?" She asked, "this has been with you for many years, make sure you rid yourself of it completely." He sat for a few more moments; he closed his eyes and eventually spat twice more into the stone. "Well done." She said encouragingly, "All done?"

"Yes, I think so." He replied. "Right, let's use our lovely stream to finish this process." She said getting up and encouraging him toward the little bridge. As they stood on the bridge she said, "Now, I'd like you to imagine all that negativity you have just expelled into the stone, stuck all around it." She shone her lantern on the babbling stream. "See the water rushing over the pebbles where it's a little shallower?" She pointed out. "Look how fast and powerful it is. I'd like you to visualise this energy that is now on the stone, then I'd like you to throw it into the stream and imagine the fast current tossing the stone down the stream and all these molecules of energy gradually being ripped off by the current and being washed randomly in different directions as it's carried downstream, all the time being more and more separated and diluted so that they simply become harmless molecules of energy that have no form or meaning"

Conrad did as she said and as he threw the stone and did his visualisation, he felt as if a massive weight had been lifted from him. He stood for a moment looking out into the darkness feeling that something quite special had happened. "Wow! That felt really powerful." He said, "Good," she nodded positively, "stay with that intention and don't let it back in, remember energy flows where attention goes. I'd now like you to burn your piece of paper." She said handing Conrad a lighter. He took the paper from his pocket, held it out in front of him and lit the bottom corner. As he did this and the flames licked up the piece of paper, Lexi continued, "Now say after me, I release the need within me for all unworthiness, I transmute and clear it across all time, space dimension and reality." He repeated her words, keeping hold of the paper until the flames licked near his fingers and then let it drop to the ground. This was now all making perfect sense to Conrad. "And now, as we walk away, you are going to leave it here." She finished.

They turned and started to head back towards the house, "Now that we've done the serious, heavy bit, let's go back and finish our Despacho." She said on a lighter note, "This will help to you fill your mind with more positive thoughts and energy." They returned to the patio, lit the fire pit and completed the Despacho and as they sat watching the flames flickering in the fire pit, Conrad felt a certain inner peace after his evening's activities.

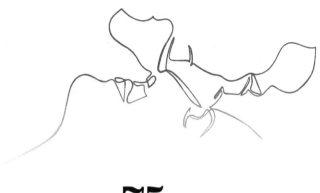

75

It was now approaching the first week in November. Lexi had just finished her 'groundwork' week for her clients arriving Sunday afternoon/evening, ready to start their full week on Monday. The timing of the intake being such that they would have the place back to themselves in good time for Christmas when both Eddie and Corrie planned to come and stay with their other halves, for the festivities and to check out this paradise they'd heard so much about on their weekly calls.

Paul was due to arrive on the Saturday afternoon, leaving straight from work. Lexi was so excited, with her first week of work having gone really well. She had a great understanding of the individual needs of those coming to stay and had spoken to them all personally via video call. Five people were staying for the one-week course, two people for two weeks, both from The States, and one staying for three weeks; this was the CEO Conrad had told Lexi about. She had checked and double-checked everything, they just had the weekend and then it was the 'real deal'. Everything she'd ever dreamed of, in the experience of turning people's lives around to a healthier, happier way of living, was about to commence.

Lexi finished in her little office and put all her paperwork away for the evening. She went into the kitchen and started to prepare their evening meal. As she sang away happily to herself, pleased with her weeks work and confident that she'd thought of absolutely everything, Conrad came in from the spa, where he had just been installing a mineral water machine.

"Okay?" she asked.

"Yep, all done, we're ready to roll lovely lady!" He said as he excitedly bounded over to her, put his arms round her waist and planted a big kiss on her cheek. She turned in his arms, draped her arms around his neck and kissed him.

"I'm so excited, I can't tell you, I feel like I'm going to burst!" She said, her voice high with excitement.

"Me too," Conrad replied, "it's gonna be brilliant, just brilliant!"

"We make a good team, don't we?" She cooed.

"We absolutely do," he agreed, pulling her in and hugging her. "And I honestly can't think of anything I'd like to do more than what I'm doing right now and who I'm doing it with. Lexi, you've changed my world in a way I would never have dreamed possible before I met you!" he said sincerely.

Lexi felt so happy to hear his words saying, "Thank you so much for giving me this opportunity. You, being here with me and us running this, it's better than everything thing I've ever dreamed of all rolled into one."

They held each other, "Thank you for being you! If I hadn't met you, I would still be chasing deals, working eighteen-hour days and probably getting quite close to my first heart attack by now, without even realising it." They kissed again and then Conrad decided to get a fire going while Lexi cooked the dinner.

With the fire roaring away, he came back into the kitchen, got a nice bottle of organic red wine and said, "I think we've earned this don't you?"

"Oh, absolutely!" she replied happily as he uncorked the bottle and took two wine glasses from the cupboard. Lexi finished dishing up the dinner and took it over to the small breakfast table they now had by the patio doors. They sat, smiled at each other, raised their glasses and both said, "Cheers!"

"Here's to us, and the rest of our lives doing exactly what we love."

"Here, here," said Lexi, and they both took a sip. Conrad started to delve into the deep pocket on the side of his trousers; he pulled out a little paper bag.

"Here, that's for you!" he said and handed the small bag over to her.

"Ooh, thank you, what is it?" she said taking it from him.

"Open it and find out!"

She opened the little bag to find a hard object wrapped in pretty pink tissue paper, she still didn't have a clue. As she unwrapped the paper, there in her hand sat the beautiful little 'trinket dish' she had admired back in the summer when they had walked round the gift shop!

"Oh, Conrad!" she said in amazement. "It's beautiful, thank you, I remember picking this up!"

"So, do I!" He winked at her.

"Oh, that's so kind, I can't believe you've done that for me, I can't believe you'd even remember!"

"I remember every moment I've spent with you," he said softly, "everything we've said and done, every kiss...

everything." She felt her heart glow at his words and reached out to touch his face, she felt loved beyond words.

With dinner eaten and cleared away, they retired to the lounge with the rest of the bottle of wine where the fire was warm and inviting. They sat on the settee with their wine, watching the flames dancing in the wood burner. Conrad got up, then returned to the settee with his guitar and started strumming away, a relaxing peaceful tune. Lexi took a sip of her wine, cozied back and lost herself in the moment, never before had she felt happier as the thought danced in her head, 'it simply doesn't get any better than this.'

'I'M LITERALLY LIVING MY DREAM'

Lexi's Appendix

There is a wealth of health to be gained by making changes in your day-to-day lifestyle. One of the biggest investments you can make in your health and wellbeing is to put excellent quality, nutritious, clean, food in your mouth and to not put anything on your skin that you wouldn't put in your mouth and eat!

Many of my clients express to me "Yes, it's all very well, but eating healthily is so much more expensive." I agree with this and feel food pricing is all the wrong way around. But until the government works out a way to make junk food higher in price, so it becomes a treat, (which would help to lessen the massive burden obesity and other poor-diet-related issues is having on the NHS) and lowers the price of unprocessed food that you cook from scratch, making healthy eating the more affordable option, there will always be this mismatch.

After being diagnosed with a condition that I had suffered with all my life, I went from being someone who had quite an unhealthy diet (although at the time I didn't consider it to be that unhealthy) to being totally obsessive about food and eating healthily. But I too, must do this on a budget. So here I'd like to share with you just a few of my recipes, starting with a bone broth base, as bone broth is one of the cheapest, yet most healthful things one can add to their diet.

Including bone broth in your daily menu is one of the kindest and most important things you can do for your body and gut. I make a large bone broth every week. Made correctly, the broth is rich in gelatine, which plays a role in healing the gut, the boiled down cartilage and bone extracts chondroitin sulphates, glucosamine and other amino acids making it good for joint pain and inflammation. It's high in calcium and magnesium for healthy bone formation and high in collagen, so it's anti-ageing as well, making you look good on the outside as well as feel good on the inside.

Much of what we throw away has an abundance of vitamins and minerals and it simply ends up in the bin. Start with your chicken carcass the next time you have a whole chicken, although bone broth can be made from any bones, preferably outdoor reared and organic, (if you get fresh bones from the butcher, they will need to be browned off in the oven first).

So now I'd like to share with you how to make a bone broth and a few of the meals I regularly make using it as the base of the meal, therefore making it the equivalent of consuming a powerful, healthful, anti-inflammatory, gut healing, multi-vitamin and mineral addition to every mouthful.

Lexi's Bone broth

Place your whole chicken in a large, lidded, Pyrex dish and fill halfway up with water. A good, slow grown, outdoor reared chicken will be much tougher than a conventional chicken (unfortunately we have become accustomed to the texture, taste and cooking of a bird that has been pumped full of growth hormones and caged so that it never develops its muscles properly, while being fed a vegetarian diet that also isn't natural to it); I find the chicken is far more tender cooked on a lower heat and slowly, 160/65 degrees for about three hours (or a bit more if you like it to really fall apart).

Alternatively, you can cook your chicken in a pressure cooker (aluminium and Teflon free ONLY). Again, place the chicken in the vessel and pour water in to three quarters of the way up the bird, add salt and pepper, a good size chicken will only take 17-20 minutes in a pressure cooker.

I then remove the liquid into a glass container, let it cool and place it in the fridge; this liquid will turn to a solid jelly once it's cooled. This is very rich in gelatine and collagen. I also take all the meat off the chicken and either use it straight away or save it to make a nice soup or curry with when the broth is ready. Place in an airtight glass container in the fridge.

Onto the broth

Place your chicken carcass or other fresh bones in a large vessel, either stainless steel, large crock-pot, or a ceramic slow cooker.

Add, three tablespoons of organic 'Apple cider vinegar' this is of utmost IMPORTANCE, it's the vinegar that 'leeches' the minerals out of the bones and into the water.

1 teaspoon of good quality salt, (Celtic or Himalayan pink) also very high in minerals, regular 'table salt' has no minerals as they are all processed out.

Organic black pepper to taste. Black pepper increases your body's ability to absorb more of the nutrients from your food by stimulating the 'villi' (hair-like protrusions on the intestine wall) to grow and be more erect. The 'villi' increase the surface area of the intestine, so there is more area to absorb the nutrients from that which passes through.

2 litres of filtered or bottled water.

Add vegetables and herbs of your choice, including any waste choppings of your vegetables. I include the stalks from cabbage leaves, broccoli stalks and top-and- tails from beans etc. Providing they are clean they can be added, they have valuable nutrition and fibre in them, which comes in handy later for thickening your sauces.

Add 1 piece of Kombu seaweed for valuable nutrients and iodine.

Bring to the boil and then turn right down, (if you are using 'browned bones' spoon off the residue that initially forms on the top of the liquid). Preferably use a slow cooker (ceramic) or an economy ring on the hob and leave for two-three days. Again, this can also be done in a fraction of the time (two and a half to three hours) in a pressure cooker, but care MUST be taken to consider the materials used in the equipment, avoid aluminium or Teflon.

When you are ready to strain your bones, chicken bones especially, will literally fall apart as you squeeze them, because now, everything that was holding them together is now held within the liquid making the nutrients highly bioavailable (available for the body to use).

The minerals from the bones, now with all the vegetable pieces and herbs makes this wonderful liquid a potent, easily digestible, multi-vitamin and mineral liquid for very little cost.

Carefully remove all the vegetables and chopping's and set them aside and blend them with a small amount of your broth so it becomes a thick paste, this will serve as a thickener for any sauces, soups or curries avoiding the need for any 'starchy' thickeners.

Then strain your bones and discard them, leaving you with a large bowl of hot broth. At this point I add the jelly that was previously removed and stored after roasting the chicken (if it's a chicken broth), this will quickly melt into the liquid. Now your broth has everything. Chicken is also very rich in cysteine, a natural amino acid that is a precursor to glutathione, the body's major antioxidant, so also healthful to the liver. Bone broth is perfect just as a drink after a workout to put much needed nutrients back in to the body and is also a perfect nutritious base for smoothies, (especially if you're lactose intolerant like me) or indeed, any dish that has a sauce.

Here are just a handful of recipes that I regularly make from my bone broth base.

Lexi's Green Smoothie

1 cup of bone broth: Due to my lactose intolerance, I've always used bone broth as my base and so, my smoothies are warm and have a more 'savoury' taste to them, but you can also use coconut or almond milk if you prefer 'traditional' tasting, cool smoothies.

1 cup of bone broth

Large handful of spinach

Half-to-one avocado

1 handful of blueberries

1 tablespoon of coconut oil

1 tablespoon of MCT oil

1 tablespoon of each sprouted linseeds and pumpkin seeds/or sesame and sunflower seeds (I rotate these on a two-weekly basis for hormone balance)

1 teaspoon turmeric

1 teaspoon chlorella

1 pinch of black pepper

First, I heat up my bone broth with the spinach in it, add the other ingredients and whizz them all up in my Nutri-Bullet.

Lexi's Chicken curry

3/4 pint of bone broth

1 cup of thickener (the blended vegetables from the broth)

500g Meat – You can use the meat from your cooked chicken or indeed, any meat you fancy.

Mushrooms sautéed in butter, or any other vegetable you prefer

1 cup of coconut milk or cream

2 dessert spoons of almond nut butter (<u>obviously not if you have a nut allergy</u> but this will also thicken your curry sauce)

1 heaped tablespoon of organic Garam masala

1 heaped teaspoon of turmeric

1 quarter teaspoon of cinnamon

1 level teaspoon of cumin

1 level teaspoon of coriander

Organic chilli (to your taste)

1-2 cloves of garlic

Two squares of organic dark chocolate

Salt and pepper to taste

> Add all the ingredients, stir and simmer.
> Serve on a bed of leafy greens sautéed in butter.

Lexi's Hot Pot- Ideal winter warmer for the slow cooker

1 pint of bone broth

1 cup of thickener (the blended vegetables with the broth)

500g organic or outdoor reared beef

1-2 chopped onions

1 punnet of peeled and chopped mushrooms/or preferred vegetables

A small glass of good-quality red wine

1 dessertspoon of organic mixed herbs

Salt and pepper to taste

Sautee the mushrooms and onions in some butter or coconut oil and add to the slow cooker. Place all the other ingredients in the slow cooker, stir and put on 'low', go to work and arrive home to the beautiful aromas when you come back in the door in the evening.

Serve on a bed of sautéed vegetables of your choice.

Lexi's Chicken livers

1 punnet of organic or outdoor reared chicken livers

1 onion/or chives

Half pint of bone broth

1 small glass of good quality red wine

1 half cup of thickener

Fresh thyme (or any herb you prefer)

Salt and pepper to taste

Organic outdoor reared, grass fed butter or organic cold pressed, virgin coconut oil to sauté

Sautee the onions in a ceramic pan, add the livers and continue. Once the livers are slightly brown to seal in their juices, add the rest of the ingredients and liquid, cover and simmer for 5-10 minutes. Serve with vegetables of your choice.

Lexi's Lamb shanks

2-4 lamb shanks depending on how many you're cooking for.

Cover them with bone broth

1 small glass of red wine

Rosemary (organic, dried or fresh)

2 chopped carrots

1-2 chopped onions

Salt and pepper to taste

Place all ingredients in the slow cooker and return home to your hearty meal, serve with vegetables of your choice.

These are just a few of my regular meals for you to try, but once the bone broth is made, portioned and refrigerated, there is no end to what you can do with it. The meals are quick and easy and you can rest safe in the knowledge that, every mouthful has an abundance of quality nutrition to nourish your cells for a happy, healthy body. Enjoy!

Lexi's Humous

Organic chickpeas 1 cup

Olive oil 1 cup

Finely chopped garlic (to personal taste)

Salt

Pepper

Cayenne pepper

2 tablespoons of organic Balsamic vinegar

Simply blend the ingredients together to your desired consistency.

Lexi's Chicken liver pate (an excellent source of B vitamins)

Organic/outdoor raised chicken livers, 1 punnet

Organic grass fed butter 2-3oz

Coconut oil 2 desertspoons

Bone broth 3 tablespoons

Salt and pepper

Herbs of your personal choice

Fry and brown the chicken livers in the butter add the herbs and bone broth salt and pepper. Lastly, stir in the cream and leave to cool a little. Transfer to your blender and blend to your personal taste of texture. Place in glass storage and stand in cold water to chill it through quickly and then refrigerate.

Sweet yummy treats

We all like to indulge ourselves with a sweet treat from time to time but it is possible to make these treats from healthier ingredients.

Try these yummy sweets:

Lexi's puddings

1 cup/tub of Coconut yogurt and mix in:

A tub of organic Blueberries

1 tablespoon of ground flaxseed

1 tablespoon of shelled hemp seeds

1 tablespoon of cacao nibs

1 teaspoon of manuka honey or organic Maple syrup

Try to source organic ingredients where possible
Stir the ingredients together and grate some dark organic chocolate over the top, yum!

Another healthy pudding

Coconut milk or gluten free Oat cream

Add:

3 heaped dessertspoons of organic milled chia seeds

2 dessertspoons of pea protein

2 dessertspoons of organic milled flaxseeds

2-3 dessertspoons of organic dried mulberries

1 dessertspoon of shelled hemp seeds

1 dessertspoon of organic Vanilla paste

Mix all ingredients together and chill for 6 hours, add organic Maple syrup to sweeten (to your taste) when dishing up.

Lexi's Banoffi pudding

1 banana sliced

Oat milk (1 pint)

2 dessertspoons Hemp protein

2 dessertspoons Pea protein

2 dessertspoons organic milled flaxseeds

2 dessertspoons organic milled chia seeds

1 heaped dessertspoon organic cacao powder

1 dessertspoon organic vanilla bean paste

Maple syrup (to personal taste).

Mix all the ingredients and chill for 6-8 hours

Chocolate brownies

I tub of almond butter 450g

2 bananas mashed

Cacao powder to taste

1 dessertspoon of maple syrup

8 drops of sweet orange essential oil, or to taste

Blend to a thick paste and place in a baking tray lined with grease proof paper, cook at 180 degrees or Gas mark 4 for 30 minutes.

Indulgent chocolate drink

Heat up one cup of coconut milk, stir in cacao powder to taste, ¼ teaspoon of cinnamon, add ¼ glass of red (organic or biodynamic) wine and honey to sweeten if needed, naughty but nice!

Blueberry Fool

2 Punnets of organic blueberries

Oat cream or coconut milk, can or carton

2 heaped tablespoons of Ground linseed

1 tablespoon Hemp protein

2 dessertspoons of Shelled hemp seeds

2 dessertspoons of Ground Chia seeds

1 dessertspoon of Pea protein

Honey to taste

Place half the blueberries in half of the liquid with 2-heaped dessertspoons of hemp seeds and blend well. Place in a vessel and add the rest of the liquid, stir in all the other ingredients and leave in the fridge for 6 hours.

Of course, there is no end to the advice and recommendations that can be given on the subject of the 'Holistic lifestyle' but for anyone who is new to this, here is a whistle-stop tour of tips and advice as an introduction to this healthful and fulfilling way of life.

One of the biggest issues we are faced with is the amount of chemicals in our commercially bought products. Chemicals are everywhere; it's impossible not to come into contact with them on a daily basis, but there is a lot you can do to reduce your own personal exposure to them.

Personal care products contain so many chemicals it's frightening! It takes 26 seconds for anything that is applied to your skin to get into your bloodstream, I can't stress enough, if you wouldn't put it in your mouth and eat it, don't put it on your skin.

There are many organic products out there. I tend to buy shower gel, shampoo and conditioner. Faith in Nature, Dr organics and Jason organics are my favourites brands, which I consider to be both good quality organic products and value for money.

Make-up can contain a huge amount of chemicals so if you wear make-up, it will serve you to buy organic make-up. Again, there are many organic makes, some of them I consider to be hugely expensive, but I've found 'Benecos' to make excellent make-up products of all kinds for a price tag on par with 'Rimmel', so it IS possible to look good and not spend a fortune.

Other personal care products I make myself with different, organic 'oil' bases and organic essential oils. The initial outlay for the oils might seem expensive, but once you have them, stored in a cool dark place, they last a long time and make up many, many batches of body lotions and face creams. Equally, I know exactly what's in the products I'm 'feeding' my skin with.

Here are a few of my homemade creams and lotions. Obviously, everybody's taste in fragrance is different and not every oil will suit everyone's skin, so care must be taken in case of skin reactions, but this will give you an idea just how easy it is to put them together.

Body oil

Organic coconut oil base. Melt a cup of coconut oil and add to a glass container.

Add:

10ml of Jojoba oil

10 drops of rose hip oil

20 drops of Frankincense (anti-inflammatory and very firming for the skin)

10 drops of Rose geranium

4 drops of roman chamomile

4-6 drops of lavender

8-10 drops of sandalwood

Mix and leave to set.
Pat your skin dry after your shower and apply all over the body.

Night-time face oil

Equal parts Jojoba oil and organic avocado oil in a small glass bottle.

Add

10 drops of rose hip oil

10-15 drops of frankincense oil

4 drops of lavender oil

4-6 drops of sandalwood oil

Shake to mix and massage into clean skin before bed.

Mouthwash

Melt a small jar of coconut oil to a liquid and add 5ml of organic oregano oil (this is powerful stuff, anti-bacterial, anti-fungal and anti-viral) this on its own will leave your mouth slightly 'tingling' but if you prefer to you can also add some mint essential oil for a fresh flavour. Note: never use undiluted Oregano oil.

Put a teaspoonful into your mouth and pull the oil back and forth through your teeth, the longer the better, maybe carry on 'oil pulling' while you're in the shower then gargle to finish.

I also use this oil to brush my teeth. Get a good dollop on your toothbrush and then dip the toothbrush head in a tub of aluminium free bicarbonate of soda, brush as normal. It cleans your teeth beautifully without harmful fluoride or other chemicals.

This mixture of coconut and oregano oil is also handy for spots and blemishes, apply directly to cleansed area.

Face toner

I've used this for years. In a glass bottle add equal parts organic apple cider vinegar and good quality (not tap) water. Shake to mix and apply to skin either with organic cotton wool pads, or use from a spay bottle, your skin will look and feel lovely.

Relaxing, cleansing and detoxing bath

Run your bath and add I cup of magnesium flakes

½ cup of organic apple cider vinegar

Two large handfuls of aluminium free bicarbonate of soda

Add essential oils of your choice (lavender, chamomile, Frankincense) Dim the light, put on some relaxing music or a meditation and soak for twenty minutes.

Drinks

Liver cleansing drink

Organic coconut milk, 1 mug, add to pan and heat.

Add

1 heaped teaspoon of turmeric

1 teaspoon of coconut or MCT oil

¼ teaspoon of cinnamon

1 pinch of cayenne pepper

1 pinch of black pepper

2-3 drops of vanilla (optional)

Whisk together as it heats in the pan, pour into a mug and add 1 teaspoon of organic, unpasteurised honey, stir and enjoy.

And of course, we can't finish without adding the bullet-proof-coffee!

It's important to have organic coffee beans as both coffee and tea are among the highest, pesticide-laden products on the market.

Only grind the amount of coffee you're going to use as coffee begins to oxidise as soon as it's cut into and the oxygen hits it, the golden rule is grind it, make it, drink it!

Grind your beans and make your coffee to your taste in strength, add a generous knob of organic butter and a heaped dessertspoon of coconut oil, whizz it up and pour into your mug, sprinkle with a small amount of cinnamon and enjoy, the fat will slow the caffeine entering the blood stream and reduce the fight or flight response whilst giving the body an injection of healthy fats.

Just a few tried and trusted recipes and homemade personal care products to help you on your way to being the happiest, healthiest version of YOU!

A Big Thank You

Before I go, I'd like to express my gratitude to the three people that had the biggest influence and most positive impact on my journey to optimal health.

Initially, I studied to be my own sports injury therapist, to learn remedial exercise to strengthen my muscles and stabilize my joints, and to manage muscle imbalances, which helped with the pain and reduced the incidence of injury quite significantly. My greatest influence in this area has been Paul Chek of the CHEK Institute. Having suffered multiple dislocations of the limbs and all manner of soft tissue injuries due to my EDS, under Paul's guidance, I took back my power and learned how to rehabilitate myself from injury and to strengthen my body in a functional way to help prevent injuries from occurring, this made a huge difference to my quality of life.

My EDS had also rendered me in and out of hospital regularly with excruciatingly painful tummy problems. After meeting Emma Lane of the 'Integrative health Education' and taking her course 'Holistic Approaches to The Fully Functional Gut' I have never had the need to go back into hospital, or indeed visit the doctor with ANY issue associated with the digestive system since, it's been eight years now. It still amazes me that an entire health system took 50 years guessing at it and were still clueless, and Emma Lane had it nailed in one weekend! That said, it wasn't 'instant', the process took some doing, but she clearly had a better understanding of how the gut works than all of the specialists I'd seen from a baby right through to fifty years of age put together. Maybe they should be taking her courses? Her knowledge is phenomenal. Her course 'Destination Wellbeing' was also a life changing one that I would whole heartedly recommend to anyone. Now at the age of 58, I manage my Elhers Danlos Syndrome extremely well and am not on any pharmaceutical drugs, not even hormones!

As I gradually learned how to lesson my physical symptoms, I was made aware of the 'mind/body' connection and that it's impossible to have a healthy body without a healthy mind. My emotional healing journey began with Louise Hay, God rest her beautiful soul. Reading her book 'You Can Heal Your Life', doing daily affirmations and listening to her many audios (available on YouTube) was my starting point and another empowering, turning point in my life. She taught me so much about myself and I developed a far healthier understanding of myself for a happier, healthier life. It seemed both fitting and a privilege that 'The Fateful Text' has been published by BalboaPress, which is the English 'arm' of Louise's Publishing company, Hay House.

I hope you have enjoyed my novel as much as I have enjoyed writing it. I hope it has bought you a little joy and also given you a gentle awareness of the principles of the holistic lifestyle and our desperate need to strive for harmony with mother nature.

Find me Georgie Gee on Facebook, also the official Facebook page The Fateful Text and The Fateful Text on Instagram

I hope you enjoy your newfound wealth of health,

Namaste.

Lightning Source UK Ltd.
Milton Keynes UK
UKHW021048170123
415494UK00015B/871